D1301342

Sinclair Lewis

# Arrowsmith

e-artnow 2019

*Sinclair Lewis*

# Arrowsmith

A Medical Novel From the Renowned Nobel Prize Winning Author & Playwright

e-artnow, 2019
Contact: info@e-artnow.org

ISBN 978-80-268-9243-4

# Contents

## Chapter 1

The driver of the wagon swaying through forest and swamp of the Ohio wilderness was a ragged girl of fourteen. Her mother they had buried near the Monongahela — the girl herself had heaped with torn sods the grave beside the river of the beautiful name. Her father lay shrinking with fever on the floor of the wagon-box, and about him played her brothers and sisters, dirty brats, tattered brats, hilarious brats.

She halted at the fork in the grassy road, and the sick man quavered, "Emmy, ye better turn down towards Cincinnati. If we could find your Uncle Ed, I guess he'd take us in."

"Nobody ain't going to take us in," she said. "We're going on jus' long as we can. Going West! They's a whole lot of new things I aim to be seeing!"

She cooked the supper, she put the children to bed, and sat by the fire, alone.

That was the great-grandmother of Martin Arrowsmith.

### II

Cross-legged in the examining-chair in Doc Vickerson's office, a boy was reading "Gray's Anatomy." His name was Martin Arrowsmith, of Elk Mills, in the state of Winnemac.

There was a suspicion in Elk Mills — now, in 1897, a dowdy red-brick village, smelling of apples — that this brown-leather adjustable seat which Doc Vickerson used for minor operations, for the infrequent pulling of teeth and for highly frequent naps, had begun life as a barber's chair. There was also a belief that its proprietor must once have been called Doctor Vickerson, but for years he had been only The Doc, and he was scurfier and much less adjustable than the chair.

Martin was the son of J. J. Arrowsmith, who conducted the New York Clothing Bazaar. By sheer brass and obstinacy he had, at fourteen, become the unofficial, also decidedly unpaid, assistant to the Doc, and while the Doc was on a country call he took charge — though what there was to take charge of, no one could ever make out. He was a slender boy, not very tall; his hair and restless eyes were black, his skin unusually white, and the contrast gave him an air of passionate variability. The squareness of his head and a reasonable breadth of shoulders saved him from any appearance of effeminacy or of that querulous timidity which artistic young gentlemen call Sensitiveness. When he lifted his head to listen, his right eyebrow, slightly higher than the left, rose and quivered in his characteristic expression of energy, of independence, and a hint that he could fight, a look of impertinent inquiry which had been known to annoy his teachers and the Sunday School superintendent.

Martin was, like most inhabitants of Elk Mills before the Slavo-Italian immigration, a Typical Pure-bred Anglo-Saxon American, which means that he was a union of German, French, Scotch, Irish, perhaps a little Spanish, conceivably a little of the strains lumped together as "Jewish," and a great deal of English, which is itself a combination of primitive Briton, Celt, Phoenician, Roman, German, Dane, and Swede.

It is not certain that, in attaching himself to Doc Vickerson, Martin was entirely and edifyingly controlled by a desire to become a Great Healer. He did awe his Gang by bandaging stone-bruises, dissecting squirrels, and explaining the astounding and secret matters to be discovered at the back of the physiology, but he was not completely free from an ambition to command such glory among them as was enjoyed by the son of the Episcopalian minister, who could smoke an entire cigar without becoming sick. Yet this afternoon he read steadily at the section on the lymphatic system, and he muttered the long and perfectly incomprehensible words in a hum which made drowsier the dusty room.

It was the central room of the three occupied by Doc Vickerson, facing on Main Street above the New York Clothing Bazaar. On one side of it was the foul waiting-room, on the other, the Doc's bedroom. He was an aged widower; for what he called "female fixings" he cared nothing; and the bedroom with its tottering bureau and its cot of frowsy blankets was cleaned only by Martin, in not very frequent attacks of sanitation.

This central room was at once business office, consultation-room, operating-theater, living-room, poker den, and warehouse for guns and fishing tackle. Against a brown plaster wall was a cabinet of zoological collections and medical curiosities, and beside it the most dreadful and fascinating object known to the boy-world of Elk Mills — a skeleton with one gaunt gold tooth. On evenings when the Doc was away, Martin would acquire prestige among the trembling Gang by leading them into the unutterable darkness and scratching a sulfur match on the skeleton's jaw.

On the wall was a home-stuffed pickerel on a home-varnished board. Beside the rusty stove, a sawdust-box cuspidor rested on a slimy oilcloth worn through to the threads. On the senile table was a pile of memoranda of debts which the Doc was always swearing he would "collect from those dead-beats right now," and which he would never, by any chance, at any time, collect from any of them. A year or two — a decade or two — a century or two — they were all the same to the plodding doctor in the bee-murmuring town.

The most unsanitary corner was devoted to the cast-iron sink, which was oftener used for washing eggy breakfast plates than for sterilizing instruments. On its ledge were a broken test-tube, a broken fishhook, an unlabeled and forgotten bottle of pills, a nail-bristling heel, a frayed cigar-butt, and a rusty lancet stuck in a potato.

The wild raggedness of the room was the soul and symbol of Doc Vickerson; it was more exciting than the flat-faced stack of shoe-boxes in the New York Bazaar: it was the lure to questioning and adventure for Martin Arrowsmith.

### III

The boy raised his head, cocked his inquisitive brow. On the stairway was the cumbersome step of Doc Vickerson. The Doc was sober! Martin would not have to help him into bed.

But it was a bad sign that the Doc should first go down the hall to his bedroom. The boy listened sharply. He heard the Doc open the lower part of the washstand, where he kept his bottle of Jamaica rum. After a long gurgle the invisible Doc put away the bottle and decisively kicked the doors shut. Still good. Only one drink. If he came into the consultation-room at once, he would be safe. But he was still standing in the bedroom. Martin sighed as the washstand doors were hastily opened again, as he heard another gurgle and a third.

The Doc's step was much livelier when he loomed into the office, a gray mass of a man with a gray mass of mustache, a form vast and unreal and undefined, like a cloud taking for the moment a likeness of humanity. With the brisk attack of one who wishes to escape the discussion of his guilt, the Doc rumbled while he waddled toward his desk-chair:

"What you doing here, young fella? What you doing here? I knew the cat would drag in something if I left the door unlocked." He gulped slightly; he smiled to show that he was being humorous — people had been known to misconstrue the Doc's humor.

He spoke more seriously, occasionally forgetting what he was talking about:

"Reading old Gray? That's right. Physician's library just three books: 'Gray's Anatomy' and Bible and Shakespeare. Study. You may become great doctor. Locate in Zenith and make five thousand dollars year — much as United States Senator! Set a high goal. Don't let things slide. Get training. Go college before go medical school. Study. Chemistry. Latin. Knowledge! I'm plug doc — got chick nor child — nobody — old drunk. But you — leadin' physician. Make five thousand dollars year.

"Murray woman's got endocarditis. Not thing I can do for her. Wants somebody hold her hand. Road's damn' disgrace. Culvert's out, beyond the grove. 'Sgrace.

"Endocarditis and —

"Training, that's what you got t' get. Fundamentals. Know chemistry. Biology. I nev' did. Mrs. Reverend Jones thinks she's got gastric ulcer. Wants to go city for operation. Ulcer, hell! She and the Reverend both eat too much.

"Why they don't repair that culvert — And don't be a booze-hoister like me, either. And get your basic science. I'll splain."

The boy, normal village youngster though he was, given to stoning cats and to playing pom-pom-pullaway, gained something of the intoxication of treasure-hunting as the Doc struggled to convey his vision of the pride of learning, the universality of biology, the triumphant exactness of chemistry. A fat old man and dirty and unvirtuous was the Doc; his grammar was doubtful, his vocabulary alarming, and his references to his rival, good Dr. Needham, were scandalous; yet he invoked in Martin a vision of making chemicals explode with much noise and stink and of seeing animalcules that no boy in Elk Mills had ever beheld.

The Doc's voice was thickening; he was sunk in his chair, blurry of eye and lax of mouth. Martin begged him to go to bed, but the Doc insisted:

"Don't need nap. No. Now you lissen. You don't appreciate but — Old man now. Giving you all I've learned. Show you collection. Only museum in whole county. Scientif' pioneer."

A hundred times had Martin obediently looked at the specimens in the brown, crackly-varnished bookcase: the beetles and chunks of mica; the embryo of a two-headed calf, the gall-stones removed from a respectable lady whom the Doc enthusiastically named to all visitors. The Doc stood before the case, waving an enormous but shaky forefinger.

"Looka that butterfly. Name is *porthesia chrysorrhoea* . Doc Needham couldn't tell you that! He don't know what butterflies are called! He don't care if you get trained. Remember that name now?" He turned on Martin. "You payin' attention? You interested? *Huh?* Oh, the devil! Nobody wants to know about my museum — not a person. Only one in county but — I'm an old failure."

Martin asserted, "Honest, it's slick!"

"Look here! Look here! See that? In the bottle? It's an appendix. First one ever took out 'round here. I did it! Old Doc Vickerson, he did the first 'pendectomy in *this* neck of the woods, you bet! And first museum. It ain't — so big — but it's start. I haven't put away money like Doc Needham, but I started first c'lection — I started it!"

He collapsed in a chair, groaning, "You're right. Got to sleep. All in." But as Martin helped him to his feet he broke away, scrabbled about on his desk, and looked back doubtfully. "Want to give you something — start your training. And remember the old man. Will anybody remember the old man?"

He was holding out the beloved magnifying glass which for years he had used in botanizing. He watched Martin slip the lens into his pocket, he sighed, he struggled for something else to say, and silently he lumbered into his bedroom.

## Chapter 2

The state of Winnemac is bounded by Michigan, Ohio, Illinois, and Indiana, and like them it is half Eastern, half Midwestern. There is a feeling of New England in its brick and sycamore villages, its stable industries, and a tradition which goes back to the Revolutionary War. Zenith, the largest city in the state, was founded in 1792. But Winnemac is Midwestern in its fields of corn and wheat, its red barns and silos, and, despite the immense antiquity of Zenith, many counties were not settled till 1860.

The University of Winnemac is at Mohalis, fifteen miles from Zenith. There are twelve thousand students; beside this prodigy Oxford is a tiny theological school and Harvard a select college for young gentlemen. The University has a baseball field under glass; its buildings are measured by the mile; it hires hundreds of young Doctors of Philosophy to give rapid instruction in Sanskrit, navigation, accountancy, spectacle-fitting, sanitary engineering, Provençal poetry, tariff schedules, rutabaga-growing, motor-car designing, the history of Voronezh, the style of Matthew Arnold, the diagnosis of *myohypertrophia kymoparalytica* , and department-store advertising. Its president is the best money-raiser and the best after-dinner speaker in the United States; and Winnemac was the first school in the world to conduct its extension courses by radio.

It is not a snobbish rich-man's college, devoted to leisurely nonsense. It is the property of the people of the state, and what they want — or what they are told they want — is a mill to turn out men and women who will lead moral lives, play bridge, drive good cars, be enterprising in business, and occasionally mention books, though they are not expected to have time to read them. It is a Ford Motor Factory, and if its products rattle a little, they are beautifully standardized, with perfectly interchangeable parts. Hourly the University of Winnemac grows in numbers and influence, and by 1950 one may expect it to have created an entirely new world-civilization, a civilization larger and brisker and purer.

### II

In 1904, when Martin Arrowsmith was an Arts and Science Junior preparing for medical school, Winnemac had but five thousand students yet it was already brisk.

Martin was twenty-one. He still seemed pale, in contrast to his black smooth hair, but he was a respectable runner, a fair basket-ball center, and a savage hockey-player. The co-eds murmured that he "looked so romantic," but as this was before the invention of sex and the era of petting-parties, they merely talked about him at a distance, and he did not know that he could have been a hero of amours. For all his stubbornness he was shy. He was not entirely ignorant of caresses but he did not make an occupation of them. He consorted with men whose virile pride it was to smoke filthy corncob pipes and to wear filthy sweaters.

The University had become his world. For him Elk Mills did not exist. Doc Vickerson was dead and buried and forgotten; Martin's father and mother were dead, leaving him only enough money for his arts and medical courses. The purpose of life was chemistry and physics and the prospect of biology next year.

His idol was Professor Edward Edwards, head of the department of chemistry, who was universally known as "Encore." Edwards' knowledge of the history of chemistry was immense. He could read Arabic, and he infuriated his fellow chemists by asserting that the Arabs had anticipated all their researches. Himself, Professor Edwards never did researches. He sat before fires and stroked his collie and chuckled in his beard.

This evening Encore was giving one of his small and popular At Homes. He lolled in a brown-corduroy Morris chair, being quietly humorous for the benefit of Martin and half a dozen other fanatical young chemists, and baiting Dr. Norman Brumfit, the instructor in English. The room was full of heartiness and beer and Brumfit.

Every university faculty must have a Wild Man to provide thrills and to shock crowded lecture-rooms. Even in so energetically virtuous an institution as Winnemac there was one Wild Man, and he was Norman Brumfit. He was permitted, without restriction, to speak of himself as immoral, agnostic and socialistic, so long as it was universally known that he remained pure, Presbyterian, and Republican. Dr. Brumfit was in form, tonight. He asserted that whenever a man showed genius, it could be proved that he had Jewish blood. Like all discussions of Judaism at Winnemac, this led to the mention of Max Gottlieb, professor of bacteriology in the medical school.

Professor Gottlieb was the mystery of the University. It was known that he was a Jew, born and educated in Germany, and that his work on immunology had given him fame in the East and in Europe. He rarely left his small brown weedy house except to return to his laboratory, and few students outside of his classes had ever identified him, but everyone had heard of his tall, lean, dark aloofness. A thousand fables fluttered about him. It was believed that he was the son of a German prince, that he had immense wealth, that he lived as sparsely as the other professors only because he was doing terrifying and costly experiments which probably had something to do with human sacrifice. It was said that he could create life in the laboratory, that he could talk to the monkeys which he inoculated, that he had been driven out of Germany as a devil-worshiper or an anarchist, and that he secretly drank real champagne every evening at dinner.

It was the tradition that faculty-members did not discuss their colleagues with students, but Max Gottlieb could not be regarded as anybody's colleague. He was impersonal as the chill northeast wind. Dr. Brumfit rattled:

"I'm sufficiently liberal, I should assume, toward the claims of science, but with a man like Gottlieb — I'm prepared to believe that he knows all about material forces, but what astounds me is that such a man can be blind to the vital force that creates all others. He says that knowledge is worthless unless it is proven by rows of figures. Well, when one of you scientific sharks can take the genius of a Ben Jonson and measure it with a yardstick, then I'll admit that we literary chaps, with our doubtless absurd belief in beauty and loyalty and the world o' dreams, are off on the wrong track!"

Martin Arrowsmith was not exactly certain what this meant and he enthusiastically did not care. He was relieved when Professor Edwards from the midst of his beardedness and smokiness made a sound curiously like "Oh, hell!" and took the conversation away from Brumfit. Ordinarily Encore would have suggested, with amiable malice, that Gottlieb was a "crapehanger" who wasted time destroying the theories of other men instead of making new ones of his own. But tonight, in detestation of such literary playboys as Brumfit, he exalted Gottlieb's long, lonely, failure-burdened effort to synthesize antitoxin, and his diabolic pleasure in disproving his own contentions as he would those of Ehrlich or Sir Almroth Wright. He spoke of Gottlieb's great book, "Immunology," which had been read by seven-ninths of all the men in the world who could possibly understand it — the number of these being nine.

The party ended with Mrs. Edwards' celebrated doughnuts. Martin tramped toward his boarding-house through a veiled spring night. The discussion of Gottlieb had roused him to a reasonless excitement. He thought of working in a laboratory at night, alone, absorbed, contemptuous of academic success and of popular classes. Himself, he believed, he had never seen the man, but he knew that Gottlieb's laboratory was in the Main Medical Building. He drifted toward the distant medical campus. The few people whom he met were hurrying with midnight timidity. He entered the shadow of the Anatomy Building, grim as a barracks, still as the dead men lying up there in the dissecting-room. Beyond him was the turreted bulk of the Main Medical Building, a harsh and blurry mass, high up in its dark wall a single light. He started. The light had gone out abruptly, as though an agitated watcher were trying to hide from him.

On the stone steps of the Main Medical, two minutes after, appeared beneath the arc-light a tall figure, ascetic, self-contained, apart. His swart cheeks were gaunt, his nose high-bridged and thin. He did not hurry, like the belated homebodies. He was unconscious of the world. He looked at Martin and through him; he moved away, muttering to himself, his shoulders stooped, his long hands clasped behind him. He was lost in the shadows, himself a shadow.

He had worn the threadbare top-coat of a poor professor, yet Martin remembered him as wrapped in a black velvet cape with a silver star arrogant on his breast.

## III

On his first day in medical school, Martin Arrowsmith was in a high state of superiority. As a medic he was more picturesque than other students, for medics are reputed to know secrets, horrors, exhilarating wickednesses. Men from the other departments go to their rooms to peer into their books. But also as an academic graduate, with a training in the basic sciences, he felt superior to his fellow medics, most of whom had but a high-school diploma, with perhaps one year in a ten-room Lutheran college among the cornfields.

For all his pride, Martin was nervous. He thought of operating, of making a murderous wrong incision; and with a more immediate, macabre fear, he thought of the dissecting-room and the stony, steely Anatomy Building. He had heard older medics mutter of its horrors: of corpses hanging by hooks, like rows of ghastly fruit, in an abominable tank of brine in the dark basement; of Henry the janitor, who was said to haul the cadavers out of the brine, to inject red lead into their veins, and to scold them as he stuffed them on the dumb-waiter.

There was prairie freshness in the autumn day but Martin did not heed. He hurried into the slate-colored hall of the Main Medical, up the wide stairs to the office of Max Gottlieb. He did not look at passing students, and when he bumped into them he grunted in confused apology. It was a portentous hour. He was going to specialize in bacteriology; he was going to discover enchanting new germs; Professor Gottlieb was going to recognize him as a genius, make him an assistant, predict for him — He halted in Gottlieb's private laboratory, a small, tidy apartment with racks of cotton-corked test-tubes on the bench, a place unimpressive and unmagical save for the constant-temperature bath with its tricky thermometer and electric bulbs. He waited till another student, a stuttering gawk of a student, had finished talking to Gottlieb, dark, lean, impassive at his desk in a cubbyhole of an office, then he plunged.

If in the misty April night Gottlieb had been romantic as a cloaked horseman, he was now testy and middle-aged. Near at hand, Martin could see wrinkles beside the hawk eyes. Gottlieb had turned back to his desk, which was heaped with shabby note-books, sheets of calculations, and a marvelously precise chart with red and green curves descending to vanish at zero. The calculations were delicate, minute, exquisitely clear; and delicate were the scientist's thin hands among the papers. He looked up, spoke with a hint of German accent. His words were not so much mispronounced as colored with a warm unfamiliar tint.

"Vell? Yes?"

"Oh, Professor Gottlieb, my name is Arrowsmith. I'm a medic freshman, Winnemac B.A. I'd like awfully to take bacteriology this fall instead of next year. I've had a lot of chemistry — "

"No. It is not time for you."

"Honest, I know I could do it now."

"There are two kinds of students the gods give me. One kind they dump on me like a bushel of potatoes. I do not like potatoes, and the potatoes they do not ever seem to have great affection for me, but I take them and teach them to kill patients. The other kind — they are very few! — they seem for some reason that is not at all clear to me to wish a liddle bit to become scientists, to work with bugs and make mistakes. Those, ah, those, I seize them, I denounce them, I teach them right away the ultimate lesson of science, which is to wait and doubt. Of the potatoes, I demand nothing; of the foolish ones like you, who think I could teach them something, I demand everything. No. You are too young. Come back next year."

"But honestly, with my chemistry — "

"Have you taken physical chemistry?"

"No, sir, but I did pretty well in organic."

"Organic chemistry! Puzzle chemistry! Stink chemistry! Drugstore chemistry! Physical chemistry is power, it is exactness, it is life. But organic chemistry — that is a trade for pot-washers. No. You are too young. Come back in a year."

Gottlieb was absolute. His talon fingers waved Martin to the door, and the boy hastened out, not daring to argue. He slunk off in misery. On the campus he met that jovial historian of chemistry, Encore Edwards, and begged, "Say, Professor, tell me, is there any value for a doctor in organic chemistry?"

"Value? Why, it seeks the drugs that allay pain! It produces the paint that slicks up your house, it dyes your sweetheart's dress — and maybe, in these degenerate days, her cherry lips! Who the dickens has been talking scandal about my organic chemistry?"

"Nobody. I was just wondering," Martin complained, and he drifted to the College Inn where, in an injured and melancholy manner, he devoured an enormous banana-split and a bar of almond chocolate, as he meditated:

"I want to take bacteriology. I want to get down to the bottom of this disease stuff. I'll learn some physical chemistry. I'll show old Gottlieb, damn him! Some day I'll discover the germ of cancer or something, and then he'll look foolish in the face!... Oh, Lord, I hope I won't take sick, first time I go into the dissecting-room.... I want to take bacteriology — now!"

He recalled Gottlieb's sardonic face; he felt and feared his quality of dynamic hatred. Then he remembered the wrinkles, and he saw Max Gottlieb not as a genius but as a man who had headaches, who became agonizingly tired, who could be loved.

"I wonder if Encore Edwards knows as much as I thought he did? What *is* Truth?" he puzzled.

## IV

Martin was jumpy on his first day of dissecting. He could not look at the inhumanly stiff faces of the starveling gray men lying on the wooden tables. But they were so impersonal, these lost old men, that in two days he was, like the other medics, calling them "Billy" and "Ike" and "the Parson," and regarding them as he had regarded animals in biology. The dissecting-room itself was impersonal: hard cement floor, walls of hard plaster between wire-glass windows. Martin detested the reek of formaldehyde; that and some dreadful subtle other odor seemed to cling about him outside the dissecting-room; but he smoked cigarettes to forget it, and in a week he was exploring arteries with youthful and altogether unholy joy.

His dissecting partner was the Reverend Ira Hinkley, known to the class by a similar but different name.

Ira was going to be a medical missionary. He was a man of twenty-nine, a graduate of Pottsburg Christian College and of the Sanctification Bible and Missions School. He had played football; he was as strong and nearly as large as a steer, and no steer ever bellowed more enormously. He was a bright and happy Christian, a romping optimist who laughed away sin and doubt, a joyful Puritan who with annoying virility preached the doctrine of his tiny sect, the Sanctification Brotherhood, that to have a beautiful church was almost as damnable as the debaucheries of card-playing.

Martin found himself viewing "Billy," their cadaver — an undersized, blotchy old man with a horrible little red beard on his petrified, vealy face — as a machine, fascinating, complex, beautiful, but a machine. It damaged his already feeble belief in man's divinity and immortality. He might have kept his doubts to himself, revolving them slowly as he dissected out the nerves of the mangled upper arm, but Ira Hinkley would not let him alone. Ira believed that he could bring even medical students to bliss, which, to Ira, meant singing extraordinarily long and unlovely hymns in a chapel of the Sanctification Brotherhood.

"Mart, my son," he roared, "do you realize that in this, what some might call a sordid task, we are learning things that will enable us to heal the bodies and comfort the souls of countless lost unhappy folks?"

"Huh! Souls. I haven't found one yet in old Billy. Honest, do you believe that junk?"

Ira clenched his fist and scowled, then belched with laughter, slapped Martin distressingly on the back, and clamored, "Brother, you've got to do better than that to get Ira's goat! You think you've got a lot of these fancy Modern Doubts. You haven't — you've only got indigestion. What you need is exercise and faith. Come on over to the Y.M.C.A. and I'll take you for a swim and pray with you. Why, you poor skinny little agnostic, here you have a chance to see the Almighty's handiwork, and all you grab out of it is a feeling that you're real smart. Buck up, young Arrowsmith. You don't know how funny you are, to a fellow that's got a serene faith!"

To the delight of Clif Clawson, the class jester, who worked at the next table, Ira chucked Martin in the ribs, patted him, very painfully, upon the head, and amiably resumed work, while Martin danced with irritation.

## V

In college Martin had been a "barb" — he had not belonged to a Greek Letter secret society. He had been "rushed," but he had resented the condescension of the aristocracy of men from the larger cities. Now that most of his Arts classmates had departed to insurance offices, law schools, and banks, he was lonely, and tempted by an invitation from Digamma Pi, the chief medical fraternity.

Digamma Pi was a lively boarding-house with a billiard table and low prices. Rough and amiable noises came from it at night, and a good deal of singing about When I Die Don't Bury Me at All; yet for three years Digams had won the valedictory and the Hugh Loizeau Medal in Experimental Surgery. This autumn the Digams elected Ira Hinkley, because they had been gaining a reputation for dissipation — girls were said to have been smuggled in late at night — and no company which included the Reverend Mr. Hinkley could possibly be taken by the Dean as immoral, which was an advantage if they were to continue comfortably immoral.

Martin had prized the independence of his solitary room. In a fraternity, all tennis rackets, trousers, and opinions are held in common. When Ira found that Martin was hesitating, he insisted, "Oh, come on in! Digam needs you. You do study hard — I'll say that for you — and think what a chance you'll have to influence The Fellows for good."

(On all occasions, Ira referred to his classmates as The Fellows, and frequently he used the term in prayers at the Y.M.C.A.)

"I don't want to influence anybody. I want to learn the doctor trade and make six thousand dollars a year."

"My boy, if you only knew how foolish you sound when you try to be cynical! When you're as old as I am, you'll understand that the glory of being a doctor is that you can teach folks high ideals while you soothe their tortured bodies."

"Suppose they don't want my particular brand of high ideals?"

"Mart, have I got to stop and pray with you?"

"No! Quit! Honestly, Hinkley, of all the Christians I ever met you take the rottenest advantages. You can lick anybody in the class, and when I think of how you're going to bully the poor heathen when you get to be a missionary, and make the kids put on breeches, and marry off all the happy lovers to the wrong people, I could bawl!"

The prospect of leaving his sheltered den for the patronage of the Reverend Mr. Hinkley was intolerable. It was not till Angus Duer accepted election to Digamma Pi that Martin himself came in.

Duer was one of the few among Martin's classmates in the academic course who had gone on with him to the Winnemac medical school. Duer had been the valedictorian. He was a silent, sharp-faced, curly-headed, rather handsome young man, and he never squandered an hour or a good impulse. So brilliant was his work in biology and chemistry that a Chicago surgeon had promised him a place in his clinic. Martin compared Angus Duer to a razor blade on a January morning; he hated him, was uncomfortable with him, and envied him. He knew that in biology Duer had been too busy passing examinations to ponder, to get any concept of biology as a whole. He knew that Duer was a tricky chemist, who neatly and swiftly completed the experiments demanded by the course and never ventured on original experiments which, leading him into a confused land of wondering, might bring him to glory or disaster. He was sure that Duer cultivated his manner of chill efficiency to impress instructors. Yet the man stood out so bleakly from a mass of students who could neither complete their experiments nor ponder nor do anything save smoke pipes and watch football-practice that Martin loved him while he hated him, and almost meekly he followed him into Digamma Pi.

Martin, Ira Hinkley, Angus Duer, Clif Clawson, the meaty class jester, and one "Fatty" Pfaff were initiated into Digamma Pi together. It was a noisy and rather painful performance, which included smelling asafetida. Martin was bored, but Fatty Pfaff was in squeaking, billowing, gasping terror.

Fatty was of all the new Freshmen candidates the most useful to Digamma Pi. He was planned by nature to be a butt. He looked like a distended hot-water bottle; he was magnificently imbecile; he believed everything, he knew nothing, he could memorize nothing; and anxiously he forgave the men who got through the vacant hours by playing jokes upon him. They persuaded him that mustard plasters were excellent for colds — solicitously they gathered about him, affixed an enormous plaster to his back, and afterward fondly removed it. They concealed the ear of a cadaver in his nice, clean, new pocket handkerchief when he went to Sunday supper at the house of a girl cousin in Zenith.... At supper he produced the handkerchief with a flourish.

Every night when Fatty retired he had to remove from his bed a collection of objects which thoughtful house-mates had stuffed between the sheets — soap, alarm clocks, fish. He was the perfect person to whom to sell useless things. Clif Clawson, who combined a brisk huckstering with his jokes, sold to Fatty for four dollars a History of Medicine which he had bought, second-hand, for two, and while Fatty never read it, never conceivably could read it, the possession of the fat red book made him feel learned. But Fatty's greatest beneficence to Digamma was his belief in spiritualism. He went about in terror of spooks. He was always seeing them emerging at night from the dissecting-room windows. His classmates took care that he should behold a great many of them flitting about the halls of the fraternity.

## VI

Digamma Pi was housed in a residence built in the expansive days of 1885. The living-room suggested a recent cyclone. Knife-gashed tables, broken Morris chairs, and torn rugs were flung about the room, and covered with backless books, hockey shoes, caps, and cigarette stubs. Above, there were four men to a bedroom, and the beds were iron double-deckers, like a steerage.

For ash-trays the Digams used sawed skulls, and on the bedroom walls were anatomical charts, to be studied while dressing. In Martin's room was a complete skeleton. He and his roommates had trustingly bought it from a salesman who came out from a Zenith surgical supply house. He was such a genial and sympathetic salesman; he gave them cigars and told G. U. stories and explained what prosperous doctors they were all going to be. They bought the skeleton gratefully, on the installment plan.... Later the salesman was less genial.

Martin roomed with Clif Clawson, Fatty Pfaff, and an earnest second-year medic named Irving Watters.

Any psychologist desiring a perfectly normal man for use in demonstrations could not have done better than to have engaged Irving Watters. He was always and carefully dull; smilingly, easily, dependably dull. If there was any cliché which he did not use, it was because he had not yet heard it. He believed in morality — except on Saturday evenings; he believed in the Episcopal Church — but not the High Church; he believed in the Constitution, Darwinism, systematic exercise in the gymnasium, and the genius of the president of the university.

Among them, Martin most liked Clif Clawson. Clif was the clown of the fraternity house, he was given to raucous laughter, he clogged and sang meaningless songs, he even practiced on the cornet, yet he was somehow a good fellow and solid, and Martin, in his detestation of Ira Hinkley, his fear of Angus Duer, his pity for Fatty Pfaff, his distaste for the amiable dullness of Irving Watters, turned to the roaring Clif as to something living and experimenting. At least Clif had reality; the reality of a plowed field, of a steaming manure-pile. It was Clif who would box with him; Clif who — though he loved to sit for hours smoking, grunting, magnificently loafing — could be persuaded to go for a five-mile walk.

And it was Clif who risked death by throwing baked beans at the Reverend Ira Hinkley at supper, when Ira was bulkily and sweetly corrective.

In the dissecting-room Ira was maddening enough with his merriment at such of Martin's ideas as had not been accepted in Pottsburg Christian College, but in the fraternity-house he was a moral pest. He never ceased trying to stop their profanity. After three years on a backwoods football team he still believed with unflinching optimism that he could sterilize young men by administering reproofs, with the nickering of a lady Sunday School teacher and the delicacy of a charging elephant.

Ira also had statistics about Clean Living.

He was full of statistics. Where he got them did not matter to him; figures in the daily papers, in the census report, or in the Miscellany Column of the *Sanctification Herald* were equally valid. He announced at supper table, "Clif, it's a wonder to me how as bright a fella as you can go on sucking that dirty old pipe. D'you realize that 67.9 per cent of all women who go to the operating table have husbands who smoke tobacco?"

"What the devil would they smoke?" demanded Clif.

"Where'd you get those figures?" from Martin.

"They came out at a medical convention in Philadelphia in 1902," Ira condescended. "Of course I don't suppose it'll make any difference to a bunch of wise galoots like you that some day you'll marry a nice bright little woman and ruin her life with your vices. Sure, keep right on — fine brave virile bunch! A poor weakling preacher like me wouldn't dare do anything so brave as smoke a pipe!"

He left them triumphantly, and Martin groaned, "Ira makes me want to get out of medicine and be an honest harness maker."

"Aw, gee now, Mart," Fatty Pfaff complained, "you oughtn't to cuss Ira out. He's awful sincere."

"Sincere? Hell! So is a cockroach!"

Thus they jabbered, while Angus Duer watched them in a superior silence that made Martin nervous. In the study of the profession to which he had looked forward all his life he found irritation and vacuity as well as serene wisdom; he saw no one clear path to Truth but a thousand paths to a thousand truths far-off and doubtful.

## Chapter 3

John A. Robertshaw, John Aldington Robertshaw, professor of physiology in the medical school, was rather deaf, and he was the only teacher in the University of Winnemac who still wore mutton-chop whiskers. He came from Back Bay; he was proud of it and let you know about it. With three other Brahmins he formed in Mohalis a Boston colony which stood for sturdy sweetness and decorously shaded light. On all occasions he remarked, "When I was studying with Ludwig in Germany — " He was too absorbed in his own correctness to heed individual students, and Clif Clawson and the other young men technically known as "hell-raisers" looked forward to his lectures on physiology.

They were held in an amphitheater whose seats curved so far around that the lecturer could not see both ends at once, and while Dr. Robertshaw, continuing to drone about blood circulation, was peering to the right to find out who was making that outrageous sound like a motor horn, far over on the left Clif Clawson would rise and imitate him, with sawing arm and stroking of imaginary whiskers. Once Clif produced the masterpiece of throwing a brick into the sink beside the platform, just when Dr. Robertshaw was working up to his annual climax about the effects of brass bands on the intensity of the knee-jerk.

Martin had been reading Max Gottlieb's scientific papers — as much of them as he could read, with their morass of mathematical symbols — and from them he had a conviction that experiments should be something dealing with the foundations of life and death, with the nature of bacterial infection, with the chemistry of bodily reactions. When Robertshaw chirped about fussy little experiments, standard experiments, maiden-aunt experiments, Martin was restless. In college he had felt that prosody and Latin Composition were futile, and he had looked forward to the study of medicine as illumination. Now, in melancholy worry about his own unreasonableness, he found that he was developing the same contempt for Robertshaw's rules of the thumb — and for most of the work in anatomy.

The professor of anatomy, Dr. Oliver O. Stout, was himself an anatomy, a dissection-chart, a thinly covered knot of nerves and blood vessels and bones. Stout had precise and enormous knowledge; in his dry voice he could repeat more facts about the left little toe than you would have thought anybody would care to learn regarding the left little toe.

No discussion at the Digamma Pi supper table was more violent than the incessant debate over the value to a doctor, a decent normal doctor who made a good living and did not worry about reading papers at medical associations, of remembering anatomical terms. But no matter what they thought, they all ground at learning the lists of names which enable a man to crawl through examinations and become an Educated Person, with a market value of five dollars an hour. Unknown sages had invented rimes which enabled them to memorize. At supper — the thirty piratical Digams sitting at a long and spotty table, devouring clam chowder and beans and codfish balls and banana layer-cake — the Freshmen earnestly repeated after a senior:

> On old Olympus' topmost top
> A fat-eared German viewed a hop.

Thus by association with the initial letters they mastered the twelve cranial nerves: olfactory, optic, oculomotor, trochlear, and the rest. To the Digams it was the world's noblest poem, and they remembered it for years after they had become practicing physicians and altogether forgotten the names of the nerves themselves.

### II

In Dr. Stout's anatomy lectures there were no disturbances, but in his dissecting-room were many pleasantries. The mildest of them was the insertion of a fire-cracker in the cadaver on which the two virginal and unhappy co-eds worked. The real excitement during Freshman year was the incident of Clif Clawson and the pancreas.

Clif had been elected class president, for the year, because he was so full of greetings. He never met a classmate in the hall of Main Medical without shouting, "How's your vermiform appendix functioning this morning?" or "I bid thee a lofty greeting, old pediculosis." With booming decorum he presided at class meetings (indignant meetings to denounce the proposal to let the "aggies" use the North Side Tennis Courts), but in private life he was less decorous.

The terrible thing happened when the Board of Regents were being shown through the campus. The Regents were the supreme rulers of the University; they were bankers and manufacturers and pastors of large churches; to them even the president was humble. Nothing gave them more interesting thrills than the dissecting-room of the medical school. The preachers spoke morally of the effect of alcohol on paupers, and the bankers of the disrespect for savings-accounts which is always to be seen in the kind of men who insist on becoming cadavers. In the midst of the tour, led by Dr. Stout and the umbrella-carrying secretary of the University, the plumpest and most educational of all the bankers stopped near Clif Clawson's dissecting-table, with his derby hat reverently held behind him, and into that hat Clif dropped a pancreas.

Now a pancreas is a damp and disgusting thing to find in your new hat, and when the banker did so find one, he threw down the hat and said that the students of Winnemac had gone to the devil. Dr. Stout and the secretary comforted him; they cleaned the derby and assured him that vengeance should be done on the man who could put a pancreas in a banker's hat.

Dr. Stout summoned Clif, as president of the Freshmen. Clif was pained. He assembled the class, he lamented that any Winnemac Man could place a pancreas in a banker's hat, and he demanded that the criminal be manly enough to stand up and confess.

Unfortunately the Reverend Ira Hinkley, who sat between Martin and Angus Duer, had seen Clif drop the pancreas. He growled, "This is outrageous! I'm going to expose Clawson, even if he is a frat-brother of mine."

Martin protested, "Cut it out. You don't want to get him fired?"

"He ought to be!"

Angus Duer turned in his seat, looked at Ira, and suggested, "Will you kindly shut up?" and, as Ira subsided, Angus became to Martin more admirable and more hateful than ever.

## III

When he was depressed by a wonder as to why he was here, listening to a Professor Robertshaw, repeating verses about fat-eared Germans, learning the trade of medicine like Fatty Pfaff or Irving Watters, then Martin had relief in what he considered debauches. Actually they were extremely small debauches; they rarely went beyond too much lager in the adjacent city of Zenith, or the smiles of a factory girl parading the sordid back avenues, but to Martin, with his pride in taut strength, his joy in a clear brain, they afterward seemed tragic.

His safest companion was Clif Clawson. No matter how much bad beer he drank, Clif was never much more intoxicated than in his normal state. Martin sank or rose to Clif's buoyancy, while Clif rose or sank to Martin's speculativeness. As they sat in a back-room, at a table glistening with beer-glass rings, Clif shook his finger and babbled, "You're only one 'at gets me, Mart. You know with all the hell-raising, and all the talk about bein' c'mmercial that I pull on these high boys like Ira Stinkley, I'm jus' sick o' c'mmercialism an' bunk as you are."

"Sure. You bet," Martin agreed with alcoholic fondness. "You're jus' like me. My God, do you get it — dough-face like Irving Watters or heartless climber like Angus Duer, and then old Gottlieb! Ideal of research! Never bein' content with what *seems* true! Alone, not carin' a damn, square-toed as a captain on the bridge, working all night, getting to the bottom of things!"

"Thash stuff. That's my idee, too. Lez have 'nother beer. Shake you for it!" observed Clif Clawson.

Zenith, with its saloons, was fifteen miles from Mohalis and the University of Winnemac; half an hour by the huge, roaring, steel interurban trolleys, and to Zenith the medical students went for their forays. To say that one had "gone into town last night" was a matter for winks and leers. But with Angus Duer, Martin discovered a new Zenith.

At supper Duer said abruptly, "Come into town with me and hear a concert."

For all his fancied superiority to the class, Martin was illimitably ignorant of literature, of painting, of music. That the bloodless and acquisitive Angus Duer should waste time listening to fiddlers was astounding to him. He discovered that Duer had enthusiasm for two composers, called Bach and Beethoven, presumably Germans, and that he himself did not yet comprehend all the ways of the world. On the interurban, Duer's gravity loosened, and he cried, "Boy, if I hadn't been born to carve up innards, I'd have been a great musician! Tonight I'm going to lead you right into Heaven!"

Martin found himself in a confusion of little chairs and vast gilded arches, of polite but disapproving ladies with programs in their laps, unromantic musicians making unpleasant noises below and, at last, incomprehensible beauty, which made for him pictures of hills and deep forests, then suddenly became achingly long-winded. He exulted, "I'm going to have 'em all — the fame of Max Gottlieb — I mean his ability — and the lovely music and lovely women — Golly! I'm going to do big things. And see the world.... Will this piece never quit?"

## IV

It was a week after the concert that he rediscovered Madeline Fox.

Madeline was a handsome, high-colored, high-spirited, opinionated girl whom Martin had known in college. She was staying on, ostensibly to take a graduate course in English, actually to avoid going back home. She considered herself a superb tennis player; she played it with energy and voluble swoopings and large lack of direction. She believed herself to be a connoisseur of literature; the fortunates to whom she gave her approval were Hardy, Meredith, Howells, and Thackeray, none of whom she had read for five years. She had often reproved Martin for his inappreciation of Howells, for wearing flannel shirts, and for his failure to hand her down from street-cars in the manner of a fiction hero. In college, they had gone to dances together, though as a dancer Martin was more spirited than accurate, and his partners sometimes had difficulty in deciding just what he was trying to dance. He liked Madeline's tall comeliness and her vigor; he felt that with her energetic culture she was somehow "good for him." During this year, he had scarcely seen her. He thought of her late in the evenings, and planned to telephone to her, and did not telephone. But as he became doubtful about medicine he longed for her sympathy, and on a Sunday afternoon of spring he took her for a walk along the Chaloosa River.

From the river bluffs the prairie stretches in exuberant rolling hills. In the long barley fields, the rough pastures, the stunted oaks and brilliant birches, there is the adventurousness of the frontier, and like young plainsmen they tramped the bluffs and told each other they were going to conquer the world.

He complained, "These damn' medics — "

"Oh, Martin, do you think 'damn' is a nice word?" said Madeline.

He did think it was a very nice word indeed, and constantly useful to a busy worker, but her smile was desirable.

"Well — these darn' studes, they aren't trying to learn science; they're simply learning a trade. They just want to get the knowledge that'll enable them to cash in. They don't talk about saving lives but about 'losing cases' — losing dollars! And they wouldn't even mind losing cases if it was a sensational operation that'd advertise 'em! They make me sick! How many of 'em do you find that're interested in the work Ehrlich is doing in Germany — yes, or that Max Gottlieb is doing right here and now! Gottlieb's just taken an awful fall out of Wright's opsonin theory."

"Has he, really?"

"*Has* he! I should say he had! And do you get any of the medics stirred up about it? You do not! They say, 'Oh, sure, science is all right in its way; helps a doc to treat his patients,' and then they begin to argue about whether they can make more money if they locate in a big city or a town, and is it better for a young doc to play the good-fellow and lodge game, or join the church and look earnest. You ought to hear Irve Watters. He's just got one idea: the fellow that gets ahead in medicine, is he the lad that knows his pathology? Oh, no; the bird that succeeds is the one that gets an office on a northeast corner, near a trolley car junction, with a 'phone number that'll be easy for patients to remember! Honest! He said so! I swear, when I graduate I believe I'll be a ship's doctor. You see the world that way, and at least you aren't racing up and down the boat trying to drag patients away from some rival doc that has an office on another deck!"

"Yes, I know; it's dreadful the way people don't have ideals about their work. So many of the English grad students just want to make money teaching, instead of enjoying scholarship the way I do."

It was disconcerting to Martin that she should seem to think that she was a superior person quite as much as himself, but he was even more disconcerted when she bubbled:

"At the same time, Martin, one does have to be practical, doesn't one! Think how much more money — no, I mean how much more social position and power for doing good a successful doctor has than one of these scientists that just putter, and don't know what's going on in the world. Look at a surgeon like Dr. Loizeau, riding up to the hospital in a lovely car with a chauffeur in uniform, and all his patients simply worshiping him, and then your Max Gottlieb — somebody pointed him out to me the other day, and he had on a dreadful old suit, and I certainly thought he could stand a hair-cut."

Martin turned on her with fury, statistics, vituperation, religious zeal, and confused metaphors. They sat on a crooked old-fashioned rail-fence where over the sun-soaked bright plantains the first insects of spring were humming. In the storm of his fanaticism she lost her airy Culture and squeaked, "Yes, I see now, I see," without stating what it was she saw. "Oh, you do have a fine mind and such fine — such integrity."

"Honest? Do you think I have?"

"Oh, indeed I do, and I'm sure you're going to have a wonderful future. And I'm so glad you aren't commercial, like the others. Don't mind what they say!"

He noted that Madeline was not only a rare and understanding spirit but also an extraordinarily desirable woman — fresh color, tender eyes, adorable slope from shoulder to side. As they walked back, he perceived that she was incredibly the right mate for him. Under his training she would learn the distinction between vague "ideals" and the hard sureness of science. They paused on the bluff, looking down at the muddy Chaloosa, a springtime Western river wild with floating branches. He yearned for her; he regretted the casual affairs of a student and determined to be a pure and extremely industrious young man, to be, in fact, "worthy of her."

"Oh, Madeline," he mourned, "you're so darn' lovely!"

She glanced at him, timidly.

He caught her hand; in a desperate burst he tried to kiss her. It was very badly done. He managed only to kiss the point of her jaw, while she struggled and begged, "Oh, don't!" They did not acknowledge, as they ambled back into Mohalis, that the incident had occurred, but there was softness in their voices and without impatience now she heard his denunciation of Professor Robertshaw as a phonograph, and he listened to her remarks on the shallowness and vulgarity of Dr. Norman Brumfit, that sprightly English instructor. At her boarding-house she sighed, "I wish I could ask you to come in, but it's almost suppertime and — Will you call me up some day?"

"You bet I will!" said Martin, according to the rules for amorous discourse in the University of Winnemac.

He raced home in adoration. As he lay in his narrow upper bunk at midnight, he saw her eyes, now impertinent, now reproving, now warm with trust in him. "I love her! I *love* her! I'll 'phone her — Wonder if I dare call her up as early as eight in the morning?"

But at eight he was too busy studying the lacrimal apparatus to think of ladies' eyes. He saw Madeline only once, and in the publicity of her boarding-house porch, crowded with coeds, red cushions, and marshmallows, before he was hurled into hectic studying for the year's final examinations.

## V

At examination-time, Digamma Pi fraternity showed its value to urgent seekers after wisdom. Generations of Digams had collected test-papers and preserved them in the sacred Quiz Book; geniuses for detail had labored through the volume and marked with red pencil the problems most often set in the course of years. The Freshmen crouched in a ring about Ira Hinkley in the Digam living-room, while he read out the questions they were most likely to get. They writhed, clawed their hair, scratched their chins, bit their fingers, and beat their temples in the endeavor to give the right answer before Angus Duer should read it to them out of the textbook.

In the midst of their sufferings they had to labor with Fatty Pfaff.

Fatty had failed in the mid-year anatomical, and he had to pass a special quiz before he could take the finals. There was a certain fondness for him in Digamma Pi; Fatty was soft, Fatty was superstitious, Fatty was an imbecile, yet they had for him the annoyed affection they might have had for a second-hand motor or a muddy dog. All of them worked on him; they tried to lift him and thrust him through the examination as through a trap-door. They panted and grunted and moaned at the labor, and Fatty panted and moaned with them.

The night before his special examination they kept him at it till two, with wet towels, black coffee, prayer, and profanity. They repeated lists — lists — lists to him; they shook their fists in his mournful red round face and howled, "Damn you, *will* you remember that the bicuspid valve is the SAME as the mitral valve and NOT another one?" They ran about the room, holding up their hands and wailing, "Won't he never remember nothing about nothing?" and charged back to purr with fictive calm, "Now no use getting fussed, Fatty. Take it easy. Just listen to this, quietly, will yuh, and try," coaxingly, "do try to remember *one* thing, anyway!"

They led him carefully to bed. He was so filled with facts that the slightest jostling would have spilled them.

When he awoke at seven, with red eyes and trembling lips, he had forgotten everything he had learned.

"There's nothing for it," said the president of Digamma Pi. "He's got to have a crib, and take his chance on getting caught with it. I thought so. I made one out for him yesterday. It's a lulu. It'll cover enough of the questions so he'll get through."

Even the Reverend Ira Hinkley, since he had witnessed the horrors of the midnight before, went his ways ignoring the crime. It was Fatty himself who protested: "Gee, I don't like to cheat. I don't think a fellow that can't get through an examination had hardly ought to be allowed to practice medicine. That's what my Dad said."

They poured more coffee into him and (on the advice of Clif Clawson, who wasn't exactly sure what the effect might be but who was willing to learn) they fed him a potassium bromide tablet. The president of Digamma, seizing Fatty with some firmness, growled, "I'm going to stick this crib in your pocket — look, here in your breast pocket, behind your handkerchief."

"I won't use it. I don't care if I fail," whimpered Fatty.

"That's all right, but you keep it there. Maybe you can absorb a little information from it through your lungs, for God knows — " The president clenched his hair. His voice rose, and in it was all the tragedy of night watches and black draughts and hopeless retreats. " — God knows you can't take it in through your head!"

They dusted Fatty, they stood him right side up, and pushed him through the door, on his way to Anatomy Building. They watched him go: a balloon on legs, a sausage in corduroy trousers.

"Is it possible he's going to be honest?" marveled Clif Clawson.

"Well, if he is, we better go up and begin packing his trunk. And this ole frat'll never have another goat like Fatty," grieved the president.

They saw Fatty stop, remove his handkerchief, mournfully blow his nose — and discover a long thin slip of paper. They saw him frown at it, tap it on his knuckles, begin to read it, stuff it back into his pocket, and go on with a more resolute step.

They danced hand in hand about the living-room of the fraternity, piously assuring one another, "He'll use it — it's all right — he'll get through or get hanged!"

He got through.

## VI

Digamma Pi was more annoyed by Martin's restless doubtings than by Fatty's idiocy, Clif Clawson's raucousness, Angus Duer's rasping, or the Reverend Ira Hinkley's nagging.

During the strain of study for examinations Martin was peculiarly vexing in regard to "laying in the best quality medical terms like the best quality sterilizers — not for use but to impress your patients." As one, the Digams suggested, "Say, if you don't like the way we study medicine, we'll be tickled to death to take up a collection and send you back to Elk Mills, where you won't be disturbed by all us lowbrows and commercialists. Look here! We don't tell you how you ought to work. Where do you get the idea you got to tell us? Oh, turn it off, will you!"

Angus Duer observed, with sour sweetness, "We'll admit we're simply carpenters, and you're a great investigator. But there's several things you might turn to when you finish science. What do you know about architecture? How's your French verbs? How many big novels have you ever read? Who's the premier of Austro-Hungary?"

Martin struggled, "I don't pretend to know anything — except I do know what a man like Max Gottlieb means. He's got the right method, and all these other hams of profs, they're simply witch doctors. You think Gottlieb isn't religious, Hinkley. Why, his just being in a lab is a prayer. Don't you idiots realize what it means to have a man like that here, making new concepts of life? Don't you — "

Clif Clawson, with a chasm of yawning, speculated, "Praying in the lab! I'll bet I get the pants took off me, when I take bacteriology, if Pa Gottlieb catches me praying during experiment hours!"

"Damn it, listen!" Martin wailed. "I tell you, you fellows are the kind that keep medicine nothing but guesswork diagnosis, and here you have a man — "

So they argued for hours, after their sweaty fact-grinding.

When the others had gone to bed, when the room was a muck-heap of flung clothing and weary young men snoring in iron bunks, Martin sat at the splintery long pine study-table, worrying. Angus Duer glided in, demanding, "Look here, old son. We're all sick of your crabbing. If you think medicine is rot, the way we study it, and if you're so confoundedly honest, why don't you get out?"

He left Martin to agonize, "He's right. I've got to shut up or get out. Do I really mean it? What do I want? What am I going to do?"

## VII

Angus Duer's studiousness and his reverence for correct manners were alike offended by Clif's bawdy singing, Clif's howling conversation, Clif's fondness for dropping things in people's soup, and Clif's melancholy inability to keep his hands washed. For all his appearance of nerveless steadiness, during the tension of examination-time Duer was as nervous as Martin, and one evening at supper, when Clif was bellowing, Duer snapped, "Will you kindly not make so much racket?"

"I'll make all the damn' racket I damn' please!" Clif asserted, and a feud was on.

Clif was so noisy thereafter that he almost became tired of his own noise. He was noisy in the living-room, he was noisy in the bath, and with some sacrifice he lay awake pretending to snore. If Duer was quiet and book-wrapped, he was not in the least timid; he faced Clif with the eye of a magistrate, and cowed him. Privily Clif complained to Martin, "Darn him, he acts like I was a worm. Either he or me has got to get out of Digam, that's a cinch, and it won't be me!"

He was ferocious and very noisy about it, and it was he who got out. He said that the Digams were a "bunch of bum sports; don't even have a decent game of poker," but he was fleeing from the hard eyes of Angus Duer. And Martin resigned from the fraternity with him, planned to room with him the coming autumn.

Clif's blustering rubbed Martin as it did Duer. Clif had no reticences; when he was not telling slimy stories he was demanding, "How much chuh pay for those shoes — must think you're a Vanderbilt!" or "D'I see you walking with that Madeline Fox femme — what chuh tryin' to do?" But Martin was alienated from the civilized, industrious, nice young men of Digamma Pi, in whose faces he could already see prescriptions, glossy white sterilizers, smart enclosed motors, and glass office-signs in the best gilt lettering. He preferred a barbarian loneliness, for next year he would be working with Max Gottlieb, and he could not be bothered.

That summer he spent with a crew installing telephones in Montana.

He was a lineman in the wire-gang. It was his job to climb the poles, digging the spurs of his leg-irons into the soft and silvery pine, to carry up the wire, lash it to the glass insulators, then down and to another pole.

They made perhaps five miles a day; at night they drove into little rickety wooden towns. Their retiring was simple — they removed their shoes and rolled up in a horse-blanket. Martin wore overalls and a flannel shirt. He looked like a farm-hand. Climbing all day long, he breathed deep, his eyes cleared of worry, and one day he experienced a miracle.

He was atop a pole and suddenly, for no clear cause, his eyes opened and he saw; as though he had just awakened he saw that the prairie was vast, that the sun was kindly on rough pasture and ripening wheat, on the old horses, the easy, broad-beamed, friendly horses, and on his red-faced jocose companions; he saw that the meadow larks were jubilant, and blackbirds shining by little pools, and with the living sun all life was living. Suppose the Angus Duers and Irving Watterses were tight tradesmen. What of it? "I'm *here*!" he gloated.

The wire-gang were as healthy and as simple as the west wind; they had no pretentiousness; though they handled electrical equipment they did not, like medics, learn a confusion of scientific terms and pretend to the farmers that they were scientists. They laughed easily and were content to be themselves, and with them Martin was content to forget how noble he was. He had for them an affection such as he had for no one at the University save Max Gottlieb.

He carried in his bag one book, Gottlieb's "Immunology." He could often get through half a page of it before he bogged down in chemical formulae. Occasionally, on Sundays or rainy days, he tried to read it, and longed for the laboratory; occasionally he thought of Madeline Fox, and became certain that he was devastatingly lonely for her. But week slipped into careless and robust week, and when he awoke in a stable, smelling the sweet hay and the horses and the lark-ringing prairie that crept near to the heart of these shanty towns, he cared only for the day's work, the day's hiking, westward toward the sunset.

So they straggled through the Montana wheatland, whole duchies of wheat in one shining field, through the cattle-country and the sagebrush desert, and suddenly, staring at a persistent cloud, Martin realized that he beheld the mountains.

Then he was on a train; the wire-gang were already forgotten; and he was thinking only of Madeline Fox, Clif Clawson, Angus Duer, and Max Gottlieb.

## Chapter 4

Professor Max Gottlieb was about to assassinate a guinea pig with anthrax germs, and the bacteriology class were nervous.

They had studied the forms of bacteria, they had handled Petri dishes and platinum loops, they had proudly grown on potato slices the harmless red cultures of *Bacillus prodigiosus* , and they had come now to pathogenic germs and the inoculation of a living animal with swift disease. These two beady-eyed guinea pigs, chittering in a battery jar, would in two days be stiff and dead.

Martin had an excitement not free from anxiety. He laughed at it, he remembered with professional scorn how foolish were the lay visitors to the laboratory, who believed that sanguinary microbes would leap upon them from the mysterious centrifuge, from the benches, from the air itself. But he was conscious that in the cotton-plugged test-tube between the instrument-bath and the bichloride jar on the demonstrator's desk were millions of fatal anthrax germs.

The class looked respectful and did not stand too close. With the flair of technique, the sure rapidity which dignified the slightest movement of his hands, Dr. Gottlieb clipped the hair on the belly of a guinea pig held by the assistant. He soaped the belly with one flicker of a hand-brush, he shaved it and painted it with iodine.

(And all the while Max Gottlieb was recalling the eagerness of his first students, when he had just returned from working with Koch and Pasteur, when he was fresh from enormous beer seidels and Korpsbrüder and ferocious arguments. Passionate, beautiful days! *Die goldene Zeit!* His first classes in America, at Queen City College, had been awed by the sensational discoveries in bacteriology; they had crowded about him reverently; they had longed to know. Now the class was a mob. He looked at them — Fatty Pfaff in the front row, his face vacant as a doorknob; the co-eds emotional and frightened; only Martin Arrowsmith and Angus Duer visibly intelligent. His memory fumbled for a pale blue twilight in Munich, a bridge and a waiting girl, and the sound of music.)

He dipped his hands in the bichloride solution and shook them — a quick shake, fingers down, like the fingers of a pianist above the keys. He took a hypodermic needle from the instrument-bath and lifted the test-tube. His voice flowed indolently, with German vowels and blurred W's:

"This, gentlemen, iss a twenty-four-hour culture of *Bacillus anthracis* . You will note, I am sure you will have noted already, that in the bottom of the tumbler there was cotton to keep the tube from being broken. I cannot advise breaking tubes of anthrax germs and afterwards getting the hands into the culture. You *might* merely get anthrax boils — "

The class shuddered.

Gottlieb twitched out the cotton plug with his little finger, so neatly that the medical students who had complained, "Bacteriology is junk; urinalysis and blood tests are all the lab stuff we need to know," now gave him something of the respect they had for a man who could do card tricks or remove an appendix in seven minutes. He agitated the mouth of the tube in the Bunsen burner, droning, "Every time you take the plug from a tube, flame the mouth of the tube. Make that a rule. It is a necessity of the technique, and technique, gentlemen, iss the beginning of all science. It iss also the least-known thing in science."

The class was impatient. Why didn't he get on with it, on to the entertainingly dreadful moment of inoculating the pig?

(And Max Gottlieb, glancing at the other guinea pig in the prison of its battery jar, meditated, "Wretched innocent! Why should I murder him, to teach *Dummköpfe* ? It would be better to experiment on that fat young man.")

He thrust the syringe into the tube, he withdrew the piston dextrously with his index finger, and lectured:

"Take one half c.c. of the culture. There are two kinds of M.D.'s — those to whom c.c. means cubic centimeter and those to whom it means compound cathartic. The second kind are more prosperous."

(But one cannot convey the quality of it: the thin drawl, the sardonic amiability, the hiss of the S's, the D's turned into blunt and challenging T's.)

The assistant held the guinea pig close; Gottlieb pinched up the skin of the belly and punctured it with a quick down thrust of the hypodermic needle. The pig gave a little jerk, a little squeak, and the co-eds shuddered. Gottlieb's wise fingers knew when the peritoneal wall was reached. He pushed home the plunger of the syringe. He said quietly, "This poor animal will now soon be dead as Moses." The class glanced at one another uneasily. "Some of you will think that it does not matter; some of you will think, like Bernard Shaw, that I am an executioner and the more monstrous because I am cool about it; and some of you will not think at all. This difference in philosophy iss what makes life interesting."

While the assistant tagged the pig with a tin disk in its ear and restored it to the battery jar, Gottlieb set down its weight in a note-book, with the time of inoculation and the age of the bacterial culture. These notes he reproduced on the blackboard, in his fastidious script, murmuring, "Gentlemen, the most important part of living is not the living but pondering upon it. And the most important part of experimentation is not doing the experiment but making notes, ve-ry accurate *quantitative* notes — in ink. I am told that a great many clever people feel they can keep notes in their heads. I have often observed with pleasure that such persons do not have heads in which to keep their notes. This iss very good, because thus the world never sees their results and science is not encumbered with them. I shall now inoculate the second guinea pig, and the class will be dismissed. Before the next lab hour I shall be glad if you will read Pater's 'Marius the Epicurean,' to derife from it the calmness which iss the secret of laboratory skill."

## II

As they bustled down the hall, Angus Duer observed to a brother Digam, "Gottlieb is an old laboratory plug; he hasn't got any imagination; he sticks here instead of getting out into the world and enjoying the fight. But he certainly is handy. Awfully good technique. He might have been a first-rate surgeon, and made fifty thousand dollars a year. As it is, I don't suppose he gets a cent over four thousand!"

Ira Hinkley walked alone, worrying. He was an extraordinarily kindly man, this huge and bumbling parson. He reverently accepted everything, no matter how contradictory to everything else, that his medical instructors told him, but this killing of animals — he hated it. By a connection not evident to him he remembered that the Sunday before, in the slummy chapel where he preached during his medical course, he had exalted the sacrifice of the martyrs and they had sung of the blood of the lamb, the fountain filled with blood drawn from Emmanuel's veins, but this meditation he lost, and he lumbered toward Digamma Pi in a fog of pondering pity.

Clif Clawson, walking with Fatty Pfaff, shouted, "Gosh, ole pig certainly did jerk when Pa Gottlieb rammed that needle home!" and Fatty begged, "Don't! Please!"

But Martin Arrowsmith saw himself doing the same experiment and, as he remembered Gottlieb's unerring fingers, his hands curved in imitation.

## III

The guinea pigs grew drowsier and drowsier. In two days they rolled over, kicked convulsively, and died. Full of dramatic expectation, the class reassembled for the necropsy. On the demonstrator's table was a wooden tray, scarred from the tacks which for years had pinned down the corpses. The guinea pigs were in a glass jar, rigid, their hair ruffled. The class tried to remember how nibbling and alive they had been. The assistant stretched out one of them with thumbtacks. Gottlieb swabbed its belly with a cotton wad soaked in lysol, slit it from belly to neck, and cauterized the heart with a red-hot spatula — the class quivered as they heard the searing of the flesh. Like a priest of diabolic mysteries, he drew out the blackened blood with a pipette. With the distended lungs, the spleen and kidneys and liver, the assistant made wavy smears on glass slides which were stained and given to the class for examination. The students who had learned to look through the microscope without having to close one eye were proud and professional, and all of them talked of the beauty of identifying the bacillus, as they twiddled the brass thumbscrews to the right focus and the cells rose from cloudiness to sharp distinctness on the slides before them. But they were uneasy, for Gottlieb remained with them that day, stalking behind them, saying nothing, watching them always, watching the disposal of the remains of the guinea pigs, and along the benches ran nervous rumors about a bygone student who had died from anthrax infection in the laboratory.

## IV

There was for Martin in these days a quality of satisfying delight; the zest of a fast hockey game, the serenity of the prairie, the bewilderment of great music, and a feeling of creation. He woke early and thought contentedly of the day; he hurried to his work, devout, unseeing.

The confusion of the bacteriological laboratory was ecstasy to him — the students in shirt-sleeves, filtering nutrient gelatine, their fingers gummed from the crinkly gelatine leaves; or heating media in an autoclave like a silver howitzer. The roaring Bunsen flames beneath the hot-air ovens, the steam from the Arnold sterilizers rolling to the rafters, clouding the windows, were to Martin lovely with activity, and to him the most radiant things in the world were rows of test-tubes filled with watery serum and plugged with cotton singed to a coffee brown, a fine platinum loop leaning in a shiny test-glass, a fantastic hedge of tall glass tubes mysteriously connecting jars, or a bottle rich with gentian violet stain.

He had begun, perhaps in youthful imitation of Gottlieb, to work by himself in the laboratory at night. ... The long room was dark, thick dark, but for the gas-mantle behind his microscope. The cone of light cast a gloss on the bright brass tube, a sheen on his black hair, as he bent over the eyepiece. He was studying trypanosomes from a rat — an eight-branched rosette stained with polychrome methylene blue; a cluster of organisms delicate as a narcissus, with their purple nuclei, their light blue cells, and the thin lines of the flagella. He was excited and a little proud; he had stained the germs perfectly, and it is not easy to stain a rosette without breaking the petal shape. In the darkness, a step, the weary step of Max Gottlieb, and a hand on Martin's shoulder. Silently Martin raised his head, pushed the microscope toward him. Bending down, a cigarette stub in his mouth — the smoke would have stung the eyes of any human being — Gottlieb peered at the preparation.

He adjusted the gas light a quarter inch, and mused, "Splendid! You have craftsmanship. Oh, there is an art in science — for a few. You Americans, so many of you — all full with ideas, but you are impatient with the beautiful dullness of long labors. I see already — and I watch you in the lab before — perhaps you may try the trypanosomes of sleeping sickness. They are very, very interesting, and very, very ticklish to handle. It is quite a nice disease. In some villages in Africa, fifty per cent of the people have it, and it is invariably fatal. Yes, I think you might work on the bugs."

Which, to Martin, was getting his brigade in battle.

"I shall have," said Gottlieb, "a little sandwich in my room at midnight. If you should happen to work so late, I should be very pleast if you would come to have a bite."

Diffidently, Martin crossed the hall to Gottlieb's immaculate laboratory at midnight. On the bench were coffee and sandwiches, curiously small and excellent sandwiches, foreign to Martin's lunch-room taste.

Gottlieb talked till Clif had faded from existence and Angus Duer seemed but an absurd climber. He summoned forth London laboratories, dinners on frosty evenings in Stockholm, walks on the Pincio with sunset behind the dome of San Pietro, extreme danger and overpowering disgust from excreta-smeared garments in an epidemic at Marseilles. His reserve slipped from him and he talked of himself and of his family as though Martin were a contemporary.

The cousin who was a colonel in Uruguay and the cousin, a rabbi, who was tortured in a pogrom in Moscow. His sick wife — it might be cancer. The three children — the youngest girl, Miriam, she was a good musician, but the boy, the fourteen-year-old, he was a worry; he was saucy, he would not study. Himself, he had worked for years on the synthesis of antibodies; he was at present in a blind alley, and at Mohalis there was no one who was interested, no one to stir him, but he was having an agreeable time massacring the opsonin theory, and that cheered him.

"No, I have done nothing except be unpleasant to people that claim too much, but I have dreams of real discoveries some day. And — No. Not five times in five years do I have students who understand craftsmanship and precision and maybe some big imagination in hypotheses. I t'ink perhaps you may have them. If I can help you — So!

"I do not t'ink you will be a good doctor. Good doctors are fine — often they are artists — but their trade, it is not for us lonely ones that work in labs. Once, I took an M.D. label. In Heidelberg that was — Herr Gott, back in 1875! I could not get much interested in bandaging legs and looking at tongues. I was a follower of Helmholtz — what a wild blithering young fellow! I tried to make researches in the physics of sound — I was bad, most unbelievable, but I learned that in this wale of tears there is nothing certain but the quantitative method. And I was a chemist — a fine stink-maker was I. And so into biology and much trouble. It has been good. I have found one or two things. And if sometimes I feel an exile, cold — I had to get out of Germany one time for refusing to sing *Die Wacht am Rhein* and trying to kill a cavalry captain — he was a stout fellow — I had to choke him — you see I am boasting, but I was a lifely *Kerl* thirty years ago! Ah! So!

"There is but one trouble of a philosophical bacteriologist. Why should we destroy these amiable pathogenic germs? Are we too sure, when we regard these oh, most unbeautiful young students attending Y.M.C.A.'s and singing dinkle-songs and wearing hats with initials burned into them — iss it worth while to protect them from the so elegantly functioning *Bacillus typhosus* with its lovely flagella? You know, once I asked Dean Silva would it not be better to let loose the pathogenic germs on the world, and so solve all economic questions. But he did not care for my met'od. Oh, well, he is older than I am; he also gives, I hear, some dinner parties with bishops and judges present, all in nice clothes. He would know more than a German Jew who loves Father Nietzsche and Father Schopenhauer (but damn him, he was teleological-minded!) and Father Koch and Father Pasteur and Brother Jacques Loeb and Brother Arrhenius. Ja! I talk foolishness. Let us go look at your slides and so good night."

When he had left Gottlieb at his stupid brown little house, his face as reticent as though the midnight supper and all the rambling talk had never happened, Martin ran home altogether drunk.

## Chapter 5

Though bacteriology was all of Martin's life now, it was the theory of the University that he was also studying pathology, hygiene, surgical anatomy, and enough other subjects to swamp a genius.

Clif Clawson and he lived in a large room with flowered wallpaper, piles of filthy clothes, iron beds, and cuspidors. They made their own breakfasts; they dined on hash at the Pilgrim Lunch Wagon or the Dew Drop Inn. Clif was occasionally irritating; he hated open windows; he talked of dirty socks; he sang "Some die of Diabetes" when Martin was studying; and he was altogether unable to say anything directly. He had to be humorous. He remarked, "Is it your combobulatory concept that we might now feed the old faces?" or "How about ingurgitating a few calories?" But he had for Martin a charm that could not be accounted for by cheerfulness, his shrewdness, his vague courage. The whole of Clif was more than the sum of his various parts.

In the joy of his laboratory work Martin thought rarely of his recent associates in Digamma Pi. He occasionally protested that the Reverend Ira Hinkley was a village policeman and Irving Watters a plumber, that Angus Duer would walk to success over his grandmother's head, and that for an idiot like Fatty Pfaff to practice on helpless human beings was criminal, but mostly he ignored them and ceased to be a pest. And when he had passed his first triumphs in bacteriology and discovered how remarkably much he did not know, he was curiously humble.

If he was less annoying in regard to his classmates, he was more so in his classrooms. He had learned from Gottlieb the trick of using the word "control" in reference to the person or animal or chemical left untreated during an experiment, as a standard for comparison; and there is no trick more infuriating. When a physician boasted of his success with this drug or that electric cabinet, Gottlieb always snorted, "Where was your control? How many cases did you have under identical conditions, and how many of them did not get the treatment?" Now Martin began to mouth it — control, control, control, where's your control? where's your control? — till most of his fellows and a few of his instructors desired to lynch him.

He was particularly tedious in materia medica.

The professor of materia medica, Dr. Lloyd Davidson, would have been an illustrious shopkeeper. He was very popular. From him a future physician could learn that most important of all things: the proper drugs to give a patient, particularly when you cannot discover what is the matter with him. His classes listened with zeal, and memorized the sacred hundred and fifty favorite prescriptions. (He was proud that this was fifty more than his predecessor had required.)

But Martin was rebellious. He inquired, and publicly, "Dr. Davidson, how do they know ichthyol is good for erysipelas? Isn't it just rotten fossil fish — isn't it like the mummy-dust and puppy-ear stuff they used to give in the olden days?"

"How do they know? Why, my critical young friend, because thousands of physicians have used it for years and found their patients getting better, and that's how they know!"

"But honest, Doctor, wouldn't the patients maybe have gotten better anyway? Wasn't it maybe a *post hoc, propter hoc* ? Have they ever experimented on a whole slew of patients together, with controls?"

"Probably not — and until some genius like yourself, Arrowsmith, can herd together a few hundred people with exactly identical cases of erysipelas, it probably never will be tried! Meanwhile I trust that you other gentlemen, who perhaps lack Mr. Arrowsmith's profound scientific attainments and the power to use such handy technical terms as 'control,' will, merely on my feeble advice, continue to use ichthyol!"

But Martin insisted, "Please, Dr. Davidson, what's the use of getting all these prescriptions by heart, anyway? We'll forget most of 'em, and besides, we can always look 'em up in the book."

Davidson pressed his lips together, then:

"Arrowsmith, with a man of your age I hate to answer you as I would a three-year-old boy, but apparently I must. Therefore, you will learn the properties of drugs and the contents of prescriptions *because I tell you to*! If I did not hesitate to waste the time of the other members of this class, I would try to convince you that my statements may be accepted, not on my humble authority, but because they are the conclusions of wise men — men wiser or certainly a little older than you, my friend — through many ages. But as I have no desire to indulge in fancy flights of rhetoric and eloquence, I shall merely say that you will accept, and you will study, and you will memorize, because I tell you to!"

Martin considered dropping his medical course and specializing in bacteriology. He tried to confide in Clif, but Clif had become impatient of his fretting, and he turned again to the energetic and willowy Madeline Fox.

## II

Madeline was at once sympathetic and sensible. Why not complete his medical course, then see what he wanted to do?

They tramped, they skated, they skied, they went to the University Dramatic Society play. Madeline's widowed mother had come to live with her, and they had taken a top-floor flat in one of the tiny apartment-houses which were beginning to replace the expansive old wooden houses of Mohalis. The flat was full of literature and decoration: a bronze Buddha from Chicago, a rubbing of Shakespeare's epitaph, a set of Anatole France in translation, a photograph of Cologne cathedral, a wicker tea-table with a samovar whose operation no one in the University understood, and a souvenir post-card album. Madeline's mother was a Main Street dowager duchess. She was stately and white-haired but she attended the Methodist Church. In Mohalis she was flustered by the chatter of the students; she longed for her home-town, for the church sociables and the meetings of the women's club — they were studying Education this year and she hated to lose all the information about university ways.

With a home and a chaperone, Madeline began to "entertain": eight-o'clock parties with coffee, chocolate cake, chicken salad, and word-games. She invited Martin, but he was jealous of his evenings, beautiful evenings of research. The first affair to which she enticed him was her big New Year's Party in January. They "did advertisements" — guessed at tableaux representing advertising pictures; they danced to the phonograph; and they had not merely a lap-supper but little tables excessively covered with doilies.

Martin was unaccustomed to such elegance. Though he had come in sulky unwillingness, he was impressed by the supper, by the frocks of the young women; he realized that his dancing was rusty, and he envied the senior who could do the new waltz called the "Boston." There was no strength, no grace, no knowledge, that Martin Arrowsmith did not covet, when consciousness of it had pierced through the layers of his absorption. If he was but little greedy for possessions, he was hungry for every skill.

His reluctant wonder at the others was drowned in his admiration for Madeline. He had known her as a jacketed outdoor girl, but this was an exquisite indoor Madeline, slender in yellow silk. She seemed to him a miracle of tact and ease as she bullied her guests into an appearance of merriment. She had need of tact, for Dr. Norman Brumfit was there, and it was one of Dr. Brumfit's evenings to be original and naughty. He pretended to kiss Madeline's mother, which vastly discomforted the poor lady; he sang a strongly improper Negro song containing the word hell; he maintained to a group of women graduate students that George Sand's affairs might perhaps be partially justified by their influence on men of talent; and when they looked shocked, he pranced a little, and his eye-glasses glittered.

Madeline took charge of him. She trilled, "Dr. Brumfit, you're terribly learned and so on and so forth, and sometimes in English classes I'm simply scared to death of you, but other times you're nothing but a bad small boy, and I won't have you teasing the girls. You can help me bring in the sherbet, that's what you can do."

Martin adored her. He hated Brumfit for the privilege of disappearing with her into the closet-like kitchen of the flat. Madeline! She was the one person who understood him! Here, where everyone snatched at her and Dr. Brumfit beamed on her with almost matrimonial fondness, she was precious, she was something he must have.

On pretense of helping her set the tables, he had a moment with her, and whimpered, "Lord, you're so lovely!"

"I'm glad you think I'm a wee bit nice." She, the rose and the adored of all the world, gave him her favor.

"Can I come call on you tomorrow evening?"

"Well, I — Perhaps."

## III

It cannot be said, in this biography of a young man who was in no degree a hero, who regarded himself as a seeker after truth yet who stumbled and slid back all his life and bogged himself in every obvious morass, that Martin's intentions toward Madeline Fox were what is called "honorable." He was not a Don Juan, but he was a poor medical student who would have to wait for years before he could make a living. Certainly he did not think of proposing marriage. He wanted — like most poor and ardent young men in such a case, he wanted all he could get.

As he raced toward her flat, he was expectant of adventure. He pictured her melting; he felt her hand glide down his cheek. He warned himself, "Don't be a fool now! Probably nothing doing at all. Don't go get all worked up and then be disappointed. She'll probably cuss you out for something you did wrong at the party. She'll probably be sleepy and wish you hadn't come. Nothing!" But he did not for a second believe it.

He rang, he saw her opening the door, he followed her down the meager hall, longing to take her hand. He came into the over-bright living-room — and he found her mother, solid as a pyramid, permanent-looking as sunless winter.

But of course Mother would obligingly go, and leave him to conquest.

Mother did not.

In Mohalis, the suitable time for young men callers to depart is ten o'clock, but from eight till a quarter after eleven Martin did battle with Mrs. Fox; talked to her in two languages, an audible gossip and a mute but furious protest, while Madeline — she was present; she sat about and looked pretty. In an equally silent tongue Mrs. Fox answered him, till the room was thick with their antagonism, while they seemed to be discussing the weather, the University, and the trolley service into Zenith.

"Yes, of course, some day I guess they'll have a car every twenty minutes," he said weightily.

("Darn her, why doesn't she go to bed? Cheers! She's doing up her knitting. Nope. Damn it! She's taking another ball of wool.")

"Oh, yes, I'm sure they'll have to have better service," said Mrs. Fox.

("Young man, I don't know much about you, but I don't believe you're the right kind of person for Madeline to go with. Anyway, it's time you went home.")

"Oh, yes, sure, you bet. Lot better service."

("I know I'm staying too long, and I know you know it, but I don't care!")

It seemed impossible that Mrs. Fox should endure his stolid persistence. He used thought-forms, will-power, and hypnotism, and when he rose, defeated, she was still there, extremely placid. They said good-by not too warmly. Madeline took him to the door; for an exhilarating half-minute he had her alone.

"I wanted so much — I wanted to talk to you!"

"I know. I'm sorry. Some time!" she muttered.

He kissed her. It was a tempestuous kiss, and very sweet.

## IV

Fudge parties, skating parties, sleighing parties, a literary party with the guest of honor a lady journalist who did the social page for the Zenith *Advocate-Times* — Madeline leaped into an orgy of jocund but extraordinarily tiring entertainments, and Martin obediently and smolderingly followed her. She appeared to have trouble in getting enough men, and to the literary evening Martin dragged the enraged Clif Clawson. Clif grumbled, "This is the damnedest zoo of sparrows I ever did time in," but he bore off treasure — he had heard Madeline call Martin by her favorite name of "Martykins." That was very valuable. Clif called him Martykins. Clif told others to call him Martykins. Fatty Pfaff and Irving Watters called him Martykins. And when Martin wanted to go to sleep, Clif croaked:

"Yuh, you'll probably marry her. She's a dead shot. She can hit a smart young M.D. at ninety paces. Oh, you'll have one fine young time going on with science after that skirt sets you at tonsil-snatching.... She's one of these literary birds. She knows all about lite'ature except maybe how to read.... She's not so bad-looking, now. She'll get fat, like her Ma."

Martin said that which was necessary, and he concluded, "She's the only girl in the graduate school that's got any pep. The others just sit around and talk, and she gets up the best parties — "

"Any kissing parties?"

"Now you look here! I'll be getting sore, first thing you know! You and I are roughnecks, but Madeline Fox — she's like Angus Duer, some ways. I realize all the stuff we're missing: music and literature, yes, and decent clothes, too — no harm to dressing well — "

"That's just what I was tellin' you! She'll have you all dolled up in a Prince Albert and a boiled shirt, diagnosing everything as rich-widowitis. How you can fall for that four-flushing dame — *Where's your control?* "

Clif's opposition stirred him to consider Madeline not merely with a sly and avaricious interest but with a dramatic conviction that he longed to marry her.

## V

Few women can for long periods keep from trying to Improve their men, and To Improve means to change a person from what he is, whatever that may be, into something else. Girls like Madeline Fox, artistic young women who do not work at it, cannot be restrained from Improving for more than a day at a time. The moment the urgent Martin showed that he was stirred by her graces, she went at his clothes — his corduroys and soft collars and eccentric old gray felt hat — at his vocabulary and his taste in fiction, with new and more patronizing vigor. Her sketchy way of saying, "Why, of course everybody knows that Emerson was the greatest thinker" irritated him the more in contrast to Gottlieb's dark patience.

"Oh, let me alone!" he hurled at her. "You're the nicest thing the Lord ever made, when you stick to things you know about, but when you spring your ideas on politics and chemotherapy — Darn it, quit bullying me! I guess you're right about slang. I'll cut out all this junk about 'feeding your face' and so on. But I will not put on a hard-boiled collar! I won't!"

He might never have proposed to her but for the spring evening on the roof.

She used the flat roof of her apartment-house as a garden. She had set out one box of geraniums and a cast-iron bench like those once beheld in cemetery plots; she had hung up two Japanese lanterns — they were ragged and they hung crooked. She spoke with scorn of the other inhabitants of the apartment-house, who were "so prosaic, so conventional, that they never came up to this darling hidey-place." She compared her refuge to the roof of a Moorish palace, to a Spanish patio, to a Japanese garden, to a "pleasaunce of old Provençal." But to Martin it seemed a good deal like a plain roof. He was vaguely ready for a quarrel, that April evening when he called on Madeline and her mother sniffily told him that she was to be found on the roof.

"Damned Japanese lanterns. Rather look at liver-sections," he grumbled, as he trudged up the curving stairs.

Madeline was sitting on the funereal iron bench, her chin in her hands. For once she did not greet him with flowery excitement but with a noncommittal "Hello." She seemed spiritless. He felt guilty for his scoffing; he suddenly saw the pathos in her pretense that this stretch of tar-paper and slatted walks was a blazing garden. As he sat beside her he piped, "Say, that's a dandy new strip of matting you've put down."

"It is not! It's mangy!" She turned toward him. She wailed, "Oh, Mart, I'm so sick of myself, tonight. I'm always trying to make people think I'm somebody. I'm not. I'm a bluff."

"What is it, dear?"

"Oh, it's lots. Dr. Brumfit, hang him — only he was right — he as good as told me that if I don't work harder I'll have to get out of the graduate school. I'm not doing a thing, he said, and if I don't have my Ph.D., then I won't be able to land a nice job teaching English in some swell school, and I'd better land one, too, because it doesn't look to poor Madeline as if anybody was going to marry her."

His arm about her, he blared, "I know exactly who — "

"No, I'm not fishing. I'm almost honest, tonight. I'm no good, Mart. I tell people how clever I am. And I don't suppose they believe it. Probably they go off and laugh at me!"

"They do not! If they did — I'd like to see anybody that tried laughing — "

"It's awfully sweet and dear of you, but I'm not worth it. The poetic Madeline. With her ree-fined vocabulary! I'm a — I'm a — Martin, I'm a tin-horn sport! I'm everything your friend Clif thinks I am. Oh, you needn't tell me. I know what he thinks. And — I'll have to go home with Mother, and I can't stand it, dear, I can't stand it! I won't go back! That town! Never anything doing! The old tabbies, and the beastly old men, always telling the same old jokes. I won't!"

Her head was in the hollow of his arm; she was weeping, hard; he was stroking her hair, not covetously now but tenderly, and he was whispering:

"Darling! I almost feel as if I dared to love you. You're going to marry me and — Take me couple more years to finish my medical course and couple in hospital, then we'll be married and — By thunder, with you helping me, I'm going to climb to the top! Be big surgeon! We're going to have everything!"

"Dearest, do be wise. I don't want to keep you from your scientific work — "

"Oh. Well. Well, I would like to keep up *some* research. But thunder, I'm not just a lab-cat. Battle o' life. Smashing your way through. Competing with real men in real he-struggle. If I can't do that and do some scientific work too, I'm no good. Course while I'm with Gottlieb, I want to take advantage of it, but afterwards — Oh, Madeline!"

Then was all reasoning lost in a blur of nearness to her.

## VI

He dreaded the interview with Mrs. Fox; he was certain that she would demand, "Young man, how do you expect to support my Maddy? And you use bad language." But she took his hand and mourned, "I hope you and my baby will be happy. She's a dear good girl, even if she is a little flighty sometimes, and I know you're nice and kind and hard-working. I shall pray you'll be happy — oh, I'll pray so hard! You young people don't seem to think much of prayer, but if you knew how it helped me — Oh, I'll petition for your sweet happiness!"

She was weeping; she kissed Martin's forehead with the dry, soft, gentle kiss of an old woman, and he was near to weeping with her.

At parting Madeline whispered, "Boy, I don't care a bit, myself, but Mother would love it if we went to church with her. Don't you think you could, just once?"

The astounded world, the astounded and profane Clif Clawson, had the spectacle of Martin in shiny pressed clothes, a painful linen collar, and an arduously tied scarf, accompanying Mrs. Fox and the chastely chattering Madeline to the Mohalis Methodist Church, to hear the Reverend Dr. Myron Schwab discourse on "The One Way to Righteousness."

They passed the Reverend Ira Hinkley, and Ira gloated with a holy gloating at Martin's captivity.

## VII

For all his devotion to Max Gottlieb's pessimistic view of the human intellect, Martin had believed that there was such a thing as progress, that events meant something, that people could learn something, that if Madeline had once admitted she was an ordinary young woman who occasionally failed, then she was saved. He was bewildered when she began improving him more airily than ever. She complained of his vulgarity and what she asserted to be his slack ambition. "You think it's terribly smart of you to feel superior. Sometimes I wonder if it isn't just laziness. You like to day-dream around labs. Why should *you* be spared the work of memorizing your materia medica and so on and so forth? All the others have to do it. No, I won't kiss you. I want you to grow up and listen to reason."

In fury at her badgering, in desire for her lips and forgiving smile, he was whirled through to the end of the term.

A week before examinations, when he was trying to spend twenty-four hours a day in making love to her, twenty-four in grinding for examinations, and twenty-four in the bacteriological laboratory, he promised Clif that he would spend that summer vacation with him, working as a waiter in a Canadian hotel. He met Madeline in the evening, and with her walked through the cherry orchard on the Agricultural Experiment Station grounds.

"You know what I think of your horrid Clif Clawson," she complained. "I don't suppose you care to hear my opinion of him."

"I've had your opinion, my beloved." Martin sounded mature, and not too pleasant.

"Well, I can tell you right now you haven't had my opinion of your being a waiter! For the life of me I can't understand why you don't get some gentlemanly job for vacation, instead of hustling dirty dishes. Why couldn't you work on a newspaper, where you'd have to dress decently and meet nice people?"

"Sure. I might edit the paper. But since you say so, I won't work at all this summer. Fool thing to do, anyway. I'll go to Newport and play golf and wear a dress suit every night."

"It wouldn't hurt you any! I do respect honest labor. It's like Burns says. But waiting on table! Oh, Mart, why are you so proud of being a roughneck? Do stop being smart, for a minute. Listen to the night. And smell the cherry blossoms.... Or maybe a great scientist like you, that's so superior to ordinary people, is too good for cherry blossoms!"

"Well, except for the fact that every cherry blossom has been gone for weeks now, you're dead right."

"Oh, they have, have they! They may be faded but — Will you be so good as to tell me what that pale white mass is up there?"

"I will. It looks to me like a hired-man's shirt."

"Martin Arrowsmith, if you think for one moment that I'm ever going to marry a vulgar, crude, selfish, microbe-grubbing smart aleck — "

"And if you think I'm going to marry a dame that keeps nag-nag-naggin' and jab-jab-jabbin' at me all day long — "

They hurt each other; they had pleasure in it; and they parted forever, twice they parted forever, the second time very rudely, near a fraternity-house where students were singing heartbreaking summer songs to a banjo.

In ten days, without seeing her again, he was off with Clif to the North Woods, and in his sorrow of losing her, his longing for her soft flesh and for her willingness to listen to him, he was only a little excited that he should have led the class in bacteriology, and that Max Gottlieb should have appointed him undergraduate assistant for the coming year.

## Chapter 6

The waiters at Nokomis Lodge, among the Ontario pines, were all of them university students. They were not supposed to appear at the Lodge dances — they merely appeared, and took the prettiest girls away from the elderly and denunciatory suitors in white flannels. They had to work but seven hours a day. The rest of the time they fished, swam, and tramped the shadowy trails, and Martin came back to Mohalis placid — and enormously in love with Madeline.

They had written to each other, politely, regretfully, and once a fortnight; then passionately and daily. For the summer she had been dragged to her home town, near the Ohio border of Winnemac, a town larger than Martin's Elk Mills but more sun-baked, more barren with little factories. She sighed, in a huge loose script dashing all over the page:

> *Perhaps we shall never see each other again but I do want you to know how much I prize all the talks we had together about science & ideals & education, etc. — I certainly appreciate them here when I listen to these stick in the muds going on, oh, it is too dreadful, about their automobiles & how much they have to pay their maids and so on & so forth. You gave me so much but I did give you something didn't I? I cant always be in the wrong can I?*

"My dear, my little girl!" he lamented. "'Can't always be in the wrong'! You poor kid, you poor dear kid!"

By midsummer they were firmly re-engaged and, though he was slightly disturbed by the cashier, a young and giggling Wisconsin school-teacher with ankles, he so longed for Madeline that he lay awake thinking of giving up his job and fleeing to her caresses — lay awake for minutes at a time.

The returning train was torturingly slow, and he dismounted at Mohalis fevered with visions of her. Twenty minutes after, they were clinging together in the quiet of her living room. It is true that twenty minutes after that, she was sneering at Clif Clawson, at fishing, and at all school-teachers, but to his fury she yielded in tears.

### II

His Junior year was a whirlwind. To attend lectures on physical diagnosis, surgery, neurology, obstetrics, and gynecology in the morning, with hospital demonstrations in the afternoon; to supervise the making of media and the sterilization of glassware for Gottlieb; to instruct a new class in the use of the microscope and filter and autoclave; to read a page now and then of scientific German or French; to see Madeline constantly; to get through it all he drove himself to hysterical hurrying, and in the dizziest of it he began his first original research — his first lyric, his first ascent of unexplored mountains.

He had immunized rabbits to typhoid, and he believed that if he mixed serum taken from these immune animals with typhoid germs, the germs would die. Unfortunately — he felt — the germs grew joyfully. He was troubled; he was sure that his technique had been clumsy; he performed his experiment over and over, working till midnight, waking at dawn to ponder on his notes. (Though in letters to Madeline his writing was an inconsistent scrawl, in his laboratory notes it was precise.) When he was quite sure that Nature was persisting in doing something she ought not to, he went guiltily to Gottlieb, protesting, "The darn' bugs ought to die in this immune serum, but they don't. There's something wrong with the theories."

"Young man, do you set yourself up against science?" grated Gottlieb, flapping the papers on his desk. "Do you feel competent, huh, to attack the dogmas of immunology?"

"I'm sorry, sir. I can't help what the dogma is. Here's my protocols. Honestly, I've gone over and over the stuff, and I get the same results, as you can see. I only know what I observe."

Gottlieb beamed. "I give you, my boy, my episcopal blessings! That is the way! Observe what you observe, and if it does violence to all the nice correct views of science — out they go! I am very pleast, Martin. But now find out the Why, the underneath principle."

Ordinarily, Gottlieb called him "Arrowsmith" or "You" or "Uh." When he was furious he called him, or any other student, "Doctor." It was only in high moments that he honored him with "Martin," and the boy trotted off blissfully, to try to find (but never to succeed in finding) the Why that made everything so.

**III**

Gottlieb had sent him into Zenith, to the huge Zenith General Hospital, to secure a strain of meningococcus from an interesting patient. The bored reception clerk — who was interested only in obtaining the names, business addresses, and religions of patients, and did not care who died or who spat on the beautiful blue and white linoleum or who went about collecting meningococci, so long as the addresses were properly entered — loftily told him to go up to Ward D. Through the long hallways, past numberless rooms from which peered yellow-faced old women sitting up in bed in linty nightgowns, Martin wandered, trying to look important, hoping to be taken for a doctor, and succeeding only in feeling extraordinarily embarrassed.

He passed several nurses rapidly, half nodding to them, in the manner (or what he conceived to be the manner) of a brilliant young surgeon who is about to operate. He was so absorbed in looking like a brilliant young surgeon that he was completely lost, and discovered himself in a wing filled with private suites. He was late. He had no more time to go on being impressive. Like all males, he hated to confess ignorance by asking directions, but grudgingly he stopped at the door of a bedroom in which a probationer nurse was scrubbing the floor.

She was a smallish and slender probationer, muffled in a harsh blue denim dress, an enormous white apron, and a turban bound about her head with an elastic — a uniform as grubby as her pail of scrub-water. She peered up with the alert impudence of a squirrel.

"Nurse," he said, "I want to find Ward D."

Lazily, "Do you?"

"I do! If I can interrupt your work — "

"Doesn't matter. The damn' superintendent of nurses put me at scrubbing, and we aren't ever *supposed* to scrub floors, because she caught me smoking a cigarette. She's an old terror. If she found a child like you wandering around here, she'd drag you out by the ear."

"My *dear* young woman, it may interest you to know — "

"Oh! 'My dear young woman, it may — ' Sounds exactly like our old prof, back home."

Her indolent amusement, her manner of treating him as though they were a pair of children making tongues at each other in a railroad station, was infuriating to the earnest young assistant of Professor Gottlieb.

"I am Dr. Arrowsmith," he snorted, "and I've been informed that even probationers learn that the first duty of a nurse is to stand when addressing doctors! I wish to find Ward D, to take a strain of — *it may interest you to know!* — a very dangerous microbe, and if you will kindly direct me — "

"Oh, gee, I've been getting fresh again. I don't seem to get along with this military discipline. All right. I'll stand up." She did. Her every movement was swiftly smooth as the running of a cat. "You go back, turn right, then left. I'm sorry I was fresh. But if you saw some of the old muffs of doctors that a nurse has to be meek to — Honestly, Doctor — if you *are* a doctor — "

"I don't see that I need to convince you!" he raged, as he stalked off. All the way to Ward D he was furious at her veiled derision. He was an eminent scientist, and it was outrageous that he should have to endure impudence from a probationer — a singularly vulgar probationer, a thin and slangy young woman apparently from the West. He repeated his rebuke: "I don't see that I need to convince you." He was proud of himself for having been lofty. He pictured himself telling Madeline about it, concluding, "I just said to her quietly, 'My dear young woman, I don't know that you are the person to whom I have to explain my mission here,' I said, and she wilted."

But her image had not wilted, when he had found the intern who was to help him and had taken the spinal fluid. She was before him, provocative, enduring. He had to see her again, and convince her — "Take a better man than she is, better man than I've ever met, to get away with being insulting to *me*!" said the modest young scientist.

He had raced back to her room and they were staring at each other before it came to him that he had not worked out the crushing things he was going to say. She had risen from her scrubbing. She had taken off her turban, and her hair was silky and honey-colored, her eyes were blue, her face childish. There was nothing of the slavey in her. He could imagine her running down hillsides, shinning up a sack of straw.

"Oh," she said gravely. "I didn't mean to be rude then. I was just — Scrubbing makes me bad-tempered. I thought you were awfully nice, and I'm sorry I hurt your feelings, but you did seem so young for a doctor."

"I'm not. I'm a medic. I was showing off."

"So was I!"

He felt an instant and complete comradeship with her, a relation free from the fencing and posing of his struggle with Madeline. He knew that this girl was of his own people. If she was vulgar, jocular, unreticent, she was also gallant, she was full of laughter at humbugs, she was capable of a loyalty too casual and natural to seem heroic. His voice was lively, though his words were only:

"Pretty hard, this training for nursing, I guess."

"Not so awful, but it's just as romantic as being a hired girl — that's what we call 'em in Dakota."

"Come from Dakota?"

"I come from the most enterprising town — three hundred and sixty-two inhabitants — in the entire state of North Dakota — Wheatsylvania. Are you in the U. medic school?"

To a passing nurse, the two youngsters would have seemed absorbed in hospital business. Martin stood at the door, she by her scrubbing pail. She had reassumed her turban; its bagginess obscured her bright hair.

"Yes, I'm a Junior medic in Mohalis. But — I don't know. I'm not much of a medic. I like the lab side. I think I'll be a bacteriologist, and raise Cain with some of the fool theories of immunology. And I don't think much of the bedside manner."

"I glad you don't. You get it here. You ought to hear some of the docs that are the sweetest old pussies with their patients — the way they bawl out the nurses. But labs — they seem sort of real. I don't suppose you can bluff a bacteria — what is it? — bacterium?"

"No, they're — What do they call you?"

"Me? Oh, it's an idiotic name — Leora Tozer."

"What's the matter with Leora? It's fine."

Sound of mating birds, sound of spring blossoms dropping in the tranquil air, the bark of sleepy dogs at midnight; who is to set them down and make them anything but hackneyed? And as natural, as conventional, as youthfully gauche, as eternally beautiful and authentic as those ancient sounds was the talk of Martin and Leora in that passionate half-hour when each found in the other a part of his own self, always vaguely missed, discovered now with astonished joy. They rattled like hero and heroine of a sticky tale, like sweat-shop operatives, like bouncing rustics, like prince and princess. Their words were silly and inconsequential, heard one by one, yet taken together they were as wise and important as the tides or the sounding wind.

He told her that he admired Max Gottlieb, that he had crossed her North Dakota on a train, and that he was an excellent hockey-player. She told him that she "adored" vaudeville, that her father, Andrew Jackson Tozer, was born in the East (by which she meant Illinois), and that she didn't particularly care for nursing. She had no especial personal ambition; she had come here because she liked adventure. She hinted, with debonair regret, that she was not too popular with the superintendent of nurses; she meant to be good but somehow she was always dragged into rebellions connected with midnight fudge or elopements. There was nothing heroic in her story but from her placid way of telling it he had an impression of gay courage.

He interrupted with an urgent, "When can you get away from the hospital for dinner? Tonight?"

"Why — "

"Please!"

"All right."

"When can I call for you?"

"Do you think I ought to — Well, seven."

All the way back to Mohalis he alternately raged and rejoiced. He informed himself that he was a moron to make this long trip into Zenith twice in one day; he remembered that he was engaged to a girl called Madeline Fox; he worried the matter of unfaithfulness; he asserted that Leora Tozer was merely an imitation nurse who was as illiterate as a kitchen wench and as impertinent as a newsboy; he decided, several times he decided, to telephone her and free himself from the engagement.

He was at the hospital at a quarter to seven.

He had to wait for twenty minutes in a reception-room like that of an undertaker. He was in a panic. What was he doing here? She'd probably be agonizingly dull, through a whole long dinner. Would he even recognize her, in mufti? Then he leaped up. She was at the door. Her sulky blue uniform was gone; she was childishly slim and light in a princess frock that was a straight line from high collar and soft young breast to her feet. It seemed natural to tuck her hand under his arm as they left the hospital. She moved beside him with a little dancing step, shyer now than she had been in the dignity of her job but looking up at him with confidence.

"Glad I came?" he demanded.

She thought it over. She had a trick of gravely thinking over obvious questions; and gravely (but with the gravity of a child, not the ponderous gravity of a politician or an office-manager) she admitted, "Yes, I am glad. I was afraid you'd go and get sore at me because I was so fresh, and I wanted to apologize and — I liked your being so crazy about your bacteriology. I think I'm a little crazy, too. The interns here — they come bothering around a lot, but they're so sort of — so sort of *soggy* , with their new stethoscopes and their brand-new dignity. Oh — " Most gravely of all: "Oh, gee, yes, I'm glad you came.... Am I an idiot to admit it?"

"You're a darling to admit it." He was a little dizzy with her. He pressed her hand with his arm.

"You won't think I let every medic and doctor pick me up, will you?"

"Leora! And you don't think I try and pick up every pretty girl I meet? I liked — I felt somehow we two could be chums. Can't we? Can't we?"

"I don't know. We'll see. Where are we going for dinner?"

"The Grand Hotel."

"We are not! It's terribly expensive. Unless you're awfully rich. You aren't, are you?"

"No, I'm not. Just enough money to get through medic school. But I want — "

"Let's go to the Bijou. It's a nice place, and it isn't expensive."

He remembered how often Madeline Fox had hinted that it would be a tasty thing to go to the Grand, Zenith's most resplendent hotel, but that was the last time he thought of Madeline that evening. He was absorbed in Leora. He found in her a casualness, a lack of prejudice, a directness, surprising in the daughter of Andrew Jackson Tozer. She was feminine but undemanding; she was never Improving and rarely shocked; she was neither flirtatious nor cold. She was indeed the first girl to whom he had ever talked without self-consciousness. It is doubtful if Leora herself had a chance to say anything, for he poured out his every confidence as a disciple of Gottlieb. To Madeline, Gottlieb was a wicked old man who made fun of the sanctities of Marriage and Easter lilies, to Clif, he was a bore, but Leora glowed as Martin banged the table and quoted his idol: "Up to the present, even in the work of Ehrlich, most research has been largely a matter of trial and error, the empirical method, which is the opposite of the scientific method, by which one seeks to establish a general law governing a group of phenomena so that he may predict what will happen."

He intoned it reverently, staring across the table at her, almost glaring at her. He insisted, "Do you see where he leaves all these detail-grubbing, machine-made researchers buzzing in the manure heap just as much as he does the commercial docs? Do you get him? Do you?"

"Yes, I think I do. Anyway, I get your enthusiasm for him. But please don't bully me so!"

"Was I bullying? I didn't mean to. Only, when I get to thinking about the way most of these damned profs don't even know what he's up to — "

Martin was off again, and if Leora did not altogether understand the relation of the synthesis of antibodies to the work of Arrhenius, yet she listened with comfortable pleasure in his zeal, with none of Madeline Fox's gently corrective admonitions.

She had to warn him that she must be at the hospital by ten.

"I've talked too much! Lord, I hope I haven't bored you," he blurted.

"I loved it."

"And I was so technical, and so noisy — Oh, I *am* a chump!"

"I like having you trust me. I'm not 'earnest,' and I haven't any brains whatever, but I do love it when my menfolks think I'm intelligent enough to hear what they really think and — Good night!"

They dined together twice in two weeks, and only twice in that time, though she telephoned to him, did Martin see his honest affianced, Madeline.

He came to know all of Leora's background. Her bed-ridden grand-aunt in Zenith, who was her excuse for coming so far to take hospital training. The hamlet of Wheatsylvania, North Dakota; one street of shanties with the red grain-elevators at the end. Her father, Andrew Jackson Tozer, sometimes known as Jackass Tozer; owner of the bank, of the creamery, and an elevator, therefore the chief person in town; pious at Wednesday evening prayer-meeting, fussing over every penny he gave to Leora or her mother. Bert Tozer, her brother; squirrel teeth, a gold eye-glass chain over his ear, cashier and all the rest of the staff in the one-room bank owned by his father. The chicken salad and coffee suppers at the United Brethren Church; German Lutheran farmers singing ancient Teutonic hymns; the Hollanders, the Bohemians and Poles. And round about the village, the living wheat, arched above by tremendous clouds. He saw Leora, always an "odd child," doing obediently enough the flat household tasks but keeping snug the belief that some day she would find a youngster with whom, in whatever danger or poverty, she would behold all the colored world.

It was at the end of her hesitating effort to make him see her childhood that he cried, "Darling, you don't have to tell me about you. I've always known you. I'm not going to let you go, no matter what. You're going to marry me — "

They said it with clasping hands, confessing eyes, in that blatant restaurant. Her first words were:

"I want to call you 'Sandy.' Why do I? I don't know why. You're as unsandy as can be, but somehow 'Sandy' means you to me and — Oh, my dear, I do like you!"

Martin went home engaged to two girls at once.

## IV

He had promised to see Madeline the next morning.

By any canon of respectable behavior he should have felt like a low dog; he assured himself that he must feel like a low dog; but he could not bring it off. He thought of Madeline's pathetic enthusiasms: her "Provençal pleasaunce" and the limp-leather volumes of poetry which she patted with fond finger-tips; of the tie she had bought for him, and her pride in his hair when he brushed it like the patent-leather heroes in magazine illustrations. He mourned that he had sinned against loyalty. But his agitation broke against the solidity of his union with Leora. Her companionship released his soul. Even when, as advocate for Madeline, he pleaded that Leora was a trivial young woman who probably chewed gum in private and certainly was careless about her nails in public, her commonness was dear to the commonness that was in himself, valid as ambition or reverence, an earthy base to her gaiety as it was to his nervous scientific curiosity.

He was absent-minded in the laboratory, that fatal next day. Gottlieb had twice to ask him whether he had prepared the new batch of medium, and Gottlieb was an autocrat, sterner with his favorites than with the ruck of students. He snarled, "Arrowsmith, you are a moon-calf! My God, am I to spend my life with *Dummköpfe*? I cannot be always alone, Martin! Are you going to fail me? Two, three days now you haf not been keen about work."

Martin went off mumbling, "I love that man!" In his tangled mood he catalogued Madeline's pretenses, her nagging, her selfishness, her fundamental ignorance. He worked himself up to a state of virtue in which it was agreeably clear to him that he must throw Madeline over, entirely as a rebuke. He went to her in the evening prepared to blaze out at her first complaining, to forgive her finally, but to break their engagement and make life resolutely simple again.

She did not complain.

She ran to him. "Dear, you're so tired — your eyes look tired. Have you been working frightfully hard? I've been so sorry you couldn't come 'round, this week. Dear, you mustn't kill yourself. Think of all the years you have ahead to do splendid things in. No, don't talk. I want you to rest. Mother's gone to the movies. Sit here. See, I'll make you so comfy with these pillows. Just lean back — go to sleep if you want to — and I'll read you 'The Crock of Gold.' You'll love it."

He was determined that he would not love it and, as he probably had no sense of humor whatever, it is doubtful whether he appreciated it, but its differentness aroused him. Though Madeline's voice was shrill and cornfieldish after Leora's lazy softness, she read so eagerly that he was sick ashamed of his intention to hurt her. He saw that it was she, with her pretenses, who was the child, and the detached and fearless Leora who was mature, mistress of a real world. The reproofs with which he had planned to crush her vanished.

Suddenly she was beside him, begging, "I've been so lonely for you, all week!"

So he was a traitor to both women. It was Leora who had intolerably roused him; it was really Leora whom he was caressing now; but it was Madeline who took his hunger to herself, and when she whimpered, "I'm so glad you're glad to be here," he could say nothing. He wanted to talk about Leora, to shout about Leora, to exult in her, his woman. He dragged out a few sound but unimpassioned flatteries; he observed that Madeline was a handsome young woman and a sound English scholar; and while she gaped with disappointment at his lukewarmness, he got himself away, at ten. He had finally succeeded very well indeed in feeling like a low dog.

He hastened to Clif Clawson.

He had told Clif nothing about Leora. He resented Clif's probable scoffing. He thought well of himself for the calmness with which he came into their room. Clif was sitting on the small of his back, shoeless feet upon the study table, reading a Sherlock Holmes story which rested on the powerful volume of Osler's Medicine which he considered himself to be reading.

"Clif! Want a drink. Tired. Let's sneak down to Barney's and see if we can rustle one."

"Thou speakest as one having tongues and who putteth the speed behind the ole rhombencephalon comprising the cerebellum and the medulla oblongata."

"Oh, cut out the cuteness! I'm in a bad temper."

"Ah, the laddie has been having a scrap with his chaste lil Madeline! Was she horrid to ickly Martykins? All right. I'll quit. Come on. Yoicks for the drink."

He told three new stories about Professor Robertshaw, all of them scurrilous and most of them untrue, on their way, and he almost coaxed Martin into cheerfulness. "Barney's" was a poolroom, a tobacco shop and, since Mohalis was dry by local option, an admirable blind-pig. Clif and the hairy-handed Barney greeted each other in a high and worthy manner:

"The benisons of eventide to you, Barney. May your circulation proceed unchecked and particularly the dorsal carpal branch of the ulnar artery, in which connection, comrade, Prof. Dr. Col. Egbert Arrowsmith and I would fain trifle with another bottle of that renowned strawberry pop."

"Gosh, Clif, you cer'nly got a swell line of jaw-music. If I ever need a' arm amputated when you get to be a doc, I'll come around and let you talk it off. Strawberry pop, gents?"

The front room of Barney's was an impressionistic painting in which a pool-table, piles of cigarettes, chocolate bars, playing cards, and pink sporting papers were jumbled in chaos. The back room was simpler: cases of sweet and thinly flavored soda, a large ice-box, and two small tables with broken chairs. Barney poured, from a bottle plainly marked Ginger Ale, two glasses of powerful and appalling raw whiskey, and Clif and Martin took them to the table in the corner. The effect was swift. Martin's confused sorrows turned to optimism. He told Clif that he was going to write a book exposing idealism, but what he meant was that he was going to do something clever about his dual engagement. He had it! He would invite Leora and Madeline to lunch together, tell them the truth, and see which of them loved him. He whooped, and had another whiskey; he told Clif that he was a fine fellow, and Barney that he was a public benefactor, and unsteadily he retired to the telephone, which was shut off from public hearing in a closet.

At the Zenith General Hospital he got the night superintendent, and the night superintendent was a man frosty and suspicious. "This is no time to be calling up a probationer! Half-past eleven! Who are you, anyway?"

Martin checked the "I'll damn' soon tell you who I am!" which was his natural reaction, and explained that he was speaking for Leora's invalid grand-aunt, that the poor old lady was very low, and if the night superintendent cared to take upon himself the murder of a blameless gentlewoman —

When Leora came to the telephone he said quickly, and soberly now, feeling as though he had come from the menace of thronging strangers into the security of her presence:

"Leora? Sandy. Meet me Grand lobby tomorrow, twelve-thirty. Must! Important! Fix 't somehow — your aunt's sick."

"All right, dear. G' night," was all she said.

It took him long minutes to get an answer from Madeline's flat, then Mrs. Fox's voice sounded, sleepily, quaveringly:

"Yes, yes?"

"'S Martin."

"Who is it? Who is it? What is it? Are you calling the Fox apartment?"

"Yes, yes! Mrs. Fox, it's Martin Arrowsmith speaking."

"Oh, oh, my dear! The 'phone woke me out of a sound sleep, and I couldn't make out what you were saying. I was so frightened. I thought maybe it was a telegram or something. I thought perhaps something had happened to Maddy's brother. What is it, dear? Oh, I do hope nothing's happened!"

Her confidence in him, the affection of this uprooted old woman bewildered in a strange land, overcame him; he lost all his whisky-colored feeling that he was a nimble fellow, and in a melancholy way, with all the weight of life again upon him, he sighed that no, nothing had happened, but he'd forgotten to tell Madeline something — so shor — so sorry call so late — could he speak Mad just minute —

Then Madeline was bubbling, "Why, Marty dear, what is it? I do hope nothing has happened! Why, dear, you just left here — "

"Listen, d-dear. Forgot to tell you. There's a — there's a great friend of mine in Zenith that I want you to meet — "

"Who is he?"

"You'll see tomorrow. Listen, I want you come in and meet — come meet um at lunch. Going," with ponderous jocularity, "going to blow you all to a swell feed at the Grand — "

"Oh, how nice!"

" — so I want you to meet me at the eleven-forty interurban, at College Square. Can you?"

Vaguely, "Oh, I'd love to but — I have an eleven o'clock, and I don't like to cut it, and I promised May Harmon to go shopping with her — she's looking for some kind of shoes that you can wear with her pink crêpe de chine but that you can walk in — and we sort of thought maybe we might lunch at Ye Kollege Karavanserai — and I'd half planned to go to the movies with her or somebody, Mother says that new Alaska film is simply dandy, she saw it tonight, and I thought I might go see it before they take it off, though Heaven knows I ought to come right home and study and not go anywhere at all — "

"Now *listen* ! It's important. Don't you trust me? Will you come or not?"

"Why, of course I trust you, dear. All right, I'll try to be there. The eleven-forty?"

"Yes."

"At College Square? Or at Bluthman's Book Shop?"

"*At College Square!* "

Her gentle "I trust you" and her wambling "I'll try to" were warring in his ears as he plunged out of the suffocating cell and returned to Clif.

"What's the grief?" Clif wondered. "Wife passed away? Or did the Giants win in the ninth? Barney, our wandering-boy-tonight looks like a necropsy. Slip him another strawberry pop, quick. Say, Doctor, I think you better call a physician."

"Oh, shut up," was all Martin had to say, and that without conviction. Before telephoning he had been full of little brightnesses; he had praised Clif's pool-playing and called Barney "old *Cimex lectularius* "; but now, while the affectionate Clif worked on him, he sat brooding save when he grumbled (with a return of self-satisfaction), "If you knew all the troubles I have — all the doggone mess a fellow can get into — *you'd* feel down in the mouth!"

Clif was alarmed. "Look here, old socks. If you've gotten in debt, I'll raise the cash, somehow. If it's — Been going a little too far with Madeline?"

"You make me sick! You've got a dirty mind. I'm not worthy to touch Madeline's hand. I regard her with nothing but respect."

"The hell you do! But never mind, if you say so. Gosh, wish there was *something* I could do for you. Oh! Have 'nother shot! Barney! Come a-runnin'!"

By several drinks Martin was warmed into a hazy carelessness, and Clif solicitously dragged him home after he had desired to fight three large academic sophomores. But in the morning he awoke with a crackling skull and a realization that he was going to face Leora and Madeline at lunch.

## V

His half-hour journey with Madeline into Zenith seemed a visible and oppressing thing, like a tornado cloud. He had not merely to get through each minute as it came; the whole grim thirty minutes were present at the same time. While he was practicing the tactful observation he was going to present two minutes from now, he could still hear the clumsy thing he had said two minutes before. He fought to keep her attention from the "great friend of his" whom they were to meet. With fatuous beaming he described a night at Barney's; without any success whatever he tried to be funny; and when Madeline lectured him on the evils of liquor and the evils of association with immoral persons, he was for once relieved. But he could not sidetrack her.

"Who is this man we're going to see? What are you so mysterious about? Oh, Martin, is it a joke? Aren't we going to meet anybody? Did you just want to run away from Mama for a while and we have a bat at the Grand together? Oh, what fun! I've always wanted to lunch at the Grand. Of course I do think it's too sort of rococo, but still, it is impressive, and — Did I guess it, darling?"

"No, there's someone — Oh, we're going to meet somebody, all right!"

"Then why don't you tell me who he is? Honestly, Mart, you make me impatient."

"Well, I'll tell you. It isn't a Him; it's a Her."

"Oh!"

"It's — You know my work takes me to the hospitals, and some of the nurses at Zenith General have been awfully helpful." He was panting. His eyes ached. Since the torture of the coming lunch was inevitable, he wondered why he should go on trying to resist his punishment. "Especially there's one nurse there who's a wonder. She's learned so much about the care of the sick, and she puts me onto a lot of good stunts, and she seems like a nice girl — Miss Tozer, her name is — I think her first name is Lee or something like that — and she's so — her father is one of the big men in North Dakota — awfully rich — big banker — I guess she just took up nursing to do her share in the world's work." He had achieved Madeline's own tone of poetic uplift. "I thought you two might like to know each other. You remember you were saying how few girls there are in Mohalis that really appreciate — appreciate ideals."

"Ye-es." Madeline gazed at something far away and, whatever it was, she did not like it. "I shall be ver' pleased to meet her, of course. *Any* friend of yours — Oh, Mart! I do hope you don't flirt; I hope you don't get too friendly with all these nurses. I don't know anything about it, of course, but I keep hearing how some of these nurses are regular man-hunters."

"Well, let me tell you right now, Leora isn't!"

"No, I'm sure, but — Oh, Martykins, you won't be silly and let these nurses just amuse themselves with you? I mean, for your own sake. They have such an advantage. Poor Madeline, she wouldn't be allowed to go hanging around men's rooms learning — things, and you think you're so psychological, Mart, but honestly, any smart woman can twist you around her finger."

"Well, I guess I can take care of myself!"

"Oh, I mean — I don't mean — But I do hope this Tozer person — I'm sure I shall like her, if you do, but — I am your own true love, aren't I, always!"

She, the proper, ignored the passengers as she clasped his hand. She sounded so frightened that his anger at her reflections on Leora turned into misery. Incidentally, her thumb was gouging painfully into the back of his hand. He tried to look tender as he protested, "Sure — sure — gosh, honest, Mad, look out. The old duffer across the aisle is staring at us."

For whatever infidelities he might ever commit he was adequately punished before they had reached the Grand Hotel.

The Grand was, in 1907, the best hotel in Zenith. It was compared by traveling salesmen to the Parker House, the Palmer House, the West Hotel. It has been humbled since by the supercilious modesty of the vast Hotel Thornleigh; dirty now is its tessellated floor and all the wild gilt tarnished, and in its ponderous leather chairs are torn seams and stogie ashes and horse-dealers. But in its day it was the proudest inn between Chicago and Pittsburgh; an oriental palace, the entrance a score of brick Moorish arches, the lobby towering from a black and white marble floor, up past gilt iron balconies, to the green, pink, pearl, and amber skylight seven stories above.

They found Leora in the lobby, tiny on an enormous couch built round a pillar. She stared at Madeline, quiet, waiting. Martin perceived that Leora was unusually sloppy — his own word. It did not matter to him how clumsily her honey-colored hair was tucked under her black hat, a characterless little mushroom of a hat, but he did see and resent the contrast between her shirtwaist, with the third button missing, her checked skirt, her unfortunate bright brown bolero jacket, and Madeline's sleekness of blue serge. The resentment was not toward Leora. Scanning them together (not haughtily, as the choosing and lofty male, but anxiously) he was more irritated than ever by Madeline. That she should be better dressed was an affront. His affection flew to guard Leora, to wrap and protect her.

And all the while he was bumbling:

" — thought you two girls ought to know each other — Miss Fox, want t' make you 'quainted with Miss Tozer — little celebration — lucky dog have two Queens of Sheba — "

And to himself, "Oh, hell!"

While they murmured nothing in particular to each other he herded them into the famous dining-room of the Grand. It was full of gilt chandeliers, red plush chairs, heavy silverware, and aged Negro retainers with gold and green waistcoats. Round the walls ran select views of Pompeii, Venice, Lake Como, and Versailles.

"Swell room!" chirped Leora.

Madeline had looked as though she intended to say the same thing in longer words, but she considered the frescoes all over again and explained, "Well, it's very large — "

He was ordering, with agony. He had appropriated four dollars for the orgy, strictly including the tip, and his standard of good food was that he must spend every cent of the four dollars. While he wondered what "Purée St. Germain" could be, and the waiter hideously stood watching behind his shoulder, Madeline fell to. She chanted with horrifying politeness:

"Mr. Arrowsmith tells me you are a nurse, Miss — Tozer."

"Yes, sort of."

"Do you find it interesting?"

"Well — yes — yes, I think it's interesting."

"I suppose it must be wonderful to relieve suffering. Of course my work — I'm taking my Doctor of Philosophy degree in English — " She made it sound as though she were taking her earldom — "it's rather dry and detached. I have to master the growth of the language and so on and so forth. With your practical training, I suppose you'd find that rather stupid."

"Yes, it must be — no, it must be very interesting."

"Do you come from Zenith, Miss — Tozer?"

"No, I come from — Just a little town. Well, hardly a town.... North Dakota."

"Oh! North Dakota!"

"Yes.... Way West."

"Oh, yes. ...Are you staying East for some time?" It was precisely what a much-resented New York cousin had once said to Madeline.

"Well, I don't — Yes, I guess I may be here quite some time."

"Do you, uh, do you find you like it here?"

"Oh, yes, it's pretty nice. These big cities — So much to see."

"'Big'? Well, I suppose it all depends on the point of view, *doesn't* it? I always think of New York as big but — Of course — Do you find the contrast to North Dakota interesting?"

"Well, of course it's different."

"Tell me what North Dakota's like. I've always wondered about these Western states." It was Madeline's second plagiarism of her cousin. "What is the general impression it makes on you?"

"I don't think I know just how you mean."

"I mean what is the general effect? The — *impression* ."

"Well, it's got lots of wheat and lots of Swedes."

"But I mean — I suppose you're all terribly virile and energetic, compared with us Easterners."

"I don't — Well, yes, maybe."

"Have you met lots of people in Zenith?"

"Not so *awfully* many."

"Oh, have you met Dr. Birchall, that operates in your hospital? He's such a nice man, and not just a good surgeon but frightfully talented. He sings won-derfully, and he comes from the most frightfully nice family."

"No, I don't think I've met him yet," Leora bleated.

"Oh, you must. And he plays the slickest — the most gorgeous game of tennis. He always goes to all these millionaire parties on Royal Ridge. Frightfully smart."

Martin now first interrupted. "Smart? Him? He hasn't got any brains whatever."

"My dear child, I didn't mean 'smart' in that sense!" He sat alone and helpless while she again turned on Leora and ever more brightly inquired whether Leora knew this son of a corporation lawyer and that famous débutante, this hatshop and that club. She spoke familiarly of what were known as the Leaders of Zenith Society, the personages who appeared daily in the society columns of the *Advocate-Times* , the Cowxes and Van Antrims and Dodsworths. Martin was astonished by the familiarity; he remembered that she had once gone to a charity ball in Zenith but he had not known that she was so intimate with the peerage. Certainly Leora had appallingly never heard of these great ones, nor even attended the concerts, the lectures, the recitals at which Madeline apparently spent all her glittering evenings.

Madeline shrugged a little, then, "Well — Of course with the fascinating doctors and everybody that you meet in the hospital, I suppose you'd find lectures frightfully tame. Well — " She dismissed Leora and looked patronizingly at Martin. "Are you planning some more work on the what-is-it with rabbits?"

He was grim. He could do it now, if he got it over quickly. "Madeline! Brought you two together because — Don't know whether you cotton to each other or not, but I wish you could, because I've — I'm not making any excuses for myself. I couldn't help it. I'm engaged to both of you, and I want to know — "

Madeline had sprung up. She had never looked quite so proud and fine. She stared at them, and walked away, wordless. She came back, she touched Leora's shoulder, and quietly kissed her. "Dear, I'm sorry for you. You've got a job! You poor baby!" She strode away, her shoulders straight.

Hunched, frightened, Martin could not look at Leora.

He felt her hand on his. He looked up. She was smiling, easy, a little mocking. "Sandy, I warn you that I'm never going to give you up. I suppose you're as bad as She says; I suppose I'm foolish — I'm a hussy. But you're mine! I warn you it isn't a bit of use your getting engaged to somebody else again. I'd tear her eyes out! Now don't think so well of yourself! I guess you're pretty selfish. But I don't care. You're mine!"

He said brokenly many things beautiful in their commonness.

She pondered, "I do feel we're nearer together than you and Her. Perhaps you like me better because you can bully me — because I tag after you and She never would. And I know your work is more important to you than I am, maybe more important than you are. But I am stupid and ordinary and She isn't. I simply admire you frightfully (Heaven knows why, but I do), while She has sense enough to make you admire Her and tag after Her."

"No! I swear it isn't because I can bully you, Leora — I swear it isn't — I don't think it is. Dearest, *don't* don't think she's brighter than you are. She's glib but — Oh, let's stop talking! I've found you! My life's begun!"

## Chapter 7

The difference between Martin's relations to Madeline and to Leora was the difference between a rousing duel and a serene comradeship. From their first evening, Leora and he depended on each other's loyalty and liking, and certain things in his existence were settled forever. Yet his absorption in her was not stagnant. He was always making discoveries about the observations of life which she kept incubating in her secret little head while she made smoke rings with her cigarettes and smiled silently. He longed for the girl Leora; she stirred him, and with gay frank passion she answered him; but to another, sexless Leora he talked more honestly than to Gottlieb or his own worried self, while with her boyish nod or an occasional word she encouraged him to confidence in his evolving ambition and disdains.

### II

Digamma Pi fraternity was giving a dance. It was understood among the anxiously whispering medics that so cosmopolitan was the University of Winnemac becoming that they were expected to wear the symbols of respectability known as "dress-suits." On the solitary and nervous occasion when Martin had worn evening clothes he had rented them from the Varsity Pantorium, but he must own them, now that he was going to introduce Leora to the world as his pride and flowering. Like two little old people, absorbed in each other and diffidently exploring new, unwelcoming streets of the city where their alienated children live, Martin and Leora edged into the garnished magnificence of Benson, Hanley and Koch's, the loftiest department store in Zenith. She was intimidated by the luminous cases of mahogany and plate glass, by the opera hats and lustrous mufflers and creamy riding breeches. When he had tried on a dinner suit and come out for her approval, his long brown tie and soft-collared shirt somewhat rustic behind the low evening waistcoat, and when the clerk had gone to fetch collars, she wailed:

"Darn it, Sandy, you're too grand for me. I just simply can't get myself to fuss over my clothes, and here you're going to go and look so spiffy I won't have a chance with you."

He almost kissed her.

The clerk, returning, warbled, "I think, Modom, you'll find that your husband will look vurry nice indeed in these wing collars."

Then, while the clerk sought ties, he did kiss her, and she sighed:

"Oh, gee, you're one of these people that get ahead. I never thought I'd have to live up to a man with a dress-suit and a come-to-Heaven collar. Oh, well, I'll tag!"

### III

For the Digamma Ball, the University Armory was extremely decorated. The brick walls were dizzv with bunting, spotty with paper chrysanthemums and plaster skulls and wooden scalpels ten feet long.

In six years at Mohalis, Martin had gone to less than a score of dances, though the refined titillations of communal embracing were the chief delight of the co-educational university. When he arrived at the Armory, with Leora timorously brave in a blue crêpe de chine made in no recognized style, he did not care whether he had a single two-step, though he did achingly desire to have the men crowd in and ask Leora, admire her and make her welcome. Yet he was too proud to introduce her about, lest he seem to be begging his friends to dance with her. They stood alone, under the balcony, disconsolately facing the vastness of the floor, while beyond them flashed the current of dancers, beautiful, formidable, desirable. Leora and he had assured each other that, for a student affair, dinner jacket and black waistcoat would be the thing, as stated in the Benson, Hanley and Koch Chart of Correct Gents' Wearing Apparel, but he grew miserable at the sight of voluptuous white waistcoats, and when that embryo famous surgeon,

Angus Duer, came by, disdainful as a greyhound and pushing on white gloves (which are the whitest, the most superciliously white objects on earth), then Martin felt himself a hobbledehoy.

"Come on, *we'll* dance," he said, as though it were a defiance to all Angus Duers.

He very much wanted to go home.

He did not enjoy the dance, though she waltzed easily and himself not too badly. He did not even enjoy having her in his arms. He could not believe that she was in his arms. As they revolved he saw Duer join a brilliance of pretty girls and distinguished-looking women about the great Dr. Silva, dean of the medical school. Angus seemed appallingly at home, and he waltzed off with the prettiest girl, sliding, swinging, deft. Martin tried to hate him as a fool, but he remembered that yesterday Angus had been elected to the honorary society of Sigma Xi.

Leora and he crept back to the exact spot beneath the balcony where they had stood before, to their den, their one safe refuge. While he tried to be nonchalant and talk up to his new clothes, he was cursing the men he saw go by laughing with girls, ignoring his Leora.

"Not many here yet," he fussed. "Pretty soon they'll all be coming, and then you'll have lots of dances."

"Oh, I don't mind."

("God, won't somebody come and ask the poor kid?")

He fretted over his lack of popularity among the dancing-men of the medical school. He wished Clif Clawson were present — Clif liked any sort of assembly, but he could not afford dress-clothes. Then, rejoicing as at sight of the best-beloved, he saw Irving Watters, that paragon of professional normality, wandering toward them, but Watters passed by, merely nodding. Thrice Martin hoped and desponded, and now all his pride was gone. If Leora could be happy —

"I wouldn't care a hoot if she fell for the gabbiest fusser in the whole U., and gave me the go-by all evening. Anything to let her have a good time! If I could coax Duer over — No, that's one thing I couldn't stand: crawling to that dirty snob — I will!"

Up ambled Fatty Pfaff, just arrived. Martin pounced on him lovingly. "H'lo, old Fat! You a stag tonight? Meet my friend Miss Tozer."

Fatty's bulbous eyes showed approval of Leora's cheeks and amber hair. He heaved, "Pleased-meetch — dance starting — have the honor?" in so flattering a manner that Martin could have kissed him.

That he himself stood alone through the dance did not occur to him. He leaned against a pillar and gloated. He felt gorgeously unselfish.... That various girl wallflowers were sitting near him, waiting to be asked, did not occur to him either.

He saw Fatty introduce Leora to a decorative pair of Digams, one of whom begged her for the next. Thereafter she had more invitations than she could take. Martin's excitement cooled. It seemed to him that she clung too closely to her partners, that she followed their steps too eagerly. After the fifth dance he was agitated. "Course! *She's* enjoying herself! Hasn't got time to notice that I just stand here — yes, by thunder, and hold her scarf! Sure! Fine for her. Fact I might like a little dancing myself — And the way she grins and gawps at that fool Brindle Morgan, the — the — the damnedest — Oh, you and I are going to have a talk, young woman! And those hounds trying to pinch her off me — the one thing I've ever loved! Just because they dance better than I can, and spiel a lot of foolishness — And that damn' orchestra playing that damn' peppery music — And she falling for all their damn' cheap compliments and — You and I are going to have one lovely little understanding!"

When she next returned to him, besieged by three capering medics, he muttered to her, "Oh, it doesn't *matter* about *me* !"

"Would you like this one? *Course* you shall have it!" She turned to him fully; she had none of Madeline's sense of having to act for the benefit of observers. Through a strained eternity of waiting, while he glowered, she babbled of the floor, the size of the room, and her "dandy partners." At the sound of the music he held out his arms.

"No," she said. "I want to talk to you." She led him to a corner and hurled at him, "Sandy, this is the last time I'm going to stand for your looking jealous. Oh, I know! See here! If we're going to stick together — and we are! — I'm going to dance with just as many men as I want to, and I'm going to be just as foolish with 'em as I want to. Dinners and those things — I suppose I'll always go on being a clam. Nothing to say. But I love dancing, and I'm going to do exactly what I want to, and if you had any sense whatever, you'd know I don't care a hang for anybody but you. Yours! Absolute. No matter what fool things you do — and they'll probably be a plenty. So when you go and get jealous on me again, you sneak off and get rid of it. Aren't you ashamed of yourself!"

"I wasn't jealous — Yes, I was. Oh, I can't help it! I love you so much. I'd be one fine lover, now wouldn't I, if I never got jealous!"

"All right. Only you've got to keep it under cover. Now we'll finish the dance."

He was her slave.

## IV

It was regarded as immoral, at the University of Winnemac, to dance after midnight, and at that hour the guests crowded into the Imperial Cafeteria. Ordinarily it closed at eight, but tonight it kept open till one, and developed a spirit of almost lascivious mirth. Fatty Pfaff did a jig, another humorous student, with a napkin over his arm, pretended to be a waiter, and a girl (but she was much disapproved) smoked a cigarette.

At the door Clif Clawson was waiting for Martin and Leora. He was in his familiar shiny gray suit, with a blue flannel shirt.

Clif assumed that he was the authority to whom all of Martin's friends must be brought for judgment. He had not met Leora. Martin had confessed his double engagement; he had explained that Leora was unquestionably the most gracious young woman on earth; but as he had previously used up all of his laudatory adjectives and all of Clif's patience on the subject of Madeline, Clif failed to listen, and prepared to dislike Leora as another siren of morality.

He eyed her now with patronizing enmity. He croaked at Martin behind her back, "Good-looking kid, I will say that for her — what's wrong with her?" When they had brought their own sandwiches and coffee and mosaic cake from the long counter, Clif rasped:

"Well, it's grand of a couple of dress-suit swells like you to assassinate with me 'mid the midmosts of sartorials and Sassiety. Gosh, it's fierce I had to miss the select pleasures of an evening with Anxious Duer and associated highboys, and merely play a low game of poker — in which Father deftly removed the sum of six simolea, point ten, from the foregathered bums and yahoos. Well, Leory, I suppose you and Martykins here have now ratiocinated all these questions of polo and, uh, Monte Carlo and so on."

She had an immense power of accepting people as they were. While Clif waited, leering, she placidly investigated the inside of a chicken sandwich and assented, "Um-huh."

"Good boy! I thought you were going to pull that 'If you are a roughneck, I don't see why you think you've got to boast about it' stuff that Mart springs on me!"

Clif turned into a jovial and (for him) unusually quiet companion.... Ex-farmhand, ex-book-agent, ex-mechanic, he had so little money yet so scratching a desire to be resplendent that he took refuge in pride in poverty, pride in being offensive. Now, when Leora seemed to look through his boasting, he liked her as quickly as had Martin, and they buzzed with gaiety. Martin was warmed to benevolence toward mankind, including Angus Duer, who was at the end of the room at a table with Dean Silva and his silvery women. Without plan, Martin sprang up, raced down the room. Holding out his hand he clamored:

"Angus, old man, want to congratulate you on getting Sigma Xi. That's fine."

Duer regarded the outstretched hand as though it was an instrument which he had seen before but whose use he could not quite remember. He picked it up and shook it tentatively. He did not turn his back; he was worse than rude — he looked patient.

"Well, good luck," said Martin, chilled and shaky.

"Very good of you. Thanks."

Martin returned to Leora and Clif, to tell them the incident as a cosmic tragedy. They agreed that Angus Duer was to be shot. In the midst of it Duer came past, trailing after Dean Silva's party, and nodded to Martin, who glared back, feeling noble and mature.

At parting, Clif held Leora's hand and urged, "Honey, I think a lot of Mart, and one time I was afraid the old kid was going to get tied up to — to parties that would turn him into a hand-shaker. I'm a hand-shaker myself. I know less about medicine than Prof Robertshaw. But this boob has some conscience to him, and I'm so darn' glad he's playing around with a girl that's real folks and — Oh, listen at me fallin' all over my clumsy feet! But I just mean I hope you won't mind Uncle Clif saying he does by golly like you a lot!"

It was almost four when Martin returned from taking Leora home and sagged into bed. He could not sleep. The aloofness of Angus Duer racked him as an insult to himself, as somehow an implied insult to Leora, but his boyish rage had passed into a bleaker worry. Didn't Duer, for all his snobbishness and shallowness, have something that he himself lacked? Didn't Clif, with his puppy-dog humor, his speech of a vaudeville farmer, his suspicion of fine manners as posing, take life too easily? Didn't Duer know how to control and drive his hard little mind? Wasn't there a technique of manners as there was of experimentation.... Gottlieb's fluent bench-technique versus the clumsy and podgy hands of Ira Hinkley.... Or was all this inquiry a treachery, a yielding to Duer's own affected standard?

He was so tired that behind his closed eyelids were flashes of fire. His whirling mind flew over every sentence he had said or heard that night, till round his twisting body there was fevered shouting.

## V

As he grumped across the medical campus next day, he came unexpectedly upon Angus and he was smitten with the guiltiness and embarrassment one has toward a person who has borrowed money and probably will not return it. Mechanically he began to blurt "Hello," but he checked it in a croak, scowled, and stumbled on.

"Oh, Mart," Angus called. He was dismayingly even. "Remember speaking to me last evening? It struck me when I was going out that you looked huffy. I was wondering if you thought I'd been rude. I'm sorry if you did. Fact is, I had a rotten headache. Look. I've got four tickets for 'As It Listeth,' in Zenith, next Friday evening — original New York cast! Like to see it? And I noticed you were with a peach, at the dance. Suppose she might like to go along with us, she and some friend of hers?"

"Why — gosh — I'll 'phone her — darn' nice of you to ask us — "

It was not till melancholy dusk, when Leora had accepted and promised to bring with her a probationer-nurse named Nelly Byers, that Martin began to brood:

"Wonder if he did have a headache last night?

"Wonder if somebody *gave* him the tickets?

"Why didn't he ask Dad Silva's daughter to go with us? Does he think Leora is some tart I've picked up?

"Sure, he never really quarrels with anybody — wants to keep us all friendly, so we'll send him surgical patients some day when we're hick G. P.'s and he's a Great and Only.

"Why did I crawl down so meekly?

"I don't care! If Leora enjoys it — Me personally, I don't care two hoots for all this trotting around — Though of course it isn't so bad to see pretty women in fine clothes, and be dressed as good as anybody — Oh, I don't *know* !"

## VI

In the slightly Midwestern city of Zenith, the appearance of a play "with the original New York cast" was an event. (What play it was did not much matter.) The Dodsworth Theatre was splendid with the aristocracy from the big houses on Royal Ridge. Leora and Nelly Byers admired the bloods — graduates of Yale and Harvard and Princeton, lawyers and bankers, motor-manufacturers and inheritors of real estate, virtuosi of golf, familiars of New York — who with their shrill and glistening women occupied the front rows. Miss Byers pointed out the Dodsworths, who were often mentioned in *Town Topics* .

Leora and Miss Byers bounced with admiration of the hero when he refused the governorship; Martin worried because the heroine was prettier than Leora; and Angus Duer (who gave an appearance of knowing all about plays without having seen more than half a dozen in his life) admitted that the set depicting "Jack Vanduzen's Camp in the Adirondacks: Sunset, the Next Day" was really very nice.

Martin was in a mood of determined hospitality. He was going to give them supper and that was all there was to it. Miss Byers explained that they had to be in the hospital by a quarter after eleven, but Leora said lazily, "Oh, I don't care. I'll slip in through a window. If you're there in the morning, the Old Cat can't prove you got in late." Shaking her head at this lying wickedness, Miss Byers fled to a trolley car, while Leora, Angus, and Martin strolled to Epstein's Alt Nuremberg Café for beer and Swiss cheese sandwiches flavored by the sight of German drinking mottos and papier-mâché armor.

Angus was studying Leora, looking from her to Martin, watching their glances of affection. That a keen young man should make a comrade of a girl who could not bring him social advancement, that such a thing as the boy and girl passion between Martin and Leora could exist, was probably inconceivable to him. He decided that she was conveniently frail. He gave Martin a refined version of a leer, and set himself to acquiring her for his own uses.

"I hope you enjoyed the play," he condescended to her.

"Oh, yes — "

"Jove, I envy you two. Of course I understand why girls fall for Martin here, with his romantic eyes, but a grind like me, I have to go on working without a single person to give me sympathy. Oh, well, I deserve it for being shy of women."

With unexpected defiance from Leora: "When anybody says that, it means they're not shy, and they despise women."

"Despise them? Why, child, honestly, I long to be a Don Juan. But I don't know how. Won't you give me a lesson?" Angus's aridly correct voice had become lulling; he concentrated on Leora as he would have concentrated on dissecting a guinea pig. She smiled at Martin now and then to say, "Don't be jealous, idiot. I'm magnificently uninterested in this conceited hypnotist." But she was flustered by Angus's sleek assurance, by his homage to her eyes and wit and reticence.

Martin twitched with jealousy. He blurted that they must be going — Leora really had to be back — The trolleys ran infrequently after midnight and they walked to the hospital through hollow and sounding streets. Angus and Leora kept up a high-strung chatter, while Martin stalked beside them, silent, sulky, proud of being sulky. Skittering through a garage alley they came out on the mass of Zenith General Hospital, a block long, five stories of bleak windows with infrequent dim blotches of light. No one was about. The first floor was but five feet from the ground, and they lifted Leora up to the limestone ledge of a half-open corridor window. She slid in, whispering, "G' night! Thanks!"

Martin felt empty, dissatisfied. The night was full of a chill mournfulness. A light was suddenly flickering in a window above them, and there was a woman's scream breaking down into moans. He felt the tragedy of parting — that in the briefness of life he should lose one moment of her living presence.

"I'm going in after her; see she gets there safe," he said.

The frigid edge of the stone sill bit his hands, but he vaulted, thrust up his knee, crawled hastily through the window. Ahead of him, in the cork-floored hallway lit only by a tiny electric globe, Leora was tiptoeing toward a flight of stairs. He ran after her, on his toes. She squeaked as he caught her arm.

"We got to say good night better than that!" he grumbled. "With that damn' Duer — "

"Ssssssh! They'd simply murder me if they caught you here. Do you want to get me fired?"

"Would you care, if it was because of me?"

"Yes — no — well — But they'd probably fire you from medic school, my lad. If — " His caressing hands could feel her shiver with anxiety. She peered along the corridor, and his quickened imagination created sneaking forms, eyes peering from doorways. She sighed, then, resolutely: "We can't talk here. We'll slip up to my room — roommate's away for the week. Stand there, in the shadow. If nobody's in sight upstairs, I'll come back."

He followed her to the floor above, to a white door, then breathlessly inside. As he closed the door he was touched by this cramped refuge, with its camp-beds and photographs from home and softly wrinkled linen. He clasped her, but with hand against his chest she forbade him, as she mourned:

"You were jealous again! How can you distrust me so? With that fool! Women not like him? They wouldn't have a chance! Likes himself too well. And then you jealous!"

"I wasn't — Yes, I was, but I don't dare! To have to sit there and grin like a hyena, with him between us, when I wanted to talk to you, to kiss you! All right! Probably I'll always be jealous. It's you that have got to trust me. I'm not easy-going; never will be. Oh, trust me — "

Their profound and unresisted kiss was the more blind in memory of that barren hour with Angus. They forgot that the superintendent of nurses might dreadfully come bursting in; they forgot that Angus was waiting. "Oh, curse Angus — let him go home!" was Martin's only reflection, as his eyes closed and his long loneliness vanished.

"Good night, dear love — my love forever," he exulted.

In the still ghostliness of the hall, he laughed as he thought of how irritably Angus must have marched away. But from the window he discovered Angus huddled on the stone steps, asleep. As he touched the ground, he whistled, but stopped short. He saw bursting from the shadow a bulky man, vaguely in a porter's uniform, who was shouting:

"I've caught yuh! Back you come into the hospital, and we'll find out what you've been up to!"

They closed. Martin was wiry, but in the watchman's clasp he was smothered. There was a reek of dirty overalls, of unbathed flesh. Martin kicked his shins, struck at his boulder of red cheek, tried to twist his arm. He broke loose, started to flee, and halted. The struggle, in its contrast to the aching sweetness of Leora, had infuriated him. He faced the watchman, raging.

From the awakened Angus, suddenly appearing beside him, there was a thin sound of disgust. "Oh, come *on* ! Let's get out of this. Why do you dirty your hands on scum like him?"

The watchman bellowed, "Oh, I'm scum, am I? I'll show you!"

He collared Angus and slapped him.

Under the sleepy street-lamp, Martin saw a man go mad. It was not the unfeeling Angus Duer who stared at the watchman; it was a killer, and his eyes were the terrible eyes of the killer, speaking to the least experienced a message of death. He gasped only, "He dared to touch me!" A pen-knife was somehow in his hands, he had leaped at the watchman, and he was busily and earnestly endeavoring to cut his throat.

As Martin tried to hold them he heard the agitated pounding of a policeman's night stick on the pavement. Martin was slim but he had pitched hay and strung telephone wire. He hit the watchman, judiciously, beside the left ear, snatched Angus's wrist, and dragged him away. They ran up an alley, across a courtyard. They came to a thoroughfare as an owl trolley glowed and rattled round the corner; they ran beside it, swung up on the steps, and were safe.

Angus stood on the back platform, sobbing. "My God, I wish I'd killed him! He laid his filthy hands on me! Martin! Hold me here on the car. I thought I'd got over that. Once when I was a kid I tried to kill a fellow — God, I wish I'd cut that filthy swine's throat!"

As the trolley came into the center of the city, Martin coaxed, "There's an all-night lunch up Oberlin Avenue where we can get some white mule. Come on. It'll straighten you up."

Angus was shaky and stumbling — Angus the punctilious. Martin led him into the lunch-room where, between catsup bottles, they had raw whisky in granite-like coffee cups. Angus leaned his head on his arm and sobbed, careless of stares, till he had drunk himself into obliteration, and Martin steered him home. Then to Martin, in his furnished room with Clif snoring, the evening became incredible and nothing more incredible than Angus Duer. "Well, he'll be a good friend of mine now, for always. Fine!"

Next morning, in the hall of the Anatomy Building, he saw Angus and rushed toward him. Angus snapped, "You were frightfully stewed last night, Arrowsmith. If you can't handle your liquor better than that, you better cut it out entirely."

He walked on, clear-eyed, unruffled.

## Chapter 8

And always Martin's work went on — assisting Max Gottlieb, instructing bacteriological students, attending lectures and hospital demonstrations — sixteen merciless hours to the day. He stole occasional evenings for original research or for peering into the stirring worlds of French and German bacteriological publications; he went proudly now and then to Gottlieb's cottage where, against rain-smeared brown wallpaper, were Blake drawings and a signed portrait of Koch. But the rest was nerve-gnawing.

Neurology, O.B., internal medicine, physical diagnosis; always a few pages more than he could drudge through before he fell asleep at his rickety study-table.

Memorizing of gynecology, of ophthalmology, till his mind was burnt raw.

Droning afternoons of hospital demonstrations, among stumbling students barked at by tired clinical professors.

The competitive exactions of surgery on dogs, in which Angus Duer lorded it with impatient perfection.

Martin admired the professor of internal medicine, T. J. H. Silva, known as "Dad" Silva, who was also dean of the medical faculty. He was a round little man with a little crescent of mustache. Silva's god was Sir William Osler, his religion was the art of sympathetic healing, and his patriotism was accurate physical diagnosis. He was a Doc Vickerson of Elk Mills, grown wiser and soberer and more sure. But Martin's reverence for Dean Silva was counterbalanced by his detestation for Dr. Roscoe Geake, professor of otolaryngology.

Roscoe Geake was a peddler. He would have done well with oil stock. As an otolaryngologist he believed that tonsils had been placed in the human organism for the purpose of providing specialists with closed motors. A physician who left the tonsils in any patient was, he felt, foully and ignorantly overlooking his future health and comfort — the physician's future health and comfort. His earnest feeling regarding the nasal septum was that it never hurt any patient to have part of it removed, and if the most hopeful examination could find nothing the matter with the patient's nose and throat except that he was smoking too much, still, in any case, the enforced rest after an operation was good for him. Geake denounced this cant about Letting Nature Alone. Why, the average well-to-do man appreciated attention! He really didn't think much of his specialists unless he was operated on now and then — just a little and not very painfully. Geake had one classic annual address in which, winging far above otolaryngology, he evaluated all medicine, and explained to grateful healers like Irving Watters the method of getting suitable fees:

"Knowledge is the greatest thing in the medical world but it's no good whatever unless you can sell it, and to do this you must first impress your personality on the people who have the dollars. Whether a patient is a new or an old friend, you must always use *salesmanship* on him. Explain to him, also to his stricken and anxious family, the hard work and thought you are giving to his case, and so make him feel that the good you have done him, or intend to do him, is even greater than the fee you plan to charge. Then, when he gets your bill, he will not misunderstand or kick."

### II

There was, as yet, no vision in Martin of serene spaciousness of the mind. Beyond doubt he was a bustling young man, and rather shrill. He had no uplifted moments when he saw himself in relation to the whole world — if indeed he realized that there was a deal of the world besides himself. His friend Clif was boorish, his beloved Leora was rustic, however gallant she might be, and he himself wasted energy in hectic busyness and in astonishment at dullness. But if he had not ripened, yet he was close to earth, he did hate pretentiousness, he did use his hands, and he did seek iron actualities with a curiosity inextinguishable.

And at infrequent times he perceived the comedy of life; relaxed for a gorgeous hour from the intensity wearing to his admirers. Such was the hour before Christmas vacation when Roscoe Geake rose to glory.

It was announced in the *Winnemac Daily News* that Dr. Geake had been called from the chair of otolaryngology to the vice-presidency of the puissant New Idea Medical Instrument and Furniture Company of Jersey City. In celebration he gave a final address to the entire medical school on "The Art and Science of Furnishing the Doctor's Office."

He was a neatly finished person, Geake, eye-glassed and enthusiastic and fond of people. He beamed on his loving students and cried:

"Gentlemen, the trouble with too many doctors, even those splendid old pioneer war-horses who through mud and storm, through winter's chill blast and August's untempered heat, go bringing cheer and surcease from pain to the world's humblest, yet even these old Nestors not so infrequently settle down in a rut and never shake themselves loose. Now that I am leaving this field where I have labored so long and happily, I want to ask every man jack of you to read, before you begin to practice medicine, not merely your Rosenau and Howell and Gray, but also, as a preparation for being that which all good citizens must be, namely, practical men, a most valuable little manual of modern psychology, 'How to Put Pep in Salesmanship,' by Grosvenor A. Bibby. For don't forget, gentlemen, and this is my last message to you, the man worth while is not merely the man who takes things with a smile but also the man who's trained in philosophy, *practical* philosophy, so that instead of day-dreaming and spending all his time talking about 'ethics,' splendid though they are, and 'charity,' glorious virtue though that be, yet he never forgets that unfortunately the world judges a man by the amount of good hard cash he can lay away. The graduates of the University of Hard Knocks judge a physician as they judge a business man, not merely by his alleged 'high ideals' but by the horsepower he puts into carrying them out — and making them pay! And from a scientific standpoint, don't overlook the fact that the impression of properly remunerated competence which you make on a patient is of just as much importance, in these days of the new psychology, as the drugs you get into him or the operations he lets you get away with. The minute he begins to see that other folks appreciate and reward your skill, that minute he must begin to feel your power and so to get well.

"Nothing is more important in inspiring him than to have such an office that as soon as he steps into it, you have begun to sell him the idea of being properly cured. I don't care whether a doctor has studied in Germany, Munich, Baltimore, and Rochester. I don't care whether he has all science at his fingertips, whether he can instantly diagnose with a considerable degree of accuracy the most obscure ailment, whether he has the surgical technique of a Mayo, a Crile, a Blake, an Ochsner, a Cushing. If he has a dirty old office, with hand-me-down chairs and a lot of second-hand magazines, then the patient isn't going to have confidence in him; he is going to resist the treatment — and the doctor is going to have difficulty in putting over and collecting an adequate fee.

"To go far below the surface of this matter into the fundamental philosophy and esthetics of office-furnishing for the doctor, there are today two warring schools, the Tapestry School and the Aseptic School, if I may venture to so denominate and conveniently distinguish them. Both of them have their merits. The Tapestry School claims that luxurious chairs for waiting patients, handsome hand-painted pictures, a bookcase jammed with the world's best literature in expensively bound sets, together with cut-glass vases and potted palms, produce an impression of that opulence which can come only from sheer ability and knowledge. The Aseptic School, on the other hand, maintains that what the patient wants is that appearance of scrupulous hygiene which can be produced only by furnishing the outer waiting-room as well as the inner offices in white-painted chairs and tables, with merely a Japanese print against a gray wall.

"But, gentlemen, it seems obvious to me, so obvious that I wonder it has not been brought out before, that the ideal reception-room is a combination of these two schools! Have your potted palms and handsome pictures — to the practical physician they are as necessary a part of his working equipment as a sterilizer or a Baumanometer. But so far as possible have everything in sanitary-looking white — and think of the color-schemes you can evolve, or the good wife for you, if she be one blessed with artistic tastes! Rich golden or red cushions, in a Morris chair enameled the purest white! A floor-covering of white enamel, with just a border of delicate rose! Recent and unspotted numbers of expensive magazines, with art covers, lying on a white table! Gentlemen, there is the idea of imaginative salesmanship which I wish to leave with you; there is the gospel which I hope to spread in my fresh field of endeavor, the New Idea Instrument Company of Jersey City, where at any time I shall be glad to see and shake by the hand any and all of you."

## III

Through the storm of his Christmas examinations, Martin had an intensified need of Leora. She had been summoned home to Dakota, perhaps for months, on the ground that her mother was unwell, and he had or thought he had, to see her daily. He must have slept less than four hours a night. Grinding at examinations on the interurban car, he dashed in to her, looking up to scowl when he thought of the lively interns and the men patients whom she met in the hospital, scorning himself for being so primitive, and worrying all over again. To see her at all, he had to wait for hours in the lobby, or walk up and down in the snow outside till she could slip to a window and peep out. When they were together, they were completely absorbed. She had a genius for frank passion; she teased him, tantalized him, but she was tender and unafraid.

He was sick lonely when he saw her off at the Union Station.

His examination papers were competent but, save in bacteriology and internal medicine, they were sketchy. He turned emptily to the laboratory for vacation time.

He had so far displayed more emotion than achievement in his tiny original researches. Gottlieb was patient. "It iss a fine system, this education. All what we cram into the students, not Koch and two *dieners* could learn. Do not worry about the research. We shall do it yet." But he expected Martin to perform a miracle or two in the whole fortnight of the holidays and Martin had no stomach with which to think. He played in the laboratory; he spent his time polishing glassware, and when he transplanted cultures from his rabbits, his notes were incomplete.

Gottlieb was instantly grim. "*Was gibt es dann?* Do you call these notes? Always when I praise a man must he stop working? Do you think that you are a Theobald Smith or a Novy that you should sit and meditate? You have the ability of Pfaff!"

For once, Martin was impenitent. He mumbled to himself, as Gottlieb stamped out like a Grand Duke, "Rats, I've got *some* rest coming to me. Gosh, most fellows, why, they go to swell homes for vacation, and have dances and fathers and everything. If Leora was here, we'd go to a show tonight."

He viciously seized his cap (a soggy and doubtful object), sought Clif Clawson, who was spending the vacation in sleeping between poker games at Barney's, and outlined a project of going into town and getting drunk. It was executed so successfully that during vacation it was repeated whenever he thought of the coming torture-wheel of uninspiring work, whenever he realized that it was only Gottlieb and Leora who held him here. After vacation, in late January, he found that whisky relieved him from the frenzy of work, from the terror of loneliness — then betrayed him and left him the more weary, the more lonely. He felt suddenly old; he was twenty-four now, he reminded himself, and a schoolboy, his real work not even begun. Clif was his refuge; Clif admired Leora and would listen to his babbling of her.

But Clif and Martin came to the misfortune of Founder's Day.

## IV

January thirtieth, the birthday of the late Dr. Warburton Stonedge, founder of the medical department of Winnemac, was annually celebrated by a banquet rich in fraternalism and speeches and large lack of wine. All the faculty reserved their soundest observations for the event, and all the students were expected to be present.

This year it was held in the large hall of the University Y.M.C.A., a moral apartment with red wall paper, portraits of whiskered alumni who had gone out to be missionaries, and long thin pine boxes intended to resemble exposed oak beams. About the famous guests — Dr. Rouncefield the Chicago surgeon, a diabetes specialist from Omaha, a Pittsburgh internist — stood massed the faculty members. They tried to look festal, but they were worn and nervous after four months of school. They had wrinkles and tired eyes. They were all in business suits, mostly unpressed. They sounded scientific and interested; they used words like phlebarteriectasia and hepatocholangioenterostomy, and they asked the guests, "So you just been in Rochester? What's, uh, what're Charley and Will doing in orthopedics?" But they were full of hunger and melancholy. It was half-past seven, and they who did not normally dine at seven, dined at six-thirty.

Upon this seedy gaiety entered a splendor, a tremendous black-bearded personage, magnificent of glacial shirt-bosom, vast of brow, wild-eyed with genius or with madness. In a marvelous great voice, with a flavor of German accent, he inquired for Dr. Silva, and sailed into the dean's group like a frigate among fishing-smacks.

"Who the dickens is that?" wondered Martin.

"Let's edge in and find out," said Clif, and they clung to the fast increasing knot about Dean Silva and the mystery, who was introduced as Dr. Benoni Carr, the pharmacologist.

They heard Dr. Carr, to the pale admiration of the school-bound assistant professors, boom genially of working with Schmiedeberg in Germany on the isolation of dihydroxypentamethylendiamin, of the possibilities of chemotherapy, of the immediate cure of sleeping sickness, of the era of scientific healing. "Though I am American-born, I have the advantage of speaking German from a child, and so perhaps I can better understand the work of my dear friend Ehrlich. I saw him receive a decoration from His Imperial Highness the Kaiser. Dear old Ehrlich, he was like a child!"

There was at this time (but it changed curiously in 1914 and 1915) an active Germanophile section of the faculty. They bent before this tornado of erudition. Angus Duer forgot that he was Angus Duer; and Martin listened with excited stimulation. Benoni Carr had all of Gottlieb's individuality, all his scorn of machine-made teachers, all his air of a great world which showed Mohalis as provincial, with none of Gottlieb's nervous touchiness. Martin wished Gottlieb were present; he wondered whether the two giants would clash.

Dr. Carr was placed at the speakers' table, near the dean. Martin was astonished to see the eminent pharmacologist, after a shocked inspection of the sour chicken and mishandled salad which made up most of the dinner, pour something into his water glass from a huge silver flask — and pour that something frequently. He became boisterous. He leaned across two men to slap the indignant dean on the shoulder; he contradicted his neighbors; he sang a stanza of "I'm Bound Away for the Wild Missourai."

Few phenomena at the dinner were so closely observed by the students as the manners of Dr. Benoni Carr.

After an hour of strained festivity, when Dean Silva had risen to announce the speakers, Carr lumbered to his feet and shouted, "Let's not have any speeches. Only fools make speeches. Wise men sing songs. Whoopee! Oh, tireolee, oh, tireolee, oh, tireolee a lady! You profs are the bunk!"

Dean Silva was to be seen beseeching him, then leading him out of the room, with the assistance of two professors and a football tackle, and in the hush of a joyful horror Clif grunted to Martin:

"Here's where I get mine! And the damn' fool promised to stay sober!"

"Huh?"

"I might of known he'd show up stewed and spill the beans. Oh, maybe the dean won't hand me hell proper!"

He explained. Dr. Benoni Carr was born Benno Karkowski. He had graduated from a medical school which gave degrees in two years. He had read vastly, but he had never been in Europe. He had been "spieler" in medicine shows, chiropodist, spiritualist medium, esoteric teacher, head of sanitariums for the diversion of neurotic women. Clif had encountered him in Zenith, when they were both drunk. It was Clif who had told Dean Silva that the celebrated pharmacologist, just back from Europe, was in Zenith for a few days and perhaps might accept an invitation —

The dean had thanked Clif ardently.

The banquet ended early, and there was inadequate attention to Dr. Rouncefield's valuable address on the Sterilization of Catgut.

Clif sat up worrying, and admitting the truth of Martin's several observations. Next day — he had a way with women when he deigned to take the trouble — he pumped the dean's girl secretary, and discovered his fate. There had been a meeting of a faculty committee; the blame for the Benoni Carr outrage had been placed on Clif; and the dean had said all the things Clif had imagined, with a number which he had not possessed the talent to conceive. But the dean was not going to summon him at once; he was going to keep him waiting in torture, then execute him in public.

"Good-by, old M.D. degree! Rats, I never thought much of the doctor business. Guess I'll be a bond salesman," said Clif to Martin. He strolled away, he went to the dean, and remarked:

"Oh, Dean Silva, I just dropped in to tell you I've decided to resign from the medic school. Been offered a big job in, uh, in Chicago, and I don't think much of the way you run the school, anyway. Too much memorizing and too little real spirit of science. Good luck, Doc. So long."

"Gggggg — " said Dean Silva.

Clif moved into Zenith, and Martin was left alone. He gave up the double room at the front of his boarding-house for a hall-room at the rear, and in that narrow den he sat and mourned in a desolation of loneliness. He looked out on a vacant lot in which a tattered advertisement of pork and beans flapped on a leaning billboard. He saw Leora's eyes and heard Clif's comfortable scoffing, and the quiet was such as he could not endure.

## Chapter 9

The persistent yammer of a motor horn drew Martin to the window of the laboratory, a late afternoon in February. He looked down on a startling roadster, all streamlines and cream paint, with enormous headlights. He slowly made out that the driver, a young man in coffee-colored loose motor coat and hectic checked cap and intense neckwear, was Clif Clawson, and that Clif was beckoning.

He hastened down, and Clif cried:

"Oh, boy! How do you like the boat? Do you diagnose this suit? Scotch heather — honest! Uncle Clif has nabbed off a twenty-five-buck-a-week job *with* commissions, selling autos. Boy, I was lost in your old medic school. I can sell anything to anybody. In a year I'll be making eighty a week. Jump in, old son. I'm going to take you in to the Grand and blow you to the handsomest feed you ever stuffed into your skinny organism."

The thirty-eight miles an hour at which Clif drove into Zenith was, in 1908, dismaying speed. Martin discovered a new Clif. He was as noisy as ever, but more sure, glowing with schemes for immediately acquiring large sums of money. His hair, once bushy and greasy in front, tending to stick out jaggedly behind, was sleek now, and his face had the pinkness of massage. He stopped at the fabulous Grand Hotel with a jar of brakes; before he left the car he changed his violent yellow driving-gauntlets for a pair of gray gloves with black stitching, which he immediately removed as he paraded through the lobby. He called the coat-girl "Sweetie," and at the dining-room door he addressed the head-waiter:

"Ah, Gus, how's the boy, how's the boy feeling tonight? How's the mucho famoso majordomoso? Gus, want to make you 'quainted with Dr. Arrowsmith. Any time the doc comes here I want you to shake a leg and hand him out that well-known service, my boy, and give him anything he wants, and if he's broke, you charge it to me. Now, Gus, I want a nice little table for two, with garage and hot and cold water, and wouldst fain have thy advice, Gustavus, on the oysters and hore duffers and all the ingredients fair of a Maecenan feast."

"Yes, sir, right this way, Mr. Clawson," breathed the head-waiter.

Clif whispered to Martin, "I've got him like that in two weeks! You watch my smoke!"

While Clif was ordering, a man stopped beside their table. He resembled an earnest traveling-man who liked to get back to his suburban bungalow every Saturday evening. He was beginning to grow slightly bald, slightly plump. His rimless eye-glasses, in the midst of a round smooth face, made him seem innocent. He stared about as though he wished he had someone with whom to dine. Clif darted up, patted the man's elbow, and bawled:

"Ah, there, Babski, old boy. Feeding with anybody? Come join the Sporting Gents' Association."

"All right, be glad to. Wife's out of town," said the man.

"Shake hands with Dr. Arrowsmith. Mart, meet George F. Babbitt, the hoch-gecelebrated Zenith real-estate king. Mr. Babbitt has just adorned his thirty-fourth birthday by buying his first benzine buggy from yours truly and beg to remain as always."

It was, at least on the part of Clif and Mr. Babbitt, a mirthful affair, and when Martin had joined them in cocktails, St. Louis beer, and highballs, he saw that Clif was the most generous person now living, and Mr. George F. Babbitt a companion of charm.

Clif explained how certain he was — apparently his distinguished medical training had something to do with it — to be president of a motor factory, and Mr. Babbitt confided:

"You fellows are a lot younger than I am, eight-ten years, and you haven't learned yet, like I have, that where the big pleasure is, is in Ideals and Service and a Public Career. Now just between you and me and the gatepost, my vogue doesn't lie in real estate but in oratory. Fact, one time I planned to study law and go right in for politics. Just between ourselves, and I don't want this to go any farther, I've been making some pretty good affiliations lately — been meeting some of the rising young Republican politicians. Of course a fellow has got to start in modestly, but I may say, *sotto voce* , that I expect to run for alderman next fall. It's practically only a step from that to mayor and then to governor of the state, and if I find the career suits me, there's no reason why in ten or twelve years, say in 1918 or 1920, I shouldn't have the honor of representing the great state of Winnemac in Washington, D. C.!"

In the presence of a Napoleon like Clif and a Gladstone like George F. Babbitt, Martin perceived his own lack of power and business skill, and when he had returned to Mohalis he was restless. Of his poverty he had rarely thought, but now, in contrast to Clif's rich ease, his own shabby clothes and his pinched room seemed shameful.

## II

A long letter from Leora, hinting that she might not be able to return to Zenith, left him the more lonely. Nothing seemed worth doing. In that listless state he was mooning about the laboratory during elementary bacteriology demonstration hour, when Gottlieb sent him to the basement to bring up six male rabbits for inoculation. Gottlieb was working eighteen hours a day on new experiments; he was jumpy and testy; he gave orders like insults. When Martin came dreamily back with six females instead of males, Gottlieb shrieked at him, "You are the worst fool that was ever in this lab!"

The groundlings, second-year men who were not unmindful of Martin's own scoldings, tittered like small animals, and jarred him into raging, "Well, I couldn't make out what you said. And it's the first time I ever fell down. I won't stand your talking to me like that!"

"You will stand anything I say! Clumsy! You can take your hat and get out!"

"You mean I'm fired as assistant?"

"I am glad you haf enough intelligence to understand that, no matter how wretched I talk!"

Martin flung away. Gottlieb suddenly looked bewildered and took a step toward Martin's retreating back. But the class, the small giggling animals, they stood delighted, hoping for more, and Gottlieb shrugged, glared them into terror, sent the least awkward of them for the rabbits, and went on, curiously quiet.

And Martin, at Barney's dive, was hotly drinking the first of the whiskys which sent him wandering all night, by himself. With each drink he admitted that he had an excellent chance to become a drunkard, and with each he boasted that he did not care. Had Leora been nearer than Wheatsylvania, twelve hundred miles away, he would have fled to her for salvation. He was still shaky next morning, and he had already taken a drink to make it possible to live through the morning when he received the note from Dean Silva bidding him report to the office at once.

The dean lectured:

"Arrowsmith, you've been discussed a good deal by the faculty council of late. Except in one or two courses — in my own I have no fault to find — you have been very inattentive. Your marks have been all right, but you could do still better. Recently you have also been drinking. You have been seen in places of very low repute, and you have been intimate with a man who took it upon himself to insult me, the Founder, our guests, and the University. Various faculty members have complained of your superior attitude — making fun of our courses right out in class! But Dr. Gottlieb has always warmly defended you. He insisted that you have a real flair for investigative science. Last night, however, he admitted that you had recently been impertinent to him. Now unless you immediately turn over a new leaf, young man, I shall have to suspend you for the rest of the year and, if that doesn't do the work, I shall have to ask for your resignation. And I think it might be a good thing for your humility — you seem to have the pride of the devil, young man! — it might be a good idea for you to see Dr. Gottlieb and start off your reformation by apologizing — "

It was the whisky spoke, not Martin:

"I'm damned if I will! He can go to the devil! I've given him my life, and then he tattles on me — "

"That's absolutely unfair to Dr. Gottlieb. He merely — "

"Sure. He merely let me down. I'll see him in hell before I'll apologize, after the way I've worked for him. And as for Clif Clawson that you were hinting at — him 'take it on himself to insult anybody'? He just played a joke, and you went after his scalp. I'm glad he did it!"

Then Martin waited for the words that would end his scientific life.

The little man, the rosy, pudgy, good little man, he stared and hummed and spoke softly:

"Arrowsmith, I could fire you right now, of course, but I believe you have good stuff in you. I decline to let you go. Naturally, you're suspended, at least till you come to your senses and apologize to me and to Gottlieb." He was fatherly; almost he made Martin repent; but he concluded, "And as for Clawson, his 'joke' regarding this Benoni Carr person — and why I never looked the fellow up is beyond me, I suppose I was too busy — his 'joke,' as you call it, was the action either of an idiot or a blackguard, and until you are able to perceive that fact, I don't think you will be ready to come back to us."

"All right," said Martin, and left the room.

He was very sorry for himself. The real tragedy, he felt, was that though Gottlieb had betrayed him and ended his career, ended the possibility of his mastering science and of marrying Leora, he still worshiped the man.

He said good-by to no one in Mohalis save his landlady. He packed, and it was a simple packing. He stuffed his books, his notes, a shabby suit, his inadequate linen, and his one glory, the dinner clothes, into his unwieldy imitation-leather bag. He remembered with drunken tears the hour of buying the dinner jacket.

Martin's money, from his father's tiny estate, came in bi-monthly checks from the bank at Elk Mills. He had now but six dollars.

In Zenith he left his bag at the interurban trolley station and sought Clif, whom he found practicing eloquence over a beautiful pearl-gray motor hearse, in which a beer-fed undertaker was jovially interested. He waited, sitting hunched and twisted on the steel running-board of a limousine. He resented but he was too listless to resent greatly the stares of the other salesmen and the girl stenographers.

Clif dashed up, bumbling, "Well, well, how's the boy? Come out and catchum little drink."

"I could use one."

Martin knew that Clif was staring at him. As they entered the bar of the Grand Hotel, with its paintings of lovely but absent-minded ladies, its mirrors, its thick marble rail along a mahogany bar, he blurted:

"Well, I got mine, too. Dad Silva's fired me, for general footlessness. I'm going to bum around a little and then get some kind of a job. God, but I'm tired and nervous! Say, can you lend me some money?"

"You bet. All I've got. How much you want?"

"Guess I'll need a hundred dollars. May drift around quite some time."

"Golly, I haven't got that much, but prob'ly I can raise it at the office. Here, sit down at this table and wait for me."

How Clif obtained the hundred dollars has never been explained, but he was back with it in a quarter-hour. They went on to dinner, and Martin had much too much whisky. Clif took him to his own boarding-house — which was decidedly less promissory of prosperity than Clif's clothes — firmly gave him a cold bath to bring him to, and put him to bed. Next morning he offered to find a job for him, but Martin refused and left Zenith by the northbound train at noon.

Always, in America, there remains from pioneer days a cheerful pariahdom of shabby young men who prowl causelessly from state to state, from gang to gang, in the power of the Wanderlust. They wear black sateen shirts, and carry bundles. They are not permanently tramps. They have home towns to which they return, to work quietly in the factory or the section-gang for a year — for a week — and as quietly to disappear again. They crowd the smoking cars at night; they sit silent on benches in filthy stations; they know all the land yet of it they know nothing, because in a hundred cities they see only the employment agencies, the all-night lunches, the blind-pigs, the scabrous lodging-houses. Into that world of voyageurs Martin vanished. Drinking steadily, only half-conscious of whither he was going, of what he desired to do, shamefully haunted by Leora and Clif and the swift hands of Gottlieb, he flitted from Zenith to the city of Sparta, across to Ohio, up into Michigan, west to Illinois. His mind was a shambles. He could never quite remember, afterward, where he had been. Once, it is clear, he was soda-fountain clerk in a Minnemagantic drug-store. Once he must have been, for a week, dishwasher in the stench of a cheap restaurant. He wandered by freight trains, on blind baggages, on foot. To his fellow prospectors he was known as "Slim," the worst-tempered and most restless of all their company.

After a time a sense of direction began to appear in his crazy drifting. He was instinctively headed westward, and to the west, toward the long prairie dusk, Leora was waiting. For a day or two he stopped drinking. He woke up feeling not like the sickly hobo called "Slim," but like Martin Arrowsmith, and he pondered, with his mind running clear, "Why shouldn't I go back? Maybe this hasn't been so bad for me. I was working too hard. I was pretty high-strung. Blew up. Like to, uh — Wonder what happened to my rabbits?... Will they ever let me do research again?"

But to return to the University before he had seen Leora was impossible. His need of her was an obsession, making the rest of earth absurd and worthless. He had, with blurry cunning, saved most of the hundred dollars he had taken from Clif; he had lived — very badly, on grease-swimming stews and soda-reeking bread — by what he earned along the way. Suddenly, on no particular day, in no particular town in Wisconsin, he stalked to the station, bought a ticket to Wheatsylvania, North Dakota, and telegraphed to Leora, "Coming 2:43 tomorrow Wednesday Sandy."

## III

He crossed the wide Mississippi into Minnesota. He changed trains at St. Paul; he rolled into gusty vastnesses of snow, cut by thin lines of fence-wire. He felt free, in release from the little fields of Winnemac and Ohio, in relaxation from the shaky nerves of midnight study and midnight booziness. He remembered his days of wire-stringing in Montana and regained that careless peace. Sunset was a surf of crimson, and by night, when he stepped from the choking railroad coach and tramped the platform at Sauk Centre, he drank the icy air and looked up to the vast and solitary winter stars. The fan of the Northern Lights frightened and glorified the sky. He returned to the coach with the energy of that courageous land. He nodded and gurgled in brief smothering sleep; he sprawled on the seat and talked with friendly fellow vagrants; he drank bitter coffee and ate enormously of buckwheat cakes at a station restaurant; and so, changing at anonymous towns, he came at last to the squatty shelters, the two wheat-elevators, the cattle-pen, the oil-tank, and the red box of a station with its slushy platform, which composed the outskirts of Wheatsylvania. Against the station, absurd in a huge coonskin coat, stood Leora. He must have looked a little mad as he stared at her from the vestibule, as he shivered with the wind. She lifted to him her two open hands, childish in red mittens. He ran down, he dropped his awkward bag on the platform and, unaware of the gaping furry fanners, they were lost in a kiss.

Years after, in a tropic noon, he remembered the freshness of her wind-cooled cheeks.

The train was gone, pounding out of the tiny station. It had stood like a dark wall beside the platform, protecting them, but now the light from the snowfields glared in on them and left them exposed and self-conscious.

"What — what's happened?" she fluttered. "No letters. I was so frightened."

"Off bumming. The dean suspended me — being fresh to profs. D' y' care?"

"Course not, if you wanted to — "

"I've come to marry you."

"I don't see how we can, dearest, but — All right. There'll be a lovely row with Dad." She laughed. "He's always so surprised and *hurt* when anything happens that he didn't plan out. It'll be nice to have you with me in the scrap, because you aren't supposed to know that he expects to plan out everything for everybody and — Oh, Sandy, I've been so lonely for you! Mother isn't really a bit sick, not the least bit, but they go on keeping me here. I think probably somebody hinted to Dad that folks were saying he must be broke, if his dear little daughter had to go off and learn nursing, and he hasn't worried it all out yet — it takes Andrew Jackson Tozer about a year to worry out anything. Oh, Sandy! You're here!"

After the clatter and jam of the train, the village seemed blankly empty. He could have walked around the borders of Wheatsylvania in ten minutes. Probably to Leora one building differed from another — she appeared to distinguish between the general store of Norblom and that of Frazier & Lamb — but to Martin the two-story wooden shacks creeping aimlessly along the wide Main Street were featureless and inappreciable. Then "There's our house, end of the next block," said Leora, as they turned the corner at the feed and implement store, and in a panic of embarrassment Martin wanted to halt. He saw a storm coming: Mr. Tozer denouncing him as a failure who desired to ruin Leora, Mrs. Tozer weeping.

"Say — say — say — have you told 'em about me?" he stammered.

"Yes. Sort of. I said you were a wonder in medic school, and maybe we'd get married when you finished your internship, and then when your wire came, they wanted to know why you were coming, and why it was you wired from Wisconsin, and what color necktie you had on when you were sending the wire, and I couldn't make 'em understand I didn't know. They discussed it. Quite a lot. They do discuss things. All through supper. Solemn. Oh, Sandy, do curse and swear some at meals."

He was in a funk. Her parents, formerly amusing figures in a story, became oppressively real in sight of the wide, brown, porchy house. A large plate-glass window with a colored border had recently been cut through the wall, as a sign of prosperity, and the garage was new and authoritative.

He tagged after Leora, expecting the blast. Mrs. Tozer opened the door, and stared at him plaintively — a thin, faded, unhumorous woman. She bowed as though he was not so much unwelcome as unexplained and doubtful.

"Will you show Mr. Arrowsmith his room, Ory, or shall I?" she peeped.

It was the kind of house that has a large phonograph but no books, and if there were any pictures, as beyond hope there must have been, Martin never remembered them. The bed in his room was lumpy but covered with a chaste figured spread, and the flowery pitcher and bowl rested on a cover embroidered in red with lambs, frogs, water lilies, and a pious motto.

He took as long as he could in unpacking things which needed no unpacking, and hesitated down the stairs. No one was in the parlor, which smelled of furnace-heat and balsam pillows; then, from nowhere apparent, Mrs. Tozer was there, worrying about him and trying to think of something polite to say.

"Did you have a comfortable trip on the train?"

"Oh, yes, it was — Well, it was pretty crowded."

"Oh, was it crowded?"

"Yes, there were a lot of people traveling."

"Were there? I suppose — Yes. Sometimes I wonder where all the people can be going that you see going places all the time. Did you — was it very cold in the Cities — in Minneapolis and St. Paul?"

"Yes, it was pretty cold."

"Oh, was it cold?"

Mrs. Tozer was so still, so anxiously polite. He felt like a burglar taken for a guest, and intensely he wondered where Leora could be. She came in serenely, with coffee and a tremendous Swedish coffee-ring voluptuous with raisins and glistening brown sugar, and she had them talking, almost easily, about the coldness of winter and the value of Fords when into the midst of all this brightness slid Mr. Andrew Jackson Tozer, and they drooped again to politeness.

Mr. Tozer was as thin and undistinguished and sun-worn as his wife, and like her he peered, he kept silence and fretted. He was astonished by everything in the world that did not bear on his grain elevator, his creamery, his tiny bank, the United Brethren Church, and the careful conduct of an Overland car. It was not astounding that he should have become almost rich, for he accepted nothing that was not natural and convenient to Andrew Jackson Tozer.

He hinted a desire to know whether Martin "drank," how prosperous he was, and how he could possibly have come all this way from the urbanities of Winnemac. (The Tozers were born in Illinois, but they had been in Dakota since childhood, and they regarded Wisconsin as the farthest, most perilous rim of the Eastern horizon.) They were so blank, so creepily polite, that Martin was able to avoid such unpleasant subjects as being suspended. He dandled an impression that he was an earnest young medic who in no time at all would be making large and suitable sums of money for the support of their Leora, but as he was beginning to lean back in his chair he was betrayed by the appearance of Leora's brother.

Bert Tozer, Albert R. Tozer, cashier and vice-president of the Wheatsylvania State Bank, auditor and vice-president of the Tozer Grain and Storage Company, treasurer and vice-president of the Star Creamery, was not in the least afflicted by the listening dubiousness of his parents. Bertie was a very articulate and modern man of affairs. He had buck teeth, and on his eye-glasses was a gold chain leading to a dainty hook behind his left ear. He believed in town-boosting, organized motor tours, Boy Scouts, baseball, and the hanging of I.W.W.'s; and his most dolorous regret was that Wheatsylvania was too small — as yet — to have a Y.M.C.A. or a Commercial Club. Plunging in beside him was his fiancée, Miss Ada Quist, daughter of the feed and implement store. Her nose was sharp, but not so sharp as her voice or the suspiciousness with which she faced Martin.

"This Arrowswith?" demanded Bert. "Huh! Well, guess you're glad to be out here in God's country!"

"Yes, it's fine — "

"Trouble with the Eastern states is, they haven't got the git, or the room to grow. You ought to see a real Dakota harvest! Look here, how come you're away from school this time of year?"

"Why — "

"I know all about school-terms. I went to business college in Grand Forks. How come you can get away now?"

"I took a little lay-off."

"Leora says you and her are thinking of getting married."

"We — "

"Got any cash outside your school-money?"

"I have not!"

"Thought so! How juh expect to support a wife?"

"I suppose I'll be practicing medicine some day."

"Some day! Then what's the use of talking about being engaged till you can support a wife?"

"That," interrupted Bert's lady-love, Miss Ada Quist, "that's just what *I* said, Ory!" She seemed to speak with her pointed nose as much as with her button of a mouth. "If Bert and I can wait, I guess other people can!"

Mrs. Tozer whimpered, "Don't be too hard on Mr. Arrowsmith, Bertie. I'm sure he wants to do the right thing."

"I'm not being hard on anybody! I'm being sensible. If Pa and you would tend to things instead of standing around fussing, I wouldn't have to butt in. I don't believe in interfering with anybody else's doings, or anybody interfering with mine. Live and let live and mind your own business is my motto, and that's what I said to Alec Ingleblad the other day when I was in there having a shave and he was trying to get funny about our holding so many mortgages, but

I'll be blamed if I'm going to allow a fellow that I don't know anything about to come snooping around My Sister till I find out something about his prospects!"

Leora crooned, "Bertie, lamb, your tie is climbing your collar again."

"Yes and *you* , Ory," shrieked Bert, "if it wasn't for me you'd have married Sam Petchek, two years ago!"

Bert further said, with instances and illustrations, that she was light-minded, and as for nursing — *Nursing!*

She said that Bert was what he was, and tried to explain to Martin the matter of Sam Petchek. (It has never yet been altogether explained.)

Ada Quist said that Leora did not care if she broke her dear parents' hearts and ruined Bert's career.

Martin said, "Look here, I — " and never got farther.

Mr. and Mrs. Tozer said they were all to be calm, and of course Bert didn't mean — But really, it was true; they had to be sensible, and how Mr. Arrowsmith could expect to support a wife —

The conference lasted till nine-thirty, which, as Mr. Tozer pointed out, was everybody's bedtime, and except for the five-minute discussion as to whether Miss Ada Quist was to stay to supper, and the debate on the saltiness of this last cornbeef, they clave faithfully to the inquiry as to whether Martin and Leora were engaged. All persons interested, which apparently did not include Martin and Leora, decided that they were not. Bert ushered Martin upstairs. He saw to it that the lovers should not have a chance for a good-night kiss; and until Mr. Tozer called down the hall, at seven minutes after ten, "You going to stay up and chew the rag the whole blessed night, Bert?" he made himself agreeable by sitting on Martin's bed, looking derisively at his shabby baggage, and demanding the details of his parentage, religion, politics, and attitude toward the horrors of card-playing and dancing.

At breakfast they all hoped that Martin would stay one more night in their home — plenty of room.

Bert stated that Martin would come down-town at ten and be shown the bank, creamery, and wheat elevator.

But at ten Martin and Leora were on the eastbound train. They got out at the county seat, Leopolis, a vast city of four thousand population, with a three-story building. At one that afternoon they were married, by the German Lutheran pastor. His study was a bareness surrounding a large, rusty wood-stove, and the witnesses, the pastor's wife and an old German who had been shoveling walks, sat on the wood-box and looked drowsy. Not till they had caught the afternoon train for Wheatsylvania did Martin and Leora escape from the ghostly apprehension which had hunted them all day. In the fetid train, huddled close, hands locked, innocently free of the alienation which the pomposity of weddings sometimes casts between lovers, they sighed, "Now what are we going to do — what *are* we going to do?"

At the Wheatsylvania station they were met by the whole family, rampant.

Bert had suspected elopement. He had searched half a dozen towns by long-distance telephone, and got through to the county clerk just after the license had been granted. It did not soften Bert's mood to have the clerk remark that if Martin and Leora were of age, there was nothing he could do, and he didn't "care a damn who's talking — I'm running this office!"

Bert had come to the station determined to make Martin perfect, even as Bert Tozer was perfect, and to do it right now.

It was a dreadful evening in the Tozer mansion.

Mr. Tozer said, with length, that Martin had undertaken responsibilities.

Mrs. Tozer wept, and said that she hoped Ory had not, for certain reasons, *had* to be married —

Bert said that if such was the case, he'd kill Martin —

Ada Quist said that Ory could now see what came of pride and boasting about going off to her old Zenith —

Mr. Tozer said that there was one good thing about it, anyway: Ory could see for herself that they couldn't let her go back to nursing school and get into more difficulties —

Martin from time to time offered remarks to the effect that he was a good young man, a wonderful bacteriologist, and able to take care of *his* wife; but no one save Leora listened.

Bert further propounded (while his father squeaked, "Now don't be *too* hard on the boy,") that if Martin *thought* for one single *second* that he was going to get one red *cent* out of the Tozers because he'd gone and butted *in* where nobody'd *invited* him, he, Bert, wanted to *know* about it, that was all, he certainly wanted to *know* about it!

And Leora watched them, turning her little head from one to another. Once she came over to press Martin's hand. In the roughest of the storm, when Martin was beginning to glare, she drew from a mysterious pocket a box of very bad cigarettes, and lighted one. None of the Tozers had discovered that she smoked. Whatever they thought about her sex morals, her infidelity to United Brethrenism, and her general dementia, they had not suspected that she could commit such an obscenity as smoking. They charged on her, and Martin caught his breath savagely.

During these fulminations Mr. Tozer had somehow made up his mind. He could at times take the lead away from Bert, whom he considered useful but slightly indiscreet, and unable to grasp the "full value of a dollar." (Mr. Tozer valued it at one dollar and ninety, but the progressive Bert at scarce more than one-fifty.) Mr. Tozer mildly gave orders:

They were to stop "scrapping." They had no proof that Martin was necessarily a bad match for Ory. They would see. Martin would return to medical school at once, and be a good boy and get through as quickly as he could and begin to earn money. Ory would remain at home and behave herself — and she certainly would never act like a Bad Woman again, and smoke cigarettes. Meantime Martin and she would have no, uh, relations. (Mrs. Tozer looked embarrassed, and the hungrily attentive Ada Quist tried to blush.) They could write to each other once a week, but that was all. They would in no way, uh, act as though they were married till he gave permission.

"Well?" he demanded.

Doubtless Martin should have defied them and with his bride in his arms have gone forth into the night. But it seemed only a moment to graduation, to beginning his practice. He had Leora now, forever. For her, he must be sensible. He would return to work, and be Practical. Gottlieb's ideals of science? Laboratories? Research? Rot!

"All right," he said.

It did not occur to him that their abstention from love began tonight; it did not come to him till, holding out his hands to Leora, smiling with virtue at having determined to be prudent, he heard Mr. Tozer cackling, "Ory, you go on up to bed now — in your own room!"

That was his bridal night; tossing in his bed, ten yards from her.

Once he heard a door open, and thrilled to her coming. He waited, taut. She did not come. He peeped out, determined to find her room. His deep feeling about his brother-in-law suddenly increased. Bert was parading the hall, on guard. Had Bert been more formidable, Martin might have killed him, but he could not face that buck-toothed and nickering righteousness. He lay and resolved to curse them all in the morning and go off with Leora, but with the coming of the three-o'clock depression he perceived that with him she would probably starve, that he was disgraced, that it was not at all certain he would not become a drunkard.

"Poor kid, I'm not going to spoil her life. God, I do love her! I'm going back, and the way I'm going to work — Can I stand this?"

That was his bridal night and the barren dawn.

Three days later he was walking into the office of Dr. Silva, dean of the Winnemac Medical School.

## Chapter 10

Dean Silva's secretary looked up delightedly, she hearkened with anticipation. But Martin said meekly, "Please, could I see the dean?" and meekly he waited, in the row of oak chairs beneath the Dawson Hunziker pharmaceutical calendar.

When he had gone solemnly through the ground-glass door to the dean's office, he found Dr. Silva glowering. Seated, the little man seemed large, so domed was his head, so full his rounding mustache.

"Well, sir!"

Martin pleaded, "I'd like to come back, if you'll let me. Honest, I do apologize to you, and I'll go to Dr. Gottlieb and apologize — though honest, I can't lay down on Clif Clawson — "

Dr. Silva bounced up from his chair, bristling. Martin braced himself. Wasn't he welcome? Had he no home, anywhere? He could not fight. He had no more courage. He was so tired after the drab journey, after restraining himself from flaring out at the Tozers. He was so tired! He looked wistfully at the dean.

The little man chuckled, "Never mind, boy. It's all right! We're glad you're back. Bother the apologies! I just wanted you to do whatever'd buck you up. It's good to have you back! I believed in you, and then I thought perhaps we'd lost you. Clumsy old man!"

Martin was sobbing, too weak for restraint, too lonely and too weak, and Dr. Silva soothed, "Let's just go over everything and find out where the trouble was. What can I do? Understand, Martin, the thing I want most in life is to help give the world as many good physicians, great healers, as I can. What started your nervousness? Where have you been?"

When Martin came to Leora and his marriage, Silva purred, "I'm delighted! She sounds like a splendid girl. Well, we must try and get you into Zenith General for your internship, a year from now, and make you able to support her properly."

Martin remembered how often, how astringently, Gottlieb had sneered at "dese merry vedding or jail bells." He went away Silva's disciple; he went away to study furiously; and the brilliant insanity of Max Gottlieb's genius vanished from his faith.

## II

Leora wrote that she had been dropped from the school of nursing for over-absence and for being married. She suspected that it was her father who had informed the hospital authorities. Then, it appeared, she had secretly sent for a shorthand book and, on pretense of helping Bert, she was using the typewriter in the bank, hoping that by next autumn she could join Martin and earn her own living as a stenographer.

Once he offered to give up medicine, to take what work he could find and send for her. She refused.

Though in his service to Leora and to the new god, Dean Silva, he had become austere, denying himself whisky, learning page on page of medicine with a frozen fury, he was always in a vacuum of desire for her, and always he ran the last block to his boarding-house, looking for a letter from her. Suddenly he had a plan. He had tasted shame — this one last shame would not matter. He would flee to her in Easter vacation; he would compel Tozer to support her while she studied stenography in Zenith; he would have her near him through the last year. He paid Clif the borrowed hundred, when the bi-monthly check came from Elk Mills, and calculated his finances to the penny. By not buying the suit he distressingly needed, he could manage it. Then for a month and more he had but two meals a day, and of those meals one was bread and butter and coffee. He washed his own linen in the bath-tub and, except for occasional fiercely delightful yieldings, he did not smoke.

His return to Wheatsylvania was like his first flight, except that he talked less with fellow tramps, and all the way, between uneasy naps in the red-plush seats of coaches, he studied the bulky books of gynecology and internal medicine. He had written certain instructions to Leora. He met her on the edge of Wheatsylvania and they had a moment's talk, a resolute kiss.

News spreads not slowly in Wheatsylvania. There is a certain interest in other people's affairs, and the eyes of citizens of whose existence Martin did not know had followed him from his arrival. When the culprits reached the bone-littered castle of the Tozer ogres, Leora's father and brother were already there, and raging. Old Andrew Jackson cried out upon them. He said that conceivably it may not have been insane in Martin to have "run away from school once, but to go and sneak back this second time was absolutely plumb crazy." Through his tirade, Martin and Leora smiled confidently.

From Bert, "By God, sir, this is too much!" Bert had been reading fiction. "I object to the use of profanity, but when you come and annoy My Sister a second time, all I can say is, by God, sir, this is too blame much!"

Martin looked meditatively out of the widow. He noticed three people strolling the muddy street. They all viewed the Tozer house with hopeful interest. Then he spoke steadily:

"Mr. Tozer, I've been working hard. Everything has gone fine. But I've decided I don't care to live without my wife. I've come to take her back. Legally, you can't prevent me. I'll admit, without any argument, I can't support her yet, if I stay in the University. She's going to study stenography. She'll be supporting herself in a few months, and meanwhile I expect you to be decent enough to send her money."

"This *is* too much," said Tozer, and Bert carried it on: "Fellow not only practically ruins a girl but comes and demands that we support her for him!"

"All right. Just as you want. In the long run it'll be better for her and for me and for you if I finish medic school and have my profession, but if you won't take care of her, I'll chuck school, I'll go to work. Oh, I'll support her, all right! Only you'll never see her again. If you go on being idiots, she and I will leave here on the night train for the Coast, and that'll be the end." For the first time in his centuries of debate with the Tozers, he was melodramatic. He shook his fist under Bert's nose. "And if you try to prevent our going, God help you! And the way this town will laugh at you!... How about it, Leora? Are you ready to go away with me — forever?"

"Yes," she said.

They discussed it, greatly. Tozer and Bert struck attitudes of defense. They couldn't, they said, be bullied by anybody. Also, Martin was an Adventurer, and how did Leora know he wasn't planning to live on the money they sent her? In the end they crawled. They decided that this new, mature Martin, this new, hard-eyed Leora were ready to throw away everything for each other.

Mr. Tozer whined a good deal, and promised to send her seventy dollars a month till she should be prepared for office-work.

At the Wheatsylvania station, looking from the train window, Martin realized that this anxious-eyed, lip-puckering Andrew Jackson Tozer did love his daughter, did mourn her going.

## III

He found for Leora a room on the frayed northern edge of Zenith, miles nearer Mohalis and the University than her hospital had been; a square white and blue room, with blotchy but shoulder-wise chairs. It looked out on breezy, stubbly waste land reaching to distant glittering railroad tracks. The landlady was a round German woman with an eye for romance. It is doubtful if she ever believed that they were married. She was a good woman.

Leora's trunk had come. Her stenography books were primly set out on her little table and her pink felt slippers were arranged beneath the white iron bed. Martin stood with her at the window, mad with the pride of proprietorship. Suddenly he was so weak, so tired, that the mysterious cement which holds cell to cell seemed dissolved, and he felt that he was collapsing. But with knees rigidly straightening, his head back, his lips tight across his teeth, he caught himself, and cried, "Our first home!"

That he should be with her, quiet, none disturbing, was intoxication.

The commonplace room shone with peculiar light; the vigorous weeds and rough grass of the waste land were radiant under the April sun, and sparrows were cheeping.

"Yes," said Leora, with voice, then hungry lips.

## IV

Leora attended the Zenith University of Business Administration and Finance, which title indicated that it was a large and quite reasonably bad school for stenographers, bookkeepers, and such sons of Zenith brewers and politicians as were unable to enter even state universities. She trotted daily to the car-line, a neat, childish figure with note-books and sharpened pencils, to vanish in the horde of students. It was six months before she had learned enough stenography to obtain a place in an insurance office.

Till Martin graduated they kept that room, their home, ever dearer. No one was so domestic as these birds of passage. At least two evenings a week Martin dashed in from Mohalis and studied there. She had a genius for keeping out of his way, for not demanding to be noticed, so that, while he plunged into his books as he never had done in Clif's rustling, grunting, expectorating company, he had ever the warm, half-conscious feeling of her presence. Sometimes, at midnight, just as he began to realize that he was hungry, he would find that a plate of sandwiches had by silent magic appeared at his elbow. He was none the less affectionate because he did not comment. She made him secure. She shut out the world that had pounded at him.

On their walks, at dinner, in the dissolute and deliciously wasteful quarter-hour when they sat on the edge of the bed with comforters wrapped about them and smoked an inexcusable cigarette before breakfast, he explained his work to her, and when her own studying was done, she tried to read whichever of his books was not in use. Knowing nothing, never learning much, of the actual details of medicine, yet she understood — better it may be than Angus Duer — his philosophy and the basis of his work. If he had given up Gottlieb-worship and his yearning for the laboratory as for a sanctuary, if he had resolved to be a practical and wealth-mastering doctor, yet something of Gottlieb's spirit remained. He wanted to look behind details and impressive-sounding lists of technical terms for the causes of things, for general rules which might reduce the chaos of dissimilar and contradictory symptoms to the orderliness of chemistry.

Saturday evening they went solemnly to the motion pictures — one- and two-reel films with Cowboy Billy Anderson and a girl later to be famous as Mary Pickford — and solemnly they discussed the non-existent plots as they returned, unconscious of other people on the streets; but when they walked into the country on a Sunday (with four sandwiches and a bottle of ginger ale in his threadbare pockets), he chased her up-hill and down-gully, and they lost their solemnity in joyous childishness. He intended, when he came to her room in the evening, to catch the owl-car to Mohalis and be near his work when he woke in the morning. He was resolute about it, always, and she admired his efficiency, but he never caught the car. The crew of the six o'clock morning interurban became used to a pale, quick-moving young man who sat hunched in a back seat, devouring large red books, absently gnawing a rather dreadful doughnut. But in this young man there was none of the heaviness of workers dragged out of bed at dawn for another gray and futile day of labor. He appeared curiously determined, curiously content.

It was all so much easier, now that he was partly freed from the tyrannical honesty of Gottliebism, from the unswerving quest for causes which, as it drove through layer below layer, seemed ever farther from the bottommost principles, from the intolerable strain of learning day by day how much he did not know. It warmed him to escape from Gottlieb's ice-box into Dean Silva's neighborly world.

Now and then he saw Gottlieb on the campus. They bowed in embarrassment and passed in haste.

## V

There seemed to be no division between his Junior and Senior years. Because of the time he had lost, he had to remain in Mohalis all summer. The year and a half from his marriage to his graduation was one whirling bewilderment, without seasons or dates.

When he had, as they put it, "cut out his nonsense and buckled down to work," he had won the admiration of Dr. Silva and all the Good Students, especially Angus Duer and the Reverend Ira Hinkley. Martin had always announced that he did not care for their approbation, for the applause of commonplace drudges, but now that he had it, he prized it. However much he scoffed, he was gratified when he was treated as a peer by Angus, who spent the summer as extern in the Zenith General Hospital, and who already had the unapproachable dignity of a successful young surgeon.

Through that hot summer Martin and Leora labored, panting, and when they sat in her room, over their books and a stout pot of beer, neither their costumes nor their language had the decorum which one ought to expect from a romantic pair devoted to science and high endeavor. They were not very modest. Leora came to use, in her casual way, such words, such ancient Anglo-Saxon monosyllables, as would have dismayed Angus or Bert Tozer. On their evenings off they went economically to an imitation Coney Island beside a scummy and stinking lake, and with grave pleasure they ate Hot Dogs, painstakingly they rode the scenic railway.

Their chief appetizer was Clif Clawson. Clif was never willingly alone or silent except when he was asleep. It is probable that his success in motor-salesmanship came entirely from his fondness for the enormous amounts of bright conversation which seem necessary in that occupation. How much of his attention to Martin and Leora was friendliness and how much of it was due to his fear of being alone cannot be determined, but certainly he entertained them and drew them out of themselves, and never seemed offended by the surly unwillingness with which Martin was sometimes guilty of greeting him.

He would come roaring up to the house in a motor, the muffler always cut out. He would shout at their window, "Come on, you guys! Come out of it! Shake a leg! Lez have a little drive and get cooled off, and then I'll buy you a feed."

That Martin had to work, Clif never comprehended. There was small excuse for Martin's occasional brutality in showing his annoyance but, now that he was fulfilled in Leora and quite thoroughly and selfishly careless as to what hungry need others might have of himself, now that he was in a rut of industry and satisfied companionship, he was bored by Clif's unchanging flood of heavy humor. It was Leora who was courteous. She had heard rather too often the seven jokes which, under varying guises, made up all of Clif's humor and philosophy, but she could sit for hours looking amiable while Clif told how clever he was at selling, and she sturdily reminded Martin that they would never have a friend more loyal or generous.

But Clif went to New York, to a new motor agency, and Martin and Leora were more completely and happily dependent on each other than ever before.

Their last agitation was removed by the complacence of Mr. Tozer. He was cordial now in all his letters, however much he irritated them by the parental advice with which he penalized them for every check he sent.

## VI

None of the hectic activities of Senior year — neurology and pediatrics, practical work in obstetrics, taking of case-histories in the hospitals, attendance on operations, dressing wounds, learning not to look embarrassed when charity patients called one "Doctor" — was quite so important as the discussion of "What shall we do after graduation?"

Is it necessary to be an intern for more than a year? Shall we remain general practitioners all our lives, or work toward becoming specialists? Which specialties are the best — that is, the best paid? Shall we settle in the country or in the city? How about going West? What about the army medical corps; salutes, riding-boots, pretty women, travel?

This discussion they harried in the corridors of Main Medical, at the hospital, at lunch-rooms; and when Martin came home to Leora he went through it all again, very learnedly, very explanatorily. Almost every evening he "reached a decision" which was undecided again by morning.

Once when Dr. Loizeau, professor of surgery, had operated before a clinic which included several renowned visiting doctors — the small white figure of the surgeon below them, slashing between life and death, dramatic as a great actor taking his curtain-call — Martin came away certain that he was for surgery. He agreed then with Angus Duer, who had just won the Hugh Loizeau Medal in Experimental Surgery, that the operator was the lion, the eagle, the soldier among doctors. Angus was one of the few who knew without wavering precisely what he was going to do: after his internship he was to join the celebrated Chicago clinic headed by Dr. Rouncefield, the eminent abdominal surgeon. He would, he said briefly, be making twenty thousand a year as a surgeon within five years.

Martin explained it all to Leora. Surgery. Drama. Fearless nerves. Adoring assistants. Save lives. Science in devising new techniques. Make money — not be commercial, of course, but provide Leora with comforts. To Europe — they two together — gray London. Viennese cafés. Leora was useful to him during his oration. She blandly agreed; and the next evening, when he sought to prove that surgery was all rot and most surgeons merely good carpenters, she agreed more amiably than ever.

Next to Angus, and the future medical missionary, Ira Hinkley, Fatty Pfaff was the first to discover what his future was. He was going to be an obstetrician — or, as the medical students called it technically, a "baby-snatcher." Fatty had the soul of a midwife; he sympathized with women in their gasping agony, sympathized honestly and almost tearfully, and he was magnificent at sitting still and drinking tea and waiting. During his first obstetrical case, when the student with him was merely nervous as they fidgeted by the bed in the hard desolation of the hospital room, Fatty was terrified, and he longed as he had never longed for anything in his flabby yet wistful life to comfort this gray-faced, straining, unknown woman, to take her pains on himself.

While the others drifted, often by chance, often through relatives, into their various classes, Martin remained doubtful. He admired Dean Silva's insistence on the physician's immediate service to mankind, but he could not forget the cool ascetic hours in the laboratory. Toward the end of Senior year, decision became necessary, and he was moved by a speech in which Dean Silva condemned too much specialization and pictured the fine old country doctor, priest and father of his people, sane under open skies, serene in self-conquest. On top of this came urgent letters from Mr. Tozer, begging Martin to settle in Wheatsylvania.

Tozer loved his daughter, apparently, and more or less liked Martin, and he wanted them near him. Wheatsylvania was a "good location," he said: solid Scandinavian and Dutch and German and Bohemian farmers who paid their bills. The nearest doctor was Hesselink, at Groningen, nine and a half miles away, and Hesselink had more than he could do. If they would come, he would help Martin buy his equipment: he would even send him a check now and then during his two-year hospital internship. Martin's capital was practically gone. Angus Duer and he had received appointments to Zenith General Hospital, where he would have an incomparable training, but Zenith General gave its interns, for the first year, nothing but board and room, and he had feared that he could not take the appointment. Tozer's offer excited him. All night Leora and he sat up working themselves into enthusiasm about the freedom of the West, about the kind hearts and friendly hands of the pioneers, about the heroism and usefulness of country doctors, and this time they reached a decision which remained decided.

They would settle in Wheatsylvania.

If he ached a little for research and Gottlieb's divine curiosity — well, he would be such a country doctor as Robert Koch! He would not degenerate into a bridge-playing, duck-hunting drone. He would have a small laboratory of his own. So he came to the end of the year and graduated, looking rather flustered in his cap and gown. Angus stood first and Martin seventh in the class. He said good-by, with lamentations and considerable beer; he found a room for Leora nearer to the hospital; and he emerged as Martin L. Arrowsmith, M.D., house physician in the Zenith General Hospital.

## Chapter 11

The Boardman Box Factory was afire. All South Zenith was agitated by the glare on the low-hung clouds, the smell of scorched timber, the infernal bells of charging fire-apparatus. Miles of small wooden houses west of the factory were threatened, and shawled women, tousled men in trousers over nightshirts, tumbled out of bed and came running with a thick mutter of footsteps in the night-chilled streets.

With professional calmness, firemen in helmets were stoking the dripping engines. Policemen tramped in front of the press of people, swinging their clubs, shouting, "Get back there, you!" The fire-line was sacred. Only the factory-owner and the reporters were admitted. A crazy-eyed factory-hand was stopped by a police sergeant.

"My tools are in there!" he shrieked.

"That don't make no never-minds," bawled the strutting sergeant. "*Nobody* can't get through here!"

But one got through. They heard the blang-blang-blang of a racing ambulance, incessant, furious, defiant. Without orders, the crowd opened, and through them, almost grazing them, slid the huge gray car. At the back, haughty in white uniform, nonchalant on a narrow seat, was The Doctor — Martin Arrowsmith.

The crowd admired him, the policemen sprang to receive him.

"Where's the fireman got hurt?" he snapped.

"Over in that shed," cried the police sergeant, running beside the ambulance.

"Drive over closer. Nev' mind the smoke!" Martin barked at the driver.

A lieutenant of firemen led him to a pile of sawdust on which was huddled an unconscious youngster, his face bloodless and clammy.

"He got a bad dose of smoke from the green lumber and keeled over. Fine kid. Is he a goner?" the lieutenant begged.

Martin knelt by the man, felt his pulse, listened to his breathing. Brusquely opening a black bag, he gave him a hypodermic of strychnin and held a vial of ammonia to his nose. "He'll come around. Here, you two, getum into the ambulance — hustle!"

The police sergeant and the newest probationer patrolman sprang together, and together they mumbled. "All right, Doc."

To Martin came the chief reporter of the *Advocate-Times*. In years he was only twenty-nine, but he was the oldest and perhaps the most cynical man in the world. He had interviewed senators: he had discovered graft in charity societies and even in prize-fights. There were fine wrinkles beside his eyes, he rolled Bull Durham cigarettes constantly, and his opinion of man's honor and woman's virtue was but low. Yet to Martin, or at least to The Doctor, he was polite.

"Will he pull through, Doc?" he twanged.

"Sure, I think so. Suffocation. Heart's still going."

Martin yelped the last words from the step at the back of the ambulance as it went bumping and rocking through the factory yard, through the bitter smoke, toward the shrinking crowd. He owned and commanded the city, he and the driver. They ignored traffic regulations, they disdained the people, returning from theaters and movies, who dotted the streets which unrolled before the flying gray hood. Let 'em get out of the way! The traffic officer at Chickasaw and Twentieth heard them coming, speeding like the Midnight Express — urrrrrr — blang-blang-blang-blang — and cleared the noisy corner. People were jammed against the curb, threatened by rearing horses and backing motors, and past them hurled the ambulance, blang-blang-blang-blang, with The Doctor holding a strap and swinging easily on his perilous seat.

At the hospital, the hall-man cried, "Shooting case in the Arbor, Doc."

"All right. Wait'll I sneak in a drink," said Martin placidly.

On the way to his room he passed the open door of the hospital laboratory, with its hacked bench, its lifeless rows of flasks and test-tubes.

"Huh! That stuff! Poking 'round labs! This is real sure-enough life," he exulted, and he did not permit himself to see the vision of Max Gottlieb waiting there, so gaunt, so tired, so patient.

## II

The six interns in Zenith General, including Martin and Angus Duer, lived in a long dark room with six camp beds, and six bureaus fantastic with photographs and ties and undarned socks. They spent hours sitting on their beds, arguing surgery versus internal medicine, planning the dinners which they hoped to enjoy on their nights off, and explaining to Martin, as the only married man, the virtues of the various nurses with whom, one by one, they fell in love.

Martin found the hospital routine slightly dull. Though he developed the Intern's Walk, that quick corridor step with the stethoscope conspicuous in the pocket, he did not, he could not, develop the bedside manner. He was sorry for the bruised, yellowed, suffering patients, always changing as to individuals and never changing as a mass of drab pain, but when he had thrice dressed a wound, he had had enough; he wanted to go on to new experiences. Yet the ambulance work outside the hospital was endlessly stimulating to his pride.

The Doctor, and The Doctor alone, was safe by night in the slum called "the Arbor." His black bag was a pass. Policemen saluted him, prostitutes bowed to him without mockery, saloon-keepers called out, "Evenin', Doc," and hold-up men stood back in doorways to let him pass. Martin had power, the first obvious power in his life. And he was led into incessant adventure.

He took a bank-president out of a dive; he helped the family conceal the disgrace; he irritably refused their bribe; and afterward, when he thought of how he might have dined with Leora, he was sorry he had refused it. He broke into hotel-rooms reeking with gas and revived would-be suicides. He drank Trinidad rum with a Congressman who advocated prohibition. He attended a policeman assaulted by strikers, and a striker assaulted by policemen. He assisted at an emergency abdominal operation at three o'clock in the morning. The operating-room — white tile walls and white tile floor and glittering frosted-glass skylight — seemed lined with fire-lit ice, and the large incandescents glared on the glass instrument cases, the cruel little knives. The surgeon, in long white gown, white turban, and pale orange rubber gloves, made his swift incision in the square of yellowish flesh exposed between towels, cutting deep into layers of fat, and Martin looked on unmoved as the first blood menacingly followed the cut. And a month after, during the Chaloosa River flood, he worked for seventy-six hours, with half-hours of sleep in the ambulance or on a police-station table.

He landed from a boat at what had been the second story of a tenement and delivered a baby on the top floor; he bound up heads and arms for a line of men; but what gave him glory was the perfectly foolhardy feat of swimming the flood to save five children marooned and terrified on a bobbing church pew. The newspapers gave him large headlines, and when he had returned to kiss Leora and sleep twelve hours, he lay and thought about research with salty self-defensive scorn.

"Gottlieb, the poor old impractical fusser! I'd like to see him swim that current!" jeered Dr. Arrowsmith to Martin.

But on night duty, alone, he had to face the self he had been afraid to uncover, and he was homesick for the laboratory, for the thrill of uncharted discoveries, the quest below the surface and beyond the moment, the search for fundamental laws which the scientist (however blasphemously and colloquially he may describe it) exalts above temporary healing as the religious exalts the nature and terrible glory of God above pleasant daily virtues. With this sadness there was envy that he should be left out of things, that others should go ahead of him, ever surer in technique, more widely aware of the phenomena of biological chemistry, more deeply daring to explain laws at which the pioneers had but fumbled and hinted.

In his second year of internship, when the thrills of fires and floods and murder became as obvious a routine as bookkeeping, when he had seen the strangely few ways in which mankind can contrive to injure themselves and slaughter one another, when it was merely wearing to have to live up to the pretentiousness of being The Doctor, Martin tried to satisfy and perhaps kill his guilty scientific lust by voluntary scrabbling about the hospital laboratory, correlating the blood counts in pernicious anemia. His trifling with the drug of research was risky. Amid the bustle of operations he began to picture the rapt quietude of the laboratory. "I better cut this out," he said to Leora, "if I'm going to settle down in Wheatsylvania and 'tend to business and make a living — and I by golly am!"

Dean Silva often came to the hospital on consultations. He passed through the lobby one evening when Leora, returned from the office where she was a stenographer, was meeting Martin for dinner. Martin introduced them, and the little man held her hand, purred at her, and squeaked, "Will you children give me the pleasure of taking you to dinner? My wife has deserted me. I am a lone and misanthropic man."

He trotted between them, round and happy. Martin and he were not student and teacher, but two doctors together, for Dean Silva was one pedagogue who could still be interested in a man who no longer sat at his feet. He led the two starvelings to a chop-house and in a settle-walled booth he craftily stuffed them with roast goose and mugs of ale.

He concentrated on Leora, but his talk was of Martin:

"Your husband must be an Artist Healer, not a picker of trifles like these laboratory men."

"But Gottlieb's no picker of trifles," insisted Martin.

"No-o. But with him — It's a difference of one's gods. Gottlieb's gods are the cynics, the destroyers — crapehangers, the vulgar call 'em: Diderot and Voltaire and Elser; great men, wonder-workers, yet men that had more fun destroying other people's theories than creating their own. But my gods now, they're the men who took the discoveries of Gottlieb's gods and turned them to the use of human beings — made them come alive!

"All credit to the men who invented paint and canvas, but there's more credit, eh? to the Raphaels and Holbeins who used those discoveries! Laënnec and Osler, those are the men! It's all very fine, this business of pure research: seeking the truth, unhampered by commercialism or fame-chasing. Getting to the bottom. Ignoring consequences and practical uses. But do you realize if you carry that idea far enough, a man could justify himself for doing nothing but count the cobblestones on Warehouse Avenue — yes, and justify himself for torturing people just to see how they screamed — and then sneer at a man who was making millions of people well and happy!

"No, no! Mrs. Arrowsmith, this lad Martin is a passionate fellow, not a drudge. He must be passionate on behalf of mankind. He's chosen the highest calling in the world, but he's a feckless, experimental devil. You must keep him at it, my dear, and not let the world lose the benefit of his passion."

After this solemnity Dad Silva took them to a musical comedy and sat between them, patting Martin's shoulder, patting Leora's arm, choking with delight when the comedian stepped into the pail of whitewash. In midnight volubility Martin and Leora sputtered their affection for him, and saw their Wheatsylvania venture as glory and salvation.

But a few days before the end of Martin's internship and their migration to North Dakota, they met Max Gottlieb on the street.

Martin had not seen him for more than a year; Leora never. He looked worried and ill. While Martin was agonizing as to whether to pass with a bow, Gottlieb stopped.

"How is everything, Martin?" he said cordially. But his eyes said, "Why have you never come back to me?"

The boy stammered something, nothing, and when Gottlieb had gone by, stooped and moving as in pain, he longed to run after him.

Leora was demanding, "Is that the Professor Gottlieb you're always talking about?"

"Yes. Say! How does he strike you?"

"I don't — Sandy, he's the greatest man I've ever seen! I don't know how I know, but he is! Dr. Silva is a darling, but that was a *great* man! I wish — I wish we were going to see him again. There's the first man I ever laid eyes on that I'd leave you for, if he wanted me. He's so — oh, he's like a sword — no, he's like a brain walking. Oh, Sandy, he looked so wretched. I wanted to cry. I'd black his shoes!"

"God! So would I!"

But in the bustle of leaving Zenith, the excitement of the journey to Wheatsylvania, the scramble of his state examinations, the dignity of being a Practicing Physician, he forgot Gottlieb, and on that Dakota prairie radiant in early June, with meadow larks on every fence post, he began his work.

## Chapter 12

At the moment when Martin met him on the street, Gottlieb was ruined.

Max Gottlieb was a German Jew, born in Saxony in 1850. Though he took his medical degree, at Heidelberg, he was never interested in practicing medicine. He was a follower of Helmholtz, and youthful researches in the physics of sound convinced him of the need of the quantitative method in the medical sciences. Then Koch's discoveries drew him into biology. Always an elaborately careful worker, a maker of long rows of figures, always realizing the presence of uncontrollable variables, always a vicious assailant of what he considered slackness or lie or pomposity, never too kindly to well-intentioned stupidity, he worked in the laboratories of Koch, of Pasteur, he followed the early statements of Pearson in biometrics, he drank beer and wrote vitriolic letters, he voyaged to Italy and England and Scandinavia, and casually, between two days, he married (as he might have bought a coat or hired a housekeeper) the patient and wordless daughter of a Gentile merchant.

Then began a series of experiments, very important, very undramatic-sounding, very long, and exceedingly unappreciated. Back in 1881 he was confirming Pasteur's results in chicken cholera immunity and, for relief and pastime, trying to separate an enzyme from yeast. A few years later, living on the tiny inheritance from his father, a petty banker, and quite carelessly and cheerfully exhausting it, he was analyzing critically the ptomain theory of disease, and investigating the mechanism of the attenuation of virulence of microorganisms. He got thereby small fame. Perhaps he was over-cautious, and more than the devil or starvation he hated men who rushed into publication unprepared.

Though he meddled little in politics, considering them the most repetitious and least scientific of human activities, he was a sufficiently patriotic German to hate the Junkers. As a youngster he had a fight or two with ruffling subalterns; once he spent a week in jail; often he was infuriated by discriminations against Jews: and at forty he went sadly off to the America which could never become militaristic or anti-Semitic — to the Hoagland Laboratory in Brooklyn, then to Queen City University as professor of bacteriology.

Here he made his first investigation of toxin-anti-toxin reactions. He announced that antibodies, excepting antitoxin, had no relation to the immune state of an animal, and while he himself was being ragingly denounced in the small but hectic world of scientists, he dealt calmly and most brutally with Yersin's and Marmorek's theories of sera.

His dearest dream, now and for years of racking research, was the artificial production of antitoxin — its production *in vitro*. Once he was prepared to publish, but he found an error and rigidly suppressed his notes. All the while he was lonely. There was apparently no one in Queen City who regarded him as other than a cranky Jew catching microbes by their little tails and leering at them — no work for a tall man at a time when heroes were building bridges, experimenting with Horseless Carriages, writing the first of the poetic Compelling Ads, and selling miles of calico and cigars.

In 1899 he was called to the University of Winnemac, as professor of bacteriology in the medical school, and here he drudged on for a dozen years. Not once did he talk of results of the sort called "practical"; not once did he cease warring on the *post hoc propter hoc* conclusions which still make up most medical lore; not once did he fail to be hated by his colleagues, who were respectful to his face, uncomfortable in feeling his ironic power, but privily joyous to call him Mephisto, Diabolist, Killjoy, Pessimist, Destructive Critic, Flippant Cynic, Scientific Bounder Lacking in Dignity and Seriousness, Intellectual Snob, Pacifist, Anarchist, Atheist, Jew. They said, with reason, that he was so devoted to Pure Science, to art for art's sake, that he would rather have people die by the right therapy than be cured by the wrong. Having built a shrine for humanity, he wanted to kick out of it all mere human beings.

The total number of his papers, in a brisk scientific realm where really clever people published five times a year, was not more than twenty-five in thirty years. They were all exquisitely finished, all easily reduplicated and checked by the doubtfulest critics.

At Mohalis he was pleased by large facilities for work, by excellent assistants, endless glassware, plenty of guinea pigs, enough monkeys; but he was bored by the round of teaching, and melancholy again in a lack of understanding friends. Always he sought someone to whom he could talk without suspicion or caution. He was human enough, when he meditated upon the exaltation of doctors bold through ignorance, of inventors who were but tinkers magnified, to be irritated by his lack of fame in America, even in Mohalis, and to complain not too nobly.

He had never dined with a duchess, never received a prize, never been interviewed, never produced anything which the public could understand, nor experienced anything since his schoolboy amours which nice people could regard as romantic. He was, in fact, an authentic scientist.

He was of the great benefactors of humanity. There will never, in any age, be an effort to end the great epidemics or the petty infections which will not have been influenced by Max Gottlieb's researches, for he was not one who tagged and prettily classified bacteria and protozoa. He sought their chemistry, the laws of their existence and destruction, basic laws for the most part unknown after a generation of busy biologists. Yet they were right who called him "pessimist," for this man who, as much as any other, will have been the cause of reducing infectious diseases to almost-zero often doubted the value of reducing infectious diseases at all.

He reflected (it was an international debate in which he was joined by a few and damned by many) that half a dozen generations nearly free from epidemics would produce a race so low in natural immunity that when a great plague, suddenly springing from almost-zero to a world-smothering cloud, appeared again, it might wipe out the world entire, so that the measures to save lives to which he lent his genius might in the end be the destruction of all human life.

He meditated that if science and public hygiene did remove tuberculosis and the other major plagues, the world was grimly certain to become so overcrowded, to become such a universal slave-packed shambles, that all beauty and ease and wisdom would disappear in a famine-driven scamper for existence. Yet these speculations never checked his work. If the future became overcrowded, the future must by birth-control or otherwise look to itself. Perhaps it would, he reflected. But even this drop of wholesome optimism was lacking in his final doubts. For he doubted all progress of the intellect and the emotions, and he doubted, most of all, the superiority of divine mankind to the cheerful dogs, the infallibly graceful cats, the unmoral and unagitated and irreligious horses, the superbly adventuring seagulls.

While medical quacks, manufacturers of patent medicines, chewing-gum salesmen, and high priests of advertising lived in large houses, attended by servants, and took their sacred persons abroad in limousines, Max Gottlieb dwelt in a cramped cottage whose paint was peeling, and rode to his laboratory on an ancient and squeaky bicycle. Gottlieb himself protested rarely. He was not so unreasonable — usually — as to demand both freedom and the fruits of popular slavery. "Why," he once said to Martin, "should the world pay me for doing what I want and what they do not want?"

If in his house there was but one comfortable chair, on his desk were letters, long, intimate, and respectful, from the great ones of France and Germany, Italy and Denmark, and from scientists whom Great Britain so much valued that she gave them titles almost as high as those with which she rewarded distillers, cigarette-manufacturers, and the owners of obscene newspapers.

But poverty kept him from fulfillment of his summer longing to sit beneath the poplars by the Rhine or the tranquil Seine, at a table on whose checkered cloth were bread and cheese and wine and dusky cherries, those ancient and holy simplicities of all the world.

## II

Max Gottlieb's wife was thick and slow-moving and mute; at sixty she had not learned to speak easy English; and her German was of the small-town bourgeois, who pay their debts and overeat and grow red. If he was not confidential with her, if at table he forgot her in long reflections, neither was he unkind or impatient, and he depended on her housekeeping, her warming of his old-fashioned nightgown. She had not been well of late. She had nausea and indigestion, but she kept on with her work. Always you heard her old slippers slapping about the house.

They had three children, all born when Gottlieb was over thirty-eight: Miriam, the youngest, an ardent child who had a touch at the piano, an instinct about Beethoven, and hatred for the "ragtime" popular in America; an older sister who was nothing in particular; and their boy Robert — Robert Koch Gottlieb. He was a wild thing and a distress. They sent him, with anxiety over the cost, to a smart school near Zenith, where he met the sons of manufacturers and discovered a taste for fast motors and eccentric clothes, and no taste whatever for studying. At home he clamored that his father was a "tightwad." When Gottlieb sought to make it clear that he was a poor man, the boy answered that out of his poverty he was always sneakingly spending money on his researches — he had no right to do that and shame his son — let the confounded University provide him with material!

### III

There were few of Gottlieb's students who saw him and his learning as anything but hurdles to be leaped as quickly as possible. One of the few was Martin Arrowsmith.

However harshly he may have pointed out Martin's errors, however loftily he may have seemed to ignore his devotion, Gottlieb was as aware of Martin as Martin of him. He planned vast things. If Martin really desired his help (Gottlieb could be as modest personally as he was egotistic and swaggering in competitive science), he would make the boy's career his own. During Martin's minute original research, Gottlieb rejoiced in his willingness to abandon conventional — and convenient — theories of immunology and in the exasperated carefulness with which he checked results. When Martin for unknown reasons became careless, when he was obviously drinking too much, obviously mixed up in some absurd personal affair, it was tragic hunger for friends and flaming respect for excellent work which drove Gottlieb to snarl at him. Of the apologies demanded by Silva he had no notion. He would have raged —

He waited for Martin to return. He blamed himself: "Fool! There was a fine spirit. You should have known one does not use a platinum loop for shoveling coal." As long as he could (while Martin was dish-washing and wandering on improbable trains between impossible towns), he put off the appointment of a new assistant. Then all his wistfulness chilled to anger. He considered Martin a traitor, and put him out of his mind.

### IV

It is possible that Max Gottlieb was a genius. Certainly he was mad as any genius. He did, during the period of Martin's internship in Zenith General, a thing more preposterous than any of the superstitions at which he scoffed.

He tried to become an executive and a reformer! He, the cynic, the anarch, tried to found an Institution, and he went at it like a spinster organizing a league to keep small boys from learning naughty words.

He conceived that there might, in this world, be a medical school which should be altogether scientific, ruled by exact quantitative biology and chemistry, with spectacle-fitting and most of surgery ignored, and he further conceived that such an enterprise might be conducted at the University of Winnemac! He tried to be practical about it; oh, he was extremely practical and plausible!

"I admit we should not be able to turn out doctors to cure village bellyaches. And ordinary physicians are admirable and altogether necessary — perhaps. But there are too many of them already. And on the 'practical' side, you gif me twenty years of a school that is precise and cautious, and we shall cure diabetes, maybe tuberculosis and cancer, and all these arthritis things that the carpenters shake their heads at them and call them 'rheumatism.' So!"

He did not desire the control of such a school, nor any credit. He was too busy. But at a meeting of the American Academy of Sciences he met one Dr. Entwisle, a youngish physiologist from Harvard, who would make an excellent dean. Entwisle admired him, and sounded him on his willingness to be called to Harvard. When Gottlieb outlined his new sort of medical school, Entwisle was fervent. "Nothing I'd like so much as to have a chance at a place like that," he fluttered, and Gottlieb went back to Mohalis triumphant. He was the more assured because (though he sardonically refused it) he was at this time offered the medical deanship of the University of West Chippewa.

So simple, or so insane, was he that he wrote to Dean Silva politely bidding him step down and hand over his school — his work, his life — to an unknown teacher in Harvard! A courteous old gentleman was Dad Silva, a fit disciple of Osier, but this incredible letter killed his patience. He replied that while he could see the value of basic research, the medical school belonged to the people of the state, and its task was to provide them with immediate and practical attention. For himself, he hinted, if he ever believed that the school would profit by his resignation he would go at once, but he needed a rather broader suggestion than a letter from one of his own subordinates!

Gottlieb retorted with spirit and indiscretion. He damned the People of the State of Winnemac. Were they, in their present condition of nincompoopery, worth any sort of attention? He unjustifiably took his demand over Silva's head to that great orator and patriot, Dr. Horace Greeley Truscott, president of the University.

President Truscott said, "Really, I'm too engrossed to consider chimerical schemes, however ingenious they may be."

"You are too busy to consider anything but selling honorary degrees to millionaires for gymnasiums," remarked Gottlieb.

Next day he was summoned to a special meeting of the University Council. As head of the medical department of bacteriology, Gottlieb was a member of this all-ruling body, and when he entered the long Council Chamber, with its gilt ceiling, its heavy maroon curtains, its somber paintings of pioneers, he started for his usual seat, unconscious of the knot of whispering members, meditating on far-off absorbing things.

"Oh, uh, Professor Gottlieb, will you please sit down there at the far end of the table?" called President Truscott.

Then Gottlieb was aware of tensions. He saw that out of the seven members of the Board of Regents, the four who lived in or near Zenith were present. He saw that sitting beside Truscott was not the dean of the academic department but Dean Silva. He saw that however easily they talked, they were looking at him through the mist of their chatter.

President Truscott announced, "Gentlemen, this joint meeting of the Council and the regents is to consider charges against Professor Max Gottlieb preferred by his dean and by myself."

Gottlieb suddenly looked old.

"These charges are: Disloyalty to his dean, his president, his regents and to the State of Winnemac. Disloyalty to recognized medical and scholastic ethics. Insane egotism. Atheism. Persistent failure to collaborate with his colleagues, and such inability to understand practical affairs as makes it dangerous to let him conduct the important laboratories and classes with which we have entrusted him. Gentlemen, I shall now prove each of these points, from Professor Gottlieb's own letters to Dean Silva."

He proved them.

The chairman of the Board of Regents suggested, "Gottlieb, I think it would simplify things if you just handed us your resignation and permitted us to part in good feeling, instead of having the unpleasant — "

"I'm damned if I will resign!" Gottlieb was on his feet, a lean fury. "Because you all haf schoolboy minds, golf-links minds, you are twisting my expression, and perfectly accurate expression, of a sound revolutionary ideal, which would personally to me be of no value or advantage whatefer, into a desire to steal promotions. That fools should judge honor — !" His long forefinger was a fish-hook, reaching for President Truscott's soul. "No! I will not resign! You can cast me out!"

"I'm afraid, then, we must ask you to leave the room while we vote." The president was very suave, for so large and strong and hearty a man.

Gottlieb rode his wavering bicycle to the laboratory. It was by telephone message from a brusque girl clerk in the president's office that he was informed that "his resignation had been accepted."

He agonized, "Discharge me? They couldn't! I'm the chief glory, the only glory, of this shopkeepers' school!" When he comprehended that apparently they very much had discharged him, he was shamed that he should have given them a chance to kick him. But the really dismaying thing was that he should by an effort to be a politician have interrupted the sacred work.

He required peace and a laboratory, at once.

They'd see what fools they were when they heard that Harvard had called him!

He was eager for the mellower ways of Cambridge and Boston. Why had he remained so long in raw Mohalis? He wrote to Dr. Entwisle, hinting that he was willing to hear an offer. He expected a telegram. He waited a week, then had a long letter from Entwisle admitting that he had been premature in speaking for the Harvard faculty. Entwisle presented the faculty's compliments and their hope that some time they might have the honor of his presence, but as things were now —

Gottlieb wrote to the University of West Chippewa that, after all, he was willing to think about their medical deanship ... and had answer that the place was filled, that they had not greatly liked the tone of his former letter, and they did not "care to go into the matter further."

At sixty-one, Gottlieb had saved but a few hundred dollars — literally a few hundred. Like any bricklayer out of work, he had to have a job or go hungry. He was no longer a genius impatient of interrupted creation but a shabby schoolmaster in disgrace.

He prowled through his little brown house, fingering papers, staring at his wife, staring at old pictures, staring at nothing. He still had a month of teaching — they had dated ahead the resignation which they had written for him — but he was too dispirited to go to the laboratory. He felt unwanted, almost unsafe. His ancient sureness was broken into self-pity. He waited from delivery to delivery for the mail. Surely there would be aid from somebody who knew what he was, what he meant. There were many friendly letters about research, but the sort of men with whom he corresponded did not listen to intercollegiate faculty tattle nor know of his need.

He could not, after the Harvard mischance and the West Chippewa rebuke, approach the universities or the scientific institutes, and he was too proud to write begging letters to the men who revered him. No, he would be business-like! He applied to a Chicago teachers' agency, and received a stilted answer promising to look about and inquiring whether he would care to take the position of teacher of physics and chemistry in a suburban high school.

Before he had sufficiently recovered from his fury to be able to reply, his household was overwhelmed by his wife's sudden agony.

She had been unwell for months. He had wanted her to see a physician, but she had refused, and all the while she was stolidly terrified by the fear that she had cancer of the stomach. Now when she began to vomit blood, she cried to him for help. The Gottlieb who scoffed at medical credos, at "carpenters" and "pill mongers," had forgotten what he knew of diagnosis, and when he was ill, or his family, he called for the doctor as desperately as any backwoods layman to whom illness was the black malignity of unknown devils.

In unbelievable simplicity he considered that, as his quarrel with Silva was not personal, he could still summon him, and this time he was justified. Silva came, full of excessive benignity, chuckling to himself, "When he's got something the matter, he doesn't run for Arrhenius or Jacques Loeb, but for me!" Into the meager cottage the little man brought strength, and Gottlieb gazed down on him trustingly.

Mrs. Gottlieb was suffering. Silva gave her morphine. Not without satisfaction he learned that Gottlieb did not even know the dose. He examined her — his pudgy hands had the sensitiveness if not the precision of Gottlieb's skeleton fingers. He peered about the airless bedroom: the dark green curtains, the crucifix on the dumpy bureau, the color-print of a virtuously voluptuous maiden. He was bothered by an impression of having recently been in the room. He remembered. It was the twin of the doleful chamber of a German grocer whom he had seen during a consultation a month ago.

He spoke to Gottlieb not as to a colleague or an enemy but as a patient, to be cheered.

"Don't think there's any tumorous mass. As of course you know, Doctor, you can tell such a lot by the differences in the shape of the lower border of the ribs, and by the surface of the belly during deep breathing."

"Oh, yesss."

"I don't think you need to worry in the least. We'd better hustle her off to the University Hospital, and we'll give her a test meal and get her X-rayed and take a look for Boas-Oppler bugs."

She was taken away, heavy, inert, carried down the cottage steps. Gottlieb was with her. Whether or not he loved her, whether he was capable of ordinary domestic affection, could not be discovered. The need of turning to Dean Silva had damaged his opinion of his own wisdom. It was the final affront, more subtle and more enervating than the offer to teach chemistry to children. As he sat by her bed, his dark face was blank, and the wrinkles which deepened across that mask may have been sorrow, may have been fear.... Nor is it known how, through the secure and uninvaded years, he had regarded his wife's crucifix, which Silva had spied on their bureau — a gaudy plaster crucifix on a box set with gilded shells.

Silva diagnosed it as probable gastric ulcer, and placed her on treatment, with light and frequent meals. She improved, but she remained in the hospital for four weeks, and Gottlieb wondered: Are these doctors deceiving us? Is it really cancer, which by Their mystic craft They are concealing from me who know naught?

Robbed of her silent assuring presence on which night by weary night he had depended, he fretted over his daughters, despaired at their noisy piano-practice, their inability to manage the slattern maid. When they had gone to bed he sat alone in the pale lamplight, unmoving, not reading. He was bewildered. His haughty self was like a robber baron fallen into the hands of rebellious slaves, stooped under a filthy load, the proud eye rheumy and patient with despair, the sword hand chopped off, obscene flies crawling across the gnawed wrist.

It was at this time that he encountered Martin and Leora on the street in Zenith.

He did not look back when they had passed him, but all that afternoon he brooded on them. "That girl, maybe it was she that stole Martin from me — from science! No! He was right. One sees what happens to the fools like me!"

On the day after Martin and Leora had started for Wheatsylvania, singing, Gottlieb went to Chicago to see the teachers' agency.

The firm was controlled by a Live Wire who had once been a county superintendent of schools. He was not much interested. Gottlieb lost his temper: "Do you make an endeavor to find positions for teachers, or do you merely send out circulars to amuse yourself? Haf you looked up my record? Do you know who I am?"

The agent roared, "Oh, we know about you, all right, all right! I didn't when I first wrote you, but — You seem to have a good record as a laboratory man, though I don't see that you've produced anything of the slightest use in medicine. We had hoped to give you a chance such as you nor nobody else ever had. John Edtooth, the Oklahoma oil magnate, has decided to found a university that for plant and endowment and individuality will beat anything that's ever been pulled off in education — biggest gymnasium in the world, with an ex-New York Giant for baseball coach! We thought maybe we might work you in on the bacteriology or the physiology — I guess you could manage to teach that, too, if you boned up on it. But we've been making some inquiries. From some good friends of ours, down Winnemac way. And we find that you're not to be trusted with a position of real responsibility. Why, they fired you for general incompetence! But now that you've had your lesson — Do you think you'd be competent to teach Practical Hygiene in Edtooth University?"

Gottlieb was so angry that he forgot to speak English, and as all his cursing was in student German, in a creaky dry voice, the whole scene was very funny indeed to the cackling bookkeeper and the girl stenographers. When he went from that place Max Gottlieb walked slowly, without purpose, and in his eyes were senile tears.

## Chapter 13

No one in the medical world had ever damned more heartily than Gottlieb the commercialism of certain large pharmaceutical firms, particularly Dawson T. Hunziker & Co., Inc., of Pittsburgh. The Hunziker Company was an old and ethical house which dealt only with reputable doctors — or practically only with reputable doctors. It furnished excellent antitoxins for diphtheria and tetanus, as well as the purest of official preparations, with the plainest and most official-looking labels on the swaggeringly modest brown bottles. Gottlieb had asserted that they produced doubtful vaccines, yet he returned from Chicago to write to Dawson Hunziker that he was no longer interested in teaching, and he would be willing to work for them on half time if he might use their laboratories, on possibly important research, for the rest of the day.

When the letter had gone he sat mumbling. He was certainly not altogether sane. "Education! Biggest gymnasium in the world! Incapable of responsibility. Teaching I can do no more. But Hunziker will laugh at me. I haf told the truth about him and I shall haf to — Dear Gott, what shall I do?"

Into this still frenzy, while his frightened daughters peered at him from doorways, hope glided.

The telephone rang. He did not answer it. On the third irascible burring he took up the receiver and grumbled, "Yes, yes, vot iss it?"

A twanging nonchalant voice: "This M. C. Gottlieb?"

"This is Dr. Gottlieb!"

"Well, I guess you're the party. Hola wire. Long distance wants yuh."

Then, "Professor Gottlieb? This is Dawson Hunziker speaking. From Pittsburgh. My dear fellow, we should be delighted to have you join our staff."

"I — But — "

"I believe you have criticized the pharmaceutical houses — oh, we read the newspaper clippings very efficiently! — but we feel that when you come to us and understand the Spirit of the Old Firm better, you'll be enthusiastic. I hope, by the way, I'm not interrupting something."

Thus, over certain hundreds of miles, from the gold and blue drawing-room of his Sewickley home, Hunziker spoke to Max Gottlieb sitting in his patched easy chair, and Gottlieb grated with a forlorn effort at dignity:

"No, it iss all right."

"Well — we shall be glad to offer you five thousand dollars a year, for a starter, and we shan't worry about the half-time arrangement. We'll give you all the space and technicians and material you need, and you just go ahead and ignore us, and work out whatever seems important to you. Our only request is that if you do find any serums which are of real value to the world, we shall have the privilege of manufacturing them, and if we lose money on 'em, it doesn't matter. We like to make money, if we can do it honestly, but our chief purpose is to serve mankind. Of course if the serums pay, we shall be only too delighted to give you a generous commission. Now about practical details — "

### II

Gottlieb, the placidly virulent hater of religious rites, had a religious-seeming custom.

Often he knelt by his bed and let his mind run free. It was very much like prayer, though certainly there was no formal invocation, no consciousness of a Supreme Being — other than Max Gottlieb. This night, as he knelt, with the wrinkles softening in his drawn face, he meditated, "I was asinine that I should ever scold the commercialists! This salesman fellow, he has his feet on the ground. How much more aut'entic the worst counter-jumper than frightened professors! Fine *dieners*! Freedom! No teaching of imbeciles! *Du Heiliger!* "

But he had no contract with Dawson Hunziker.

In the medical periodicals the Dawson Hunziker Company published full-page advertisements, most starchy and refined in type, announcing that Professor Max Gottlieb, perhaps the most distinguished immunologist in the world, had joined their staff.

In his Chicago clinic, one Dr. Rouncefield chuckled, "That's what becomes of these super-highbrows. Pardon me if I seem to grin."

In the laboratories of Ehrlich and Roux, Bordet and Sir David Bruce, sorrowing men wailed, "How could old Max have gone over to that damned pill-peddler? Why didn't he come to us? Oh, well, if he didn't want to — *Voilà!* He is dead."

In the village of Wheatsylvania, in North Dakota, a young doctor protested to his wife, "Of all the people in the world! I wouldn't have believed it! Max Gottlieb falling for those crooks!"

"I don't care!" said his wife. "If he's gone into business he had some good reason for it. I told you, I'd leave you for — "

"Oh, well," sighingly, "give and forgive. I learned a lot from Gottlieb and I'm grateful for — God, Leora, I wish *he* hadn't gone wrong!"

And Max Gottlieb, with his three young and a pale, slow-moving wife, was arriving at the station in Pittsburgh, tugging a shabby wicker bag, an immigrant bundle, and a Bond Street dressing-case. From the train he had stared up at the valiant cliffs, down to the smoke-tinged splendor of the river, and his heart was young. Here was fiery enterprise, not the flat land and flat minds of Winnemac. At the station-entrance every dingy taxicab seemed radiant to him, and he marched forth a conqueror.

## III

In the Dawson Hunziker building, Gottlieb found such laboratories as he had never planned, and instead of student assistants he had an expert who himself had taught bacteriology, as well as three swift technicians, one of them German-trained. He was received with acclaim in the private office of Hunziker, which was remarkably like a minor cathedral. Hunziker was bald and business-like as to skull but tortoise-spectacled and sentimental of eye. He stood up at his Jacobean desk, gave Gottlieb a Havana cigar, and told him that they had awaited him pantingly.

In the enormous staff dining-room Gottlieb found scores of competent young chemists and biologists who treated him with reverence. He liked them. If they talked too much of money — of how much this new tincture of cinchona ought to sell, and how soon their salaries would be increased — yet they were free of the careful pomposities of college instructors. As a youngster, the cap-tilted young Max had been a laughing man, and now in gusty arguments his laughter came back.

His wife seemed better; his daughter Miriam found an excellent piano teacher; the boy Robert entered college that autumn; they had a spacious though decrepit house; the relief from the droning and the annually repeated, inevitable routine of the classroom was exhilarating; and Gottlieb had never in his life worked so well. He was unconscious of everything outside of his laboratory and a few theaters and concert-halls.

Six months passed before he realized that the young technical experts resented what he considered his jolly thrusts at their commercialism. They were tired of his mathematical enthusiasms and some of them viewed him as an old bore, muttered of him as a Jew. He was hurt, for he liked to be merry with fellow workers. He began to ask questions and to explore the Hunziker building. He had seen nothing of it save his laboratory, a corridor or two, the dining-room, and Hunziker's office.

However abstracted and impractical, Gottlieb would have made an excellent Sherlock Holmes — if anybody who would have made an excellent Sherlock Holmes would have been willing to be a detective. His mind burned through appearances to actuality. He discovered now that the Dawson Hunziker Company was quite all he had asserted in earlier days. They did make excellent antitoxins and ethical preparations, but they were also producing a new "cancer remedy" manufactured from the orchid, pontifically recommended and possessing all the value of mud. And to various billboard-advertising beauty companies they sold millions of bottles of a complexion-cream guaranteed to turn a Canadian Indian guide as lily-fair as the angels. This treasure cost six cents a bottle to make and a dollar over the counter, and the name of Dawson Hunziker was never connected with it.

It was at this time that Gottlieb succeeded in his masterwork after twenty years of seeking. He produced antitoxin in the test-tube, which meant that it would be possible to immunize against certain diseases without tediously making sera by the inoculation of animals. It was a revolution, the revolution, in immunology ... if he was right.

He revealed it at a dinner for which Hunziker had captured a general, a college president, and a pioneer aviator. It was an expansive dinner, with admirable hock, the first decent German wine Gottlieb had drunk in years. He twirled the slender green glass affectionately; he came out of his dreams and became excited, gay, demanding. They applauded him, and for an hour he was a Great Scientist. Of them all, Hunziker was most generous in his praise. Gottlieb wondered if someone had not tricked this good bald man into intrigues with the beautifiers.

Hunziker summoned him to the office next day. Hunziker did his summoning very well indeed (unless it happened to be merely a stenographer). He sent a glossy morning-coated male secretary, who presented Mr. Hunziker's compliments to the much less glossy Dr. Gottlieb, and hinted with the delicacy of a lilac bud that if it was quite altogether convenient, if it would not in the least interfere with Dr. Gottlieb's experiments, Mr. Hunziker would be flattered to see him in the office at a quarter after three.

When Gottlieb rambled in, Hunziker motioned the secretary out of existence and drew up a tall Spanish chair.

"I lay awake half the night thinking about your discovery, Dr. Gottlieb. I've been talking to the technical director and sales-manager and we feel it's the time to strike. We'll patent your method of synthesizing antibodies and immediately put them on the market in large quantities, with a great big advertising campaign — you know — not circus it, of course — strictly high-class ethical advertising. We'll start with anti-diphtheria serum. By the way, when you receive your next check you'll find we've raised your honorarium to seven thousand a year." Hunziker was a large purring pussy now, and Gottlieb death-still. "Need I say, my dear fellow, that if there's the demand I anticipate, you will have exceedingly large commissions coming!"

Hunziker leaned back with a manner of "How's that for glory, my boy?"

Gottlieb spoke nervously: "I do not approve of patenting serological processes. They should be open to all laboratories. And I am strongly against premature production or even announcement. I think I am right, but I must check my technique, perhaps improve it — be *sure*. Then, I should think there should be no objection to market production, but in ve-ry small quantities and in fair competition with others, not under patents, as if this was a dinglebat toy for the Christmas tradings!"

"My dear fellow, I quite sympathize. Personally I should like nothing so much as to spend my whole life in just producing one priceless scientific discovery, without consideration of mere profit. But we have our duty toward the stockholders of the Dawson Hunziker Company to make money for them. Do you realize that they have — and many of them are poor widows and orphans — invested their Little All in our stock, and that we must keep faith? I am helpless; I am but their Humble Servant. And on the other side: I think we've treated you rather well, Dr. Gottlieb, and we've given you complete freedom. And we intend to go on treating you well! Why, man, you'll be rich; you'll be one of us! I don't like to make any demands, but on this point it's my duty to insist, and I shall expect you at the earliest possible moment to start manufacturing — "

Gottlieb was sixty-two. The defeat at Winnemac had done something to his courage.... And he had no contract with Hunziker.

He protested shakily, but as he crawled back to his laboratory it seemed impossible for him to leave this sanctuary and face the murderous brawling world, and quite as impossible to tolerate a cheapened and ineffective imitation of his antitoxin. He began, that hour, a sordid strategy which his old proud self would have called inconceivable; he began to equivocate, to put off announcement and production till he should have "cleared up a few points," while week on week Hunziker became more threatening. Meantime he prepared for disaster. He moved his family to a smaller house, and gave up every luxury, even smoking.

Among his economies was the reduction of his son's allowance.

Robert was a square-rigged, swart, tempestuous boy, arrogant where there seemed to be no reason for arrogance, longed for by the anemic, milky sort of girls, yet ever supercilious to them. While his father was alternately proud and amiably sardonic about his own Jewish blood, the boy conveyed to his classmates in college that he was from pure and probably noble German stock. He was welcomed, or half welcomed, in a motoring, poker-playing, country-club set, and he had to have more money. Gottlieb missed twenty dollars from his desk. He who ridiculed conventional honor had the honor, as he had the pride, of a savage old squire. A new misery stained his incessant bitterness at having to deceive Hunziker. He faced Robert with, "My boy, did you take the money from my desk?"

Few youngsters could have faced that jut of his hawk nose, the red-veined rage of his sunken eyes. Robert spluttered, then shouted:

"Yes, I did! And I've got to have some more! I've got to get some clothes and stuff. It's your fault. You bring me up to train with a lot of fellows that have all the cash in the world, and then you expect me to dress like a hobo!"

"Stealing — "

"Rats! What's stealing! You're always making fun of these preachers that talk about Sin and Truth and Honesty and all those words that've been used so much they don't mean a darn' thing and — I don't care! Daws Hunziker, the old man's son, he told me his dad said you could be a millionaire, and then you keep us strapped like this, and Mom sick — Let me tell you, back in Mohalis Mom used to slip me a couple of dollars almost every week and — I'm tired of it! If you're going to keep me in rags, I'm going to cut out college!"

Gottlieb stormed, but there was no force in it. He did not know, all the next fortnight, what his son was going to do, what himself was going to do.

Then, so quietly that not till they had returned from the cemetery did they realize her passing, his wife died, and the next week his oldest daughter ran off with a worthless laughing fellow who lived by gambling.

Gottlieb sat alone. Over and over he read the Book of Job. "Truly the Lord hath smitten me and my house," he whispered. When Robert came in, mumbling that he would be good, the old man lifted to him a blind face, unhearing. But as he repeated the fables of his fathers it did not occur to him to believe them, or to stoop in fear before their God of Wrath — or to gain ease by permitting Hunziker to defile his discovery.

He arose, in time, and went silently to his laboratory. His experiments were as careful as ever, and his assistants saw no change save that he did not lunch in hall. He walked blocks away, to a vile restaurant at which he could save thirty cents a day.

## IV

Out of the dimness which obscured the people about him, Miriam emerged.

She was eighteen, the youngest of his brood, squat, and in no way comely save for her tender mouth. She had always been proud of her father, understanding the mysterious and unreasoning compulsions of his science, but she had been in awe till now, when he walked heavily and spoke rarely. She dropped her piano lessons, discharged the maid, studied the cookbook, and prepared for him the fat crisp dishes that he loved. Her regret was that she had never learned German, for he dropped now and then into the speech of his boyhood.

He eyed her, and at length: "So! One is with me. Could you endure the poverty if I went away — to teach chemistry in a high school!"

"Yes. Of course. Maybe I could play the piano in a movie theater."

He might not have done it without her loyalty, but when Dawson Hunziker next paraded into the laboratory, demanding, "Now look here. We've fussed long enough. We got to put your stuff on the market," then Gottlieb answered, "No. If you wait till I have done all I can — maybe one year, probably three — you shall have it. But not till I am sure. No."

Hunziker went off huffily, and Gottlieb prepared for sentence.

Then the card of Dr. A. DeWitt Tubbs, Director of the McGurk Institute of Biology, of New York, was brought to him.

Gottlieb knew of Tubbs. He had never visited McGurk but he considered it, next to Rockefeller and McCormick, the soundest and freest organization for pure scientific research in the country, and if he had pictured a Heavenly laboratory in which good scientists might spend eternity in happy and thoroughly impractical research, he would have devised it in the likeness of McGurk. He was mildly pleased that its director should have called on him.

Dr. A. DeWitt Tubbs was tremendously whiskered on all visible spots save his nose and temples and the palms of his hands, short but passionately whiskered, like a Scotch terrier. Yet they were not comic whiskers; they were the whiskers of dignity; and his eyes were serious, his step an earnest trot, his voice a piping solemnity.

"Dr. Gottlieb, this is a great pleasure. I have heard your papers at the Academy of Sciences but, to my own loss, I have hitherto failed to have an introduction to you."

Gottlieb tried not to sound embarrassed.

Tubbs looked at the assistants, like a plotter in a political play, and hinted, "May we have a talk — "

Gottlieb led him to his office, overlooking a vast bustle of side-tracks, of curving rails and brown freight-cars, and Tubbs urged:

"It has come to our attention, by a curious chance, that you are on the eve of your most significant discovery. We all wondered, when you left academic work, at your decision to enter the commercial field. We wished that you had cared to come to us."

"You would have taken me in? I needn't at all have come here?"

"Naturally! Now from what we hear, you are not giving your attention to the commercial side of things, and that tempts us to wonder whether you could be persuaded to join us at McGurk. So I just sprang on a train and ran down here. We should be delighted to have you become a member of the institute, and chief of the Department of Bacteriology and Immunology. Mr. McGurk and I desire nothing but the advancement of science. You would, of course, have absolute freedom as to what researches you thought it best to pursue, and I think we could provide as good assistance and material as would be obtainable anywhere in the world. In regard to salary — permit me to be business-like and perhaps blunt, as my train leaves in one hour — I don't suppose we could equal the doubtless large emolument which the Hunziker people are able to pay you, but we can go to ten thousand dollars a year — "

"Oh, my God, do not talk of the money! I shall be wit' you in New York one week from today. You see," said Gottlieb, "I haf no contract here!"

## Chapter 14

All afternoon they drove in the flapping buggy across the long undulations of the prairie. To their wandering there was no barrier, neither lake nor mountain nor factory-bristling city, and the breeze about them was flowing sunshine.

Martin cried to Leora, "I feel as if all the Zenith dust and hospital lint were washed out of my lungs. Dakota. Real man's country. Frontier. Opportunity. America!"

From the thick swale the young prairie chickens rose. As he watched them sweep across the wheat, his sun-drowsed spirit was part of the great land, and he was almost freed of the impatience with which he had started out from Wheatsylvania.

"If you're going driving, don't forget that supper is six o'clock sharp," Mrs. Tozer had said, smiling to sugar-coat it.

On Main Street, Mr. Tozer waved to them and shouted, "Be back by six. Supper at six o'clock sharp."

Bert Tozer ran out from the bank, like a country schoolmaster skipping from a one-room schoolhouse, and cackled, "Say, you folks better not forget to be back at six o'clock for supper or the Old Man'll have a fit. He'll expect you for supper at six o'clock sharp, and when he says six o'clock *sharp* , he means six o'clock *sharp* , and not five minutes *past* six!"

"Now that," observed Leora, "is funny, because in my twenty-two years in Wheatsylvania I remember three different times when supper was as late as seven minutes after six. Let's get out of this, Sandy.... I wonder were we so wise to live with the family and save money?"

Before they had escaped from the not very extensive limits of Wheatsylvania they passed Ada Quist, the future Mrs. Bert Tozer, and through the lazy air they heard her voice slashing: "Better be home by six."

Martin would be heroic. "We'll by golly get back when we're by golly good and ready!" he said to Leora; but on them both was the cumulative dread of the fussing voices, beyond every breezy prospect was the order, "Be back at six sharp"; and they whipped up to arrive at eleven minutes to six, as Mr. Tozer was returning from the creamery, full thirty seconds later than usual.

"Glad to see you among us," he said. "Hustle now and get that horse in the livery stable. Supper's at six — sharp!"

Martin survived it sufficiently to sound domestic when he announced at the supper-table:

"We had a bully drive. I'm going to like it here. Well, I've loafed for a day and a half, and now I've got to get busy. First thing is, I must find a location for my office. What is there vacant, Father Tozer?"

Mrs. Tozer said brightly, "Oh, I have such a nice idea, Martin. Why can't we fix up an office for you out in the barn? It'd be so handy to the house, for you to get to meals on time, and you could keep an eye on the house if the girl was out and Ory and I went out visiting or to the Embroidery Circle."

"In the barn!"

"Why, yes, in the old harness room. It's partly ceiled, and we could put in some nice tar paper or even beaver board."

"Mother Tozer, what the dickens do you think I'm planning to do? I'm not a hired man in a livery stable, or a kid looking for a place to put his birds' eggs! I was thinking of opening an office as a physician!"

Bert made it all easy: "Yuh, but you aren't much of a physician yet. You're just getting your toes in."

"I'm one hell of a good physician! Excuse me for cussing, Mother Tozer, but — Why, nights in the hospital, I've held hundreds of lives in my hand! I intend — "

"Look here, Mart," said Bertie. "As we're putting up the money — I don't want to be a tightwad but after all, a dollar is a dollar — if we furnish the dough, we've got to decide the best way to spend it."

Mr. Tozer looked thoughtful and said helplessly, "That's so. No sense taking a risk, with the blame farmers demanding all the money they can get for their wheat and cream, and then deliberately going to work and not paying the interest on their loans. I swear, it don't hardly pay to invest in mortgages any longer. No sense putting on lugs. Stands to reason you can look at a fellow's sore throat or prescribe for an ear-ache just as well in a nice simple little office as in some fool place all fixed up like a Moorhead saloon. Mother will see you have a comfortable corner in the barn — "

Leora intruded: "Look here, Papa. I want you to lend us one thousand dollars, outright, to use as we see fit." The sensation was immense. "We'll pay you six per cent — no, we won't; we'll pay you five; that's enough."

"And mortgages bringing six, seven, and eight!" Bert quavered.

"Five's enough. And we want our own say, absolute, as to how we use it — to fit up an office or anything else."

Mr. Tozer began, "That's a foolish way to — "

Bert took it away from him: "Ory, you're crazy! I suppose we'll have to lend you some money, but you'll blame well come to us for it from time to time, and you'll blame well take our advice — "

Leora rose. "Either you do what I say, just exactly what I say, or Mart and I take the first train and go back to Zenith, and I mean it! Plenty of places open for him there, with a big salary, so we won't have to be dependent on anybody!"

There was much conversation, most of which sounded like all the rest of it. Once Leora started for the stairs, to go up and pack; once Martin and she stood waving their napkins as they shook their fists, the general composition remarkably like the Laocoön.

Leora won.

They settled down to the most solacing fussing.

"Did you bring your trunk up from the depot?" asked Mr. Tozer.

"No sense leaving it there — paying two bits a day storage!" fumed Bert.

"I got it up this morning," said Martin.

"Oh, yes, Martin had it brought up this morning," agreed Mrs. Tozer.

"You had it brought? Didn't you bring it up yourself?" agonized Mr. Tozer.

"No. I had the fellow that runs the lumberyard haul it up for me," said Martin.

"Well, gosh almighty, you could just as well've put it on a wheelbarrow and brought it up yourself and saved a quarter!" said Bert.

"But a doctor has to keep his dignity," said Leora.

"Dignity, rats! Blame sight more dignified to be seen shoving a wheelbarrow than smoking them dirty cigarettes all the time!"

"Well, anyway — Where'd you put it?" asked Mr. Tozer.

"It's up in our room," said Martin.

"Where'd you think we better put it when it's unpacked? The attic is awful' full," Mr. Tozer submitted to Mrs. Tozer.

"Oh, I think Martin could get it in there."

"Why couldn't he put it in the barn?"

"Oh, not a nice new trunk like that!"

"What's the matter with the barn?" said Bert. "It's all nice and dry. Seems a shame to waste all that good space in the barn, now that you've gone and decided he mustn't have his dear little office there!"

"Bertie," from Leora, "I know what we'll do. You seem to have the barn on your brain. You move your old bank there, and Martin'll take the bank building for his office."

"That's entirely different — "

"Now there's no sense you two showing off and trying to be smart," protested Mr. Tozer. "Do you ever hear your mother and I scrapping and fussing like that? When do you think you'll have your trunk unpacked, Mart?" Mr. Tozer could consider barns and he could consider trunks but his was not a brain to grasp two such complicated matters at the same time.

"I can get it unpacked tonight, if it makes any difference — "

"Well, I don't suppose it really makes any special difference, but when you start to *do* a thing — "

"Oh, what difference does it make whether he — "

"If he's going to look for an office, instead of moving right into the barn, he can't take a month of Sundays getting unpacked and — "

"Oh, good Lord, I'll get it done tonight — "

"And I think we can get it in the attic — "

"I tell you it's jam full already — "

"We'll go take a look at it after supper — "

"Well now, I tell you when I tried to get that duck-boat in — "

Martin probably did not scream, but he heard himself screaming. The free and virile land was leagues away and for years forgotten.

## II

To find an office took a fortnight of diplomacy, and of discussion brightening three meals a day, every day. (Not that office-finding was the only thing the Tozers mentioned. They went thoroughly into every moment of Martin's day; they commented on his digestion, his mail, his walks, his shoes that needed cobbling, and whether he had yet taken them to the farmer-trapper-cobbler, and how much the cobbling ought to cost, and the presumable theology, politics, and marital relations of the cobbler.)

Mr. Tozer had from the first known the perfect office. The Norbloms lived above their general store, and Mr. Tozer knew that the Norbloms were thinking of moving. There was indeed nothing that was happening or likely to happen in Wheatsylvania which Mr. Tozer did not know and explain. Mrs. Norblom was tired of keeping house, and she wanted to go to Mrs. Beeson's boarding house (to the front room, on the right as you went along the upstairs hall, the room with the plaster walls and the nice little stove that Mrs. Beeson bought from Otto Krag for seven dollars and thirty-five cents — no, seven and a quarter it was).

They called on the Norbloms and Mr. Tozer hinted that "it might be nice for the Doctor to locate over the store, if the Norbloms were thinking of making any change — "

The Norbloms stared at each other, with long, bleached, cautious, Scandinavian stares, and grumbled that they "didn't *know* — of course it was the finest location in town — " Mr. Norblom admitted that if, against all probability, they ever considered moving, they would probably ask twenty-five dollars a month for the flat, unfurnished.

Mr. Tozer came out of the international conference as craftily joyful as any Mr. Secretary Tozer or Lord Tozer in Washington or London:

"Fine! Fine! We made him commit himself! Twenty-five, he says. That means, when the time's ripe, we'll offer him eighteen and close for twenty-one-seventy-five. If we just handle him careful, and give him time to go see Mrs. Beeson and fix up about boarding with her, we'll have him just where we want him!"

"Oh, if the Norbloms can't make up their minds, then let's try something else," said Martin. "There's a couple of vacant rooms behind the *Eagle* office."

"What? Go chasing around, after we've given the Norbloms reason to think we're serious, and make enemies of 'em for life? Now that would be a fine way to start building up a practice, wouldn't it? And I must say I wouldn't blame the Norbloms one bit for getting wild if you let 'em down like that. This ain't Zenith, where you can go yelling around expecting to get things done in two minutes!"

Through a fortnight, while the Norbloms agonized over deciding to do what they had long ago decided to do, Martin waited, unable to begin work. Until he should open a certified and recognizable office, most of the village did not regard him as a competent physician but as "that son-in-law of Andy Tozer's." In the fortnight he was called only once: for the sick-headache of Miss Agnes Ingleblad, aunt and housekeeper of Alec Ingleblad the barber. He was delighted, till Bert Tozer explained:

"Oh, so *she* called you in, eh? She's always doctorin' around. There ain't a thing the matter with her, but she's always trying out the latest stunt. Last time it was a fellow that come through here selling pills and liniments out of a Ford, and the time before that it was a faith-healer, crazy loon up here at Dutchman's Forge, and then for quite a spell she doctored with an osteopath in Leopolis — though I tell you there's something to this osteopathy — they cure a lot of folks that you regular docs can't seem to find out what's the matter with 'em, don't you think so?"

Martin remarked that he did not think so.

"Oh, you docs!" Bert crowed in his most jocund manner, for Bert could be very joky and bright. "You're all alike, especially when you're just out of school and think you know it all. You can't see any good in chiropractic or electric belts or bone-setters or anything, because they take so many good dollars away from you."

Then behold the Dr. Martin Arrowsmith who had once infuriated Angus Duer and Irving Watters by his sarcasm on medical standards upholding to a lewdly grinning Bert Tozer the benevolence and scientific knowledge of all doctors; proclaiming that no medicine had ever (at least by any Winnemac graduate) been prescribed in vain nor any operation needlessly performed.

He saw a good deal of Bert now. He sat about the bank, hoping to be called on a case, his fingers itching for bandages. Ada Quist came in with frequency and Bert laid aside his figuring to be coy with her:

"You got to be careful what you even think about, when the doc is here, Ade. He's been telling me what a whale of a lot of neurology and all that mind-reading stuff he knows. How about it, Mart? I'm getting so scared that I've changed the combination on the safe."

"Heh!" said Ada. "He may fool some folks but he can't fool me. Anybody can learn things in books, but when it comes to practicing 'em — Let me tell you, Mart, if you ever have one-tenth of the savvy that old Dr. Winter of Leopolis has, you'll live longer than I expect!"

Together they pointed out that for a person who felt his Zenith training had made him so "gosh-awful smart that he sticks up his nose at us poor hicks of dirt-farmers," Martin's scarf was rather badly tied.

All of his own wit and some of Ada's Bert repeated at the supper table.

"You oughtn't to ride the boy so hard. Still, that was pretty cute about the necktie — I guess Mart does think he's some punkins," chuckled Mr. Tozer.

Leora took Martin aside after supper. "Darlin', can you stand it? We'll have our own house, soon as we can. Or shall we vamoose?"

"I'm by golly going to stand it!"

"Um. Maybe. Dear, when you hit Bertie, do be careful — they'll hang you."

He ambled to the front porch. He determined to view the rooms behind the *Eagle* office. Without a retreat in which to be safe from Bert he could not endure another week. He could not wait for the Norbloms to make up their minds, though they had become to him dread and eternal figures whose enmity would crush him; prodigious gods shadowing this Wheatsylvania which was the only perceptible world.

He was aware, in the late sad light, that a man was tramping the plank walk before the house, hesitating and peering at him. The man was one Wise, a Russian Jew known to the village as "Wise the Polack." In his shack near the railroad he sold silver stock and motor-factory stock, bought and sold farmlands and horses and muskrat hides. He called out, "That you, Doc?"

"Yup!"

Martin was excited. A patient!

"Say, I wish you'd walk down a ways with me. Couple things I'd like to talk to you about. Or say, come on over to my place and sample some new cigars I've got." He emphasized the word "cigars." North Dakota was, like Mohalis, theoretically dry.

Martin was pleased. He had been sober and industrious so long now!

Wise's shack was a one-story structure, not badly built, half a block from Main Street, with nothing but the railroad track between it and open wheat country. It was lined with pine, pleasant-smelling under the stench of old pipe-smoke. Wise winked — he was a confidential, untrustworthy wisp of a man — and murmured, "Think you could stand a little jolt of first-class Kentucky bourbon?"

"Well, I wouldn't get violent about it."

Wise pulled down the sleazy window-shades and from a warped drawer of his desk brought up a bottle out of which they both drank, wiping the mouth of the bottle with circling palms. Then Wise, abruptly:

"Look here, Doc. You're not like these hicks; you understand that sometimes a fellow gets mixed up in crooked business he didn't intend to. Well, make a long story short, I guess I've sold too much mining stock, and they'll be coming down on me. I've got to be moving — curse it — hoped I could stay settled for couple of years, this time. Well, I hear you're looking for an office. This place would be ideal. Ideal! Two rooms at the back besides this one. I'll rent it to you, furniture and the whole shooting-match, for fifteen dollars a month, if you'll pay me one year in advance. Oh, this ain't phony. Your brother-in-law knows all about my ownership."

Martin tried to be very business-like. Was he not a young doctor who would soon be investing money, one of the most Substantial Citizens in Wheatsylvania? He returned home, and under the parlor lamp, with its green daisies on pink glass, the Tozers listened acutely, Bert stooping forward with open mouth.

"You'd be safe renting it for a year, but that ain't the point," said Bert.

"It certainly isn't! Antagonize the Norbloms, now that they've almost made up their minds to let you have their place? Make me a fool, after all the trouble I've taken?" groaned Mr. Tozer.

They went over it and over it till almost ten o'clock, but Martin was resolute, and the next day he rented Wise's shack.

For the first time in his life he had a place utterly his own, his and Leora's.

In his pride of possession this was the most lordly building on earth, and every rock and weed and doorknob was peculiar and lovely. At sunset he sat on the back stoop (a very interesting and not too broken soap-box) and from the flamboyant horizon the open country flowed across the thin band of the railroad to his feet. Suddenly Leora was beside him, her arm round his neck, and he hymned all the glory of their future:

"Know what I found in the kitchen here? A dandy old auger, hardly rusty a bit, and I can take a box and make a test-tube rack ... of my own!"

## Chapter 15

With none of the profane observations on "medical peddlers" which had annoyed Digamma Pi, Martin studied the catalogue of the New Idea Instrument and Furniture Company, of Jersey City. It was a handsome thing. On the glossy green cover, in red and black, were the portraits of the president, a round quippish man who loved all young physicians; the general manager, a cadaverous scholarly man who surely gave all his laborious nights and days to the advancement of science; and the vice-president, Martin's former preceptor, Dr. Roscoe Geake, who had a lively, eye-glassed, forward-looking modernity all his own. The cover also contained in surprisingly small space, a quantity of poetic prose, and the inspiring promise:

> *Doctor, don't be buffaloed by the unenterprising. No reason why* YOU *should lack the equipment which impresses patients, makes practice easy, and brings honor and riches. All the high-class supplies which distinguish the Leaders of the Profession from the Dubs are within* YOUR *reach right* NOW *by the famous New Idea Financial System: "Just a little down and the rest* FREE *— out of the increased earnings which New Idea apparatus will bring you!"*

Above, in a border of laurel wreaths and Ionic capitals, was the challenge:

> *Sing not the glory of soldiers or explorers or statesmen for who can touch the doctor — wise, heroic, uncontaminated by common greed. Gentlemen, we salute you humbly and herewith offer you the most up-to-the-jiffy catalogue ever presented by any surgical supply house.*

The back cover, though it was less glorious with green and red, was equally arousing. It presented illustrations of the Bindledorf Tonsillectomy Outfit and of an electric cabinet, with the demand:

> *Doctor, are you sending your patients off to specialists for tonsil removal or to sanitoriums for electric, etc., treatment? If so, you are losing the chance to show yourself one of the distinguished powers in the domain of medical advancement in your locality, and losing a lot of big fees. Don't you* WANT *to be a high-class practitioner? Here's the Open Door.*
>
> *The Bindledorf Outfit is not only useful but exquisitely beautiful, adorns and gives class to any office. We guarantee that by the installation of a Bindledorf Outfit and a New Idea Panaceatic Electro-Therapeutic Cabinet (see details on pp. 34 and 97) you can increase your income from a thousand to ten thousand annually and please patients more than by the most painstaking plugging.*
>
> *When the Great Call sounds, Doctor, and it's time for you to face your reward, will you be satisfied by a big Masonic funeral and tributes from Grateful Patients if you have failed to lay up provision for the kiddies, and faithful wife who has shared your tribulations?*
>
> *You may drive through blizzard and August heat, and go down into the purple-shadowed vale of sorrow and wrestle with the ebon-cloaked Powers of Darkness for the lives of your patients, but that heroism is incomplete without Modern Progress, to be obtained by the use of a Bindledorf Tonsillectomy Outfit and the New Idea Panaceatic Cabinet, to be obtained on small payment down, rest on easiest terms known in history of medicine!*

### II

This poetry of passion Martin neglected, for his opinion of poetry was like his opinion of electric cabinets, but excitedly he ordered a steel stand, a sterilizer, flasks, test-tubes, and a white-enameled mechanism with enchanting levers and gears which transformed it from examining-chair to operating-table. He yearned over the picture of a centrifuge while Leora was admiring the "stunning seven-piece Reception Room fumed oak set, upholstered in genuine Barcelona Longware Leatherette, will give your office the class and distinction of any high-grade New York specialist's."

"Aw, let 'em sit on plain chairs," Martin grunted.

In the attic Mrs. Tozer found enough seedy chairs for the reception-room, and an ancient bookcase which, when Leora had lined it with pink fringed paper, became a noble instrument-cabinet. Till the examining-chair should arrive, Martin would use Wise's lumpy couch, and Leora busily covered it with white oilcloth. Behind the front room of the tiny office-building were two cubicles, formerly bedroom and kitchen. Martin made them into consultation-room and laboratory. Whistling, he sawed out racks for the glassware and turned the oven of a discarded kerosene stove into a hot-air oven for sterilizing glassware.

"But understand, Lee, I'm not going to go monkeying with any scientific research. I'm through with all that."

Leora smiled innocently. While he worked she sat outside in the long wild grass, sniffing the prairie breeze, her hands about her ankles, but every quarter-hour she had to come in and admire.

Mr. Tozer brought home a package at suppertime. The family opened it, babbling. After supper Martin and Leora hastened with the new treasure to the office and nailed it in place. It was a plate-glass sign; on it in gold letters, "M. Arrowsmith, M.D." They looked up, arms about each other, squealing softly, and in reverence he grunted, "There — by — jiminy!"

They sat on the back stoop, exulting in freedom from Tozers. Along the railroad bumped a freight train with a cheerful clanking. The fireman waved to them from the engine, a brakeman from the platform of the red caboose. After the train there was silence but for the crickets and a distant frog.

"I've never been so happy," he murmured.

## III

He had brought from Zenith his own Ochsner surgical case. As he laid out the instruments he admired the thin, sharp, shining bistoury, the strong tenotome, the delicate curved needles. With them was a dental forceps. Dad Silva had warned his classes, "Don't forget the country doctor often has to be not only physician but dentist, yes, and priest, divorce lawyer, blacksmith, chauffeur, and road engineer, and if you are too lily-handed for those trades, don't get out of sight of a trolley line and a beauty parlor." And the first patient whom Martin had in the new office, the second patient in Wheatsylvania, was Nils Krag, the carpenter, roaring with an ulcerated tooth. This was a week before the glass sign was up, and Martin rejoiced to Leora, "Begun already! You'll see 'em tumbling in now."

They did not see them tumbling in. For ten days Martin tinkered at his hot-air oven or sat at his desk, reading and trying to look busy. His first joy passed into fretfulness, and he could have yelped at the stillness, the inactivity.

Late one afternoon, when he was in a melancholy way preparing to go home, into the office stamped a grizzled Swedish farmer who grumbled, "Doc, I got a fish-hook caught in my thumb and its all swole." To Arrowsmith, intern in Zenith General Hospital with its out-patient clinic treating hundreds a day, the dressing of a hand had been less important than borrowing a match, but to Dr. Arrowsmith of Wheatsylvania it was a hectic operation, and the farmer a person remarkable and very charming. Martin shook his left hand violently and burbled, "Now if there's anything, you just 'phone me — you just 'phone me."

There had been, he felt, a rush of admiring patients sufficient to justify them in the one thing Leora and he longed to do, the thing about which they whispered at night: the purchase of a motor car for his country calls.

They had seen the car at Frazier's store.

It was a Ford, five years old, with torn upholstery, a gummy motor, and springs made by a blacksmith who had never made springs before. Next to the chugging of the gas engine at the creamery, the most familiar sound in Wheatsylvania was Frazier's closing the door of his Ford. He banged it flatly at the store, and usually he had to shut it thrice again before he reached home.

But to Martin and Leora, when they had tremblingly bought the car and three new tires and a horn, it was the most impressive vehicle on earth. It was their own; they could go when and where they wished.

During his summer at a Canadian hotel Martin had learned to drive the Ford station wagon, but it was Leora's first venture. Bert had given her so many directions that she had refused to drive the family Overland. When she first sat at the steering wheel, when she moved the hand-throttle with her little finger and felt in her own hands all this power, sorcery enabling her to go as fast as she might desire (within distinct limits), she transcended human strength, she felt that she could fly like the wild goose — and then in a stretch of sand she killed the engine.

Martin became the demon driver of the village. To ride with him was to sit holding your hat, your eyes closed, waiting for death. Apparently he accelerated for corners, to make them more interesting. The sight of anything on the road ahead, from another motor to a yellow pup, stirred in him a frenzy which could be stilled only by going up and passing it. The village adored, "The Young Doc is quite some driver, all right." They waited, with amiable interest, to hear that he had been killed. It is possible that half of the first dozen patients who drifted into his office came because of awe at his driving ... the rest because there was nothing serious the matter, and he was nearer than Dr. Hesselink at Groningen.

## IV

With his first admirers he developed his first enemies.

When he met the Norbloms on the street (and in Wheatsylvania it is difficult not to meet everyone on the street every day), they glared. Then he antagonized Pete Yeska.

Pete conducted what he called a "drug store," devoted to the sale of candy, soda water, patent medicines, fly paper, magazines, washing-machines, and Ford accessories, yet Pete would have starved if he had not been postmaster also. He alleged that he was a licensed pharmacist but he so mangled prescriptions that Martin burst into the store and addressed him piously.

"You young docs make me sick," said Pete. "I was putting up prescriptions when you was in the cradle. The old doc that used to be here sent everything to me. My way o' doing things suits me, and I don't figure on changing it for you or any other half-baked young string-bean."

Thereafter Martin had to purchase drugs from St. Paul, over-crowd his tiny laboratory, and prepare his own pills and ointments, looking in a homesick way at the rarely used test-tubes and the dust gathering on the bell glass of his microscope, while Pete Yeska joined with the Norbloms in whispering, "This new doc here ain't any good. You better stick to Hesselink."

## V

So blank, so idle, had been the week that when he heard the telephone at the Tozers', at three in the morning, he rushed to it as though he were awaiting a love message.

A hoarse and shaky voice: "I want to speak to the doctor."

"Yuh — yuh — 'S the doctor speaking."

"This is Henry Novak, four miles northeast, on the Leopolis road. My little girl, Mary, she has a terrible sore throat. I think maybe it is croup and she look awful and — Could you come right away?"

"You bet. Be right there."

Four miles — he would do it in eight minutes.

He dressed swiftly, dragging his worn brown tie together, while Leora beamed over the first night call. He furiously cranked the Ford, banged and clattered past the station and into the wheat prairie. When he had gone six miles by the speedometer, slackening at each rural box to look for the owner's name, he realized that he was lost. He ran into a farm driveway and stopped under the willows, his headlight on a heap of dented milk-cans, broken harvester wheels, cord-wood, and bamboo fishing-poles. From the barn dashed a woolly anomalous dog, barking viciously, leaping up at the car.

A frowsy head protruded from a ground-floor window. "What you want?" screamed a Scandinavian voice.

"This is The Doctor. Where does Henry Novak live?"

"Oh! The Doctor! Dr. Hesselink?"

"No! Dr. Arrowsmith."

"Oh. Dr. Arrowsmith. From Wheatsylvania? Um. Well, you went right near his place. You yoost turn back one mile and turn to the right by the brick schoolhouse, and it's about forty rods up the road — the house with a cement silo. Somebody sick by Henry's?"

"Yuh — yuh — girl's got croup — thanks — "

"Yoost keep to the right. You can't miss it."

Probably no one who has listened to the dire "you can't miss it" has ever failed to miss it.

Martin swung the Ford about, grazing a slashed chopping-block; he rattled up the road, took the corner that side of the schoolhouse instead of this, ran half a mile along a boggy trail between pastures, and stopped at a farmhouse. In the surprising fall of silence, cows were to be heard feeding, and a white horse, startled in the darkness, raised its head to wonder at him. He had to arouse the house with wild squawkings of his horn, and an irate farmer who bellowed, "Who's there? I've got a shotgun!" sent him back to the country road.

It was forty minutes from the time of the telephone call when he rushed into a furrowed driveway and saw on the doorstep, against the lamplight, a stooped man who called, "The Doctor? This is Novak."

He found the child in a newly finished bedroom of white plastered walls and pale varnished pine. Only an iron bed, a straight chair, a chromo of St. Anne, and a shadeless hand-lamp on a rickety stand broke the staring shininess of the apartment, a recent extension of the farmhouse. A heavy-shouldered woman was kneeling by the bed. As she lifted her wet red face, Novak urged:

"Don't cry now; he's here!" And to Martin: "The little one is pretty bad but we done all we could for her. Last night and tonight we steam her throat, and we put her here in our own bedroom!"

Mary was a child of seven or eight. Martin found her lips and finger-tips blue, but in her face no flush. In the effort to expel her breath she writhed into terrifying knots, then coughed up saliva dotted with grayish specks. Martin worried as he took out his clinical thermometer and gave it a professional-looking shake.

It was, he decided, laryngeal croup or diphtheria. Probably diphtheria. No time now for bacteriological examination, for cultures and leisurely precision. Silva the healer bulked in the room, crowding out Gottlieb the inhuman perfectionist. Martin leaned nervously over the child on the tousled bed, absent-mindedly trying her pulse again and again. He felt helpless without the equipment of Zenith General, its nurses and Angus Duer's sure advice. He had a sudden respect for the lone country doctor.

He had to make a decision, irrevocable, perhaps perilous. He would use diphtheria antitoxin. But certainly he could not obtain it from Pete Yeska's in Wheatsylvania.

Leopolis?

"Hustle up and get me Blassner, the druggist at Leopolis, on the 'phone," he said to Novak, as calmly as he could contrive. He pictured Blassner driving through the night, respectfully bringing the antitoxin to The Doctor. While Novak bellowed into the farm-line telephone in the dining-room, Martin waited — waited — staring at the child; Mrs. Novak waited for him to do miracles; the child's tossing and hoarse gasping became horrible; and the glaring walls, the glaring lines of pale yellow woodwork, hypnotized him into sleepiness. It was too late for anything short of antitoxin or tracheotomy. Should he operate; cut into the wind-pipe that she might breathe? He stood and worried; he drowned in sleepiness and shook himself awake. He had to do something, with the mother kneeling there, gaping at him, beginning to look doubtful.

"Get some hot cloths — towels, napkins — and keep 'em around her neck. I wish to God he'd get that telephone call!" he fretted.

As Mrs. Novak, padding on thick slippered feet, brought in the hot cloths, Novak appeared with a blank "Nobody sleeping at the drug store, and Blassner's house-line is out of order."

"Then listen. I'm afraid this may be serious. I've got to have antitoxin. Going to drive t' Leopolis and get it. You keep up these hot applications and — Wish we had an atomizer. And room ought to be moister. Got 'n alcohol stove? Keep some water boiling in here. No use of medicine. B' right back."

He drove the twenty-four miles to Leopolis in thirty-seven minutes. Not once did he slow down for a cross-road. He defied the curves, the roots thrusting out into the road, though always one dark spot in his mind feared a blow-out and a swerve. The speed, the casting away of all caution, wrought in him a high exultation, and it was blessed to be in the cool air and alone, after the strain of Mrs. Novak's watching. In his mind all the while was the page in Osler regarding diphtheria, the very picture of the words: "In severe cases the first dose should be from 8,000 — " No. Oh, yes: " — from 10,000 to 15,000 units."

He regained confidence. He thanked the god of science for antitoxin and for the gas motor. It was, he decided, a Race with Death.

"I'm going to do it — going to pull it off and save that poor kid!" he rejoiced.

He approached a grade crossing and hurled toward it, ignoring possible trains. He was aware of a devouring whistle, saw sliding light on the rails, and brought up sharp. Past him, ten feet from his front wheels, flung the Seattle Express like a flying volcano. The fireman was stoking, and even in the thin clearness of coming dawn the glow from the fire-box was appalling on the under side of the rolling smoke. Instantly the apparition was gone and Martin sat trembling, hands trembling on the little steering-wheel, foot trembling like St. Vitus's dance on the brake. "That was an awful' close thing!" he muttered, and thought of a widowed Leora, abandoned to Tozers. But the vision of the Novak child, struggling for each terrible breath, overrode all else. "Hell! I've killed the engine!" he groaned. He vaulted over the side, cranked the car, and dashed into Leopolis.

To Crynssen County, Leopolis with its four thousand people was a metropolis, but in the pinched stillness of the dawn it was a tiny graveyard: Main Street a sandy expanse, the low shops desolate as huts. He found one place astir; in the bleak office of the Dakota Hotel the night clerk was playing poker with the 'bus-driver and the town policeman.

They wondered at his hysterical entrance.

"Dr. Arrowsmith, from Wheatsylvania. Kid dying from diphtheria. Where's Blassner live? Jump in my car and show me."

The constable was a lanky old man, his vest swinging open over a collarless shirt, his trousers in folds, his eyes resolute. He guided Martin to the home of the druggist, he kicked the door, then, standing with his lean and bristly visage upraised in the cold early light, he bawled, "Ed! Hey, you, Ed! Come out of it!"

Ed Blassner grumbled from the upstairs window. To him, death and furious doctors had small novelty. While he drew on his trousers and coat he was to be heard discoursing to his drowsy wife on the woes of druggists and the desirability of moving to Los Angeles and going into real estate. But he did have diphtheria antitoxin in his shop, and sixteen minutes after Martin's escape from being killed by a train he was speeding to Henry Novak's.

## VI

The child was still alive when he came brusquely into the house.

All the way back he had seen her dead and stiff. He grunted "Thank God!" and angrily called for hot water. He was no longer the embarrassed cub doctor but the wise and heroic physician who had won the Race with Death, and in the peasant eyes of Mrs. Novak, in Henry's nervous obedience, he read his power.

Swiftly, smoothly, he made intravenous injection of the antitoxin, and stood expectant.

The child's breathing did not at first vary, as she choked in the labor of expelling her breath. There was a gurgle, a struggle in which her face blackened, and she was still. Martin peered, incredulous. Slowly the Novaks began to glower, shaky hands at their lips. Slowly they knew the child was gone.

In the hospital, death had become indifferent and natural to Martin. He had said to Angus, he had heard nurses say one to another, quite cheerfully, "Well, fifty-seven has just passed out." Now he raged with desire to do the impossible. She *couldn't* be dead. He'd do something — All the while he was groaning, "I should've operated — I should have." So insistent was the thought that for a time he did not realize that Mrs. Novak was clamoring, "She is dead? Dead?"

He nodded, afraid to look at the woman.

"You killed her, with that needle thing! And not even tell us, so we could call the priest!"

He crawled past her lamentations and the man's sorrow and drove home, empty of heart.

"I shall never practice medicine again," he reflected.

"I'm through," he said to Leora. "I'm no good. I should of operated. I can't face people, when they know about it. I'm through. I'll go get a lab job — Dawson Hunziker or some place."

Salutary was the tartness with which she protested, "You're the most conceited man that ever lived! Do you think you're the only doctor that ever lost a patient? I know you did everything you could." But he went about next day torturing himself, the more tortured when Mr. Tozer whined at supper, "Henry Novak and his woman was in town today. They say you ought to have saved their girl. Why didn't you give your mind to it and manage to cure her somehow? Ought to tried. Kind of too bad, because the Novaks have a lot of influence with all these Pole and Hunky farmers."

After a night when he was too tired to sleep, Martin suddenly drove to Leopolis.

From the Tozers he had heard almost religious praise of Dr. Adam Winter of Leopolis, a man of nearly seventy, the pioneer physician of Crynssen County, and to this sage he was fleeing. As he drove he mocked furiously his melodramatic Race with Death, and he came wearily into the dust-whirling Main Street. Dr. Winter's office was above a grocery, in a long "block" of bright red brick stores with an Egyptian cornice — of tin. The darkness of the broad hallway was soothing after the prairie heat and incandescence. Martin had to wait till three respectful patients had been received by Dr. Winter, a hoary man with a sympathetic bass voice, before he was admitted to the consultation-room.

The examining-chair was of doubtful superiority to that once used by Doc Vickerson of Elk Mills, and sterilizing was apparently done in a wash-bowl, but in a corner was an electric therapeutic cabinet with more electrodes and pads than Martin had ever seen.

He told the story of the Novaks, and Winter cried, "Why, Doctor, you did everything you could have and more too. Only thing is, next time, in a crucial case, you better call some older doctor in consultation — not that you need his advice, but it makes a hit with the family, it divides the responsibility, and keeps 'em from going around criticizing. I, uh, I frequently have the honor of being called by some of my younger colleagues. Just wait. I'll 'phone the editor of the *Gazette* and give him an item about the case."

When he had telephoned, Dr. Winter shook hands ardently. He indicated his electric cabinet. "Got one of those things yet? Ought to, my boy. Don't know as I use it very often, except with the cranks that haven't anything the matter with 'em, but say, it would surprise you how it impresses folks. Well, Doctor, welcome to Crynssen County. Married? Won't you and your wife come take dinner with us some Sunday noon? Mrs. Winter will be real pleased to meet you. And if I ever can be of service to you in a consultation — I only charge a very little more than my regular fee, and it looks so well, talking the case over with an older man."

Driving home, Martin fell into vain and wicked boasting:

"You bet I'll stick to it! At worst, I'll never be as bad as that snuffling old fee-splitter!"

Two weeks after, the *Wheatsylvania Eagle* , a smeary four-page rag, reported:

> *Our enterprising contemporary, the* Leopolis Gazette, *had as follows last week to say of one of our townsmen who we recently welcomed to our midst.*
>
> "*Dr. M. Arrowsmith of Wheatsylvania is being congratulated, we are informed by our valued pioneer local physician, Dr. Adam Winter, by the medical fraternity all through the Pony River Valley, there being no occupation or profession more unselfishly appreciative of each other's virtues than the medical gentlemen, on the courage and enterprise he recently displayed in addition to his scientific skill.*
>
> "*Being called to attend the little daughter of Henry Norwalk of near Delft the well-known farmer and finding the little one near death with diphtheria he made a desperate attempt to save it by himself bringing antitoxin from Blassner our ever popular druggist, who had on hand a full and fresh supply. He drove out and back in his gasoline chariot, making the total distance of 48 miles in 79 minutes.*
>
> "*Fortunately our ever alert policeman, Joe Colby, was on the job and helped Dr. Arrowsmith find Mr. Blassner's bungalow on Red River Avenue and this gentleman rose from bed and hastened to supply the doctor with the needed article but unfortunately the child was already too low to be saved but it is by such incidents of pluck and quick thinking as well as knowledge which make the medical profession one of our greatest blessings.* "

Two hours after this was published, Miss Agnes Ingleblad came in for another discussion of her non-existent ailments, and two days later Henry Novak appeared, saying proudly:

"Well, Doc, we all done what we could for the poor little girl, but I guess I waited too long calling you. The woman is awful' cut up. She and I was reading that piece in the *Eagle* about it. We showed it to the priest. Say, Doc, I wish you'd take a look at my foot. I got kind of a rheumatic pain in the ankle."

## Chapter 16

When he had practiced medicine in Wheatsylvania for one year, Martin was an inconspicuous but not discouraged country doctor. In summer Leora and he drove to the Pony River for picnic suppers and a swim, very noisy, splashing, and immodest; through autumn he went duck-hunting with Bert Tozer, who became nearly tolerable when he stood at sunset on a pass between two slews; and with winter isolating the village in a sun-blank desert of snow, they had sleigh-rides, card-parties, "sociables" at the churches.

When Martin's flock turned to him for help, their need and their patient obedience made them beautiful. Once or twice he lost his temper with jovial villagers who bountifully explained to him that he was less aged than he might have been; once or twice he drank too much whisky at poker parties in the back room of the Co-operative Store; but he was known as reliable, skillful, and honest — and on the whole he was rather less distinguished than Alec Ingleblad the barber, less prosperous than Nils Krag the carpenter, and less interesting to his neighbors than the Finnish garageman.

Then one accident and one mistake made him famous for full twelve miles about.

He had gone fishing, in the spring. As he passed a farmhouse a woman ran out shrieking that her baby had swallowed a thimble and was choking to death. Martin had for surgical kit a large jack-knife. He sharpened it on the farmer's oilstone, sterilized it in the tea-kettle, operated on the baby's throat, and saved its life.

Every newspaper in the Pony River Valley had a paragraph, and before this sensation was over he cured Miss Agnes Ingleblad of her desire to be cured.

She had achieved cold hands and a slow circulation, and he was called at midnight. He was soggily sleepy, after two country drives on muddy roads, and in his torpor he gave her an overdose of strychnin, which so shocked and stimulated her that she decided to be well. It was so violent a change that it made her more interesting than being an invalid — people had of late taken remarkably small pleasure in her symptoms. She went about praising Martin, and all the world said, "I hear this Doc Arrowsmith is the only fellow Agnes ever doctored with that's done her a mite of good."

He gathered a practice small, sound, and in no way remarkable. Leora and he moved from the Tozers' to a cottage of their own, with a parlor-dining-room which displayed a nickeled stove on bright, new, pleasant-smelling linoleum, and a golden-oak sideboard with a souvenir match-holder from Lake Minnetonka. He bought a small Roentgen ray outfit; and he was made a director of the Tozer bank. He became too busy to long for his days of scientific research, which had never existed, and Leora sighed:

"It's fierce, being married. I did expect I'd have to follow you out on the road and be a hobo, but I never expected to be a Pillar of the Community. Well, I'm too lazy to look up a new husband. Only I warn you: when you become the Sunday School superintendent, you needn't expect me to play the organ and smile at the cute jokes you make about Willy's not learning his Golden Text."

### II

So did Martin stumble into respectability.

In the autumn of 1912, when Mr. Debs, Mr. Roosevelt, Mr. Wilson, and Mr. Taft were campaigning for the presidency, when Martin Arrowsmith had lived in Wheatsylvania for a year and a half, Bert Tozer became a Prominent Booster. He returned from the state convention of the Modern Woodmen of America with notions. Several towns had sent boosting delegations to the convention, and the village of Groningen had turned out a motor procession of five cars, each with an enormous pennant, "Groningen for White Men and Black Dirt."

Bert came back clamoring that every motor in town must carry a Wheatsylvania pennant. He had bought thirty of them and they were on sale at the bank at seventy-five cents apiece.

This, Bert explained to everyone who came into the bank, was exactly cost-price, which was within eleven cents of the truth. He came galloping at Martin, demanding that he be the first to display a pennant.

"I don't want one of those fool things flopping from my 'bus," protested Martin. "What's the idea, anyway?"

"What's the *idea* ? To advertise your own town, of course!"

"What is there to advertise? Do you think you're going to make strangers believe Wheatsylvania is a metropolis like New York or Jimtown by hanging a dusty rag behind a second-hand tin Lizzie?"

"You never did have any patriotism! Let me tell you, Mart, if you don't put on a banner I'll see to it that everybody in town notices it!"

While the other rickety cars of the village announced to the world, or at least to several square miles of the world, that Wheatsylvania was the "Wonder Town of Central N. D.," Martin's clattering Ford went bare; and when his enemy Norblom remarked, "I like to see a fellow have some public spirit and appreciate the place he gets his money outa," the citizenry nodded and spat, and began to question Martin's fame as a worker of miracles.

## III

He had intimates — the barber, the editor of the *Eagle* , the garageman — to whom he talked comfortably of hunting and the crops, and with whom he played poker. Perhaps he was too intimate with them. It was the theory of Crynssen County that it was quite all right for a young professional man to take a timely drink providing he kept it secret and made up for it by yearning over the clergy of the neighborhood. But with the clergy Martin was brief, and his drinking and poker he never concealed.

If he was bored by the United Brethren minister's discourse on doctrine, on the wickedness of movies, and the scandalous pay of pastors, it was not at all because he was a distant and supersensitive young man but because he found more savor in the garageman's salty remarks on the art of remembering to ante in poker.

Through all the state there were celebrated poker players, rustic-looking men with stolid faces, men who sat in shirtsleeves, chewing tobacco: men whose longest remark was "By me," and who delighted to plunder the gilded and condescending traveling salesmen. When there was news of a "big game on," the county sports dropped in silently and went to work — the sewing-machine agent from Leopolis, the undertaker from Vanderheide's Grove, the bootlegger from St. Luke, the red fat man from Melody who had no known profession.

Once (still do men tell of it gratefully, up and down the Valley), they played for seventy-two unbroken hours, in the office of the Wheatsylvania garage. It had been a livery-stable; it was littered with robes and long whips, and the smell of horses mingled with the reek of gasoline.

The players came and went, and sometimes they slept on the floor for an hour or two, but they were never less than four in the game. The stink of cheap feeble cigarettes and cheap powerful cigars hovered about the table like a malign spirit; the floor was scattered with stubs, matches, old cards, and whisky bottles. Among the warriors were Martin, Alec Ingleblad the barber, and a highway engineer, all of them stripped to flannel undershirts, not moving for hour on hour, ruffling their cards, eyes squinting and vacant.

When Bert Tozer heard of the affair, he feared for the good fame of Wheatsylvania, and to everyone he gossiped about Martin's evil ways and his own patience. Thus it happened that while Martin was at the height of his prosperity and credit as a physician, along the Pony River Valley sinuated the whispers that he was a gambler, that he was a "drinking man," that he never went to church; and all the godly enjoyed mourning, "Too bad to see a decent young man like that going to the dogs."

Martin was as impatient as he was stubborn. He resented the well-meant greetings: "You ought to leave a little hooch for the rest of us to drink, Doc," or "I s'pose you're too busy playing poker to drive out to the house and take a look at the woman." He was guilty of an absurd and boyish tactlessness when he heard Norblom observing to the postmaster, "A fellow that calls himself a doctor just because he had luck with that fool Agnes Ingleblad, he hadn't ought to go getting drunk and disgracing — "

Martin stopped. "Norblom! You talking about me?"

The storekeeper turned slowly. "I got more important things to do 'n talk about you," he cackled.

As Martin went on he heard laughter.

He told himself that these villagers were generous; that their snooping was in part an affectionate interest, and inevitable in a village where the most absorbing event of the year was the United Brethren Sunday School picnic on Fourth of July. But he could not rid himself of twitchy discomfort at their unending and maddeningly detailed comments on everything. He felt as though the lightest word he said in his consultation-room would be megaphoned from flapping ear to ear all down the country roads.

He was contented enough in gossiping about fishing with the barber, nor was he condescending to meteorologicomania, but except for Leora he had no one with whom he could talk of his work. Angus Duer had been cold, but Angus had his teeth into every change of surgical technique, and he was an acrid debater. Martin saw that, unless he struggled, not only would he harden into timid morality under the pressure of the village, but be fixed in a routine of prescriptions and bandaging.

He might find a stimulant in Dr. Hesselink of Groningen.

He had seen Hesselink only once, but everywhere he heard of him as the most honest practitioner in the Valley. On impulse Martin drove down to call on him.

Dr. Hesselink was a man of forty, ruddy, tall, broad-shouldered. You knew immediately that he was careful and that he was afraid of nothing, however much he might lack in imagination. He received Martin with no vast ebullience, and his stare said, "Well, what do you want? I'm a busy man."

"Doctor," Martin chattered, "do you find it hard to keep up with medical developments?"

"No. Read the medical journals."

"Well, don't you — gosh, I don't want to get sentimental about it, but don't you find that without contact with the Big Guns you get mentally lazy — sort of lacking in inspiration?"

"I do not! There's enough inspiration for me in trying to help the sick."

To himself Martin was protesting, "All right, if you don't want to be friendly, go to the devil!" But he tried again:

"I know. But for the game of the thing, for the pleasure of increasing medical knowledge, how can you keep up if you don't have anything but routine practice among a lot of farmers?"

"Arrowsmith, I may do you an injustice, but there's a lot of you young practitioners who feel superior to the farmers, that are doing their own jobs better than you are. You think that if you were only in the city with libraries and medical meetings and everything, you'd develop. Well, I don't know of anything to prevent your studying at home! You consider yourself so much better educated than these rustics, but I notice you say 'gosh' and 'Big Guns' and that sort of thing. How much do you read? Personally, I'm extremely well satisfied. My people pay me an excellent living wage, they appreciate my work, and they honor me by election to the schoolboard. I find that a good many of these farmers think a lot harder and squarer than the swells I meet in the city. Well! I don't see any reason for feeling superior, or lonely either!"

"Hell, I don't!" Martin mumbled. As he drove back he raged at Hesselink's superiority about not feeling superior, but he stumbled into uncomfortable meditation. It was true; he was half-educated. He was supposed to be a college graduate but he knew nothing of economics, nothing of history, nothing of music or painting. Except in hasty bolting for examinations he had read no poetry save that of Robert Service, and the only prose besides medical journalism at which he looked nowadays was the baseball and murder news in the Minneapolis papers and Wild West stories in the magazines.

He reviewed the "intelligent conversation" which, in the desert of Wheatsylvania, he believed himself to have conducted at Mohalis. He remembered that to Clif Clawson it had been pretentious to use any phrase which was not as colloquial and as smutty as the speech of a truck-driver, and that his own discourse had differed from Clif's largely in that it had been less fantastic and less original. He could recall nothing save the philosophy of Max Gottlieb, occasional scoldings of Angus Duer, one out of ten among Madeline Fox's digressions, and the councils of Dad Silva which was above the level of Alec Ingleblad's barber-shop.

He came home hating Hesselink but by no means loving himself; he fell upon Leora and, to her placid agreement, announced that they were "going to get educated, if it kills us." He went at it as he had gone at bacteriology.

He read European history aloud at Leora, who looked interested or at least forgiving; he worried the sentences in a copy of "The Golden Bowl" which an unfortunate school-teacher had left at the Tozers'; he borrowed a volume of Conrad from the village editor and afterward, as he drove the prairie roads, he was marching into jungle villages — sun helmets, orchids, lost temples of obscene and dog-faced deities, secret and sun-scarred rivers. He was conscious of his own mean vocabulary. It cannot be said that he became immediately and conspicuously articulate, yet it is possible that in those long intense evenings of reading with Leora he advanced a step or two toward the tragic enchantments of Max Gottlieb's world — enchanting sometimes and tragic always.

But in becoming a schoolboy again he was not so satisfied as Dr. Hesselink.

## IV

Gustaf Sondelius was back in America.

In medical school, Martin had read of Sondelius, the soldier of science. He held reasonable and lengthy degrees, but he was a rich man and eccentric, and neither toiled in laboratories nor had a decent office and a home and a lacy wife. He roamed the world fighting epidemics and founding institutions and making inconvenient speeches and trying new drinks. He was a Swede by birth, a German by education, a little of everything by speech, and his clubs were in London, Paris, Washington, and New York. He had been heard of from Batoum and Fuchau, from Milan and Bechuanaland, from Antofagasta and Cape Romanzoff. Manson on Tropical Diseases mentions Sondelius's admirable method of killing rats with hydrocyanic acid gas, and *The Sketch* once mentioned his atrocious system in baccarat.

Gustaf Sondelius shouted, in high places and low, that most diseases could be and must be wiped out; that tuberculosis, cancer, typhoid, the plague, influenza, were an invading army against which the world must mobilize — literally; that public health authorities must supersede generals and oil kings. He was lecturing through America, and his exclamatory assertions were syndicated in the press.

Martin sniffed at most newspaper articles touching on science or health but Sondelius's violence caught him, and suddenly he was converted, and it was an important thing for him, that conversion.

He told himself that however much he might relieve the sick, essentially he was a business man, in rivalry with Dr. Winter of Leopolis and Dr. Hesselink of Groningen; that though they might be honest, honesty and healing were less their purpose than making money; that to get rid of avoidable disease and produce a healthy population would be the worst thing in the world for them; and that they must all be replaced by public health officials.

Like all ardent agnostics, Martin was a religious man. Since the death of his Gottlieb-cult he had unconsciously sought a new passion, and he found it now in Gustaf Sondelius's war on disease. Immediately he became as annoying to his patients as he had once been to Digamma Pi.

He informed the farmers at Delft that they had no right to have so much tuberculosis.

This was infuriating, because none of their rights as American citizens was better established, or more often used, than the privilege of being ill. They fumed, "Who does he think he is?

We call him in for doctoring, not for bossing. Why, the damn' fool said we ought to burn down our houses — said we were committing a crime if we had the con. here! Won't stand for nobody talking to me like that!"

Everything became clear to Martin — too clear. The nation must make the best physicians autocratic officials, at once, and that was all there was to it. As to how the officials were to become perfect executives, and how people were to be persuaded to obey them, he had no suggestions but only a beautiful faith. At breakfast he scolded, "Another idiotic day of writing prescriptions for bellyaches that ought never to have happened! If I could only get into the Big Fight, along with men like Sondelius! It makes me tired!"

Leora murmured, "Yes, darling. I'll promise to be good. I won't have any little bellyaches or T.B. or anything, so please don't lecture me!"

Even in his irritability he was gentle, for Leora was with child.

## V

Their baby was coming in five months. Martin promised to it everything he had missed.

"He's going to have a real education!" he gloated, as they sat on the porch in spring twilight. "He'll learn all this literature and stuff. We haven't done much ourselves — here we are, stuck in this two-by-twice crossroads for the rest of our lives — but maybe we've gone a little beyond our dads, and he'll go way beyond us."

He was worried, for all his flamboyance. Leora had undue morning sickness. Till noon she dragged about the house, pea-green and tousled and hollow-faced. He found a sort of maid, and came home to help, to wipe the dishes and sweep the front walk. All evening he read to her, not history now and Henry James but "Mrs. Wiggs of the Cabbage Patch," which both of them esteemed a very fine tale. He sat on the floor by the grubby second-hand couch on which she lay in her weakness; he held her hand and crowed:

"Golly, we — No, not 'golly.' Well, what *can* you say except 'golly'? Anyway: Some day we'll save up enough money for a couple months in Italy and all those places. All those old narrow streets and old castles! There must be scads of 'em that are couple hundred years old or older! And we'll take the boy ... Even if he turns out to be a girl, darn him!... And he'll learn to chatter Wop and French and everything like a regular native, and his dad and mother'll be so proud! Oh, we'll be a fierce pair of old birds! We never did have any more morals 'n a rabbit, either of us, and probably when we're seventy we'll sit out on the doorstep and smoke pipes and snicker at all the respectable people going by, and tell each other scandalous stories about 'em till they want to take a shot at us, and our boy — he'll wear a plug hat and have a chauffeur — he won't dare to recognize us!"

Trained now to the false cheerfulness of the doctor, he shouted, when she was racked and ghastly with the indignity of morning sickness, "There, that's fine, old girl! Wouldn't be making a good baby if you weren't sick. Everybody is." He was lying, and he was nervous. Whenever he thought of her dying, he seemed to die with her. Barren of her companionship, there would be nothing he wanted to do, nowhere to go. What would be the worth of having all the world if he could not show it to her, if she was not there —

He denounced Nature for her way of tricking human beings, by every gay device of moonlight and white limbs and reaching loneliness, into having babies, then making birth as cruel and clumsy and wasteful as she could. He was abrupt and jerky with patients who called him into the country. With their suffering he was sympathetic as he had never been, for his eyes had opened to the terrible beauty of pain, but he must not go far from Leora's need.

Her morning sickness turned into pernicious vomiting. Suddenly, while she was torn and inhuman with agony, he sent for Dr. Hesselink, and that horrible afternoon when the prairie spring was exuberant outside the windows of the poor iodoform-reeking room, they took the baby from her, dead.

Had it been possible, he might have understood Hesselink's success then, have noted that gravity and charm, that pity and sureness, which made people entrust their lives to him. Not cold and blaming was Hesselink now, but an older and wiser brother, very compassionate. Martin saw nothing. He was not a physician. He was a terrified boy, less useful to Hesselink than the dullest nurse.

When he was certain that Leora would recover, Martin sat by her bed, coaxing, "We'll just have to make up our minds we never can have a baby now, and so I want — Oh, I'm no good! And I've got a rotten temper. But to you, I want to be everything!"

She whispered, scarce to be heard:

"He would have been such a sweet baby. Oh, I know! I saw him so often. Because I knew he was going to be like you, when you were a baby." She tried to laugh. "Perhaps I wanted him because I could boss him. I've never had anybody that would let me boss him. So if I can't have a real baby, I'll have to bring you up. Make you a great man that everybody will wonder at, like your Sondelius.... Darling, I worried so about your worrying — "

He kissed her, and for hours they sat together, unspeaking, eternally understanding, in the prairie twilight.

## Chapter 17

Dr. Coughlin of Leopolis had a red mustache, a large heartiness, and a Maxwell which, though it was three years old this May and deplorable as to varnish, he believed to be the superior in speed and beauty of any motor in Dakota.

He came home in high cheerfulness, rode the youngest of his three children pickaback, and remarked to his wife:

"Tessie, I got a swell idea."

"Yes, and you got a swell breath, too. I wish you'd quit testing that old Spirits Frumentus bottle at the drug store!"

"'At a girl! But honest, listen!"

"I will not!" She bussed him heartily. "Nothing doing about driving to Los Angeles this summer. Too far, with all the brats squalling."

"Sure. All right. But I mean: Let's pack up and light out and spend a week touring 'round the state. Say tomorrow or next day. Got nothing to keep me now except that obstetrical case, and we'll hand that over to Winter."

"All right. We can try out the new thermos bottles!"

Dr. Coughlin, his lady, and the children started at four in the morning. The car was at first too well arranged to be interesting, but after three days, as he approached you on the flat road that without an inch of curving was slashed for leagues through the grassy young wheat, you saw the doctor in his khaki suit, his horn-rimmed spectacles, and white linen boating hat; his wife in a green flannel blouse and a lace boudoir cap. The rest of the car was slightly confused. While you motored by you noticed a canvas Egyptian Water Bottle, mud on wheels and fenders, a spade, two older children leaning perilously out and making tongues at you, the baby's diapers hanging on a line across the tonneau, a torn copy of *Snappy Stories* , seven lollypop sticks, a jack, a fish-rod, and a rolled tent.

Your last impression was of two large pennants labeled "Leopolis, N. D.," and "Excuse Our Dust."

The Coughlins had agreeable adventures. Once they were stuck in a mud-hole. To the shrieking admiration of the family, the doctor got them out by making a bridge of fence rails. Once the ignition ceased and, while they awaited a garageman summoned by telephone, they viewed a dairy farm with an electrical milking machine. All the way they were broadened by travel, and discovered the wonders of the great world: the movie theater at Roundup, which had for orchestra not only a hand-played piano but also a violin; the black fox farm at Melody; and the Severance water-tower, which was said to be the tallest in Central North Dakota.

Dr. Coughlin "dropped in to pass the time of day," as he said, with all the doctors. At St. Luke he had an intimate friend in Dr. Tromp — at least they had met twice, at the annual meetings of the Pony River Valley Medical Association. When he told Tromp how bad they had found the hotels, Tromp looked uneasy and conscientious, and sighed, "If the wife could fix it up somehow, I'd like to invite you all to stay with us tonight."

"Oh, don't want to impose on you. Sure it wouldn't be any trouble?" said Coughlin.

After Mrs. Tromp had recovered from her desire to call her husband aside and make unheard but vigorous observations, and after the oldest Tromp boy had learned that "it wasn't nice for a little gentleman to kick his wee guests that came from so far, far away," they were all very happy. Mrs. Coughlin and Mrs. Tromp bewailed the cost of laundry soap and butter, and exchanged recipes for pickled peaches, while the men, sitting on the edge of the porch, their knees crossed, eloquently waving their cigars, gave themselves up to the ecstasy of shop-talk:

"Say, Doctor, how do you find collections?"

(It was Coughlin speaking — or it might have been Tromp.)

"Well, they're pretty good. These Germans pay up first rate. Never send 'em a bill, but when they've harvested they come in and say, 'How much do I owe you, Doctor?'"

"Yuh, the Germans are pretty good pay."

"Yump, they certainly are. Not many dead-beats among the Germans."

"Yes, that's a fact. Say, tell me, Doctor, what do you do with your jaundice cases?"

"Well, I'll tell you, Doctor: if it's a persistent case I usually give ammonium chlorid."

"Do you? I've been giving ammonium chlorid but here the other day I see a communication in the *Journal of the A.M.A.* where a fellow was claiming it wasn't any good."

"Is that a fact! Well, well! I didn't see that. Hum. Well. Say, Doctor, do you find you can do much with asthma?"

"Well now, Doctor, just in confidence, I'm going to tell you something that may strike you as funny, but I believe that foxes' lungs are fine for asthma, and T.B. too. I told that to a Sioux City pulmonary specialist one time and he laughed at me — said it wasn't scientific — and I said to him, 'Hell!' I said, 'scientific!' I said, 'I don't know if it's the latest fad and wrinkle in science or not,' I said, 'but I get results, and that's what I'm looking for 's results!' I said. I tell you a plug G.P. may not have a lot of letters after his name, but he sees a slew of mysterious things that he can't explain, and I swear I believe most of these damn' alleged scientists could learn a whale of a lot from the plain country practitioners, let me tell you!"

"Yuh, that's a fact. Personally I'd rather stay right here in the country and be able to do a little hunting and take it easy than be the classiest specialist in the cities. One time I kind of figured on becoming an X-ray specialist — place in New York where you can take the whole course in eight weeks — and maybe settling in Butte or Sioux Falls, but I figured that even if I got to making eight-ten thousand a year, 'twouldn't hardly mean more than three thousand does here and so — And a fellow has to consider his duty to his old patients."

"That's so.... Say, Doctor, say, what sort of fellow is McMinturn, down your way?"

"Well, I don't like to knock any fellow practitioner, and I suppose he's well intentioned, but just between you and me he does too confounded much guesswork. Now you take you and me, we apply *science* to a case, instead of taking a chance and just relying on experience and going off half-cocked. But McMinturn, he doesn't know enough. And *say* , that wife of his, she's a caution — she's got the meanest tongue in four counties, and the way she chases around drumming up business for Mac — Well, I suppose that's their way of doing business."

"Is old Winter keeping going?"

"Oh, yes, in a sort of way. You know how he is. Of course he's about twenty years behind the times, but he's a great hand-holder — keep some fool woman in bed six weeks longer than he needs to, and call around twice a day and chin with her — absolutely unnecessary."

"I suppose you get your biggest competition from Silzer, Doctor?"

"Don't you believe it. Doctor! He isn't beginning to do the practice he lets on to. Trouble with Silzer is, he's too brash — shoots off his mouth too much — likes to hear himself talk. Oh, say, by the way, have you run into this new fellow — will been located here about two years now — at Wheatsylvania — Arrowsmith?"

"No, but they say he's a good bright young fellow."

"Yes, they claim he's a brainy man — very well-informed — and I hear his wife is a nice brainy little woman."

"I hear Arrowsmith hits it up too much though — likes his booze awful' well."

"Yes, so they say. Shame, for a nice hustling young fellow. I like a nip myself, now and then, but a Drinking Man — ! Suppose he's drunk and gets called out on a case! And a fellow from down there was telling me Arrowsmith is great on books and study, but he's a freethinker — never goes to church."

"Is that a fact! Hm. Great mistake for any doctor to not identify himself with some good solid religious denomination, whether he believes the stuff or not. I tell you a priest or a preacher can send you an awful lot of business."

"You bet he can! Well, this fellow said Arrowsmith was always arguing with the preachers — he told some Reverend that everybody ought to read this immunologist Max Gottlieb, and this Jacques Loeb — you know — the fellow that, well, I don't recall just exactly what it was, but he claimed he could create living fishes out of chemicals."

"Sure! There you got it! That's the kind of delusions these laboratory fellows get unless they have some practical practice to keep 'em well balanced. Well, if Arrowsmith falls for that kind of fellow, no wonder people don't trust him."

"That's so. Hm. Well, it's too bad Arrowsmith goes drinking and helling around and neglecting his family and his patients. I can see his finish. Shame. Well — wonder what time o' night it's getting to be?"

## II

Bert Tozer wailed, "Mart, what you been doing to Dr. Coughlin of Leopolis? Fellow told me he was going around saying you were a booze-hoister and so on."

"Did he? People do sort of keep an eye on one another around here, don't they?"

"You bet your life they do, and that's why I tell you you ought to cut out the poker and the booze. You don't see me needing any liquor, do you?"

Martin more desperately than ever felt the whole county watching him. He was not a praise-eater; he was not proud that he should feel misplaced; but however sturdily he struggled he saw himself outside the picture of Wheatsylvania and trudging years of country practice.

Suddenly, without planning it, forgetting in his admiration for Sondelius and the health war his pride of the laboratory, he was thrown into a research problem.

## III

There was blackleg among the cattle in Crynssen County. The state veterinarian had been called and Dawson Hunziker vaccine had been injected, but the disease spread. Martin heard the farmers wailing. He noted that the injected cattle showed no inflammation nor rise in temperature. He was roused by a suspicion that the Hunziker vaccine had insufficient living organisms, and he went yelping on the trail of his hypothesis.

He obtained (by misrepresentations) a supply of the vaccine and tested it in his stuffy closet of a laboratory. He had to work out his own device for growing anaerobic cultures, but he had been trained by the Gottlieb who remarked, "Any man dat iss unable to build a filter out of toot'-picks, if he has to, would maybe better buy his results along with his fine equipment." Out of a large fruit-jar and a soldered pipe Martin made his apparatus.

When he was altogether sure that the vaccine did not contain living blackleg organisms, he was much more delighted than if he had found that good Mr. Dawson Hunziker was producing honest vaccine.

With no excuse and less encouragement he isolated blackleg organisms from sick cattle and prepared an attenuated vaccine of his own. It took much time. He did not neglect his patients but certainly he failed to appear in the stores, at the poker games. Leora and he dined on a sandwich every evening and hastened to the laboratory, to heat the cultures in the improvised water-bath, an ancient and leaky oatmeal-cooker with an alcohol lamp. The Martin who had been impatient of Hesselink was of endless patience as he watched his results. He whistled and hummed, and the hours from seven to midnight were a moment. Leora, frowning placidly, the tip of her tongue at the corner of her mouth, guarded the temperature like a good little watchdog.

After three efforts with two absurd failures, he had a vaccine which satisfied him, and he injected a stricken herd. The blackleg stopped, which was for Martin the end and the reward, and he turned his notes and supply of vaccine over to the state veterinarian. For others, it was not the end. The veterinarian of the county denounced him for intruding on their right to save or kill cattle; the physicians hinted, "That's the kind of monkey-business that ruins the dignity of the profession. I tell you Arrowsmith's a medical nihilist and a notoriety-seeker, that's what he is. You mark my words, instead of his sticking to decent regular practice, you'll be hearing of his opening a quack sanitarium, one of these days!"

He commented to Leora:

"Dignity, hell! If I had my way I'd be doing research — oh, not this cold detached stuff of Gottlieb but really practical work — and then I'd have some fellow like Sondelius take my results and jam 'em down people's throats, and I'd make them and their cattle and their tabby-cats healthy whether they wanted to be or not, that's what I'd do!"

In this mood he read in his Minneapolis paper, between a half column on the marriage of the light middleweight champion and three lines devoted to the lynching of an I.W.W. agitator, the announcement:

> *Gustave Sundelios, well-known authority on cholera prevention, will give an address on "Heroes of Health" at the University summer school next Friday evening.*

He ran into the house gloating, "Lee! Sondelius going to lecture in Minneapolis. I'm going! Come on! We'll hear him and have a bat and everything!"

"No, you run down by yourself. Be fine for you to get away from the town and the family and me for a while. I'll go down with you in the fall. Honestly. If I'm not in the way, maybe you can manage to have a good long talk with Dr. Sondelius."

"Fat chance! The big city physicians and the state health authorities will be standing around him ten deep. But I'm going."

## IV

The prairie was hot, the wheat rattled in a weary breeze, the day-coach was gritty with cinders. Martin was cramped by the hours of slow riding. He drowsed and smoked and meditated. "I'm going to forget medicine and everything else," he vowed. "I'll go up and talk to somebody in the smoker and tell him I'm a shoe-salesman."

He did. Unfortunately his confidant happened to be a real shoe-salesman, with a large curiosity as to what firm Martin represented, and he returned to the day coach with a renewed sense of injury. When he reached Minneapolis, in mid-afternoon, he hastened to the University and besought a ticket to the Sondelius lecture before he had even found a hotel, though not before he had found the long glass of beer which he had been picturing for a hundred miles.

He had an informal but agreeable notion of spending his first evening of freedom in dissipation. Somewhere he would meet a company of worthies who would succor him with laughter and talk and many drinks — not too many drinks, of course — and motor very rapidly to Lake Minnetonka for a moonlight swim. He began his search for the brethren by having a cocktail at a hotel bar and dinner in a Hennepin Avenue restaurant. Nobody looked at him, nobody seemed to desire a companion. He was lonely for Leora, and all his state of grace, all his earnest and simple-hearted devotion to carousal, degenerated into sleepiness.

As he turned and turned in his hotel bed he lamented, "And probably the Sondelius lecture will be rotten. Probably he's simply another Roscoe Geake."

## V

In the hot night desultory students wandered up to the door of the lecture-hall, scanned the modest Sondelius poster, and ambled away. Martin was half minded to desert with them, and he went in sulkily. The hall was a third full of summer students and teachers, and men who might have been doctors or school-principals. He sat at the back, fanning with his straw hat, disliking the man with side-whiskers who shared the row with him, disapproving of Gustaf Sondelius, and as to himself having no good opinions whatever.

Then the room was charged with vitality. Down the central aisle, ineffectively attended by a small fussy person, thundered a man with a smile, a broad brow, and a strawpile of curly flaxen hair — a Newfoundland dog of a man. Martin sat straight. He was strengthened to endure even the depressing man with side-whiskers as Sondelius launched out, in a musical bellow with Swedish pronunciation and Swedish sing-song:

"The medical profession can have but one desire: to destroy the medical profession. As for the laymen, they can be sure of but one thing: nine-tenths of what they know about health is not so, and with the other tenth they do nothing. As Butler shows in 'Erewhon' — the swine stole that idea from me, too, maybe thirty years before I ever got it — the only crime for w'ich we should hang people is having toobercoolosis."

"Umph!" grunted the studious audience, doubtful whether it was fitting to be amused, offended, bored, or edified.

Sondelius was a roarer and a playboy, but he knew incantations. With him Martin watched the heroes of yellow fever, Reed, Agramonte, Carroll, and Lazear; with him he landed in a Mexican port stilled with the plague and famished beneath the virulent sun; with him rode up the mountain trails to a hill town rotted with typhus; with him, in crawling August, when babies were parched skeletons, fought an ice trust beneath the gilt and blunted sword of the law.

"That's what I want to do! Not just tinker at a lot of worn-out bodies but make a new world!" Martin hungered. "Gosh, I'd follow him through fire! And the way he lays out the crapehangers that criticize public health results! If I could only manage to meet him and talk to him for a couple o' minutes — "

He lingered after the lecture. A dozen people surrounded Sondelius on the platform; a few shook hands; a few asked questions; a doctor worried, "But how about the danger of free clinics and all those things drifting into socialism?" Martin stood back till Sondelius had been deserted. A janitor was closing the windows, very firmly and suggestively. Sondelius looked about, and Martin would have sworn that the Great Man was lonely. He shook hands with him, and quaked:

"Sir, if you aren't due some place, I wonder if you'd like to come out and have a — a — "

Sondelius loomed over him in solar radiance and rumbled, "Have a drink? Well, I think maybe I would. How did the joke about the dog and his fleas go tonight? Do you think they liked it?"

"Oh, sure, you bet."

The warrior who had been telling of feeding five thousand Tatars, of receiving a degree from a Chinese university and refusing a decoration from quite a good Balkan king, looked affectionately on his band of one disciple and demanded, "Was it all right — was it? Did they like it? So hot tonight, and I been lecturing nine time a week — Des Moines, Fort Dodge, LaCrosse, Elgin, Joliet [but he pronounced it Zho-lee-ay] and — I forget. Was it all right? Did they like it?"

"Simply corking! Oh, they just ate it up! Honestly, I've never enjoyed anything so much in my life!"

The prophet crowed, "Come! I buy a drink. As a hygienist, I war on alcohol. In excessive quantities it is almost as bad as coffee or even ice cream soda. But as one who is fond of talking, I find a nice long whisky and soda a great solvent of human idiocy. Is there a cool place with some Pilsener here in Detroit — no; where am I tonight? — Minneapolis?"

"I understand there's a good beer-garden. And we can get the trolley right near here."

Sondelius stared at him. "Oh, I have a taxi waiting."

Martin was abashed by this luxury. In the taxi-cab he tried to think of the proper things to say to a celebrity.

"Tell me, Doctor, do they have city health boards in Europe?"

Sondelius ignored him. "Did you see that girl going by? What ankles! What shoulders! Is it good beer at the beer-garden? Have they any decent cognac? Do you know Courvoisier 1865 cognac? Oof! Lecturing! I swear I will give it up. And wearing dress clothes a night like this! You know, I mean all the crazy things I say in my lectures, but let us now forget being earnest, let us drink, let us sing 'Der Graf von Luxemburg,' let us detach exquisite girls from their escorts, let us discuss the joys of 'Die Meistersinger,' which only I appreciate!"

In the beer-garden the tremendous Sondelius discoursed of the Cosmos Club, Halle's investigation of infant mortality, the suitability of combining benedictine and apple-jack, Biarritz, Lord Haldane, the Doane-Buckley method of milk examination, George Gissing, and *homard thermidor*. Martin looked for a connection between Sondelius and himself, as one does with the notorious or with people met abroad. He might have said, "I think I met a man who knows you," or "I have had the pleasure of reading all your articles," but he fished with "Did you ever run into the two big men in my medical school — Winnemac — Dean Silva and Max Gottlieb?"

"Silva? I don't remember. But Gottlieb — you know him? Oh!" Sondelius waved his mighty arms. "The greatest! The spirit of science! I had the pleasure to talk with him at McGurk. He would not sit here bawling like me! He makes me like a circus clown! He takes all my statements about epidemiology and shows me I am a fool! Ho, ho, ho!" He beamed, and was off on a denunciation of high tariff.

Each topic had its suitable refreshment. Sondelius was a fantastic drinker, and zinc-lined. He mixed Pilsener, whisky, black coffee, and a liquid which the waiter asserted to be absinthe. "I should go to bed at midnight," he lamented, "but it is a cardinal sin to interrupt good talk. Yoost tempt me a little! I am an easy one to be tempted! But I must have five hours' sleep. Absolute! I lecture in — it's some place in Iowa — tomorrow evening. Now that I am past fifty, I cannot get along with three hours as I used to, and yet I have found so many new things that I want to talk about."

He was more eloquent than ever; then he was annoyed. A surly-looking man at the next table listened and peered, and laughed at them. Sondelius dropped from Haffkine's cholera serum to an irate:

"If that fellow stares at me some more, I am going over and kill him! I am a peaceful man, now that I am not so young, but I do not like starers. I will go and argue with him. I will yoost hit him a little!"

While the waiters came rushing, Sondelius charged the man, threatened him with enormous fists, then stopped, shook hands repeatedly, and brought him back to Martin.

"This is a born countryman of mine, from Gottenborg. He is a carpenter. Sit down, Nilsson, sit down and have a drink. Herumph! VAI-ter!"

The carpenter was a socialist, a Swedish Seventh Day Adventist, a ferocious arguer, and fond of drinking aquavit. He denounced Sondelius as an aristocrat, he denounced Martin for his ignorance of economics, he denounced the waiter concerning the brandy; Sondelius and Martin and the waiter answered with vigor; and the conversation became admirable. Presently they were turned out of the beer-garden and the three of them crowded into the still waiting taxicab, which shook to their debating. Where they went, Martin could never trace. He may have dreamed the whole tale. Once they were apparently in a roadhouse on a long street which must have been University Avenue; once in a saloon on Washington Avenue South, where three tramps were sleeping at the end of the bar; once in the carpenter's house, where an unexplained man made coffee for them.

Wherever they might be, they were at the same time in Moscow and Curaçao and Murwillumbah. The carpenter created communistic states, while Sondelius, proclaiming that he did not care whether he worked under socialism or an emperor so long as he could bully people into being well, annihilated tuberculosis and by dawn had cancer fleeing.

They parted at four, tearfully swearing to meet again, in Minnesota or Stockholm, in Rio or on the southern seas, and Martin started for Wheatsylvania to put an end to all this nonsense of allowing people to be ill.

And the great god Sondelius had slain Dean Silva, as Silva had slain Gottlieb, Gottlieb had slain "Encore" Edwards the playful chemist, Edwards had slain Doc Vickerson, and Vickerson had slain the minister's son who had a real trapeze in his barn.

## Chapter 18

Dr. Woestijne of Vanderheide's Grove acted in spare time as Superintendent of Health for Crynssen County, but the office was not well paid and it did not greatly interest him. When Martin burst in and offered to do all the work for half the pay, Woestijne accepted with benevolence, assuring him that it would have a great effect on his private practice.

It did. It almost ruined his private practice.

There was never an official appointment. Martin signed Woestijne's name (spelling it in various interesting ways, depending on how he felt) to papers, and the Board of County Commissioners recognized Martin's limited power, but the whole thing was probably illegal.

There was small science and considerably less heroism in his first furies as a health officer, but a great deal of irritation for his fellow-townsmen. He poked into yards, he denounced Mrs. Beeson for her reeking ash-barrels, Mr. Norblom for piling manure on the street, and the schoolboard for the school ventilation and lack of instruction in tooth-brushing. The citizens had formerly been agitated by his irreligion, his moral looseness, and his lack of local patriotism, but when they were prodded out of their comfortable and probably beneficial dirt, they exploded.

Martin was honest and appallingly earnest, but if he had the innocence of the dove he lacked the wisdom of the serpent. He did not make them understand his mission; he scarce tried to make them understand. His authority, as Woestijne's *alter ego* , was imposing on paper but feeble in action, and it was worthless against the stubbornness which he aroused.

He advanced from garbage-spying to a drama of infection.

The community at Delft had a typhoid epidemic which slackened and continually reappeared. The villagers believed that it came from a tribe of squatters six miles up the creek, and they considered lynching the offenders, as a practical protest and an interesting break in wheat-farming. When Martin insisted that in six miles the creek would purify any waste and that the squatters were probably not the cause, he was amply denounced.

"He's a fine one, he is, to go around blatting that we'd ought to have more health precautions! Here we go and show him where there's some hellhounds that ought to be shot, and them only Bohunks anyway, and he doesn't do a darn' thing but shoot a lot of hot air about germicidal effect or whatever the fool thing is," remarked Kaes, the wheat-buyer at the Delft elevator.

Flashing through the county, not neglecting but certainly not enlarging his own practice, Martin mapped every recent case of typhoid within five miles of Delft. He looked into milk-routes and grocery deliveries. He discovered that most of the cases had appeared after the visits of an itinerant seamstress, a spinster virtuous and almost painfully hygienic. She had had typhoid four years before.

"She's a chronic carrier of the bugs. She's got to be examined," he announced.

He found her sewing at the house of an old farmer-preacher.

With modest indignation she refused to be examined, and as he went away she could be heard weeping at the insult, while the preacher cursed him from the doorstep. He returned with the township police officer and had the seamstress arrested and confined in the segregation ward of the county poor-farm. In her discharges he found billions of typhoid bacilli.

The frail and decent body was not comfortable in the board-lined whitewashed ward. She was shamed and frightened. She had always been well beloved, a gentle, shabby, bright-eyed spinster who brought presents to the babies, helped the overworked farmwives to cook dinner, and sang to the children in her thin sparrow voice. Martin was reviled for persecuting her. "He wouldn't dare pick on her if she wasn't so poor," they said, and they talked of a jail-delivery.

Martin fretted. He called upon the seamstress at the poor-farm, he tried to make her understand that there was no other place for her, he brought her magazines and sweets. But he was firm. She could not go free. He was convinced that she had caused at least one hundred cases of typhoid, with nine deaths.

The county derided him. Cause typhoid now, when she had been well for four years? The County Commissioners and the County Board of Health called Dr. Hesselink in from the next county. He agreed with Martin and his maps. Every meeting of the Commissioners was a battle now, and it was uncertain whether Martin would be ruined or throned.

Leora saved him and the seamstress. "Why not take up a collection to send her off to some big hospital where she can be treated, or where they can keep her if she can't be cured?" said she.

The seamstress entered a sanitarium — and was amiably forgotten by everyone for the rest of her life — and his recent enemies said of Martin, "He's mighty smart, and right on the job." Hesselink drove over to inform him, "You did pretty well this time, Arrowsmith. Glad to see you're settling down to business."

Martin was slightly cocky, and immediately bounded after a fine new epidemic. He was so fortunate as to have a case of small-pox and several which he suspected. Some of these lay across the border in Mencken County, Hesselink's domain, and Hesselink laughed at him. "It's probably chicken-pox, except your one case. Mighty rarely you get small-pox in summer," he chuckled, while Martin raged up and down the two counties, proclaiming the scourge, imploring everyone to be vaccinated, thundering, "There's going to be all hell let loose here in ten or fifteen days!"

But the United Brethren parson, who served chapels in Wheatsylvania and two other villages, was an anti-vaccinationist and he preached against it. The villages sided with him. Martin went from house to house, beseeching them, offering to treat them without charge. As he had never taught them to love him and follow him as a leader, they questioned, they argued long and easily on doorsteps, they cackled that he was drunk. Though for weeks his strongest draft had been the acrid coffee of the countryside, they peeped one to another that he was drunk every night, that the United Brethren minister was about to expose him from the pulpit.

And ten dreadful days went by and fifteen, and all but the first case did prove to be chicken-pox. Hesselink gloated and the village roared and Martin was the butt of the land.

He had only a little resented their gossip about his wickedness, only in evenings of slow depression had he meditated upon fleeing from them, but at their laughter he was black furious.

Leora comforted him with cool hands. "It'll pass over," she said. But it did not pass.

By autumn it had become such a burlesque epic as peasants love through all the world. He had, they mirthfully related, declared that anybody who kept hogs would die of small-pox; he had been drunk for a week, and diagnosed everything from gall-stones to heart-burn as small-pox. They greeted him, with no meaning of offense in their snickering, "Got a pimple on my chin, Doc. What is 't — small-pox?"

More terrible than their rage is the people's laughter, and if it rends tyrants, with equal zest it pursues the saint and wise man and befouls their treasure.

When the neighborhood suddenly achieved a real epidemic of diphtheria and Martin shakily preached antitoxin, one-half of them remembered his failure to save Mary Novak and the other half clamored, "Oh, give us a rest! You got epidemics on the brain!" That a number of children quite adequately died did not make them relinquish their comic epic.

Then it was that Martin came home to Leora and said quietly, "I'm licked. I've got to get out. Nothing more I can do here. Take years before they'd trust me again. They're so damned *humorous*! I'm going to go get a real job — public health."

"I'm so glad! You're too good for them here. We'll find some big place where they'll appreciate your work."

"No, that's not fair. I've learned a little something. I've failed here. I've antagonized too many people. I didn't know how to handle them. We could stick it out, and I would, except that life is short and I think I'm a good worker in some ways. Been worrying about being a coward, about running away, 'turning my —' What is it? '— turning my hand from the plow.' I don't care now! By God, I know what I can do! Gottlieb saw it! And I want to get to work. On we go. All right?"

"Of course!"

## II

He had read in the *Journal of the American Medical Association* that Gustaf Sondelius was giving a series of lectures at Harvard. He wrote asking whether he knew of a public health appointment. Sondelius answered, in a profane and blotty scrawl, that he remembered with joy their Minneapolis vacation, that he disagreed with Entwisle of Harvard about the nature of metathrombin, that there was an excellent Italian restaurant in Boston, and that he would inquire among his health-official friends as to a position.

Two days later he wrote that Dr. Almus Pickerbaugh, Director of Public Health in the city of Nautilus, Iowa, was looking for a second-in-command, and would probably be willing to send particulars.

Leora and Martin swooped on an almanac.

"Gosh! Sixty-nine thousand people in Nautilus! Against three hundred and sixty-six here — no, wait, it's three hundred and sixty-seven now, with that new baby of Pete Yeska's that the dirty swine called in Hesselink for. People! People that can talk! Theaters! Maybe concerts! Leora, we'll be like a pair of kids let loose from school!"

He telegraphed for details, to the enormous interest of the station agent, who was also telegraph operator.

The mimeographed form which was sent to him said that Dr. Pickerbaugh required an assistant who would be the only full-time medical officer besides Pickerbaugh himself, as the clinic and school doctors were private physicians working part-time. The assistant would be epidemiologist, bacteriologist, and manager of the office clerks, the nurses, and the lay inspectors of dairies and sanitation. The salary would be twenty-five hundred dollars a year — against the fifteen or sixteen hundred Martin was making in Wheatsylvania.

Proper recommendations were desired.

Martin wrote to Sondelius, to Dad Silva, and to Max Gottlieb, now at the McGurk Institute in New York.

Dr. Pickerbaugh informed him, "I have received very pleasant letters from Dean Silva and Dr. Sondelius about you, but the letter from Dr. Gottlieb is quite remarkable. He says you have rare gifts as a laboratory man. I take great pleasure in offering you the appointment; kindly wire."

Not till then did Martin completely realize that he was leaving Wheatsylvania — the tedium of Bert Tozer's nagging — the spying of Pete Yeska and the Norbloms — the inevitability of turning, as so many unchanging times he had turned, south from the Leopolis road at the Two Mile Grove and following again that weary, flat, unbending trail — the superiority of Dr. Hesselink and the malice of Dr. Coughlin — the round which left him no time for his dusty laboratory — leaving it all for the achievement and splendor of the great city of Nautilus.

"Leora, we're going! We're really going!"

## III

Bert Tozer said:

"You know by golly there's folks that would call you a traitor, after all we've done for you, even if you did pay back the thousand, to let some other doc come in here and get all that influence away from the Family."

Ada Quist said:

"I guess if you ain't any too popular with the folks around here you'll have one fine time in a big city like Nautilus! Well Bert and me are going to get married next year and when you two swells make a failure of it I suppose we'll have to take care of you at our house when you come sneaking back do you think we could get your house at the same rent you paid for it oh Bert why couldn't we take Mart's office instead it would save money well I've always said since we were in school together you couldn't stand a decent regular life Ory."

Mr. Tozer said:

"I simply can't understand it, with everything going so nice. Why, you'd be making three-four thousand a year some day, if you just stuck to it. Haven't we tried to treat you nice? I don't like to have my little girl go away and leave me alone, now I'm getting on in years. And Bert gets so cranky with me and Mother, but you and Ory would always kind of listen to us. Can't you fix it somehow so you could stay?"

Pete Yeska said:

"Doc, you could of knocked me down with a feather when I heard you were going! Course you and me have scrapped about this drug business, but Lord! I been kind of half thinking about coming around some time and offering you a partnership and let you run the drug end to suit yourself, and we could get the Buick agency, maybe, and work up a nice little business. I'm real sorry you're going to leave us.... Well, come back some day and we'll take a shot at the ducks, and have a good laugh about that bull you made over the small-pox. I never will forget that! I was saying to the old woman just the other day, when she had an ear-ache, 'Ain't got small-pox, have yuh, Bess!' "

Dr. Hesselink said:

"Doctor, what's this I hear? You're not going away? Why, you and I were just beginning to bring medical practice in this neck of the woods up to where it ought to be, so I drove over tonight — Huh? We panned you? Ye-es, I suppose we did, but that doesn't mean we didn't appreciate you. Small place like here or Gronigen, you have to roast your neighbors to keep busy. Why, Doctor, I've been watching you develop from an unlicked cub to a real upstanding physician, and now you're going away — you don't know how I feel!"

Henry Novak said:

"Why, Doc, you ain't going to *leave* us? And we got a new baby coming, and I said to the woman, just the other day, 'It's a good thing we got a doctor that hands you out the truth and not all this guff we used to get from Doc Winter.'"

The wheat-buyer at Delft said:

"Doc, what's this I hear? You ain't going *away*? A fellow told me you was and I says to him, 'Don't be more of a damn' fool than the Lord meant you to be,' I says. But I got to worrying about it, and I drove over and — Doc, I fire off my mouth pretty easy, I guess. I was agin you in the typhoid epidemic, when you said that seamstress was carrying the sickness around, and then you showed me up good. Doc, if you'd like to be state senator, and if you'll stay — I got quite a little influence — believe me, I'll get out and work my shirt off for you!"

Alec Ingleblad said:

"You're a lucky guy!"

All the village was at the train when they left for Nautilus.

For a hundred autumn-blazing miles Martin mourned his neighbors. "I feel like getting off and going back. Didn't we used to have fun playing Five Hundred with the Fraziers! I hate to think of the kind of doctor they may get. I swear, if some quack settles there or if Woestijne neglects the health work again, I'll go back and run 'em both out of business! And be kind of fun to be state senator, some ways."

But as evening thickened and nothing in all the rushing world existed save the yellow Pintsch gas globes above them in the long car, they saw ahead of them great Nautilus, high honor and achievement, the making of a radiant model city and the praise of Sondelius — perhaps even of Max Gottlieb.

## Chapter 19

Midmost of the black-soiled Iowa plain, watered only by a shallow and insignificant creek, the city of Nautilus bakes and rattles and glistens. For hundreds of miles the tall corn springs in a jungle of undeviating rows, and the stranger who sweatily trudges the corn-walled roads is lost and nervous with the sense of merciless growth.

Nautilus is to Zenith what Zenith is to Chicago.

With seventy thousand people, it is a smaller Zenith but no less brisk. There is one large hotel to compare with the dozen in Zenith, but that one is as busy and standardized and frenziedly modern as its owner can make it. The only authentic difference between Nautilus and Zenith is that in both cases all the streets look alike but in Nautilus they do not look alike for so many miles.

The difficulty in defining its quality is that no one has determined whether it is a very large village or a very small city. There are houses with chauffeurs and Bacardi cocktails, but on August evenings all save a few score burghers sit in their shirt-sleeves on front porches. Across from the ten-story office building, in which a little magazine of the New Prose is published by a young woman who for five months lived in the cafés of Montparnasse, is an old frame mansion comfortable with maples, and a line of Fords and lumber-wagons in which the overalled farmers have come to town.

Iowa has the richest land, the lowest illiteracy rate, the largest percentages of native-born whites and motor-car owners, and the most moral and forward-looking cities of all the States, and Nautilus is the most Iowan city in Iowa. One out of every three persons above the age of sixty has spent a winter in California, and among them are the champion horseshoe pitcher of Pasadena and the woman who presented the turkey which Miss Mary Pickford, the cinema princess, enjoyed at her Christmas dinner in 1912.

Nautilus is distinguished by large houses with large lawns and by an astounding quantity of garages and lofty church spires. The fat fields run up to the edge of the city, and the scattered factories, the innumerable railroad side-tracks, and the scraggly cottages for workmen are almost amid the corn. Nautilus manufactures steel windmills, agricultural implements, including the celebrated Daisy Manure Spreader, and such corn-products as Maize Mealies, the renowned breakfast-food. It makes brick, it sells groceries wholesale, and it is the headquarters of the Cornbelt Co-operative Insurance Company.

One of its smallest but oldest industries is Mugford Christian College, which has two hundred and seventeen students, and sixteen instructors, of whom eleven are ministers of the Church of Christ. The well-known Dr. Tom Bissex is football coach, health director, and professor of hygiene, chemistry, physics, French, and German. Its shorthand and piano departments are known far beyond the limits of Nautilus, and once, though that was some years ago, Mugford held the Grinnell College baseball team down to a score of eleven to five. It has never been disgraced by squabbles over teaching evolutionary biology — it never has thought of teaching biology at all.

### II

Martin left Leora at the Sims House, the old-fashioned, second-best hotel in Nautilus, to report to Dr. Pickerbaugh, Director of the Department of Public Health.

The department was on an alley, in a semi-basement at the back of that large graystone fungus, the City Hall. When he entered the drab reception-office he was highly received by the stenographer and the two visiting nurses. Into the midst of their flutterings — "Did you have a good trip, Doctor? Dr. Pickerbaugh didn't hardly expect you till tomorrow, Doctor. Is Mrs. Arrowsmith with you, Doctor?" — charged Pickerbaugh, thundering welcomes.

Dr. Almus Pickerbaugh was forty-eight. He was a graduate of Mugford College and of the Wassau Medical School. He looked somewhat like President Roosevelt, with the same squareness and the same bristly mustache, and he cultivated the resemblance. He was a man who never merely talked: he either bubbled or made orations.

He received Martin with four "Well's," which he gave after the manner of a college cheer; he showed him through the Department, led him into the Director's private office, gave him a cigar, and burst the dam of manly silence:

"Doctor, I'm delighted to have a man with your scientific inclinations. Not that I should consider myself entirely without them. In fact I make it a regular practice to set aside a period for scientific research, without a certain amount of which even the most ardent crusade for health methods would scarcely make much headway."

It sounded like the beginning of a long seminar. Martin settled in his chair. He was doubtful about his cigar, but he found that it helped him to look more interested.

"But with me, I admit, it's a matter of temperament. I have often hoped that, without any desire whatever for mere personal aggrandizement, the powers above may yet grant me the genius to become at once the Roosevelt and the Longfellow of the great and universally growing movement for public health measures is your cigar too mild, Doctor? or perhaps it would be better to say the Kipling of public health rather than the Longfellow, because despite the beautiful passages and high moral atmosphere of the Sage of Cambridge, his poetry lacked the swing and punch of Kipling.

"I assume you agree with me, or you will when you have had an opportunity to see the effect our work has on the city, and the success we have in selling the idea of Better Health, that what the world needs is a really inspired, courageous, overtowering leader — say a Billy Sunday of the movement — a man who would know how to use sensationalism properly and wake the people out of their sloth. Sometimes the papers, and I can only say they flatter me when they compare me with Billy Sunday, the greatest of all evangelists and Christian preachers — sometimes they claim that I'm too sensational. Huh! If they only could understand it, trouble is I can't be sensational enough! Still, I try, I try, and — Look here. Here's a placard, it was painted by my daughter Orchid and the poetry is my own humble effort, and let me tell you it gets quoted around everywhere:

*You can't get health*
*By a pussyfoot stealth.*
*So let's every health-booster*
*Crow just like a rooster.*

"Then there's another — this is a minor thing; it doesn't try to drive home general abstract principles, but it'd surprise you the effect it's had on careless housewives, who of course don't mean to neglect the health of their little ones and merely need instruction and a little pep put into them, and when they see a card like this, it makes 'em think:

*Boil the milk bottles or by gum*
*You better buy your ticket to Kingdom Come.*

"I've gotten quite a lot of appreciation in my small way for some of these things that didn't hardly take me five minutes to dash off. Some day when you get time, glance over this volume of clippings — just to show you, Doctor, what you can do if you go at the Movement in the up-to-date and scientific manner. This one, about the temperance meeting I addressed in Des Moines — say, I had that hall, and it was jam-pack-full, lifting right up on their feet when I proved by statistics that ninety-three per cent of all insanity is caused by booze! Then this — well, it hasn't anything to do with health, directly, but it'll just indicate the opportunity you'll have here to get in touch with all the movements for civic weal."

He held out a newspaper clipping in which, above a pen-and-ink caricature portraying him with large mustached head on a tiny body, was the headline:

DOC PICKERBAUGH BANNER BOOSTER
OF EVANGELINE COUNTY LEADS BIG
GO-TO-CHURCH DEMONSTRATION HERE

Pickerbaugh looked it over, reflecting, "That was a dandy meeting! We increased church attendance here seventeen per cent! Oh, Doctor, you went to Winnemac and had your internship in Zenith, didn't you? Well, this might interest you then. It's from the *Zenith Advocate-Times* , and it's by Chum Frink, who, I think you'll agree with me, ranks with Eddie Guest and Walt Mason as the greatest, as they certainly are the most popular, of all our poets, showing that you can bank every time on the literary taste of the American Public. Dear old Chum! That was when I was in Zenith to address the national convention of Congregational Sunday-schools, I happen to be a Congregationalist myself, on 'The Morality of A1 Health.' So Chum wrote this poem about me:"

*Zenith welcomes with high hurraw*
*A friend in Almus Pickerbaugh,*
*The two-fisted fightin' poet doc*
*Who stands for health like Gibraltar's rock.*
*He's jammed with figgers and facts and fun,*
*The plucky old, lucky old son — of — a — gun!*

For a moment the exuberant Dr. Pickerbaugh was shy.

"Maybe it's kind of immodest in me to show that around. And when I read a poem with such originality and swing, when I find a genu-ine vest-pocket masterpiece like this, then I realize that I'm not a poet at all, no matter how much my jingles may serve to jazz up the Cause of Health. My brainchildren may teach sanitation and do their little part to save thousands of dear lives, but they aren't literature, like what Chum Frink turns out. No, I guess I'm nothing but just a plain scientist in an office.

"Still you'll readily see how one of these efforts of mine, just by having a good laugh and a punch and some melody in it, does gild the pill and make careless folks stop spitting on the sidewalks, and get out into God's great outdoors and get their lungs packed full of ozone and lead a real hairy-chested he-life. In fact you might care to look over the first number of a little semi-yearly magazine I'm just starting — I know for a fact that a number of newspaper editors are going to quote from it and so carry on the good work as well as boost my circulation."

He handed to Martin a pamphlet entitled *Pickerbaugh Pickings* .

In verse and aphorism, *Pickings* recommended good health, good roads, good business, and the single standard of morality. Dr. Pickerbaugh backed up his injunctions with statistics as impressive as those the Reverend Ira Hinkley had once used at Digamma Pi. Martin was edified by an item which showed that among all families divorced in Ontario, Tennessee, and Southern Wyoming in 1912, the appalling number of fifty-three per cent of the husbands drank at least one glass of whisky daily.

Before this warning had sunk in, Pickerbaugh snatched *Pickings* from him with a boyish, "Oh, you won't want to read any more of my rot. You can look it over some future time. But this second volume of my clippings may perhaps interest you, just as a hint of what a fellow can do."

While he considered the headlines in the scrapbook, Martin realized that Dr. Pickerbaugh was vastly better known than he had realized. He was exposed as the founder of the first Rotary Club in Iowa; superintendent of the Jonathan Edwards Congregational Sunday School of Nautilus; president of the Moccasin Ski and Hiking Club, of the West Side Bowling Club, and the 1912 Bull Moose and Roosevelt Club; organizer and cheerleader of a Joint Picnic of the Woodmen, Moose, Elks, Masons, Odd Fellows, Turnverein, Knights of Columbus, B'nai Brith, and the Y.M.C.A.; and winner of the prizes both for reciting the largest number of Biblical texts and for dancing the best Irish jig at the Harvest Moon Soiree of the Jonathan Edwards Bible Class for the Grown-ups.

Martin read of him as addressing the Century Club of Nautilus on "A Yankee Doctor's Trip Through Old Europe," and the Mugford College Alumni Association on "Wanted: A Man-sized Feetball Coach for Old Mugford." But outside of Nautilus as well, there were loud alarums of his presence.

He had spoken at the Toledo Chamber of Commerce Weekly Luncheon on "More Health — More Bank Clearings." He had edified the National Interurban Trolley Council, meeting at Wichita, on "Health Maxims for Trolley Folks." Seven thousand, six hundred Detroit automobile mechanics had listened to his observations on "Health First, Safety Second, and Booze Nowhere A-tall." And in a great convention at Waterloo he had helped organize the first regiment in Iowa of the Anti-rum Minute Men.

The articles and editorials regarding him, in newspapers, house organs, and one rubber-goods periodical, were accompanied by photographs of himself, his buxom wife, and his eight bounding daughters, depicted in Canadian winter costumes among snow and icicles, in modest but easy athletic costumes, playing tennis in the backyard, and in costumes of no known genus whatever, frying bacon against a background of Northern Minnesota pines.

Martin felt strongly that he would like to get away and recover.

He walked back to the Sims House. He realized that to a civilized man the fact that Pickerbaugh advocated any reform would be sufficient reason for ignoring it.

When he had gone thus far, Martin pulled himself up, cursed himself for what he esteemed his old sin of superiority to decent normal people.... Failure. Disloyalty. In medical school, in private practice, in his bullying health administration. Now again?

He urged, "This pep and heartiness stuff of Pickerbaugh's is exactly the thing to get across to the majority of people the scientific discoveries of the Max Gottliebs. What do I care how much Pickerbaugh gases before conventions of Sunday School superintendents and other morons, as long as he lets me do my work in the lab and dairy inspection?"

He pumped up enthusiasm and came quite cheerfully and confidently into the shabby, high-ceilinged hotel bedroom where Leora sat in a rocker by the window.

"Well?" she said.

"It's fine — gave me fine welcome. And they want us to come to dinner tomorrow evening."

"What's he like?"

"Oh, he's awfully optimistic — he puts things over — he — Oh, Leora, am I going to be a sour, cranky, unpopular, rotten failure again?"

His head was buried in her lap and he clung to her affection, the one reality in a world of chattering ghosts.

## III

When the maples fluttered beneath their window in the breeze that sprang up with the beginning of twilight, when the amiable citizens of Nautilus had driven home to supper in their shaky Fords, Leora had persuaded him that Pickerbaugh's flamboyance would not interfere with his own work, that in any case they would not remain in Nautilus forever, that he was impatient, and that she loved him dearly. So they descended to supper, an old-fashioned Iowa supper with corn fritters and many little dishes which were of interest after the loving but misinformed cooking of Leora, and they went to the movies and held hands and were not ill content.

The next day Dr. Pickerbaugh was busier and less buoyant. He gave Martin a notion of the details of his work.

Martin had thought of himself, freed from tinkering over cut fingers and ear-aches, as spending ecstatic days in the laboratory, emerging only to battle with factory-owners who defied sanitation. But he found that it was impossible to define his work, except that he was to do a little of everything that Pickerbaugh, the press, or any stray citizen of Nautilus might think of.

He was to placate voluble voters who came in to complain of everything from the smell of sewer-gas to the midnight beer parties of neighbors; he was to dictate office correspondence to the touchy stenographer, who was not a Working Girl but a Nice Girl Who Was Working; to give publicity to the newspapers; to buy paper-clips and floor-wax and report-blanks at the lowest prices; to assist, in need, the two part-time physicians in the city clinic; to direct the nurses and the two sanitary inspectors; to scold the Garbage Removal Company; to arrest — or at least to jaw at — all public spitters; to leap into a Ford and rush out to tack placards on houses in which were infectious diseases; to keep a learned implacable eye on epidemics from Vladivostok to Patagonia, and to prevent (by methods not very clearly outlined) their coming in to slay the yeomanry and even halt the business activities of Nautilus.

But there was a little laboratory work: milk tests, Wassermanns for private physicians, the making of vaccines, cultures in suspected diphtheria.

"I get it," said Leora, as they dressed for dinner at Pickerbaugh's. "Your job will only take about twenty-eight hours a day, and the rest of the time you're perfectly welcome to spend in research, unless somebody interrupts you."

## IV

The home of Dr. and Mrs. Almus Pickerbaugh, on the steeple-prickly West Side, was a Real Old-Fashioned Home. It was a wooden house with towers, swings, hammocks, rather mussy shade trees, a rather mangy lawn, a rather damp arbor, and an old carriage-house with a line of steel spikes along the ridge pole. Over the front gate was the name: UNEEDAREST.

Martin and Leora came into a shambles of salutations and daughters. The eight girls, from pretty Orchid aged nineteen to the five-year-old twins, surged up in a tidal wave of friendly curiosity and tried to talk all at once.

Their hostess was a plump woman with an air of worried trustfulness. Her conviction that everything was all right was constantly struggling with her knowledge that a great many things seemed to be all wrong. She kissed Leora while Pickerbaugh was pump-handling Martin. Pickerbaugh had a way of pressing his thumb into the back of your hand which was extraordinarily cordial and painful.

He immediately drowned out even his daughters by an oration on the Home Nest:

"Here you've got an illustration of Health in the Home. Look at these great strapping girls, Arrowsmith! Never been sick a day in their lives — practically — and though Mother does have her sick-headaches, that's to be attributed to the early neglect of her diet, because while her father, the old deacon — and a fine upstanding gentleman of the old school he was, too, if there ever was one, and a friend of Nathaniel Mugford, to whom more than any other we owe not only the foundation of Mugford College but also the tradition of integrity and industry which have produced our present prosperity — BUT he had no knowledge of diet or sanitation, and I've always thought — "

The daughters were introduced as Orchid, Verbena, Daisy, Jonquil, Hibisca, Narcissa, and the twins, Arbuta and Gladiola.

Mrs. Pickerbaugh sighed:

"I suppose it would be dreadfully conventional to call them My Jewels — I do so hate these conventional phrases that everybody uses, don't you? — but that's what they really are to their mother, and the Doctor and I have sometimes wished — Of course when we'd started giving them floral names we had to keep it up, but if we'd started with jewels, just think of all the darling names we might have used, like Agate and Cameo and Sardonyx and Beryl and Topaz and Opal and Esmeralda and Chrysoprase — it *is* Chrysoprase, isn't it, not Chrysalis? Oh, well, many people have congratulated us on their names as it is. You know the girls are getting quite famous — their pictures in so many papers, and we have a Pickerbaugh Ladies' Baseball Team all our own — only the Doctor has to play on it now, because I'm beginning to get a little stout."

Except by their ages, it was impossible to tell the daughters apart. They were all bouncing, all blond, all pretty, all eager, all musical, and not merely pure but clamorously clean-minded. They all belonged to the Congregational Sunday School, and to either the Y.W.C.A. or the Camp

Fire Girls; they were all fond of picnicking; and they could all of them, except the five-year-old twins, quote practically without error the newest statistics showing the evils of alcohol.

"In fact," said Dr. Pickerbaugh, "*we* think they're a very striking brood of chickabiddies."

"They certainly are!" quivered Martin.

"But best of all, they are able to help me put over the doctrine of the *Mens Sana* in the *Corpus Sano* . Mrs. Pickerbaugh and I have trained them to sing together, both in the home and publicly, and as an organization we call them the Healthette Octette."

"Really?" said Leora, when it was apparent that Martin had passed beyond speech.

"Yes, and before I get through with it I hope to popularize the name Healthette from end to end of this old nation, and you're going to see bands of happy young women going around spreading their winged message into every dark corner. Healthette Bands! Beautiful and pure-minded and enthusiastic and good basket-ball players! I tell you, *they'll* make the lazy and willful stir their stumps! They'll shame the filthy livers and filthy talkers into decency! I've already worked out a poem-slogan for the Healthette Bands. Would you like to hear it?"

*Winsome young womanhood wins with a smile*
*Boozers, spitters, and gamblers from things that are vile.*
*Our parents and teachers have explained the cause of life,*
*So against the evil-minded we'll also make strife.*
*We'll shame them, reclaim them, from bad habits, you bet!*
*Better watch out, Mr. Loafer, I am a Healthette!*

"But of course an even more important Cause is — and I was one of the first to advocate it — having a Secretary of Health and Eugenics in the cabinet at Washington — "

On the tide of this dissertation they were swept through a stupendous dinner. With a hearty "Nonsense, nonsense, man, of course you want a second helping — this is Hospitality Hall!" Pickerbaugh so stuffed Martin and Leora with roast duck, candied sweet potatoes, and mince pie that they became dangerously ill and sat glassy-eyed. But Pickerbaugh himself did not seem to be affected. While he carved and gobbled, he went on discoursing till the dining-room, with its old walnut buffet, its Hoffmann pictures of Christ, and its Remington pictures of cowpunchers, seemed to vanish, leaving him on a platform beside a pitcher of ice-water.

Not always was he merely fantastic. "Dr. Arrowsmith, I tell you we're lucky men to be able to get a living out of doing our honest best to make the people in a he-town like this well and vital. I could be pulling down eight or ten thousand a year in private practice, and I've been told I could make more than that in the art of advertising, yet I'm glad, and my dear ones are glad with me, to take a salary of four thousand. Think of our having a job where we've got nothing to sell but honesty and decency and the brotherhood o' man!"

Martin perceived that Pickerbaugh meant it, and the shame of the realization kept him from leaping up, seizing Leora, and catching the first freight train out of Nautilus.

After dinner the younger daughters desired to love Leora, in swarms. Martin had to take the twins on his knees and tell them a story. They were remarkably heavy twins, but no heavier than the labor of inventing a plot. Before they went to bed, the entire Healthette Octette sang the famous Health Hymn (written by Dr. Almus Pickerbaugh) which Martin was to hear on so many bright and active public occasions in Nautilus. It was set to the tune of "The Battle Hymn of the Republic," but as the twins' voices were energetic and extraordinarily shrill, it had an effect all its own:

*Oh, are you out for happiness or are you out for pelf?*
*You owe it to the grand old flag to cultivate yourself,*
*To train the mind, keep clean the streets, and ever guard your health.*
*Then we'll all go marching on.*

*A healthy mind in A clean body,*
*A healthy mind in A clean body,*
*A healthy mind in A clean body,*
*The slogan for one and all.*

As a bedtime farewell, the twins then recited, as they had recently at the Congregational Festival, one of their father's minor lyrics:

*What does little birdie say*
*On the sill at break o' day?*
*"Hurrah for health in Nautilus*
*For Pa and Ma and all of us,*
*Hurray, hurray, hurray!"*

"There, my popsywopsies, up to bed we go!" said Mrs. Pickerbaugh. "Don't you think, Mrs. Arrowsmith, they're natural-born actresses? They're not afraid of any audience, and the way they throw themselves into it — perhaps not Broadway, but the more refined theaters in New York would just love them, and maybe they've been sent to us to elevate the drama. Upsy go."

During her absence the others gave a brief musical program.

Verbena, the second oldest, played Chaminade. ("Of course we all love music, and popularize it among the neighbors, but Verby is perhaps the only real musical genius in the family.") But the unexpected feature was Orchid's cornet solo.

Martin dared not look at Leora. It was not that he was sniffily superior to cornet solos, for in Elk Mills, Wheatsylvania, and surprisingly large portions of Zenith, cornet solos were done by the most virtuous females. But he felt that he had been in a madhouse for dozens of years.

"I've never been so drunk in my life. I wish I could get at a drink and sober up," he agonized. He made hysterical and completely impractical plans for escape. Then Mrs. Pickerbaugh, returning from the still audible twins, sat down at the harp.

While she played, a faded woman and thickish, she fell into a great dreaming, and suddenly Martin had a picture of her as a gay, good, dove-like maiden who had admired the energetic young medical student, Almus Pickerbaugh. She must have been a veritable girl of the late eighties and the early nineties, the naïve and idyllic age of Howells, when young men were pure, when they played croquet and sang Swanee River; a girl who sat on a front porch enchanted by the sweetness of lilacs, and hoped that when Almus and she were married they would have a nickel-plated baseburner stove and a son who would become a missionary or a millionaire.

For the first time that evening, Martin managed to put a respectable heartiness into his "Enjoyed that s' much." He felt victorious, and somewhat recovered from his weakness. But the evening's orgy was only begun.

They played word-games, which Martin hated and Leora did very badly indeed. They acted charades, at which Pickerbaugh was tremendous. The sight of him on the floor in his wife's fur coat, being a seal on an ice-floe, was incomparable. Then Martin, Orchid, and Hibisca (aged twelve) had to present a charade, and there were complications.

Orchid was as full of simple affections, of smilings and pattings and bouncings, as her younger sisters, but she was nineteen and not altogether a child. Doubtless she was as pure-minded and as devoted to Clean and Wholesome Novels as Dr. Pickerbaugh stated, and he stated it with frequency, but she was not unconscious of young men, even though they were married.

She planned to enact the word *doleful*, with a beggar asking a dole, and a corncrib full. As they skipped upstairs to dress, she hugged Martin's arm, frisked beside him, and murmured, "Oh, Doctor, I'm so glad Daddy has you for assistant — somebody that's young and good-looking. Oh, was that dreadful of me? But I mean: you look so athletic and everything, and the other assistant director — don't tell Daddy I said so, but he was an old crank!"

He was conscious of brown eyes and unshadowed virginal lips. As Orchid put on her agreeably loose costume as a beggar, he was also conscious of ankles and young bosom. She smiled at him, as one who had long known him, and said loyally, "We'll show 'em! I know you're a dan-dy actor!"

When they bustled downstairs, as she did not take his arm, he took hers, and he pressed it slightly and felt alarmed and relinquished it with emphasis.

Since his marriage he had been so absorbed in Leora, as lover, as companion, as helper, that till this hour his most devastating adventure had been a glance at a pretty girl in a train. But the flushed young gaiety of Orchid disturbed him. He wanted to be rid of her, he hoped that he would not be altogether rid of her, and for the first time in years he was afraid of Leora's eyes.

There were acrobatic feats later, and a considerable prominence of Orchid, who did not wear stays, who loved dancing, and who praised Martin's feats in the game of "Follow the Leader."

All the daughters save Orchid were sent to bed, and the rest of the fête consisted of what Pickerbaugh called "a little quiet scientific conversation by the fireside," made up of his observations on good roads, rural sanitation, Ideals in politics, and methods of letter filing in health departments. Through this placid hour, or it may have been an hour and a half, Martin saw that Orchid was observing his hair, his jaw, his hands, and he had, and dismissed, and had again a thought about the innocent agreeableness of holding her small friendly paw.

He also saw that Leora was observing both of them, and he suffered a good deal, and had practically no benefit whatever from Pickerbaugh's notes on the value of disinfectants. When Pickerbaugh predicted for Nautilus, in fifteen years, a health department thrice as large, with many full-time clinic and school physicians and possibly Martin as director (Pickerbaugh himself having gone off to mysterious and interesting activities in a Larger Field), Martin merely croaked, "Yes, that'd be — be fine," while to himself he was explaining, "Damn that girl, I wish she wouldn't shake herself at me."

At half-past eight he had pictured his escape as life's highest ecstasy; at twelve he took leave with nervous hesitation.

They walked to the hotel. Free from the sight of Orchid, brisk in the coolness, he forgot the chit and pawed again the problem of his work in Nautilus.

"Lord, I don't know whether I can do it. To work under that gas-bag, with his fool pieces about boozers — "

"They weren't so bad," protested Leora.

"Bad? Why, he's probably the worst poet that ever lived, and he certainly knows less about epidemiology than I thought any one man could ever learn, all by himself. But when it comes to this — what was it Clif Clawson used to call it? — by the way, wonder what's ever become of Clif; haven't heard from him for a couple o' years — when it comes to this 'overpowering Christian Domesticity' — Oh, let's hunt for a blind-pig and sit around with the nice restful burglars."

She insisted, "I thought his poems were kind of cute."

"Cute! What a word!"

"It's no worse than the cuss-words you're always using! But the cornet yowling by that awful oldest daughter — Ugh!"

"Well, now she played darn' well!"

"Martin, the cornet is the kind of instrument my brother would play. And you so superior about the doctor's poetry and my saying 'cute'! You're just as much a backwoods hick as I am, and maybe more so!"

"Why, gee, Leora, I never knew you to get sore about nothing before! And can't you understand how important — You see, a man like Pickerbaugh makes all public health work simply ridiculous by his circusing and his ignorance. If he said that fresh air was a good thing, instead of making me open my windows it'd make me or any other reasonable person close 'em. And to use the word 'science' in those flop-eared limericks or whatever you call 'em — it's sacrilege!"

"Well, if you want to *know*, Martin Arrowsmith, I'll have no more of these high jinks with that Orchid girl! Practically hugging her when you came downstairs, and then mooning at her all evening! I don't mind your cursing and being cranky and even getting drunk, in a reasonable sort of way, but ever since the lunch when you told me and that Fox woman, 'I hope you girls won't mind, but I just happen to remember that I'm engaged to both of you' — You're mine, and I won't have any trespassers. I'm a cavewoman, and you'd better learn it, and as for that Orchid, with her simper and her stroking your arm and her great big absurd feet — Orchid! She's no orchid! She's a bachelor's button!"

"But, honest, I don't even remember which of the eight she was."

"Huh! Then you've been making love to all of 'em, that's why. Drat her! Well, I'm not going to go on scrapping about it. I just wanted to warn you, that's all."

At the hotel, after giving up the attempt to find a short, jovial, convincing way of promising that he would never flirt with Orchid, he stammered, "If you don't mind, I think I'll stay down and walk a little more. I've got to figure this health department business out."

He sat in the Sims House office — singularly dismal it was, after midnight, and singularly smelly.

"That fool Pickerbaugh! I wish I'd told him right out that we know hardly anything about the epidemiology of tuberculosis, for instance.

"Just the same, she's a darling child. Orchid! She's like an orchid — no, she's too healthy. Be a great kid to go hunting with. Sweet. And she acted as if I were her own age, not an old doctor. I'll be good, oh, I'll be good, but — I'd like to kiss her once, *good* ! She likes me. Those darling lips, like — like rosebuds!

"Poor Leora. I nev' was so astonished in my life. Jealous. Well, she's got a right to be! No woman ever stood by a man like — Lee, sweet, can't you see, idiot, if I skipped round the corner with seventeen billion Orchids, it'd be you I loved, and never anybody but you!

"I can't go round singing Healthette Octette Pantalette stuff. Even if it did instruct people, which it don't. Be almost better to let 'em die than have to live and listen to —

"Leora said I was a 'backwoods hick.' Let me tell you, young woman, as it happens I am a Bachelor of Arts, and you may recall the kind of books the 'backwoods hick' was reading to you last winter, and even Henry James and everybody and — Oh, she's right. I am. I do know how to make pipets and agar, but — And yet some day I want to travel like Sondelius —

"Sondelius! God! If it were he I was working for, instead of Pickerbaugh, I'd slave for him —

"Or does he pull the bunk, too?

"Now that's just what I mean. That kind of phrase. 'Pull the bunk'! Horrible!

"Hell! I'll use any kind of phrase I want to! I'm not one of your social climbers like Angus. The way Sondelius cusses, for instance, and yet he's used to all those highbrows —

"And I'll be so busy here in Nautilus that I won't even be able to go on reading. Still — I don't suppose they read much, but there must be quite a few of these rich men here that know about nice houses. Clothes. Theaters. That stuff.

"Rats!"

He wandered to an all-night lunch-wagon, where he gloomily drank coffee. Beside him, seated at the long shelf which served as table, beneath the noble red-glass window with a portrait of George Washington, was a policeman who, as he gnawed a Hamburger sandwich, demanded:

"Say, ain't you this new doctor that's come to assist Pickerbaugh? Seen you at City Hall."

"Yes. Say, uh, say, how does the city like Pickerbaugh? How do you like him? Tell me honestly, because I'm just starting in, and, uh — You get me."

With his spoon held inside the cup by a brawny thumb, the policeman gulped his coffee and proclaimed, while the greasy friendly cook of the lunch-wagon nodded in agreement:

"Well, if you want the straight dope, he hollers a good deal, but he's one awful brainy man. He certainly can sling the Queen's English, and jever hear one of his poems? They're darn' bright. I'll tell you: There's some people say Pickerbaugh pulls the song and dance too much, but way I figure it, course maybe for you and me, Doctor, it'd be all right if he just looked after the milk and the garbage and the kids' teeth. But there's a lot of careless, ignorant, foreign slobs that need to be jollied into using their konks about these health biznai, so's they won't go getting sick with a lot of these infectious diseases and pass 'em on to the rest of us, and believe me, old Doc Pickerbaugh is the boy that gets the idea into their noodles!

"Yes, sir, he's a great old coot — he ain't a clam like some of these docs. Why, say, one day he showed up at the St. Patrick picnic, even if he is a dirty Protestant, and him and Father Costello chummed up like two old cronies, and darn' if he didn't wrestle a fellow half his age, and awful' near throw him, yes, you bet he did, he certainly give that young fellow a run for his money all right! We fellows on the Force all like him, and we have to grin, the way he comes around and soft-soaps us into doing a lot of health work that by law we ain't hardly supposed to do, you might say, instead of issuing a lot of fool orders. You bet. He's a real guy."

"I see," said Martin, and as he returned to the hotel he meditated:

"But think of what Gottlieb would say about him.

"Damn Gottlieb! Damn everybody except Leora!

"I'm not going to fail here, way I did in Wheatsylvania.

"Some day Pickerbaugh will get a bigger job — Huh! He's just the kind of jollying four-flusher that *would* climb! But anyway, I'll have my training then, and maybe I'll make a real health department here.

"Orchid said we'd go skating this winter —

"*Damn* Orchid!"

## Chapter 20

Martin found in Dr. Pickerbaugh a generous chief. He was eager to have Martin invent and clamor about his own Causes and Movements. His scientific knowledge was rather thinner than that of the visiting nurses, but he had little jealousy, and he demanded of Martin only the belief that a rapid and noisy moving from place to place is the means (and possibly the end) of Progress.

In a two-family house on Social Hill, which is not a hill but a slight swelling in the plain, Martin and Leora found an upper floor. There was a simple pleasantness in these continuous lawns, these wide maple-shaded streets, and a joy in freedom from the peering whispers of Wheatsylvania.

Suddenly they were being courted by the Nice Society of Nautilus.

A few days after their arrival Martin was summoned to the telephone to hear a masculine voice rasping:

"Hello. Martin? I bet you can't guess who this is!"

Martin, very busy, restrained his desire to observe, "You win — g' by!" and he buzzed, with the cordiality suitable to a new Assistant Director:

"No, I'm afraid I can't."

"Well, make a guess."

"Oh — Clif Clawson?"

"Nope. Say, I see you're looking fine. Oh, I guess I've got you guessing this time! Go on! Have another try!"

The stenographer was waiting to take letters, and Martin had not yet learned to become impersonal and indifferent in her presence. He said with a perceptible tartness:

"Oh, I suppose it's President Wilson. Look here — "

"Well, Mart, it's Irve Watters! What do you know about that!"

Apparently the jester expected large gratification, but it took ten seconds for Martin to remember who Irving Watters might be. Then he had it: Watters, the appalling normal medical student whose faith in the good, the true, the profitable, had annoyed him at Digamma Pi. He made his response as hearty as he could:

"Well, well, what you doing here, Irve?"

"Why, I'm settled here. Been here ever since internship. And got a nice little practice, too. Look, Mart, Mrs. Watters and I want you and your wife — I believe you are married, aren't you? — to come up to the house for dinner, tomorrow evening, and I'll put you onto all the local slants."

The dread of Watters's patronage enabled Martin to lie vigorously:

"Awfully sorry — awfully sorry — got a date for tomorrow evening and the next evening."

"Then come have lunch with me tomorrow at the Elks' Club, and you and your wife take dinner with us Sunday noon."

Hopelessly, "I don't think I can make it for lunch but — Well, we'll dine with you Sunday."

It is one of the major tragedies that nothing is more discomforting than the hearty affection of the Old Friends who never were friends. Martin's imaginative dismay at being caught here by Watters was not lessened when Leora and he reluctantly appeared on Sunday at one-thirty and were by a fury of Old Friendship dragged back into the days of Digamma Pi.

Watters's house was new, and furnished in a highly built-in and leaded-glass manner. He had in three years of practice already become didactic and incredibly married; he had put on weight and infallibility; and he had learned many new things about which to be dull. Having been graduated a year earlier than Martin and having married an almost rich wife, he was kind and hospitable with an emphasis which aroused a desire to do homicide. His conversation was a series of maxims and admonitions:

"If you stay with the Department of Public Health for a couple of years and take care to meet the right people, you'll be able to go into very lucrative practice here. It's a fine town — prosperous — so few dead beats.

"You want to join the country club and take up golf. Best opportunity in the world to meet the substantial citizens. I've picked up more than one high-class patient there.

"Pickerbaugh is a good active man and a fine booster but he's got a bad socialistic tendency. These clinics — outrageous — the people that go to them that can afford to pay! Pauperize people. Now this may startle you — oh, you had a lot of crank notions when you were in school, but you aren't the only one that does some thinking for himself! — sometimes I believe it'd be better for the general health situation if there weren't any public health departments at all, because they get a lot of people into the habit of going to free clinics instead of to private physicians, and cut down the earnings of the doctors and reduce their number, so there are less of us to keep a watchful eye on sickness.

"I guess by this time you've gotten over the funny ideas you used to have about being practical — 'commercialism' you used to call it. You can see now that you've got to support your wife and family, and if you don't, nobody else is going to.

"Any time you want a straight tip about people here, you just come to me. Pickerbaugh is a crank — he won't give you the right dope — the people you want to tie up with are the good, solid, conservative, successful business men."

Then Mrs. Watters had her turn. She was meaty with advice, being the daughter of a prosperous person, none other than Mr. S. A. Peaseley, the manufacturer of the Daisy Manure Spreader.

"You haven't any children?" she sobbed at Leora. "Oh, you must! Irving and I have two, and you don't know what an interest they are to us, and they keep us so young."

Martin and Leora looked at each other pitifully.

After dinner, Irving insisted on their recalling the "good times we used to have together at the dear old U." He took no denial. "You always want to make folks think you're eccentric, Mart. You pretend you haven't any college patriotism, but I know better — I know you're showing off — you admire the old place and our profs just as much as anybody. Maybe I know you better than you do yourself! Come on, now; let's give a long cheer and sing 'Winnemac, Mother of Brawny Men.' "

And, "Don't be silly; of course you're going to sing," said Mrs. Watters, as she marched to the piano, with which she dealt in a firm manner.

When they had politely labored through the fried chicken and brick ice cream, through the maxims, gurglings and memories, Martin and Leora went forth and spoke in tongues:

"Pickerbaugh must be a saint, if Watters roasts him. I begin to believe he has sense enough to come in when it rains."

In their common misery they forgot that they had been agitated by a girl named Orchid.

## II

Between Pickerbaugh and Irving Watters, Martin was drafted into many of the associations, clubs, lodges, and "causes" with which Nautilus foamed; into the Chamber of Commerce, the Moccasin Ski and Hiking Club, the Elks' Club, the Odd Fellows, and the Evangeline County Medical society. He resisted, but they said in a high hurt manner, "Why, my boy, if you're going to be a public official, and if you have the slightest appreciation of their efforts to make you welcome here — "

Leora and he found themselves with so many invitations that they, who had deplored the dullness of Wheatsylvania, complained now that they could have no quiet evenings at home. But they fell into the habit of social ease, of dressing, of going places without nervous anticipation. They modernized their rustic dancing; they learned to play bridge, rather badly, and tennis rather well; and Martin, not by virtue and heroism but merely by habit, got out of the way of resenting the chirp of small talk.

Probably they were never recognized by their hostesses as pirates, but considered a Bright Young Couple who, since they were protégés of Pickerbaugh, must be earnest and forward-looking, and who, since they were patronized by Irving and Mrs. Watters, must be respectable.

Watters took them in hand and kept them there. He had so thick a rind that it was impossible for him to understand that Martin's frequent refusals of his invitations could conceivably mean that he did not wish to come. He detected traces of heterodoxy in Martin, and with affection, diligence, and an extraordinarily heavy humor he devoted himself to the work of salvation. Frequently he sought to entertain other guests by urging, "Come on now, Mart, let's hear some of those crazy ideas of yours!"

His friendly zeal was drab compared with that of his wife. Mrs. Watters had been reared by her father and by her husband to believe that she was the final fruit of the ages, and she set herself to correct the barbarism of the Arrowsmiths. She rebuked Martin's damns, Leora's smoking, and both their theories of bidding at bridge. But she never nagged. To have nagged would have been to admit that there were persons who did not acknowledge her sovereignty. She merely gave orders, brief, humorous, and introduced by a strident "Now don't be silly," and she expected that to settle the matter.

Martin groaned, "Oh, Lord, between Pickerbaugh and Irve, it's easier to become a respectable member of society than to go on fighting."

But Watters and Pickerbaugh were not so great a compulsion to respectability as the charms of finding himself listened to in Nautilus as he never had been in Wheatsylvania, and of finding himself admired by Orchid.

## III

He had been seeking a precipitation test for the diagnosis of syphilis which should be quicker and simpler than the Wassermann. His slackened fingers and rusty mind were becoming used to the laboratory and to passionate hypotheses when he was dragged away to help Pickerbaugh in securing publicity. He was coaxed into making his first speech: an address on "What the Laboratory Teaches about Epidemics" for the Sunday Afternoon Free Lecture Course of the Star of Hope Universalist Church.

He was flustered when he tried to prepare his notes, and on the morning of the affair he was chill as he remembered the dreadful thing he would do this day, but he was desperate with embarrassment when he came up to the Star of Hope Church.

People were crowding in; mature, responsible people. He quaked, "They're coming to hear *me*, and I haven't got a darn' thing to say to 'em!" It made him feel the more ridiculous that they who presumably wished to listen to him should not be aware of him, and that the usher, profusely shaking hands at the Byzantine portal, should bluster, "You'll find plenty room right up the side aisles, young man."

"I'm the speaker for the afternoon."

"Oh, oh, yes, oh, yes, Doctor. Right round to the Bevis Street entrance, if you please, Doctor."

In the parlors he was unctuously received by the pastor and a committee of three, wearing morning clothes and a manner of Christian intellectuality.

They held his hand in turn, they brought up rustling women to meet him, they stood about him in a polite and twittery circle, and dismayingly they expected him to say something intelligent. Then, suffering, ghastly frightened, dumb, he was led through an arched doorway into the auditorium. Millions of faces were staring at his apologetic insignificance — faces in the curving lines of pews, faces in the low balcony, eyes which followed him and doubted him and noted that his heels were run down.

The agony grew while he was prayed over and sung over.

The pastor and the lay chairman of the Lecture Course opened with suitable devotions. While Martin trembled and tried to look brazenly at the massed people who were looking at him, while he sat nude and exposed and unprotected on the high platform, the pastor made announcement of the Thursday Missionary Supper and the Little Lads' Marching Club. They sang a brief cheerful hymn or two — Martin wondering whether to sit or stand — and the chairman prayed that "our friend who will address us today may have power to put his Message across." Through the prayer Martin sat with his forehead in his hand, feeling foolish, and raving, "I guess this is the proper attitude — they're all gawping at me — gosh, won't he ever quit? — oh, damn it, now what was that point I was going to make about fumigation? — oh, Lord, he's winding up and I've got to shoot!"

Somehow, he was standing by the reading-desk, holding it for support, and his voice seemed to be going on, producing reasonable words. The blur of faces cleared and he saw individuals. He picked out a keen old man and tried to make him laugh and marvel.

He found Leora, toward the back, nodding to him, reassuring him. He dared to look away from the path of faces directly in front of him. He glanced at the balcony —

The audience perceived a young man who was being earnest about sera and vaccines but, while his voice buzzed on, that churchly young man had noted two silken ankles distinguishing the front row of the balcony, had discovered that they belonged to Orchid Pickerbaugh and that she was flashing down admiration.

At the end Martin had the most enthusiastic applause ever known — all lecturers, after all lectures, are gratified by that kind of applause — and the chairman said the most flattering things ever uttered, and the audience went out with the most remarkable speed ever witnessed, and Martin discovered himself holding Orchid's hand in the parlors while she warbled, in the most adorable voice ever heard, "Oh, Dr. Arrowsmith, you were just wonderful! Most of these lecturers are old stuffs, but you put it right over! I'm going to do a dash home and tell Dad. He'll be so tickled!"

Not till then did he find that Leora had made her way to the parlors and was looking at them like a wife.

As they walked home Leora was eloquently silent.

"Well, did you like my spiel?" he said, after a suitable time of indignant waiting.

"Yes, it wasn't bad. It must have been awfully hard to talk to all those stupid people."

"Stupid? What d'you mean by 'stupid'? They got me splendidly. They were fine."

"Were they? Well anyway, thank Heaven, you won't have to keep up this silly gassing. Pickerbaugh likes to hear himself talk too well to let you in on it very often."

"I didn't mind it. Fact, don't know but what it's a good thing to have to express myself publicly now and then. Makes you think more lucidly."

"As for instance the nice, lovely, lucid politicians!"

"Now you look here, Lee! Of course we know your husband is a mutt, and no good outside the laboratory, but I do think you might *pretend* to be a little enthusiastic over the first address he's ever made — the very first he's ev-er tackled — when it went off so well."

"Why, silly, I was enthusiastic. I applauded a lot. I thought you were terribly smart. It's just — There's other things I think you can do better. What shall we do tonight; have a cold snack at home or go to the cafeteria?"

Thus was he reduced from hero to husband, and he had all the pleasures of inappreciation.

He thought about his indignities the whole week, but with the coming of winter there was a fever of dully sprightly dinners and safely wild bridge and their first evening at home, their first opportunity for secure and comfortable quarreling, was on Friday. They sat down to what he announced as "getting back to some real reading, like physiology and a little of this fellow Arnold Bennett — nice quiet reading," but which consisted of catching up on the news notes in the medical journals.

He was restless. He threw down his magazine. He demanded:

"What're you going to wear at Pickerbaugh's snow picnic tomorrow?"

"Oh, I haven't — I'll find something."

"Lee, I want to ask you: Why the devil did you say I talked too much at Dr. Strafford's last evening? I know I've got most of the faults going, but I didn't know talking too much was one of 'em."

"It hasn't been, till now."

"'Till now'!"

"You look here, Sandy Arrowsmith! You've been pouting like a bad brat all week. What's the matter with you?"

"Well, I — Gosh, it makes me tired! Here everybody is so enthusiastic about my Star of Hope spiel — that note in the *Morning Frontiersman* , and Pickerbaugh says Orchid said it was a corker — and you never so much as peep!"

"Didn't I applaud? But — It's just that I hope you aren't going to keep up this drooling."

"You do, do you! Well, let me tell you I *am* going to keep it up! Not that I'm going to talk a lot of hot air. I gave 'em straight science, last Sunday, and they ate it up. I hadn't realized it isn't necessary to be mushy, to hold an audience. And the amount of good you can do! Why, I got across more Health Instruction and ideas about the value of the lab in that three-quarters of an hour than — I don't care for being a big gun but it's fine to have people where they have to listen to what you've got to say and can't butt in, way they did in Wheatsylvania. You bet I'm going to keep up what you so politely call my damn' fool drooling — "

"Sandy, it may be all right for some people, but not for you. I can't tell you — that's one reason I haven't said more about your talk — I can't tell you how astonished I am to hear you, who're always sneering at what you call sentimentality, simply weeping over the Dear Little Tots!"

"I never said that — never used the phrase and you know it. And by God! *You* talk about sneering! Just let me tell you that the Public Health Movement, by correcting early faults in children, by looking after their eyes and tonsils and so on, can save millions of lives and make a future generation — "

"I know it! I love children much more than you do! But I mean all this ridiculous simpering — "

"Well, gosh, somebody has to do it. You can't work with people till you educate 'em. There's where old Pick, even if he is an imbecile, does such good work with his poems and all that stuff. Prob'ly be a good thing if I could write 'em — golly, wonder if I couldn't learn to?"

"They're horrible!"

"Now there's a fine consistency for you! The other evening you called 'em 'cute.'"

"I don't have to be consistent. I'm a mere woman. You, Martin Arrowsmith, you'd be the first to tell me so. And for Dr. Pickerbaugh they're all right, but not for you. You belong in a laboratory, finding out things, not advertising them. Do you remember once in Wheatsylvania for five minutes you almost thought of joining a church and being a Respectable Citizen? Are you going on for the rest of your life, stumbling into respectability and having to be dug out again? Will you never learn you're a barbarian?"

"By God, I am! And — what was that other lovely thing you called me? — I'm also, soul of my soul, a damn' backwoods hick! And a fine lot you help! When I want to settle down to a decent and useful life and not go 'round antagonizing people, you, the one that ought to believe in me, you're the first one to crab!"

"Maybe Orchid Pickerbaugh would help you better."

"She probably would! Believe me, she's a darling, and she did appreciate my spiel at the church, and if you think I'm going to sit up all night listening to you sneering at my work and my friends — I'm going to have a hot bath. Good *night* !"

In the bath he gasped that it was impossible he should have been quarreling with Leora. Why! She was the only person in the world, besides Gottlieb and Sondelius and Clif Clawson — by the way, where was Clif? still in New York? didn't Clif owe him a letter? but anyway — He was a fool to have lost his temper, even if she was so stubborn that she wouldn't adjust her opinions, couldn't see that he had a gift for influencing people. Nobody would ever stand by him as she had, and he loved her —

He dried himself violently; he dashed in with repentances; they told each other that they were the most reasonable persons living; they kissed with eloquence; and then Leora reflected:

"Just the same, my lad, I'm not going to help you fool yourself. You're not a booster. You're a lie-hunter. Funny, you'd think to hear about these lie-hunters, like Professor Gottlieb and your old Voltaire, they couldn't be fooled. But maybe they were like you: always trying to get away from the tiresome truth, always hoping to settle down and be rich, always selling their souls to the devil and then going and doublecrossing the poor devil. I think — I think — " She sat up in bed, holding her temples in the labor of articulation. "You're different from Professor Gottlieb. He never makes mistakes or wastes time on — "

"He wasted time at Hunziker's nostrum factory all right, and his title is 'Doctor,' not 'Professor,' if you *must* give him a — "

"If he went to Hunziker's he had some good reason. He's a genius; he couldn't be wrong. Or could he, even he? But *anyway* : you, Sandy, you have to stumble every so often; have to learn by making mistakes. I will say one thing: you learn from your crazy mistakes. But I get a little tired, sometimes, watching you rush up and put your neck in every noose — like being a blinking orator or yearning over your Orchid."

"Well, by golly! After I come in here trying to make peace! It's a good thing *you* never make any mistakes! But one perfect person in a household is enough!"

He banged into bed. Silence. Soft sounds of "Mart — *Sandy!* " He ignored her, proud that he could be hard with her, and so fell asleep. At breakfast, when he was ashamed and eager, she was curt.

"I don't care to discuss it," she said.

In that wry mood they went on Saturday afternoon to the Pickerbaughs' snow picnic.

## IV

Dr. Pickerbaugh owned a small log cabin in a scanty grove of oaks among the hillocks north of Nautilus. A dozen of them drove out in a bob-sled filled with straw and blue woolly robes. The sleigh bells were exciting and the children leaped out to run beside the sled.

The school physician, a bachelor, was attentive to Leora; twice he tucked her in, and that, for Nautilus, was almost compromising. In jealousy Martin turned openly and completely to Orchid.

He grew interested in her not for the sake of disciplining Leora but for her own rosy sweetness. She was wearing a tweed jacket, with a tam, a flamboyant scarf, and the first breeches any girl had dared to display in Nautilus. She patted Martin's knee, and when they rode behind the sled on a perilous toboggan, she held his waist, resolutely.

She was calling him "Dr. Martin" now, and he had come to a warm "Orchid."

At the cabin there was a clamor of disembarkation. Together Martin and Orchid carried in the hamper of food; together they slid down the hillocks on skis. When their skis were entangled, they rolled into a drift, and as she clung to him, unafraid and unembarrassed, it seemed to him that in the roughness of tweeds she was but the softer and more wonderful — eyes fearless, cheeks brilliant as she brushed the coating of wet snow from them, flying legs of a slim boy, shoulders adorable in their pretense of sturdy boyishness —

But "I'm a sentimental fool! Leora was right!" he snarled at himself. "I thought you had some originality! And poor little Orchid — she'd be shocked if she knew how sneak-minded you are!"

But poor little Orchid was coaxing, "Come on, Dr. Martin, let's shoot off that high bluff. We're the only ones that have any pep."

"That's because we're the only young ones."

"It's because you're so young. I'm dreadfully old. I just sit and moon when you rave about your epidemics and things."

He saw that, with her infernal school physician, Leora was sliding on a distant slope. It may have been pique and it may have been relief that he was licensed to be alone with Orchid, but he ceased to speak to her as though she were a child and he a person laden with wisdom; ceased to speak to her as though he were looking over his shoulder. They raced to the high bluff. They skied down it and fell; they had one glorious swooping slide, and wrestled in the snow.

They returned to the cabin together, to find the others away. She stripped off her wet sweater and patted her soft blouse. They ferreted out a thermos of hot coffee, and he looked at her as though he was going to kiss her, and she looked back at him as though she did not mind. As they laid out the food they hummed with the intimacy of understanding, and when she trilled, "Now hurry up, lazy one, and put those cups on that horrid old table," it was as one who was content to be with him forever.

They said nothing compromising, they did not hold hands, and as they rode home in the electric snow-flying darkness, though they sat shoulder by shoulder he did not put his arms about her except when the bob-sled slewed on sharp corners. If Martin was exalted with excitement, it was presumably caused by the wholesome exercises of the day. Nothing happened and nobody looked uneasy. At parting all their farewells were cheery and helpful.

And Leora made no comments, though for a day or two there was about her a chill air which the busy Martin did not investigate.

## Chapter 21

Nautilus was one of the first communities in the country to develop the Weeks habit, now so richly grown that we have Correspondence School Week, Christian Science Week, Osteopathy Week, and Georgia Pine Week.

A Week is not merely a week.

If an aggressive, wide-awake, live-wire, and go-ahead church or chamber of commerce or charity desires to improve itself, which means to get more money, it calls in those few energetic spirits who run any city, and proclaims a Week. This consists of one month of committee meetings, a hundred columns of praise for the organization in the public prints, and finally a day or two on which athletic persons flatter inappreciative audiences in churches or cinema theaters, and the prettiest girls in town have the pleasure of being allowed to talk to male strangers on the street corners, apropos of giving them extremely undecorative tags in exchange for the smallest sums which those strangers think they must pay if they are to be considered gentlemen.

The only variation is the Weeks in which the object is not to acquire money immediately by the sale of tags but by general advertising to get more of it later.

Nautilus had held a Pep Week, during which a race of rapidly talking men, formerly book-agents but now called Efficiency Engineers, went about giving advice to shopkeepers on how to get money away from one another more rapidly, and Dr. Almus Pickerbaugh addressed a prayer-meeting on "The Pep of St. Paul, the First Booster." It had held a Gladhand Week, when everybody was supposed to speak to at least three strangers daily, to the end that infuriated elderly traveling salesmen were back-slapped all day long by hearty and powerful unknown persons. There had also been an Old Home Week, a Write to Mother Week, a We Want Your Factory in Nautilus Week, an Eat More Corn Week, a Go to Church Week, a Salvation Army Week, and an Own Your Own Auto Week.

Perhaps the bonniest of all was Y. Week, to raise eighty thousand dollars for a new Y.M.C.A. building.

On the old building were electric signs, changed daily, announcing "You Must Come Across," "Young Man Come Along" and "Your Money Creates 'Appiness." Dr. Pickerbaugh made nineteen addresses in three days, comparing the Y.M.C.A. to the Crusaders, the Apostles, and the expeditions of Dr. Cook — who, he believed, really had discovered the North Pole. Orchid sold three hundred and nineteen Y. tags, seven of them to the same man, who afterward made improper remarks to her. She was rescued by a Y.M.C.A. secretary, who for a considerable time held her hand to calm her.

No organization could rival Almus Pickerbaugh in the invention of Weeks.

He started in January with a Better Babies Week, and a very good Week it was, but so hotly followed by Banish the Booze Week, Tougher Teeth Week, and Stop the Spitter Week that people who lacked his vigor were heard groaning, "My health is being ruined by all this fretting over health."

During Clean-up Week, Pickerbaugh spread abroad a new lyric of his own composition:

*Germs come by stealth*
*And ruin health,*
*So listen, pard,*
*Just drop a card*
*To some man who'll clean up your yard*
*And that will hit the old germs hard.*

Swat the Fly Week brought him, besides the joy of giving prizes to the children who had slaughtered the most flies, the inspiration for two verses. Posters admonished:

*Sell your hammer and buy a horn,*
*But hang onto the old fly-swatter.*

*If you don't want disease sneaking into the Home*
*Then to kill the fly you gotter!*

It chanced that the Fraternal Order of Eagles were holding a state convention at Burlington that week, and Pickerbaugh telegraphed to them:

*Just mention fly-prevention*
*At the good old Eagles' convention.*

This was quoted in ninety-six newspapers, including one in Alaska, and waving the clippings Pickerbaugh explained to Martin, "Now you see the way a fellow can get the truth across, if he goes at it right."

Three Cigars a Day Week, which Pickerbaugh invented in midsummer, was not altogether successful, partly because an injudicious humorist on a local newspaper wanted to know whether Dr. Pickerbaugh really expected all babes in arms to smoke as many as three cigars a day, and partly because the cigar-manufacturers came around to the Department of Health with strong remarks about Common Sense. Nor was there thorough satisfaction in Can the Cat and Doctor the Dog Week.

With all his Weeks, Pickerbaugh had time to preside over the Program Committee of the State Convention of Health Officers and Agencies.

It was he who wrote the circular letter sent to all members:

*Brother Males and Shemales* :

*Are you coming to the Health Bee? It will be the livest Hop-to-it that this busy lil ole planet has ever see. And it's going to be Practical. We'll kiss out on all these glittering generalities and get messages from men as kin talk, so we can lug a think or two (2) home wid us.*

*Luther Botts, the famous community-sing leader, will be there to put Wim an Wigor neverything into the program. John F. Zeisser, M.A., M.D., nall the rest of the alphabet (part your hair Jack and look cute, the ladies will love you) will unlimber a coupla keynotes. (On your tootsies, fellers, thar she blows!) From time to time, if the brakes hold, we will, or shall in the infinitive, hie oursellufs from wherein we are at to thither, and grab a lunch with Wild Wittles.*

*Do it sound like a good show? It do! Barber, you're next. Let's have those cards saying you're coming.*

This created much enthusiasm and merriment. Dr. Feesons of Clinton wrote to Pickerbaugh:

*I figure it was largely due to your snappy come-on letter that we pulled such an attendance and with all modesty I think we may say it was the best health convention ever held in the world. I had to laugh at one old hen, Bostonian or somepun, who was howling that your letter was "undignified"! Can you beat it! I think people as hypercritical and lacking in humor as her should be treated with the dignified contempt they deserve, the damn fool!*

## II

Martin was enthusiastic during Better Babies Week. Leora and he weighed babies, examined them, made out diet charts, and in each child saw the baby they could never have. But when it came to More Babies Week, then he was argumentative. He believed, he said, in birth-control. Pickerbaugh answered with theology, violence, and the example of his own eight beauties.

Martin was equally unconvinced by Anti-Tuberculosis Week. He liked his windows open at night and he disliked men who spat tobacco juice on sidewalks, but he was jarred by hearing these certainly esthetic and possibly hygienic reforms proposed with holy frenzy and bogus statistics.

Any questioning of his fluent figures about tuberculosis, any hint that the cause of decline in the disease may have been natural growth of immunity and not the crusades against spitting and stale air, Pickerbaugh regarded as a criticism of his honesty in making such crusades. He had the personal touchiness of most propagandists; he believed that because he was sincere, therefore his opinions must always be correct. To demand that he be accurate in his statements, to quote Raymond Pearl's dictum: "As a matter of objective scientific fact, extremely little is known about why the mortality from tuberculosis has declined" — this was to be a scoundrel who really liked to befoul the pavements.

Martin was so alienated that he took an anti-social and probably vicious joy in discovering that though the death-rate in tuberculosis certainly had decreased during Pickerbaugh's administration in Nautilus, it had decreased at the same rate in most villages of the district, with no speeches about spitting, no Open Your Windows parades.

It was fortunate for Martin that Pickerbaugh did not expect him to take much share in his publicity campaigns, but rather to be his substitute in the office during them. They stirred in Martin the most furious and complicated thoughts that had ever afflicted him.

Whenever he hinted criticism, Pickerbaugh answered, "What if my statistics aren't always exact? What if my advertising, my jollying of the public, does strike some folks as vulgar? It all does good; it's all on the right side. No matter what methods we use, if we can get people to have more fresh air and cleaner yards and less alcohol, we're justified."

To himself, a little surprised, Martin put it, "Yes, does it really matter? Does truth matter — clean, cold, unfriendly truth, Max Gottlieb's truth? Everybody says, 'Oh, you mustn't tamper with the truth,' and everybody is furious if you hint that they themselves are tampering with it. Does anything matter, except making love and sleeping and eating and being flattered?

"I think truth does matter to me, but if it does, isn't the desire for scientific precision simply my hobby, like another man's excitement about his golf? Anyway, I'm going to stick by Pickerbaugh."

To the defense of his chief he was the more impelled by the attitude of Irving Watters and such other physicians as attacked Pickerbaugh because they feared that he really would be successful, and reduce their earnings. But all the while Martin was weary of unchecked statistics.

He estimated that according to Pickerbaugh's figures on bad teeth, careless motoring, tuberculosis, and seven other afflictions alone, every person in the city had a one hundred and eighty per cent chance of dying before the age of sixteen and he could not startle with much alarm when Pickerbaugh shouted, "Do you realize that the number of people who died from yaws in Pickens County, Mississippi, last year alone, was twenty-nine and that they might all have been saved, yes, sir, *saved* , by a daily cold shower?"

For Pickerbaugh had the dreadful habit of cold showers, even in winter, though he might have known that nineteen men between the ages of seventeen and forty-two died of cold showers in twenty-two years in Milwaukee alone.

To Pickerbaugh the existence of "variables," a word which Martin now used as irritatingly as once he had used "control," was without significance. That health might be determined by temperature, heredity, profession, soil, natural immunity, or by anything save health-department campaigns for increased washing and morality, was to him inconceivable.

"Variables! Huh!" Pickerbaugh snorted. "Why, every enlightened man in the public service *knows* enough about the causes of disease — matter now of acting on that knowledge."

When Martin sought to show that they certainly knew very little about the superiority of fresh air to warmth in schools, about the hygienic dangers of dirty streets, about the real danger of alcohol, about the value of face-masks in influenza epidemics, about most of the things they tub-thumped in their campaigns, Pickerbaugh merely became angry, and Martin wanted to resign, and saw Irving Watters again, and returned to Pickerbaugh with new zeal, and was in general as agitated and wretched as a young revolutionist discovering the smugness of his leaders.

He came to question what Pickerbaugh called "the proven practical value" of his campaigns as much as the accuracy of Pickerbaugh's biology. He noted how bored were most of the newspapermen by being galvanized into a new saving of the world once a fortnight, and how incomparably bored was the Man in the Street when the nineteenth pretty girl in twenty days had surged up demanding that he buy a tag to support an association of which he had never heard.

But more dismaying was the slimy trail of the dollar which he beheld in Pickerbaugh's most ardent eloquence.

When Martin suggested that all milk should be pasteurized, that certain tenements known to be tuberculosis-breeders should be burnt down instead of being fumigated in a fiddling useless way, when he hinted that these attacks would save more lives than ten thousand sermons and ten years of parades by little girls carrying banners and being soaked by the rain, then Pickerbaugh worried, "No, no, Martin, don't think we could do that. Get so much opposition from the dairymen and the landlords. Can't accomplish anything in this work unless you keep from offending people."

When Pickerbaugh addressed a church or the home circle he spoke of "the value of health in making life more joyful," but when he addressed a business luncheon he changed it to "the value in good round dollars and cents of having workmen who are healthy and sober, and therefore able to work faster at the same wages." Parents' associations he enlightened upon "the saving in doctors' bills of treating the child before maladjustments go too far," but to physicians he gave assurance that public health agitation would merely make the custom of going regularly to doctors more popular.

To Martin, he spoke of Pasteur, George Washington, Victor Vaughan, and Edison as his masters, but in asking the business men of Nautilus — the Rotary Club, the Chamber of Commerce, the association of wholesalers — for their divine approval of more funds for his department, he made it clear that they were his masters and lords of all the land, and fatly, behind cigars, they accepted their kinghood.

Gradually Martin's contemplation moved beyond Almus Pickerbaugh to all leaders, of armies or empires, of universities or churches, and he saw that most of them were Pickerbaughs. He preached to himself, as Max Gottlieb had once preached to him, the loyalty of dissent, the faith of being very doubtful, the gospel of not bawling gospels, the wisdom of admitting the probable ignorance of one's self and of everybody else, and the energetic acceleration of a Movement for going very slow.

## III

A hundred interruptions took Martin out of his laboratory. He was summoned into the reception-room of the department to explain to angry citizens why the garage next door to them should smell of gasoline; he went back to his cubbyhole to dictate letters to school-principals about dental clinics; he drove out to Swede Hollow to see what attention the food and dairy inspector had given to the slaughter-houses; he ordered a family in Shantytown quarantined; and escaped at last into the laboratory.

It was well lighted, convenient, well stocked. Martin had little time for anything but cultures, blood-tests, and Wassermanns for the private physicians of the city, but the work rested him, and now and then he struggled over a precipitation test which was going to replace Wassermanns and make him famous.

Pickerbaugh apparently believed that this research would take six weeks; Martin had hoped to do it in two years; and with the present interruptions it would require two hundred, by which time the Pickerbaughs would have eradicated syphilis and made the test useless.

To Martin's duties was added the entertainment of Leora in the strange city of Nautilus.

"Do you manage to keep busy all day?" he encouraged her, and, "Any place you'd like to go this evening?"

She looked at him suspiciously. She was as easily and automatically contented by herself as a pussy cat, and he had never before worried about her amusement.

## IV

The Pickerbaugh daughters were always popping into Martin's laboratory. The twins broke test-tubes, and made doll tents out of filter paper. Orchid lettered the special posters for her father's Weeks, and the laboratory, she said, was the quietest place in which to work. While Martin stood at his bench he was conscious of her, humming at a table in the corner. They talked, tremendously, and he listened with fatuous enthusiasm to opinions which, had Leora produced them, he would have greeted with "That's a damn' silly remark!"

He held a clear, claret-red tube of hemolyzed blood up to the light, thinking half of its color and half of Orchid's ankles as she bent over the table, absurdly patient with her paintbrushes, curling her legs in a fantastic knot.

Absurdly he asked her, "Look here, honey. Suppose you — suppose a kid like you were to fall in love with a married man. What d'you think she ought to do? Be nice to him? Or chuck him?"

"Oh, she ought to chuck him. No matter how much she suffered. Even if she liked him terribly. Because even if she liked him, she oughtn't to wrong his wife."

"But suppose the wife never knew, or maybe didn't care?" He had stopped his pretense of working; he was standing before her, arms akimbo, dark eyes demanding.

"Well, if she didn't know — But it isn't that. I believe marriages really and truly are made in Heaven, don't you? Some day Prince Charming will come, the perfect lover — " She was so young, her lips were so young, so very sweet! " — and of course I want to keep myself for him. It would spoil everything if I made light of love before my Hero came."

But her smile was caressing.

He pictured them thrown together in a lonely camp. He saw her parroted moralities forgotten. He went through a change as definite as religious conversion or the coming of insane frenzy in war; the change from shamed reluctance to be unfaithful to his wife, to a determination to take what he could get. He began to resent Leora's demand that she, who had eternally his deepest love, should also demand his every wandering fancy. And she did demand it. She rarely spoke of Orchid, but she could tell (or nervously he thought she could tell) when he had spent an afternoon with the child. Her mute examination of him made him feel illicit. He who had never been unctuous was profuse and hearty as he urged her, "Been home all day? Well, we'll just skip out after dinner and take in a movie. Or shall we call up somebody and go see 'em? Whatever you'd like."

He heard his voice being flowery, and he hated it and knew that Leora was not cajoled. Whenever he drifted into one of his meditations on the superiority of his brand of truth to Pickerbaugh's, he snarled, "You're a fine bird to think about truth, you liar!"

He paid, in fact, an enormous price for looking at Orchid's lips, and no amount of anxiety about the price kept him from looking at them.

In early summer, two months before the outbreak of the Great War in Europe, Leora went to Wheatsylvania for a fortnight with her family. Then she spoke:

"Sandy, I'm not going to ask you any questions when I come back, but I hope you won't look as foolish as you've been looking lately. I don't think that bachelor's button, that ragweed, that lady idiot of yours is worth our quarreling. Sandy darling, I do want you to be happy, but unless I up and die on you some day, I'm not going to be hung up like an old cap. I warn you. Now about ice. I've left an order for a hundred pounds a week, and if you want to get your own dinners sometimes — "

When she had gone, nothing immediately happened, though a good deal was always about to happen. Orchid had the flapper's curiosity as to what a man was likely to do, but she was satisfied by exceedingly small thrills.

Martin swore, that morning of June, that she was a fool and a flirt, and he "hadn't the slightest intention of going near her." No! He would call on Irving Watters in the evening, or read, or have a walk with the school-clinic dentist.

But at half-past eight he was loitering toward her house.

If the elder Pickerbaughs were there — Martin could hear himself saying, "Thought I'd just drop by, Doctor, and ask you what you thought about — " Hang it! Thought about what? Pickerbaugh never thought about anything.

On the low front steps he could see Orchid. Leaning over her was a boy of twenty, one Charley, a clerk.

"Hello, Father in?" he cried, with a carelessness on which he could but pride himself.

"I'm terribly sorry; he and Mama won't be back till eleven. Won't you sit down and cool off a little?"

"Well — " He did sit down, firmly, and tried to make youthful conversation, while Charley produced sentiments suitable, in Charley's opinion, to the aged Dr. Arrowsmith, and Orchid made little purry interested sounds, an art in which she was very intelligent.

"Been, uh, been seeing many of the baseball games?" said Martin.

"Oh, been getting in all I can," said Charley. "How's things going at City Hall? Been nailing a lot of cases of small-pox and winkulus pinkulus and all those fancy diseases?"

"Oh, keep busy," grunted old Dr. Arrowsmith.

He could think of nothing else. He listened while Charley and Orchid giggled cryptically about things which barred him out and made him feel a hundred years old: references to Mamie and Earl, and a violent "Yeh, that's all right, but any time you see me dancing with her you just tell me about it, will yuh!" At the corner, Verbena Pickerbaugh was yelping, and observing, "Now you quit!" to persons unknown.

"Hell! It isn't worth it! I'm going home," Martin sighed, but at the moment Charley screamed, "Well, ta, ta, be good; gotta toddle along."

He was left to Orchid and peace and a silence rather embarrassing.

"It's so nice to be with somebody that has brains and doesn't always try to flirt, like Charley," said Orchid.

He considered, "Splendid! She's going to be just a nice good girl. And I've come to my senses. We'll just have a little chat and I'll go home."

She seemed to have moved nearer. She whispered at him, "I was so lonely, especially with that horrid slangy boy, till I heard your step on the walk. I knew it the second I heard it."

He patted her hand. As his pats were becoming more ardent than might have been expected from the assistant and friend of her father, she withdrew her hand, clasped her knees, and began to chatter.

Always it had been so in the evenings when he had drifted to the porch and found her alone. She was ten times more incalculable than the most complex woman. He managed to feel guilty toward Leora without any of the reputed joys of being guilty.

While she talked he tried to discover whether she had any brains whatever. Apparently she did not have enough to attend a small Midwestern denominational college. Verbena was going to college this autumn, but Orchid, she explained, thought she "ought to stay home and help Mama take care of the chickabiddies."

"Meaning," Martin reflected, "that she can't even pass the Mugford entrance exams!" But his opinion of her intelligence was suddenly enlarged as she whimpered, "Poor little me, prob'ly I'll always stay here in Nautilus, while you — oh, with your knowledge and your frightfully strong will-power, I know you're going to conquer the world!"

"Nonsense, I'll never conquer any world, but I do hope to pull off a few good health measures. Honestly, Orchid honey, do you think I have much will-power?"

The full moon was spacious now behind the maples. The seedy Pickerbaugh domain was enchanted; the tangled grass was a garden of roses, the ragged grape-arbor a shrine to Diana, the old hammock turned to fringed cloth of silver, the bad-tempered and sputtering lawn-sprinkler a fountain, and over all the world was the proper witchery of moonstruck love. The little city, by day as noisy and busy as a pack of children, was stilled and forgotten. Rarely had Martin been inspired to perceive the magic of a perfect hour, so absorbed was he ever in irascible pondering, but now he was caught, and lifted in rapture.

He held Orchid's quiet hand — and was lonely for Leora.

The belligerent Martin who had carried off Leora had not thought about romance, because in his clumsy way he had been romantic. The Martin who, like a returned warrior scented and enfeebled, yearned toward a girl in the moonlight, now desirously lifted his face to romance and was altogether unromantic.

He felt the duty of making love. He drew her close, but when she sighed, "Oh, please don't," there was in him no ruthlessness and no conviction with which to go on. He considered the moonlight again, but also he considered being at the office early in the morning, and he wondered if he could without detection slip out his watch and see what time it was. He managed it. He stooped to kiss her good-night, and somehow didn't quite kiss her, and found himself walking home.

As he went, he was ruthless and convinced enough regarding himself. He had never, he raged, however stumbling he might have been, expected to find himself a little pilferer of love, a peeping, creeping area-sneak, and not even successful in his sneaking, less successful than the soda-clerks who swanked nightly with the virgins under the maples. He told himself that Orchid was a young woman of no great wisdom, a signer and drawer-out of her M's and O's, but once he was in his lonely flat he longed for her, thought of miraculous and completely idiotic ways of luring her here tonight, and went to bed yearning, "Oh, Orchid — "

Perhaps he had paid too much attention to moonlight and soft summer, for quite suddenly, one day when Orchid came swarming all over the laboratory and perched on the bench with a whisk of stockings, he stalked to her, masterfully seized her wrists, and kissed her as she deserved to be kissed.

He immediately ceased to be masterful. He was frightened. He stared at her wanly. She stared back, shocked, eyes wide, lips uncertain.

"Oh!" she profoundly said.

Then, in a tone of immense interest and some satisfaction:

"Martin — oh — my dear — do you think you ought to have done that?"

He kissed her again. She yielded and for a moment there was nothing in the universe, neither he nor she, neither laboratory nor fathers nor wives nor traditions, but only the intensity of their being together.

Suddenly she babbled, "I know there's lots of conventional people that would say we'd done wrong, and perhaps I'd have thought so, one time, but — Oh, I'm terribly glad I'm liberal! Of course I wouldn't hurt dear Leora or do anything *really* wrong for the world, but isn't it wonderful that with so many bourgeois folks all around, we can rise above them and realize the call that strength makes to strength and — But I've simply *got* to be at the Y.W.C.A. meeting. There's a woman lawyer from New York that's going to tell us about the Modern Woman's Career."

When she had gone Martin viewed himself as a successful lover. "I've won her," he gloated.... Probably never has gloating been so shakily and badly done.

That evening, when he was playing poker in his flat with Irving Watters, the school-clinic dentist, and a young doctor from the city clinic, the telephone bell summoned him to an excited but saccharine:

"This is Orchid. Are you glad I called up?"

"Oh, yes, yes, mighty glad you called up." He tried to make it at once amorously joyful, and impersonal enough to beguile the three coatless, beer-swizzling, grinning doctors.

"Are you doing anything this evening, Marty?"

"Just, uh, couple fellows here for a little game cards."

"Oh!" It was acute. "Oh, then you — I was such a baby to call you up, but Daddy is away and Verbena and everybody, and it was such a lovely evening, and I just thought — *Do* you think I'm an awful little silly?"

"No — no — sure not."

"I'm so glad you don't. I'd hate it if I thought you thought I was just a silly to call you up. You don't, do you?"

"No — no — course not. Look, I've got to — "

"I know. I mustn't keep you. But I just wanted you to tell me whether you thought I was a silly to — "

"No! Honest! Really!"

Three fidgety minutes later, deplorably aware of masculine snickers from behind him, he escaped. The poker-players said all the things considered suitable in Nautilus: "Oh, you little Don Jewen!" and "Can you beat it — his wife only gone for a week!" and "Who is she, Doctor? Go on, you tightwad, bring her up here!" and "Say, I know who it is; it's that little milliner on Prairie Avenue."

Next noon she telephoned from a drug store that she had lain awake all night, and on profound contemplation decided that they "musn't ever do that sort of thing again" — and would he meet her at the corner of Crimmins Street and Missouri Avenue at eight, so that they might talk it all over?

In the afternoon she telephoned and changed the tryst to half-past eight.

At five she called up just to remind him —

In the laboratory that day Martin transplanted cultures no more. He was too confusedly human to be a satisfactory experimenter, too coldly thinking to be a satisfactory sinful male, and all the while he longed for the sure solace of Leora.

"I can go as far as I like with her tonight.

"But she's a brainless man-chaser.

"All the better. I'm tired of being a punk philosopher.

"I wonder if these other lucky lovers that you read about in all this fiction and poetry feel as glum as I do?

"I will *not* be middle-aged and cautious and monogamic and moral! It's against my religion. I demand the right to be free —

"Hell! These free souls that have to slave at being free are just as bad as their Methodist dads. I have enough sound natural immorality in me so I can afford to be moral. I want to keep my brain clear for work. I don't want it blurred by dutifully running around trying to kiss everybody I can.

"Orchid is too easy. I hate to give up the right of being a happy sinner, but my way was so straight, with just Leora and my work, and I'm not going to mess it. God help any man that likes his work and his wife! He's beaten from the beginning."

He met Orchid at eight-thirty, and the whole matter was unkind. He was equally distasteful of the gallant Martin of two days ago and the prosy cautious Martin of tonight. He went home desolately ascetic, and longed for Orchid all the night.

A week later Leora returned from Wheatsylvania.

He met her at the station.

"It's all right," he said. "I feel a hundred and seven years old. I'm a respectable, moral young man, and Lord how I'd hate it, if it wasn't for my precipitation test and you and — *Why* do you always lose your trunk check? I suppose I am a bad example for others, giving up so easily. No, no, darling, can't you *see*, that's the transportation check the conductor gave you!"

## Chapter 22

This summer Pickerbaugh had shouted and hand-shaken his way through a brief Chautauqua tour in Iowa, Nebraska, and Kansas. Martin realized that though he seemed, in contrast to Gustaf Sondelius, an unfortunately articulate and generous lout, he was destined to be ten times better known in America than Sondelius could ever be, a thousand times better known than Max Gottlieb.

He was a correspondent of many of the nickel-plated Great Men whose pictures and sonorous aphorisms appeared in the magazines: the advertising men who wrote little books about Pep and Optimism, the editor of the magazine which told clerks how to become Goethes and Stonewall Jacksons by studying correspondence-courses and never touching the manhood-rotting beer, and the cornfield sage who was equally an authority on finance, peace, biology, editing, Peruvian ethnology, and making oratory pay. These intellectual rulers recognized Pickerbaugh as one of them; they wrote quippish letters to him: and when he answered he signed himself "Pick," in red pencil.

The *Onward March Magazine* , which specialized in biographies of Men Who Have Made Good, had an account of Pickerbaugh among its sketches of the pastor who built his own beautiful Neo-Gothic church out of tin cans, the lady who had in seven years kept 2,698 factory-girls from leading lives of shame, and the Oregon cobbler who had taught himself to read Sanskrit, Finnish, and Esperanto.

"Meet Ol' Doc Almus Pickerbaugh, a he-man whom Chum Frink has hailed as 'the two-fisted, fighting poet doc,' a scientist who puts his remarkable discoveries right over third base, yet who, as a regular old-fashioned Sunday-school superintendent, rebukes the atheistic so-called scientists that are menacing the foundations of our religion and liberties by their smart-aleck cracks at everything that is noble and improving," chanted the chronicler.

Martin was reading this article, trying to realize that it was actually exposed in a fabulous New York magazine, with a million circulation, when Pickerbaugh summoned him.

"Mart," he said, "do you feel competent to run this Department?"

"Why, uh — "

"Do you think you can buck the Interests and keep a clean city all by yourself?"

"Why, uh — "

"Because it looks as if I were going to Washington, as the next congressman from this district!"

"Really?"

"Looks that way. Boy, I'm going to take to the whole nation the Message I've tried to ram home here!"

Martin got out quite a good "I congratulate you." He was so astonished that it sounded fervent. He still had a fragment of his boyhood belief that congressmen were persons of intelligence and importance.

"I've just been in conference with some of the leading Republicans of the district. Great surprise to me. Ha, ha, ha! Maybe they picked me because they haven't anybody else to run this year. Ha, ha, ha!"

Martin also laughed. Pickerbaugh looked as though that was not exactly the right response, but he recovered and caroled on:

"I said to them, 'Gentlemen, I must warn you that I am not sure I possess the rare qualifications needful in a man who shall have the high privilege of laying down, at Washington, the rules and regulations for the guidance, in every walk of life, of this great nation of a hundred million people. However, gentlemen,' I said, 'the impulse that prompts me to consider, in all modesty, your unexpected and probably undeserved honor is the fact that it seems to me that what Congress needs is more forward-looking scientists to plan and more genu-ine trained business men to execute the improvements demanded by our evolving commonwealth, and also the possibility of persuading the Boys there at Washington of the pre-eminent and crying need of a Secretary of Health who shall completely control —'"

But no matter what Martin thought about it, the Republicans really did nominate Pickerbaugh for Congress.

## II

While Pickerbaugh went out campaigning, Martin was in charge of the Department, and he began his reign by getting himself denounced as a tyrant and a radical.

There was no more sanitary and efficient dairy in Iowa than that of old Klopchuk, on the outskirts of Nautilus. It was tiled and drained and excellently lighted; the milking machines were perfect; the bottles were super-boiled; and Klopchuk welcomed inspectors and the tuberculin test. He had fought the dairymen's union and kept his dairy open-shop by paying more than the union scale. Once, when Martin attended a meeting of the Nautilus Central Labor Council as Pickerbaugh's representative, the secretary of the council confessed that there was no plant which they would so like to unionize and which they were so unlikely to unionize as Klopchuk's Dairy.

Now Martin's labor sympathies were small. Like most laboratory men, he believed that the reason why workmen found less joy in sewing vests or in pulling a lever than he did in a long research was because they were an inferior race, born lazy and wicked. The complaint of the unions was the one thing to convince him that at last he had found perfection.

Often he stopped at Klopchuk's merely for the satisfaction of it. He noted but one thing which disturbed him: a milker had a persistent sore throat. He examined the man, made cultures, and found hemolytic streptococcus. In a panic he hurried back to the dairy, and after cultures he discovered that there was streptococcus in the udders of three cows.

When Pickerbaugh had saved the health of the nation through all the smaller towns in the congressional district and had returned to Nautilus, Martin insisted on the quarantine of the infected milker and the closing of the Klopchuk Dairy till no more infection should be found.

"Nonsense! Why, that's the cleanest place in the city," Pickerbaugh scoffed. "Why borrow trouble? There's no sign of an epidemic of strep."

"There darn' well will be! Three cows infected. Look at what's happened in Boston and Baltimore, here recently. I've asked Klopchuk to come in and talk it over."

"Well, you know how busy I am, but —"

Klopchuk appeared at eleven, and to Klopchuk the affair was tragic. Born in a gutter in Poland, starving in New York, working twenty hours a day in Vermont, in Ohio, in Iowa, he had made this beautiful thing, his dairy.

Seamed, drooping, twirling his hat, almost in tears, he protested, "Dr. Pickerbaugh, I do everything the doctors say is necessary. I know dairies! Now comes this young man and he says because one of my men has a cold, I kill little children with diseased milk! I tell you, this is my life, and I would sooner hang myself than send out one drop of bad milk. The young man has some wicked reason. I have asked questions. I find he is a great friend from the Central Labor Council. Why, he go to their meetings! And they want to break me!"

To Martin the trembling old man was pitiful, but he had never before been accused of treachery. He said grimly:

"You can take up the personal charges against me later, Dr. Pickerbaugh. Meantime I suggest you have in some expert to test my results; say Long of Chicago or Brent of Minneapolis or somebody."

"I — I — I —" The Kipling and Billy Sunday of health looked as distressed as Klopchuk. "I'm sure our friend here doesn't really mean to make charges against you, Mart. He's overwrought, naturally. Can't we just treat the fellow that has the strep infection and not make everybody uncomfortable?"

"All right, if you want a bad epidemic here, toward the end of your campaign!"

"You know cussed well I'd do anything to avoid — Though I want you to distinctly understand it has nothing to do with my campaign for Congress! It's simply that I owe my city the most scrupulous performance of duty in safeguarding it against disease, and the most fearless enforcement — "

At the end of his oratory Pickerbaugh telegraphed to Dr. J. C. Long, the Chicago bacteriologist.

Dr. Long looked as though he had made the train journey in an ice-box. Martin had never seen a man so free from the poetry and flowing philanthropy of Almus Pickerbaugh. He was slim, precise, lipless, lapless, and eye-glassed, and his hair was parted in the middle. He coolly listened to Martin, coldly listened to Pickerbaugh, icily heard Klopchuk, made his inspection, and reported, "Dr. Arrowsmith seems to know his business perfectly, there is certainly a danger here, I advise closing the dairy, my fee is one hundred dollars, thank you no I shall not stay to dinner I must catch the evening train."

Martin went home to Leora snarling, "That man was just as lovable as a cucumber salad, but my God, Lee, with his freedom from bunk he's made me wild to get back to research; away from all these humanitarians that are so busy hollering about loving the dear people that they let the people die! I hated him, but — Wonder what Max Gottlieb's doing this evening? The old German crank! I'll bet — I'll bet he's talking music or something with some terrible highbrow bunch. Wouldn't you like to see the old coot again? You know, just couple minutes. D'I ever tell you about the time I made the dandy stain of the trypanosomes — Oh, did I?"

He assumed that with the temporary closing of the dairy the matter was ended. He did not understand how hurt was Klopchuk. He knew that Irving Watters, Klopchuk's physician, was unpleasant when they met, grumbling, "What's the use going on being an alarmist, Mart?" But he did not know how many persons in Nautilus had been trustily informed that this fellow Arrowsmith was in the pay of labor-union thugs.

### III

Two months before, when Martin had been making his annual inspection of factories, he had encountered Clay Tredgold, the president (by inheritance) of the Steel Windmill Company. He had heard that Tredgold, an elaborate but easy-spoken man of forty-five, moved as one clad in purple on the loftiest planes of Nautilus society. After the inspection Tredgold urged, "Sit down, Doctor; have a cigar and tell me all about sanitation."

Martin was wary. There was in Tredgold's affable eye a sardonic flicker.

"What d'you want to know about sanitation?"

"Oh, all about it."

"The only thing I know is that your men must like you. Of course you haven't enough wash-bowls in that second-floor toilet room, and the whole lot of 'em swore you were putting in others immediately. If they like you enough to lie against their own interests, you must be a good boss, and I think I'll let you get away with it — till my next inspection! Well, got to hustle."

Tredgold beamed on him. "My dear man, I've been pulling that dodge on Pickerbaugh for three years. I'm glad to have seen you. And I think I really may put in some more bowls — just before your next inspection. Good-by!"

After the Klopchuk affair, Martin and Leora encountered Clay Tredgold and that gorgeous slim woman, his wife, in front of a motion-picture theater.

"Give you a lift, Doctor?" cried Tredgold.

On the way he suggested, "I don't know whether you're dry, like Pickerbaugh, but if you'd like I'll run you out to the house and present you with the noblest cocktail conceived since Evangeline County went dry. Does it sound reasonable?"

"I haven't heard anything so reasonable for years," said Martin.

The Tredgold house was on the highest knoll (fully twenty feet above the general level of the plain) in Ashford Grove, which is the Back Bay of Nautilus. It was a Colonial structure, with a sun-parlor, a white-paneled hall, and a blue and silver drawing-room. Martin tried to look casual as they were wafted in on Mrs. Tredgold's chatter, but it was the handsomest house he had ever entered.

While Leora sat on the edge of her chair in the manner of one likely to be sent home, and Mrs. Tredgold sat forward like a hostess, Tredgold flourished the cocktail-shaker and performed courtesies:

"How long you been here now, Doctor?"

"Almost a year."

"Try that. Look here, it strikes me you're kind of different from Salvation Pickerbaugh."

Martin felt that he ought to praise his chief but, to Leora's gratified amazement, he sprang up and ranted in something like Pickerbaugh's best manner:

"Gentlemen of the Steel Windmill Industries, than which there is no other that has so largely contributed to the prosperity of our commonwealth, while I realize that you are getting away with every infraction of the health laws that the inspector doesn't catch you at, yet I desire to pay a tribute to your high respect for sanitation, patriotism, and cocktails, and if I only had an assistant more earnest than young Arrowsmith, I should, with your permission, become President of the United States."

Tredgold clapped. Mrs. Tredgold asserted, "If that isn't exactly like Dr. Pickerbaugh!" Leora looked proud, and so did her husband.

"I'm so glad you're free from this socialistic clap-trap of Pickerbaugh's," said Tredgold.

The assumption roused something sturdy and defensive in Martin:

"Oh, I don't care a hang how socialistic he is — whatever that means. Don't know anything about socialism. But since I've gone and given an imitation of him — I suppose it was probably disloyal — I must say I'm not very fond of oratory that's so full of energy it hasn't any room for facts. But mind you, Tredgold, it's partly the fault of people like your Manufacturers' Association. You encourage him to rant. I'm a laboratory man — or rather, I sometimes wish I were. I like to deal with exact figures."

"So do I. I was keen on mathematics in Williams," said Tredgold.

Instantly Martin and he were off on education, damning the universities for turning out graduates like sausages. Martin found himself becoming confidential about "variables," and Tredgold proclaimed that he had not wanted to take up the ancestral factory, but to specialize in astronomy.

Leora was confessing to the friendly Mrs. Tredgold how cautiously the wife of an assistant director has to economize and with that caressing voice of hers Mrs. Tredgold comforted, "I know. I was horribly hard-up after Dad died. Have you tried the little Swedish dressmaker on Crimmins Street, two doors from the Catholic church? She's awfully clever, and so cheap."

Martin had found, for the first time since marriage, a house in which he was altogether happy; Leora had found, in a woman with the easy smartness which she had always feared and hated, the first woman to whom she could talk of God and the price of toweling. They came out from themselves and were not laughed at.

It was at midnight, when the charms of bacteriology and toweling were becoming pallid, that outside the house sounded a whooping, wheezing motor horn, and in lumbered a ruddy fat man who was introduced as Mr. Schlemihl, president of the Cornbelt Insurance Company of Nautilus.

Even more than Clay Tredgold was he a leader of the Ashford Grove aristocracy, but, while he stood like an invading barbarian in the blue and silver room, Schlemihl was cordial:

"Glad meet yuh, Doctor. Well, say, Clay, I'm tickled to death you've found another highbrow to gas with. Me, Arrowsmith, I'm simply a poor old insurance salesman. Clay is always telling me what an illiterate boob I am. Look here, Clay darling, do I get a cocktail or don't I? I seen your lights! I seen you in here telling what a smart guy you are! Come on! *Mix!* "

Tredgold mixed, extensively. Before he had finished, young Monte Mugford, great-grandson of the sainted but side-whiskered Nathaniel Mugford who had founded Mugford College, also came in, uninvited. He wondered at the presence of Martin, found him human, told him he was human, and did his rather competent best to catch up on the cocktails.

Thus it happened that at three in the morning Martin was singing to a commendatory audience the ballad he had learned from Gustaf Sondelius:

*She'd a dark and a roving eye,*
*And her hair hung down in ringlets,*
*A nice girl, a decent girl,*
*But one of the rakish kind.*

At four, the Arrowsmiths had been accepted by the most desperately Smart Set of Nautilus, and at four-thirty they were driven home, at a speed neither legal nor kind, by Clay Tredgold.

## IV

There was in Nautilus a country club which was the axis of what they called Society, but there was also a tribe of perhaps twelve families in the Ashford Grove section who, though they went to the country club for golf, condescended to other golfers, kept to themselves, and considered themselves as belonging more to Chicago than to Nautilus. They took turns in entertaining one another. They assumed that they were all welcome at any party given by any of them, and to none of their parties was anyone outside the Group invited except migrants from larger cities and occasional free lances like Martin. They were a tight little garrison in a heathen town.

The members of the Group were very rich, and one of them, Montgomery Mugford, knew something about his great-grandfather. They lived in Tudor manor houses and Italian villas so new that the scarred lawns had only begun to grow. They had large cars and larger cellars, though the cellars contained nothing but gin, whisky, vermouth, and a few sacred bottles of rather sweet champagne. Everyone in the Group was familiar with New York — they stayed at the St. Regis or the Plaza and went about buying clothes and discovering small smart restaurants — and five of the twelve couples had been in Europe; had spent a week in Paris, intending to go to art galleries and actually going to the more expensive fool-traps of Montmartre.

In the Group Martin and Leora found themselves welcomed as poor relations. They were invited to choric dinners, to Sunday lunches at the country club. Whatever the event, it always ended in rapidly motoring somewhere, having a number of drinks, and insisting that Martin again "give that imitation of Doc Pickerbaugh."

Besides motoring, drinking, and dancing to the Victrola, the chief diversion of the Group was cards. Curiously, in this completely unmoral set, there were no flirtations; they talked with considerable freedom about "sex," but they all seemed monogamic, all happily married or afraid to appear unhappily married. But when Martin knew them better he heard murmurs of husbands having "times" in Chicago, of wives picking up young men in New York hotels, and he scented furious restlessness beneath their superior sexual calm.

It is not known whether Martin ever completely accepted as a gentleman-scholar the Clay Tredgold who was devoted to everything about astronomy except studying it, or Monte Mugford as the highly descended aristocrat, but he did admire the Group's motor cars, shower baths, Fifth Avenue frocks, tweed plus-fours, and houses somewhat impersonally decorated by daffodillic young men from Chicago. He discovered sauces and old silver. He began to consider Leora's clothes not merely as convenient coverings, but as a possible expression of charm, and irritably he realized how careless she was.

In Nautilus, alone, rarely saying much about herself, Leora had developed an intense mute little life of her own. She belonged to a bridge club, and she went solemnly by herself to the movies, but her ambition was to know France and it engrossed her. It was an old desire, mysterious in source and long held secret, but suddenly she was sighing:

"Sandy, the one thing I want to do, maybe ten years from now, is to see Touraine and Normandy and Carcassonne. Could we, do you think?"

Rarely had Leora asked for anything. He was touched and puzzled as he watched her reading books on Brittany, as he caught her, over a highly simplified French grammar, breathing "J'ay — j'aye — damn it, whatever it is!"

He crowed, "Lee, dear if you want to go to France — Listen! Some day we'll shoot over there with a couple of knapsacks on our backs, and we'll see that ole country from end to end!"

Gratefully yet doubtfully: "You know if you got bored, Sandy, you could go see the work at the Pasteur Institute. Oh, I would like to tramp, just once, between high plastered walls, and come to a foolish little café and watch the men with funny red sashes and floppy blue pants go by. Really, do you think maybe we could?"

Leora was strangely popular in the Ashford Grove Group, though she possessed nothing of what Martin called their "elegance." She always had at least one button missing. Mrs. Tredgold, best natured as she was least pious of women, adopted her complete.

Nautilus had always doubted Clara Tredgold. Mrs. Almus Pickerbaugh said that she "took no part in any movement for the betterment of the city." For years she had seemed content to grow her roses, to make her startling hats, to almond-cream her lovely hands, and listen to her husband's improper stories — and for years she had been a lonely woman. In Leora she perceived an interested casualness equal to her own. The two women spent afternoons sitting on the sun-porch, reading, doing their nails, smoking cigarettes, saying nothing, trusting each other.

With the other women of the Group Leora was never so intimate as with Clara Tredgold, but they liked her, the more because she was a heretic whose vices, her smoking, her indolence, her relish of competent profanity, disturbed Mrs. Pickerbaugh and Mrs. Irving Watters. The Group rather approved all unconventionalities — except such economic unconventionalities as threatened their easy wealth. Leora had tea, or a cocktail, alone with nervous young Mrs. Monte Mugford, who had been the lightest-footed débutante in Des Moines four years before and who hated now the coming of her second baby; and it was to Leora that Mrs. Schlemihl, though publicly she was rompish and serene with her porker of a husband, burst out, "If that man would only quit pawing me — reaching for me — slobbering on me! I hate it here! I *will* have my winter in New York — alone!"

The childish Martin Arrowsmith, so unworthy of Leora's old quiet wisdoms, was not content with her acceptance by the Group. When she appeared with a hook unfastened or her hair like a crow's nest, he worried, and said things about her "sloppiness" which he later regretted.

"Why can't you take a little time to make yourself attractive? God knows you haven't anything else to do! Great Jehoshaphat, can't you even sew on buttons?"

But Clara Tredgold laughed, "Leora, I do think you have the sweetest back, but do you mind if I pin you up before the others come?"

It happened after a party which lasted till two, when Mrs. Schlemihl had worn the new frock from Lucile's and Jack Brundidge (by day vice-president and sales-manager of the Maize Mealies Company) had danced what he belligerently asserted to be a Finnish polka, that when Martin and Leora were driving home in a borrowed Health Department car he snarled, "Lee, why can't you ever take any trouble with what you wear? Here this morning — or yesterday morning — you were going to mend that blue dress, and as far as I can figure out you haven't done a darn' thing the whole day but sit around and read, and then you come out with that ratty embroidery — "

"Will you stop the car!" she cried.

He stopped it, astonished. The headlights made ridiculously important a barbed-wire fence, a litter of milkweeds, a bleak reach of gravel road.

She demanded, "Do you want me to become a harem beauty? I could. I could be a floosey. But I've never taken the trouble. Oh, Sandy, I won't go on fighting with you. Either I'm the foolish sloppy wife that I am, or I'm nothing. What do you want? Do you want a real princess like Clara Tredgold, or do you want me, that don't care a hang where we go or what we do as long as we stand by each other? You do such a lot of worrying. I'm tired of it. Come on now. What do you want?"

"I don't want anything but you. But can't you understand — I'm not just a climber — I want us both to be equal to anything we run into. I certainly don't see why we should be inferior to this bunch, in *anything*. Darling, except for Clara, maybe, they're nothing but rich bookkeepers! But we're real soldiers of fortune. Your France that you love so much — some day we'll go there, and the French President will be at the N.P. depot to meet us! Why should we let anybody do anything better than we can? Technique!"

They talked for an hour in that drab place, between the poisonous lines of barbed wire.

Next day, when Orchid came into his laboratory and begged, with the wistfulness of youth, "Oh, Dr. Martin, aren't you ever coming to the house again?" he kissed her so briskly, so cheerfully, that even a flapper could perceive that she was unimportant.

## V

Martin realized that he was likely to be the next Director of the Department. Pickerbaugh had told him, "Your work is very satisfactory. There's only one thing you lack, my boy: enthusiasm for getting together with folks and giving a long pull and a strong pull, all together. But perhaps that'll come to you when you have more responsibility."

Martin sought to acquire a delight in giving long strong pulls all together, but he felt like a man who has been dragooned into wearing yellow tights at a civic pageant.

"Gosh, I may be up against it when I become Director," he fretted. "I wonder if there's people who become what's called 'successful' and then hate it? Well, anyway, I'll start a decent system of vital statistics in the department before they get me. I won't lay down! I'll fight! I'll make myself succeed!"

## Chapter 23

It may have been a yearning to give one concentrated dose of inspiration so powerful that no citizen of Nautilus would ever again dare to be ill, or perhaps Dr. Pickerbaugh desired a little reasonable publicity for his congressional campaign, but certainly the Health Fair which the good man organized was overpowering.

He got an extra appropriation from the Board of Aldermen; he bullied all the churches and associations into co-operation; he made the newspapers promise to publish three columns of praise each day.

He rented the rather dilapidated wooden "tabernacle" in which the Reverend Mr. Billy Sunday, an evangelist, had recently wiped out all the sin in the community. He arranged for a number of novel features. The Boy Scouts were to give daily drills. There was a W.C.T.U. booth at which celebrated clergymen and other physiologists would demonstrate the evils of alcohol. In a bacteriology booth, the protesting Martin (in a dinky white coat) was to do jolly things with test-tubes. An anti-nicotine lady from Chicago offered to kill a mouse every half-hour by injecting ground-up cigarette paper into it. The Pickerbaugh twins, Arbuta and Gladiola, now aged six, were to show the public how to brush its teeth, and in fact they did, until a sixty-year-old farmer of whom they had lovingly inquired, "Do you brush your teeth daily?" made thunderous answer, "No, but I'm going to paddle your bottoms daily, and I'm going to start in right now."

None of these novelties was so stirring as the Eugenic Family, who had volunteered to give, for a mere forty dollars a day, an example of the benefits of healthful practices.

They were father, mother, and five children, all so beautiful and powerful that they had recently been presenting refined acrobatic exhibitions on the Chautauqua Circuit. None of them smoked, drank, spit upon pavements, used foul language, or ate meat. Pickerbaugh assigned to them the chief booth on the platform once sacerdotally occupied by the Reverend Mr. Sunday.

There were routine exhibits: booths with charts and banners and leaflets. The Pickerbaugh Healthette Octette held song recitals, and daily there were lectures, most of them by Pickerbaugh or by his friend Dr. Bissex, football coach and professor of hygiene and most other subjects in Mugford College.

A dozen celebrities, including Gustaf Sondelius and the governor of the state, were invited to come and "give their messages," but it happened, unfortunately, that none of them seemed able to get away that particular week.

The Health Fair opened with crowds and success. There was a slight misunderstanding the first day. The Master Bakers' Association spoke strongly to Pickerbaugh about the sign "Too much pie makes pyorrhea" on the diet booth. But the thoughtless and prosperity-destroying sign was removed at once, and the Fair was thereafter advertised in every bakery in town.

The only unhappy participant, apparently, was Martin. Pickerbaugh had fitted up for him an exhibition laboratory which, except that it had no running water and except that the fire laws forbade his using any kind of a flame, was exactly like a real one. All day long he poured a solution of red ink from one test-tube into another, with his microscope carefully examined nothing at all, and answered the questions of persons who wished to know how you put bacterias to death once you had caught them swimming about.

Leora appeared as his assistant, very pretty and demure in a nurse's costume, very exasperating as she chuckled at his low cursing. They found one friend, the fireman on duty, a splendid person with stories about pet cats in the fire-house and no tendency to ask questions in bacteriology. It was he who showed them how they could smoke in safety. Behind the Clean Up and Prevent Fires exhibit, consisting of a miniature Dirty House with red arrows to show where a fire might start and an extremely varnished Clean House, there was an alcove with a broken window which would carry off the smoke of their cigarettes. To this sanctuary Martin, Leora, and the bored fireman retired a dozen times a day, and thus wore through the week.

One other misfortune occurred. The detective sergeant coming in not to detect but to see the charming spectacle of the mouse dying in agony from cigarette paper, stopped before the booth of the Eugenic Family, scratched his head, hastened to the police station, and returned with certain pictures. He growled to Pickerbaugh:

"Hm. That Eugenic Family. Don't smoke or booze or anything?"

"Absolutely! And look at their perfect health."

"Hm. Better keep an eye on 'em. I won't spoil your show, Doc — we fellows at City Hall had all ought to stick together. I won't run 'em out of town till after the Fair. But they're the Holton gang. The man and woman ain't married, and only one of the kids is theirs. They've done time for selling licker to the Indians, but their specialty, before they went into education, used to be the badger game. I'll detail a plain-clothes man to keep 'em straight. Fine show you got here, Doc. Ought to give this city a lasting lesson in the value of up-to-date health methods. Good luck! Say, have you picked your secretary yet, for when you get to Congress? I've got a nephew that's a crackajack stenographer and a bright kid and knows how to keep his mouth shut about stuff that don't concern him. I'll send him around to have a talk with you. So long."

But, except that once he caught the father of the Eugenic Family relieving the strain of being publicly healthy by taking a long, gurgling, ecstatic drink from a flask, Pickerbaugh found nothing wrong in their conduct, till Saturday. There was nothing wrong with anything, till then.

Never had a Fair been such a moral lesson, or secured so much publicity. Every newspaper in the congressional district gave columns to it, and all the accounts, even in the Democratic papers, mentioned Pickerbaugh's campaign.

Then, on Saturday, the last day of the Fair, came tragedy.

There was terrific rain, the roof leaked without restraint, and the lady in charge of the Healthy Housing Booth, which also leaked, was taken home threatened with pneumonia. At noon, when the Eugenic Family were giving a demonstration of perfect vigor, their youngest blossom had an epileptic fit, and before the excitement was over, upon the Chicago anti-nicotine lady as she triumphantly assassinated a mouse charged an anti-vivisection lady, also from Chicago.

Round the two ladies and the unfortunate mouse gathered a crowd. The anti-vivisection lady called the anti-nicotine lady a murderer, a wretch, and an atheist, all of which the anti-nicotine lady endured, merely weeping a little and calling for the police. But when the anti-vivisection lady wound up, "And as for your pretensions to know anything about science, you're no scientist at all!" then with a shriek the anti-nicotine lady leaped from her platform, dug her fingers into the anti-vivisection lady's hair, and observed with distinctness, "I'll show you whether I know anything about science!"

Pickerbaugh tried to separate them. Martin, standing happily with Leora and their friend the fireman on the edge, distinctly did not. Both ladies turned on Pickerbaugh and denounced him, and when they had been removed he was the center of a thousand chuckles, in decided danger of never going to Congress.

At two o'clock, when the rain had slackened, when the after-lunch crowd had come in and the story of the anti ladies was running strong, the fireman retired behind the Clean Up and Prevent Fires exhibit for his hourly smoke. He was a very sleepy and unhappy little fireman; he was thinking about the pleasant fire-house and the unending games of pinochle. He dropped the match, unextinguished, on the back porch of the model Clean House. The Clean House had been so handsomely oiled that it was like kindling soaked in kerosene. It flared up, and instantly the huge and gloomy Tabernacle was hysterical with flames. The crowd rushed toward the exits.

Naturally, most of the original exits of the Tabernacle had been blocked by booths. There was a shrieking panic, and children were being trampled.

Almus Pickerbaugh was neither a coward nor slothful. Suddenly, coming from nowhere, he was marching through the Tabernacle at the head of his eight daughters, singing "Dixie," his head up, his eyes terrible, his arms wide in pleading. The crowd weakly halted. With the voice of a clipper captain he unsnarled them and ushered them safely out, then charged back into the spouting flames.

The rain-soaked building had not caught. The fireman, with Martin and the head of the Eugenic Family, was beating the flames. Nothing was destroyed save the Clean House, and the crowd which had fled in agony came back in wonder. Their hero was Pickerbaugh.

Within two hours the Nautilus papers vomited specials which explained that not merely had Pickerbaugh organized the greatest lesson in health ever seen, but he had also, by his courage and his power to command, saved hundreds of people from being crushed, which latter was probably the only completely accurate thing that has been said about Dr. Almus Pickerbaugh in ten thousand columns of newspaper publicity.

Whether to see the Fair, Pickerbaugh, the delightful ravages of a disaster, or another fight between the anti ladies, half the city struggled into the Tabernacle that evening, and when Pickerbaugh took the platform for his closing lecture he was greeted with frenzy. Next day, when he galloped into the last week of his campaign, he was overlord of all the district.

## II

His opponent was a snuffy little lawyer whose strength lay in his training. He had been state senator, lieutenant governor, county judge. But the Democratic slogan, "Pickerbaugh the Pick-up Candidate," was drowned in the admiration for the hero of the health fair. He dashed about in motors, proclaiming, "I am not running because I want office, but because I want the chance to take to the whole nation my ideals of health." Everywhere was plastered:

*For Congress*
*PICKERBAUGH*
*The two-fisted fighting poet doc*

*Just elect him for a term*
*And all through the nation he'll swat the germ.*

Enormous meetings were held. Pickerbaugh was ample and vague about his Policies. Yes, he was opposed to our entering the European War, but he assured them, he certainly did assure them, that he was for using every power of our Government to end this terrible calamity. Yes, he was for high tariff, but it must be so adjusted that the farmers in his district could buy everything cheaply. Yes, he was for high wages for each and every workman, but he stood like a rock, like a boulder, like a moraine, for protecting the prosperity of all manufacturers, merchants, and real-estate owners.

While this larger campaign thundered, there was proceeding in Nautilus a smaller and much defter campaign, to re-elect as mayor one Mr. Pugh, Pickerbaugh's loving chief. Mr. Pugh sat nicely at desks, and he was pleasant and promissory to everybody who came to see him; clergymen, gamblers, G.A.R. veterans, circus advance-agents, policemen, and ladies of reasonable virtue — everybody except perhaps socialist agitators, against whom he staunchly protected the embattled city. In his speeches Pickerbaugh commended Pugh for "that firm integrity and ready sympathy with which His Honor had backed up every movement for the public weal," and when Pickerbaugh (quite honestly) begged, "Mr. Mayor, if I go to Congress you must appoint Arrowsmith in my place; he knows nothing about politics but he's incorruptible," then Pugh gave his promise, and amity abode in that land.... Nobody said anything at all about Mr. F. X. Jordan.

F. X. Jordan was a contractor with a generous interest in politics. Pickerbaugh called him a grafter, and the last time Pugh had been elected — it had been on a Reform Platform, though since that time the reform had been coaxed to behave itself and be practical — both Pugh and Pickerbaugh had denounced Jordan as a "malign force." But so kindly was Mayor Pugh that in the present election he said nothing that could hurt Mr. Jordan's feelings, and in return what could Mr. Jordan do but speak forgivingly about Mr. Pugh to the people in blind-pigs and houses of ill fame?

On the evening of the election, Martin and Leora were among the company awaiting the returns at the Pickerbaughs'. They were confident. Martin had never been roused by politics, but he was stirred now by Pickerbaugh's twitchy pretense of indifference, by the telephoned report from the newspaper office, "Here's Willow Grove township — Pickerbaugh leading, two to one!" by the crowds which went past the house howling, "Pickerbaugh, Pickerbaugh, Pickerbaugh!"

At eleven the victory was certain, and Martin, his bowels weak with unconfidence, realized that he was now Director of Public Health, with responsibility for seventy thousand lives.

He looked wistfully toward Leora and in her still smile found assurance.

Orchid had been airy and distant with Martin all evening, and dismayingly chatty and affectionate with Leora. Now she drew him into the back parlor and "So I'm going off to Washington — and you don't care a bit!" she said, her eyes blurred and languorous and undefended. He held her, muttering, "You darling child, I can't let you go!" As he walked home he thought less of being Director than of Orchid's eyes.

In the morning he groaned, "Doesn't anybody ever learn anything? Must I watch myself and still be a fool, all my life? Doesn't any story ever end?"

He never saw her afterward, except on the platform of the train.

Leora surprisingly reflected, after the Pickerbaughs had gone, "Sandy dear, I know how you feel about losing your Orchid. It's sort of Youth going. She really is a peach. Honestly, I can appreciate how you feel, and sympathize with you — I mean, of course, providin' you aren't ever going to see her again."

### III

Over the *Nautilus Cornfield's* announcement was the vigorous headline:

*ALMUS PICKERBAUGH WINS*
*First Scientist Ever Elected*
*to Congress*

*Side-kick of Darwin and Pasteur*
*Gives New Punch to Steering*
*Ship of State*

Pickerbaugh's resignation was to take effect at once; he was, he explained, going to Washington before his term began, to study legislative methods and start his propaganda for the creation of a national Secretaryship of Health. There was a considerable struggle over the appointment of Martin in his stead. Klopchuk the dairyman was bitter; Irving Watters whispered to fellow doctors that Martin was likely to extend the socialistic free clinics; F. X. Jordan had a sensible young doctor as his own candidate. It was the Ashford Grove Group, Tredgold, Schlemihl, Monte Mugford, who brought it off.

Martin went to Tredgold worrying, "Do the people want me? Shall I fight Jordan or get out?"

Tredgold said balmily, "Fight? What about? I own a good share of the bank that's lent various handy little sums to Mayor Pugh. You leave it to me."

Next day Martin was appointed, but only as Acting Director, with a salary of thirty-five hundred instead of four thousand.

That he had been put in by what he would have called "crooked politics" did not occur to him.

Mayor Pugh called him in and chuckled:

"Doc, there's been a certain amount of opposition to you, because you're pretty young and not many folks know you. I haven't any doubt I can give you the full appointment later — if we find you're competent and popular. Meantime you better avoid doing anything brash. Just come and ask my advice. I know this town and the people that count better than you do."

## IV

The day of Pickerbaugh's leaving for Washington was made a fiesta. At the Armory, from twelve to two, the Chamber of Commerce gave to everybody who came a lunch of hot wienies, doughnuts, and coffee, with chewing gum for the women and, for the men, Schweinhügel's Little Dandy Nautilus-made Cheroots.

The train left at three-fifty-five. The station was, to the astonishment of innocent passengers gaping from the train windows, jammed with thousands.

By the rear platform, on a perilous packing box, Mayor Pugh held forth. The Nautilus Silver Cornet Band played three patriotic selections, then Pickerbaugh stood on the platform, his family about him. As he looked on the crowd, tears were in his eyes.

"For once," he stammered, "I guess I can't make a speech. D-darn it, I'm all choked up! I meant to orate a lot, but all I can say is — I love you all, I'm mighty grateful, I'll represent you my level best, neighbors! God bless you!"

The train moved out, Pickerbaugh waving as long as he could see them.

And Martin to Leora, "Oh, he's a fine old boy. He — No, I'm hanged if he is! The world's always letting people get away with asininities because they're kind-hearted. And here I've sat back like a coward, not saying a word, and watched 'em loose that wind-storm on the whole country. Oh, curse it, isn't anything in the world simple? Well, let's go to the office, and I'll begin to do things conscientiously and all wrong."

## Chapter 24

It cannot be said that Martin showed any large ability for organization, but under him the Department of Public Health changed completely. He chose as his assistant Dr. Rufus Ockford, a lively youngster recommended by Dean Silva of Winnemac. The routine work, examination of babies, quarantines, anti-tuberculosis placarding, went on as before.

Inspection of plumbing and food was perhaps more thorough, because Martin lacked Pickerbaugh's buoyant faith in the lay inspectors, and one of them he replaced, to the considerable displeasure of the colony of Germans in the Homedale district. Also he gave thought to the killing of rats and fleas, and he regarded the vital statistics as something more than a recording of births and deaths. He had notions about their value which were most amusing to the health department clerk. He wanted a record of the effect of race, occupation, and a dozen other factors upon the disease rate.

The chief difference was that Martin and Rufus Ockford found themselves with plenty of leisure. Martin estimated that Pickerbaugh must have used half his time in being inspirational and eloquent.

He made his first mistake in assigning Ockford to spend part of the week in the free city clinic, in addition to the two half-time physicians. There was fury in the Evangeline County Medical Society. At a restaurant, Irving Watters came over to Martin's table.

"I hear you've increased the clinic staff," said Dr. Watters.

"Yuh."

"Thinking of increasing it still more?"

"Might be a good idea."

"Now you see here, Mart. As you know, Mrs. Watters and I have done everything in our power to make you and Leora welcome. Glad to do anything I can for a fellow alumnus of old Winnemac. But at the same time, there are limits, you know! Not that I've got any objection to your providing free clinical facilities. Don't know but what it's a good thing to treat the damn', lazy, lousy pauper-class free, and keep the D.B.'s off the books of the regular physicians. But same *time*, when you begin to make a practice of encouraging a lot of folks, that can afford to pay, to go and get free treatment, and practically you attack the integrity of the physicians of this city, that have been giving God knows how much of their time to charity — "

Martin answered neither wisely nor competently: "Irve, sweetheart, you can go straight to hell!"

After that hour, when they met there was nothing said between them.

Without disturbing his routine work, he found himself able to sink blissfully into the laboratory. At first he merely tinkered, but suddenly he was in full cry, oblivious of everything save his experiment.

He was playing with cultures isolated from various dairies and various people, thinking mostly of Klopchuk and streptococcus. Accidentally he discovered the lavish production of hemolysin in sheep's blood as compared with the blood of other animals. Why should streptococcus dissolve the red blood corpuscles of sheep more easily than those of rabbits?

It is true that a busy health-department bacteriologist has no right to waste the public time in being curious, but the irresponsible sniffing beagle in Martin drove out the faithful routineer.

He neglected the examination of an ominously increasing number of tubercular sputums; he set out to answer the question of the hemolysin. He wanted the streptococcus to produce its blood-destroying poison in twenty-four-hour cultures.

He beautifully and excitedly failed, and sat for hours meditating. He tried a six-hour culture. He mixed the supernatant fluid from a centrifugated culture with a suspension of red blood corpuscles and placed it in the incubator. When he returned, two hours later, the blood cells were dissolved.

He telephoned to Leora: "Lee! Got something! C'n you pack up sandwich and come down here f'r evening?"

"Sure," said Leora.

When she appeared he explained to her that his discovery was accidental, that most scientific discoveries were accidental, and that no investigator, however great, could do anything more than see the value of his chance results.

He sounded mature and rather angry.

Leora sat in the corner, scratching her chin, reading a medical journal. From time to time she reheated coffee, over a doubtful Bunsen flame. When the office staff arrived in the morning they found something that had but rarely occurred during the régime of Almus Pickerbaugh: the Director of the Department was transplanting cultures, and on a long table was his wife, asleep.

Martin blared at Dr. Ockford, "Get t'hell out of this, Rufus, and take charge of the department for today — I'm out — I'm dead — and oh, say, get Leora home and fry her a couple o' eggs, and you might bring me a Denver sandwich from the Sunset Trail Lunch, will you?"

"You bet, chief," said Ockford.

Martin repeated his experiment, testing the cultures for hemolysin after two, four, six, eight, ten, twelve, fourteen, sixteen, and eighteen hours of incubation. He discovered that the maximum production of hemolysin occurred between four and ten hours. He began to work out the formula of production — and he was desolate. He fumed, raged, sweated. He found that his mathematics was childish, and all his science rusty. He pottered with chemistry, he ached over his mathematics, and slowly he began to assemble his results. He believed that he might have a paper for the *Journal of Infectious Diseases* .

Now Almus Pickerbaugh had published scientific papers — often. He had published them in the *Midwest Medical Quarterly* , of which he was one of fourteen editors. He had discovered the germ of epilepsy and the germ of cancer — two entirely different germs of cancer. Usually it took him a fortnight to make the discovery, write the report, and have it accepted. Martin lacked this admirable facility.

He experimented, he re-experimented, he cursed, he kept Leora out of bed, he taught her to make media, and was ill-pleased by her opinions on agar. He was violent to the stenographer; not once could the pastor of the Jonathan Edwards Congregational Church get him to address the Bible Class; and still for months his paper was not complete.

The first to protest was His Honor the Mayor. Returning from an extremely agreeable game of chemin de fer with F. X. Jordan, taking a short cut through the alley behind the City Hall, Mayor Pugh saw Martin at two in the morning drearily putting test-tubes in the incubator, while Leora sat in a corner smoking. Next day he summoned Martin, and protested.

"Doc, I don't want to butt in on your department — my specialty is never butting in — but it certainly strikes me that after being trained by a seventy-horsepower booster like Pickerbaugh, you ought to know that it's all damn' foolishness to spend so much time in the laboratory, when you can hire an A1 laboratory fellow for thirty bucks a week. What you ought to be doing is jollying along these sobs that are always panning the administration. Get out and talk to the churches and clubs, and help me put across the ideas that we stand for."

"Maybe he's right," Martin considered. "I'm a rotten bacteriologist. Probably I never will get this experiment together. My job here is to keep tobacco-chewers from spitting. Have I the right to waste the tax-payers' money on anything else?"

But that week he read, as an announcement issued by the McGurk Institute of Biology of New York, that Dr. Max Gottlieb had synthesized antibodies *in vitro* .

He pictured the saturnine Gottlieb not at all enjoying the triumph but, with locked door, abusing the papers for their exaggerative reports of his work; and as the picture became sharp Martin was like a subaltern stationed in a desert isle when he learns that his old regiment is going off to an agreeable Border war.

Then the McCandless fury broke.

## II

Mrs. McCandless had once been a "hired girl"; then nurse, then confidante, then wife to the invalid Mr. McCandless, wholesale grocer and owner of real estate. When he died she inherited everything. There was a suit, of course, but she had an excellent lawyer.

She was a grim, graceless, shady, mean woman, yet a nymphomaniac. She was not invited into Nautilus society, but in her unaired parlor, on the mildewed couch, she entertained seedy, belching, oldish married men, a young policeman to whom she often lent money, and the contractor-politician, F. X. Jordan.

She owned, in Swede Hollow, the filthiest block of tenements in Nautilus. Martin had made a tuberculosis map of these tenements, and in conferences with Dr. Ockford and Leora he denounced them as murder-holes. He wanted to destroy them, but the police power of the Director of Public Health was vague. Pickerbaugh had enjoyed the possession of large power only because he never used it.

Martin sought a court decision for the demolition of the McCandless tenements. Her lawyer was also the lawyer of F. X. Jordan, and the most eloquent witness against Martin was Dr. Irving Watters. But it chanced, because of the absence of the proper judge, that the case came before an ignorant and honest person who quashed the injunction secured by Mrs. McCandless's lawyer and instructed the Department of Public Health that it might use such methods as the city ordinances provided for emergencies.

That evening Martin grumbled to young Ockford, "You don't suppose for a moment, do you, Rufus, that McCandless and Jordan won't appeal the case? Let's get rid of the tenements while it's comparatively legal, heh?"

"You bet, chief," said Ockford, and, "Say, let's go out to Oregon and start practice when we get kicked out. Well, we can depend on our sanitary inspector, anyway. Jordan seduced his sister, here 'bout six years back."

At dawn a gang headed by Martin and Ockford, in blue overalls, joyful and rowdyish, invaded the McCandless tenements, drove the tenants into the street, and began to tear down the flimsy buildings. At noon, when lawyers appeared and the tenants were in new flats commandeered by Martin, the wreckers set fire to the lower stories, and in half an hour the buildings had been annihilated.

F. X. Jordan came to the scene after lunch. A filthy Martin and a dusty Ockford were drinking coffee brought by Leora.

"Well, boys," said Jordan, "you've put it all over us. Only if you ever pull this kind of stunt again, use dynamite and save a lot of time. You know, I like you boys — I'm sorry for what I've got to do to you. But may the saints help you, because it's just a question of time when I learn you not to monkey with the buzz-saw."

## III

Clay Tredgold admired their amateur arson and rejoiced, "Fine! I'm going to back you up in everything the D.P.H. does."

Martin was not too pleased by the promise, for Tredgold's set were somewhat exigent. They had decided that Martin and Leora were free spirits like themselves, and amusing, but they had also decided, long before the Arrowsmiths had by coming to Nautilus entered into authentic existence, that the Group had a monopoly of all Freedom and Amusingness, and they expected the Arrowsmiths to appear for cocktails and poker every Saturday and Sunday evening. They could not understand why Martin should desire to spend his time in a laboratory, drudging over something called "streptolysin," which had nothing to do with cocktails, motors, steel windmills, or insurance.

On an evening perhaps a fortnight after the destruction of the McCandless tenements, Martin was working late in the laboratory. He wasn't even doing experiments which might have diverted the Group — causing bacterial colonies to cloud liquids, or making things change color. He was merely sitting at a table, looking at logarithmic tables. Leora was not there, and he was mumbling, "Confound her, why did she have to go and be sick today?"

Tredgold and Schemihl and their wives were bound for the Old Farmhouse Inn. They had telephoned to Martin's flat and learned where he was. From the alley behind City Hall they could peer in and see him, dreary and deserted.

"We'll take the old boy out and brighten him up. First, let's rush home and shake up a few cocktails and bring 'em down to surprise him," was Tredgold's inspiration.

Tredgold came into the laboratory, a half-hour later, with much clamor.

"This is a nice way to put in a moonlit spring evening, young Narrowsmith! Come on, we'll all go out and dance a little. Grab your hat."

"Gosh, Clay, I'd like to, but honestly I can't. I've got to work; simply got to."

"Rats! Don't be silly. You've been working too hard. Here — look what Father's brought. Be reasonable. Get outside of a nice long cocktail and you'll have a new light on things."

Martin was reasonable up to that point, but he did not have a new light. Tredgold would not take No. Martin continued to refuse, affectionately, then a bit tartly. Outside, Schlemihl pressed down the button of the motor horn and held it, producing a demanding, infuriating yawp which made Martin cry, "For God's sake go out and make 'em quit that, will you, and let me alone! I've got to work, I told you!"

Tredgold stared a moment. "I certainly shall! I'm not accustomed to force my attentions on people. Pardon me for disturbing you!"

By the time Martin sulkily felt that he must apologize, the car was gone. Next day and all the week, he waited for Tredgold to telephone, and Tredgold waited for him to telephone, and they fell into a circle of dislike. Leora and Clara Tredgold saw each other once or twice, but they were uncomfortable, and a fortnight later, when the most prominent physician in town dined with the Tredgolds and attacked Martin as a bumptious and narrow-visioned young man, both the Tredgolds listened and agreed.

Opposition to Martin developed all at once.

Various physicians were against him, not only because of the enlarged clinics, but because he rarely asked their help and never their advice. Mayor Pugh considered him tactless. Klopchuk and F. X. Jordan were assailing him as crooked. The reporters disliked him for his secrecy and occasional brusqueness. And the Group had ceased to defend him. Of all these forces Martin was more or less aware, and behind them he fancied that doubtful business men, sellers of impure ice-cream and milk, owners of unsanitary shops and dirty tenements, men who had always hated Pickerbaugh but who had feared to attack him because of his popularity, were gathering to destroy the entire Department of Public Health.... He appreciated Pickerbaugh in those days, and loved soldier-wise the Department.

There came from Mayor Pugh a hint that he would save trouble by resigning. He would not resign. Neither would he go to the citizens begging for support. He did his work, and leaned on Leora's assurance, and tried to ignore his detractors. He could not.

News-items and three-line editorial squibs dug at his tyranny, his ignorance, his callowness. An old women died after treatment at the clinic, and the coroner hinted that it had been the fault of "our almighty health-officer's pet cub assistant." Somewhere arose the name "the Schoolboy Czar" for Martin, and it stuck.

In the gossip at luncheon clubs, in discussions at the Parents' and Teachers' Association, in one frank signed protest sent to the Mayor, Martin was blamed for too strict an inspection of milk, for insufficiently strict inspection of milk; for permitting garbage to lie untouched, for persecuting the overworked garbage collectors; and when a case of small-pox appeared in the Bohemian section, there was an opinion that Martin had gone out personally and started it.

However vague the citizens were as to the nature of his wickedness, once they lost faith in him they lost it completely and with joy, and they welcomed an apparently spontaneously generated rumor that he had betrayed his benefactor, their beloved Dr. Pickerbaugh, by seducing Orchid.

At this interesting touch of immorality, he had all the fashionable churches against him. The pastor of the Jonathan Edwards Church touched up a sermon about Sin in High Places by a reference to "one who, while like a Czar he pretends to be safeguarding the city from entirely imaginary dangers, yet winks at the secret vice rampant in hidden places; who allies himself with the forces of graft and evil and the thugs who batten on honest but deluded Labor; one who cannot arise, a manly man among men, and say, 'I have a clean heart and clean hands.' "

It is true that some of the delighted congregation thought that this referred to Mayor Pugh, and others applied it to F. X. Jordan, but wise citizens saw that it was a courageous attack on that monster of treacherous lewdness, Dr. Arrowsmith.

In all the city there were exactly two ministers who defended him: Father Costello of the Irish Catholic Church and Rabbi Rovine. They were, it happened, very good friends, and not at all friendly with the pastor of the Jonathan Edwards Church. They bullied their congregations; each of them asserted, "People come sneaking around with criticisms of our new Director of Health. If you want to make charges, make them openly. I will not listen to cowardly hints. And let me tell you that this city is lucky in having for health-officer a man who is honest and who actually knows something!"

But their congregations were poor.

Martin realized that he was lost. He tried to analyze his unpopularity.

"It isn't just Jordan's plotting and Tredgold's grousing and Pugh's weak spine. It's my own fault. I can't go out and soft-soap the people and get their permission to help keep them well. And I won't tell them what a hell of an important thing my work is — that I'm the one thing that saves the whole lot of 'em from dying immediately. Apparently an official in a democratic state has to do those things. Well, I don't! But I've got to think up something or they'll emasculate the whole Department."

One inspiration he did have. If Pickerbaugh were here, he could crush, or lovingly smother, the opposition. He remembered Pickerbaugh's farewell: "Now, my boy, even if I'm way off there in Washington, this Work will be as close to my heart as it ever was, and if you should really need me, you just send for me and I'll drop everything and come."

Martin wrote hinting that he was much needed.

Pickerbaugh replied by return mail — good old Pickerbaugh! — but the reply was, "I cannot tell you how grieved I am that I cannot for the moment possibly get away from Washington but am sure that in your earnestness you exaggerate strength of opposition, write me freely, at any time."

"That's my last shot," Martin said to Leora. "I'm done. Mayor Pugh will fire me, just as soon as he comes back from his fishing trip. I'm a failure again, darling."

"You're not a failure, and you must eat some of this nice steak, and what shall we do now — time for us to be moving on, anyway — I hate staying in one place," said Leora.

"I don't know what we'll do. Maybe I could get a job at Hunziker's. Or go back to Dakota and try to work up a practice. What I'd like is to become a farmer and get me a big shotgun and drive every earnest Christian citizen off the place. But meantime I'm going to stick here. I might win yet — with just a couple of miracles and a divine intervention. Oh, God, I am so tired! Are you coming back to the lab with me this evening? Honest, I'll quit early — before eleven, maybe."

He had completed his paper on the streptolysin research, and he took a day off to go to Chicago and talk it over with an editor of the *Journal of Infectious Diseases*. As he left Nautilus he was confused. He had caught himself rejoicing that he was free of Wheatsylvania and bound for great Nautilus. Time bent back, progress was annihilated, and he was mazed with futility.

The editor praised his paper, accepted it, and suggested only one change. Martin had to wait for his train. He remembered that Angus Duer was in Chicago, with the Rouncefield Clinic — a private organization of medical specialists, sharing costs and profits.

The clinic occupied fourteen rooms in a twenty-story building constructed (or so Martin certainly remembered it) of marble, gold, and rubies. The clinic reception-room, focused on a vast stone fireplace, was like the drawing-room of an oil magnate, but it was not a place of leisure. The young woman at the door demanded Martin's symptoms and address. A page in buttons sped with his name to a nurse, who flew to the inner offices. Before Angus appeared, Martin had to wait a quarter-hour in a smaller, richer, still more abashing reception-room. By this time he was so awed that he would have permitted the clinic surgeons to operate on him for any ill which at the moment they happened to fancy.

In medical school and Zenith General Hospital, Angus Duer had been efficient enough, but now he was ten times as self-assured. He was cordial; he invited Martin to step out for a dish of tea as though he almost meant it; but beside him Martin felt young, rustic, inept.

Angus won him by pondering, "Irving Watters? He was Digam? I'm not sure I remember him. Oh, yes — he was one of these boneheads that are the curse of every profession."

When Martin had sketched his conflict at Nautilus, Angus suggested, "You better come join us here at Rouncefield, as pathologist. Our pathologist is leaving in a few weeks. You could do the job, all right. You're getting thirty-five hundred a year now? Well, I think I could get you forty-five hundred, as a starter, and some day you'd become a regular member of the clinic and get in on all the profits. Let me know if you want it. Rouncefield told me to dig up a man."

With this resource and with an affection for Angus, Martin returned to Nautilus and open war. When Mayor Pugh returned he did not discharge Martin, but he appointed over him, as full director, Pickerbaugh's friend, Dr. Bissex, the football coach and health director of Mugford College.

Dr. Bissex first discharged Rufus Ockford, which took five minutes, went out and addressed a Y.M.C.A. meeting, then bustled in and invited Martin to resign.

"I will like hell!" said Martin. "Come on, be honest, Bissex. If you want to fire me, do it, but let's have things straight. I won't resign, and if you do fire me I think I'll take it to the courts, and maybe I can turn enough light on you and His Honor and Frank Jordan to keep you from taking all the guts out of the work here."

"Why, Doctor, what a way to talk! Certainly I won't fire you," said Bissex, in the manner of one who has talked to difficult students and to lazy football teams. "Stay with us as long as you like. Only, in the interests of economy, I reduce your salary to eight hundred dollars a year!"

"All right, reduce and be damned," said Martin.

It sounded particularly fine and original when he said it, but less so when Leora and he found that, with their rent fixed by their lease, they could not by whatever mean economies live on less than a thousand a year.

Now that he was free from responsibility he began to form his own faction, to save the Department. He gathered Rabbi Rovine, Father Costello, Ockford, who was going to remain in town and practice, the secretary of the Labor Council, a banker who regarded Tredgold as "fast," and that excellent fellow the dentist of the school clinic.

"With people like that behind me, I can do something," he gloated to Leora. "I'm going to stick by it. I'm not going to have the D.P.H. turned into a Y.M.C.A. Bissex has all of Pickerbaugh's mush without his honesty and vigor. I can beat him! I'm not much of an executive, but I was beginning to visualize a D.P.H. that would be solid and not gaseous — that would save kids and prevent epidemics. I won't give it up. You watch me!"

His committee made representations to the Commercial Club, and for a time they were certain that the chief reporter of the *Frontiersman* was going to support them, "as soon as he could get his editor over being scared of a row." But Martin's belligerency was weakened by shame, for he never had enough money to meet his bills, and he was not used to dodging irate grocers, receiving dunning letters, standing at the door arguing with impertinent bill-collectors. He, who had been a city dignitary a few days before, had to endure, "Come on now, you pay up, you dead beat, or I'll get a cop!" When the shame had grown to terror, Dr. Bissex suddenly reduced his salary another two hundred dollars.

Martin stormed into the mayor's office to have it out, and found F. X. Jordan sitting with Pugh. It was evident that they both knew of the second reduction and considered it an excellent joke.

He reassembled his committee. "I'm going to take this into the courts," he raged.

"Fine," said Father Costello; and Rabbi Rovine: "Jenkins, that radical lawyer, would handle the case free."

The wise banker observed, "You haven't got anything to take into the courts till they discharge you without cause. Bissex has a legal right to reduce your salary all he wants to. The city regulations don't fix the salary of anybody except the Director and the inspectors. You haven't a thing to say."

With a melodramatic flourish Martin protested, "And I suppose I haven't a thing to say if they wreck the Department!"

"Not a thing, if the city doesn't care."

"Well, I care! I'll starve before I'll resign!"

"You'll starve if you don't resign, and your wife, too. Now here's my plan," said the banker. "You go into private practice here — I'll finance your getting an office and so on — and when the time comes, maybe in five or ten years from now, we'll all get together again and have you put in as full Director."

"Ten years of waiting — in *Nautilus*? Nope. I'm licked. I'm a complete failure — at thirty-two! I'll resign. I'll wander on," said Martin.

"I know I'm going to love Chicago," said Leora.

## IV

He wrote to Angus Duer. He was appointed pathologist in the Rouncefield Clinic. But, Angus wrote, "they could not at the moment see their way clear to pay him forty-five hundred a year, though they were glad to go to twenty-five hundred."

Martin accepted.

## V

When the Nautilus papers announced that Martin had resigned, the good citizens chuckled, "Resigned? He got kicked out, that's what happened." One of the papers had an innocent squib:

> *Probably a certain amount of hypocrisy is inevitable in us sinful human critters, but when a public official tries to pose as a saint while indulging in every vice, and tries to cover up his gross ignorance and incompetence by pulling political wires, and makes a holy show of himself by not even doing a first-class job of wire-pulling, then even the cussedest of us old scoundrels begins to holler for the meat-ax.*

Pickerbaugh wrote to Martin from Washington:

> *I greatly regret to hear that you have resigned your post. I cannot tell you how disappointed I am, after all the pains I took in breaking you in and making you acquainted with my ideals. Bissex informs me that, because of crisis in city finances, he had to reduce your salary temporarily. Well personally I would rather work for the D.P.H. for nothing a year and earn my keep by being a night watchman than give up the fight for everything that is decent and constructive. I am sorry. I had a great liking for you, and your defection, your going back to private practice merely for commercial gain, your selling out for what I presume is a very high emolument, is one of the very greatest blows I have recently had to sustain.*

## VI

As they rode up to Chicago Martin thought aloud:

"I never knew I could be so badly licked. I never want to see a laboratory or a public health office again. I'm done with everything but making money.

"I suppose this Rouncefield Clinic is probably nothing but a gilded boob-trap — scare the poor millionaire into having all the fancy kinds of examinations and treatments the traffic will bear. I hope it is! I expect to be a commercial-group doctor the rest of my life. I hope I have the sense to be!

"All wise men are bandits. They're loyal to their friends, but they despise the rest. Why not, when the mass of people despise them if they *aren't* bandits? Angus Duer had the sense to see this from the beginning, way back in medic school. He's probably a perfect technician as a surgeon, but he knows you get only what you grab. Think of the years it's taken me to learn what he savvied all the time!

"Know what I'll do? I'll stick to the Rouncefield Clinic till I'm making maybe thirty thousand a year, and then I'll get Ockford and start my own clinic, with myself as internist and head of the whole shooting-match, and collect every cent I can.

"All right, if what people want is a little healing and a lot of tapestry, they shall have it — and pay for it.

"I never thought I could be such a failure — to become a commercialist and not want to be anything else. And I don't want to be anything else, believe me! I'm through!"

## Chapter 25

Then for a year with each day longer than a sleepless night, yet the whole year speeding without events or seasons or eagerness, Martin was a faithful mechanic in that most competent, most clean and brisk and visionless medical factory, the Rouncefield Clinic. He had nothing of which to complain. The clinic did, perhaps, give over-many roentgenological examinations to socially dislocated women who needed children and floor-scrubbing more than pretty little skiagraphs; they did, perhaps, view all tonsils with too sanguinary a gloom; but certainly no factory could have been better equipped or more gratifyingly expensive, and none could have routed its raw human material through so many processes so swiftly. The Martin Arrowsmith who had been supercilious toward Pickerbaugh and old Dr. Winters had for Rouncefield and Angus Duer and the other keen taut specialists of the clinic only the respect of the poor and uncertain for the rich and shrewd.

He admired Angus's firmness of purpose and stability of habit.

Angus had a swim or a fencing lesson daily; he swam easily and fenced like a still-faced demon. He was in bed before eleven-thirty; he never took more than one drink a day; and he never read anything or said anything which would not contribute to his progress as a Brilliant Young Surgeon. His underlings knew that Dr. Duer would not fail to arrive precisely on time, precisely well dressed, absolutely sober, very cool, and appallingly unpleasant to any nurse who made a mistake or looked for a smile.

Martin would without fear have submitted to the gilded and ardent tonsil-snatcher of the clinic, would have submitted to Angus for abdominal surgery or to Rouncefield for any operation of the head or neck, providing he was himself quite sure the operation was necessary, but he was never able to rise to the clinic's faith that any portions of the body without which people could conceivably get along should certainly be removed at once.

The real flaw in his year of Chicago was that through all his working day he did not live. With quick hands, and one-tenth of his brain, he made blood counts, did urinalyses and Wassermanns and infrequent necropsies, and all the while he was dead, in a white-tiled coffin. Amid the blattings of Pickerbaugh and the peepings of Wheatsylvania, he had lived, had fought his environment. Now there was nothing to fight.

After hours, he almost lived. Leora and he discovered the world of book-shops and print-shops and theaters and concerts. They read novels and history and travel; they talked, at dinners given by Rouncefield or Angus, to journalists, engineers, bankers, merchants. They saw a Russian play, and heard Mischa Elman, and read Gottlieb's beloved Rabelais. Martin learned to flirt without childishness, and Leora went for the first time to a hair-dresser and to a manicure, and began her lessons in French. She had called Martin a "lie-hunter," a "truth-seeker." They decided now, talking it over in their tight little two-and-quarter room flat, that most people who call themselves "truth-seekers" — persons who scurry about chattering of Truth as though it were a tangible separable thing, like houses or salt or bread — did not so much desire to find Truth as to cure their mental itch. In novels, these truth-seekers quested the "secret of life" in laboratories which did not seem to be provided with Bunsen flames or reagents; or they went, at great expense and much discomfort from hot trains and undesirable snakes, to Himalayan monasteries, to learn from unaseptic sages that the Mind can do all sorts of edifying things if one will but spend thirty or forty years in eating rice and gazing on one's navel.

To these high matters Martin responded, "Rot!" He insisted that there is no Truth but only many truths; that Truth is not a colored bird to be chased among the rocks and captured by its tail, but a skeptical attitude toward life. He insisted that no one could expect more than, by stubbornness or luck, to have the kind of work he enjoyed and an ability to become better acquainted with the facts of that work than the average job-holder.

His mechanistic philosophy did not persuade him that he was progressing adequately. When he tried to match himself with the experts of the clinic or with their professional friends, he was even more uncomfortable than he had been under the disconcerting scorn of Dr. Hesselink of Groningen. At clinic luncheons he met surgeons from London, New York, Boston; men with limousines and social positions and the offensive briskness of the man who has numerous engagements, or the yet more offensive quietness of the person who is amused by his inferiors; master technicians, readers of papers at medical congresses, executives and controllers, unafraid to operate before a hundred peering doctors, or to give well-bred and exceedingly final orders to subordinates; captain-generals of medicine, never doubting themselves; great priests and healers; men mature and wise and careful and blandly cordial.

In their winged presences, Max Gottlieb seemed an aged fusser, Gustaf Sondelius a mountebank, and the city of Nautilus unworthy of passionate warfare. As their suave courtesy smothered him, Martin felt like a footman.

In long hours of increasing frankness and lucidity he discussed with Leora the question of "What is this Martin Arrowsmith and whither is he going?" and he admitted that the sight of the Famous Surgeons disturbed his ancient faith that he was somehow a superior person. It was Leora who consoled him:

"I've got a lovely description for your dratted Famous Surgeons. You know how polite and important they are, and they smile so carefully? Well, don't you remember you once said that Professor Gottlieb called all such people like that 'men of measured merriment'?"

He caught up the phrase; they sang it together; and they made of it a beating impish song:

"Men of measured merriment! Men of measured merriment! Damn the great executives, the men of measured merriment, damn the men with careful smiles, damn the men that run the shops, oh, damn their measured merriment, the men with measured merriment, oh, damn their measured merriment, and DAMN their careful smiles!"

## II

While Martin developed in a jagged way from the boy of Wheatsylvania to mature man, his relations to Leora developed from loyal boy-and-girl adventurousness to lasting solidity. They had that understanding of each other known only to married people, a few married people, wherein for all their differences they were as much indissoluble parts of a whole as are the eye and hand. Their identification did not mean that they dwelt always in rosy bliss. Because he was so intimately fond of her and so sure of her, because anger and eager hot injustices are but ways of expressing trust, Martin was irritated by her and querulous with her as he would not have endured being with any other woman, any charming Orchid.

He stalked out now and then after a quarrel, disdaining to answer her, and for hours he left her alone, enjoying the knowledge that he was hurting her, that she was alone, waiting, perhaps weeping. Because he loved her and also was fond of her, he was annoyed when she was less sleek, less suave, than the women he encountered at Angus Duer's.

Mrs. Rouncefield was a worthy old waddler — beside her, Leora was shining and exquisite. But Mrs. Duer was of amber and ice. She was a rich young woman, she dressed with distinction, she spoke with finishing-school mock-melodiousness, she was ambitious, and she was untroubled by the possession of a heart or a brain. She was, indeed, what Mrs. Irving Watters believed herself to be.

In the simple gorgeousness of the Nautilus smart set, Mrs. Clay Tredgold had petted Leora and laughed at her if she lacked a shoe-buckle or split an infinitive, but the gold-slippered Mrs. Duer was accustomed to sneer at carelessness with the most courteous and unresentable and unmistakable sneers.

As they returned by taxicab from the Duers', Martin flared:

"Don't you ever learn anything? I remember once in Nautilus we stopped on a country road and talked till — oh, darn' near dawn, and you were going to be so energetic, but here we are again tonight, with just the same thing — Good God, couldn't you even take the trouble to notice you had a spot of soot on your nose tonight? Mrs. Duer noticed it, all right! Why are you so sloppy? Why can't you take a little care? And why can't you make an effort, anyway, to have something to say? You just sit there at dinner — you just sit and look healthy! Don't you want to help me? Mrs. Duer will probably help Angus to become president of the American Medical Association, in about twenty years, and by that time I suppose you'll have me back in Dakota as assistant to Hesselink!"

Leora had been snuggling beside him in the unusual luxury of a taxicab. She sat straight now, and when she spoke she had lost the casual independence with which she usually regarded life:

"Dear, I'm awfully sorry. I went out this afternoon, I went out and had a facial massage, so as to look nice for you, and then I knew you like conversation, so I got my little book about modern painting that I bought and I studied it terribly hard, but tonight I just couldn't seem to get the conversation around to modern painting — "

He was sobbing, with her head on his shoulder, "Oh, you poor, scared, bullied kid, trying to be grown-up with these dollar-chasers!"

## III

After the first daze of white tile and bustling cleverness at the Rouncefield Clinic, Martin had the desire to tie up a few loose knots of his streptolysin research.

When Angus Duer discovered it he hinted, "Look here, Martin, I'm glad you're keeping on with your science, but if I were you I wouldn't, I think, waste too much energy on mere curiosity. Dr. Rouncefield was speaking about it the other day. We'd be glad to have you do all the research you want, only we'd like it if you went at something practical. Take for instance: if you could make a tabulation of the blood-counts in a couple of hundred cases of appendicitis and publish it, that'd get somewhere, and you could sort of bring in a mention of the clinic, and we'd all receive a little credit — and incidentally maybe we could raise you to three thousand a year then."

This generosity had the effect of extinguishing Martin's desire to do any research whatever.

"Angus is right. What he means is: as a scientist I'm finished. I am. I'll never try to do anything original again."

It was at this time, when Martin had been with the clinic for a year, that his streptolysin paper was published in the *Journal of Infectious Diseases*. He gave reprints to Rouncefield and to Angus. They said extremely nice things which showed that they had not read the paper, and again they suggested his tabulating blood-counts.

He also sent a reprint to Max Gottlieb, at the McGurk Institute of Biology.

Gottlieb wrote to him, in that dead-black spider-web script:

*Dear Martin* :

*I have read your paper with great pleasure. The curves of the relation of hemolysin production to age of culture are illuminating. I have spoken about you to Tubbs. When are you coming to us — to me? Yor laboratory and diener are waiting for you here. The last thing I want to be is a mystic, but I feel when I see your fine engraved letterhead of a clinic and a Rouncefield that you should be tired of trying to be a good citizen and ready to come back to work. We shall be glad, & Dr. Tubbs, if you can come.*

*Truly yours,*

*M. Gottlieb.*

"I'm simply going to adore New York," said Leora.

## Chapter 26

The McGurk Building. A sheer wall, thirty blank stories of glass and limestone, down in the pinched triangle whence New York rules a quarter of the world.

Martin was not overwhelmed by his first hint of New York; after a year in the Chicago Loop, Manhattan seemed leisurely. But when from the elevated railroad he beheld the Woolworth Tower, he was exalted. To him architecture had never existed; buildings were larger or smaller bulks containing more or less interesting objects. His most impassioned architectural comment had been, "There's a cute bungalow; be nice place to live." Now he pondered, "Like to see that tower every day — clouds and storms behind it and everything — so sort of satisfying."

He came along Cedar Street, among thunderous trucks portly with wares from all the world; came to the bronze doors of the McGurk Building and a corridor of intemperately colored terracotta, with murals of Andean Indians, pirates booming up the Spanish Main, guarded gold-trains, and the stout walls of Cartagena. At the Cedar Street end of the corridor, a private street, one block long, was the Bank of the Andes and Antilles (Ross McGurk, chairman of the board), in whose gold-crusted sanctity red-headed Yankee exporters drew drafts on Quito, and clerks hurled breathless Spanish at bulky women. A sign indicated, at the Liberty Street end, "Passenger Offices, McGurk Line, weekly sailings for the West Indies and South America."

Born to the prairies, never far from the sight of the cornfields, Martin was conveyed to blazing lands and portentous enterprises.

One of the row of bronze-barred elevators was labeled "Express to McGurk Institute." He entered it proudly, feeling himself already a part of the godly association. They rose swiftly, and he had but half-second glimpses of ground glass doors with the signs of mining companies, lumber companies, Central American railroad companies.

The McGurk Institute is probably the only organization for scientific research in the world which is housed in an office building. It has the twenty-ninth and thirtieth stories of the McGurk Building, and the roof is devoted to its animal house and to tiled walks along which (above a world of stenographers and bookkeepers and earnest gentlemen who desire to sell Better-bilt Garments to the golden dons of the Argentine) saunter rapt scientists dreaming of osmosis in Spirogyra.

Later, Martin was to note that the reception-room of the Institute was smaller, yet more forbiddingly polite, in its white paneling and Chippendale chairs, than the lobby of the Rouncefield Clinic, but now he was unconscious of the room, of the staccato girl attendant, of everything except that he was about to see Max Gottlieb, for the first time in five years.

At the door of the laboratory he stared hungrily.

Gottlieb was thin-cheeked and dark as ever, his hawk nose bony, his fierce eyes demanding, but his hair had gone gray, the flesh round his mouth was sunken, and Martin could have wept at the feebleness with which he rose. The old man peered down at him, his hand on Martin's shoulder, but he said only:

"Ah! Dis is good.... Your laboratory is three doors down the hall.... But I object to one thing in the good paper you send me. You say, "The regularity of the rate at which the streptolysin disappears suggests that an equation may be found — ""

"But it can, sir!"

"Then why did you not make the equation?"

"Well — I don't know. I wasn't enough of a mathematician."

"Then you should not have published till you knew your math!"

"I — Look, Dr. Gottlieb, do you really think I know enough to work here? I want terribly to succeed."

"Succeed? I have heard that word. It is English? Oh, yes, it is a word that liddle schoolboys use at the University of Winnemac. It means passing examinations. But there are no examinations to pass here.... Martin, let us be clear. You know something of laboratory technique; you have heard about dese bacilli; you are not a good chemist, and mathematics — pfui! — most terrible! But you have curiosity and you are stubborn. You do not accept rules. Therefore I t'ink you will either make a very good scientist or a very bad one, and if you are bad enough, you will be popular with the rich ladies who rule this city, New York, and you can gif lectures for a living or even become, if you get to be plausible enough, a college president. So anyvay, it will be interesting."

Half an hour later they were arguing ferociously, Martin asserting that the whole world ought to stop warring and trading and writing and get straightway into laboratories to observe new phenomena; Gottlieb insisting that there were already too many facile scientists, that the one thing necessary was the mathematical analysis (and often the destruction) of phenomena already observed.

It sounded bellicose, and all the while Martin was blissful with the certainty that he had come home.

The laboratory in which they talked (Gottlieb pacing the floor, his long arms fantastically knotted behind his thin back; Martin leaping on and off tall stools) was not in the least remarkable — a sink, a bench with racks of numbered test-tubes, a microscope, a few note-books and hydrogen-ion charts, a grotesque series of bottles connected by glass and rubber tubes on an ordinary kitchen table at the end of the room — yet now and then during his tirades Martin looked about reverently.

Gottlieb interrupted their debate: "What work do you want to do here?"

"Why, sir, I'd like to help you, if I can. I suppose you're cleaning up some things on the synthesis of antibodies."

"Yes, I t'ink I can bring immunity reactions under the mass action law. But you are not to help me. You are to do your own work. What do you want to do? This is not a clinic; wit' patients going through so neat in a row!"

"I want to find a hemolysin for which there's an antibody. There isn't any for streptolysin. I'd like to work with staphylolysin. Would you mind?"

"I do not care what you do — if you just do not steal my staph cultures out of the ice-box, and if you will look mysterious all the time, so Dr. Tubbs, our Director, will t'ink you are up to something big. So! I haf only one suggestion: when you get stuck in a problem, I have a fine collection of detective stories in my office. But no. Should I be serious — this once, when you are just come?

"Perhaps I am a crank, Martin. There are many who hate me. There are plots against me — oh, you t'ink I imagine it, but you shall see! I make many mistakes. But one thing I keep always pure: the religion of a scientist.

"To be a scientist — it is not just a different job, so that a man should choose between being a scientist and being an explorer or a bond-salesman or a physician or a king or a farmer. It is a tangle of ver-y obscure emotions, like mysticism, or wanting to write poetry; it makes its victim all different from the good normal man. The normal man, he does not care much what he does except that he should eat and sleep and make love. But the scientist is intensely religious — he is so religious that he will not accept quarter-truths, because they are an insult to his faith.

"He wants that everything should be subject to inexorable laws. He is equal opposed to the capitalists who t'ink their silly money-grabbing is a system, and to liberals who t'ink man is not a fighting animal; he takes both the American booster and the European aristocrat, and he ignores all their blithering. Ignores it! All of it! He hates the preachers who talk their fables, but he iss not too kindly to the anthropologists and historians who can only make guesses, yet they have the nerf to call themselves scientists! Oh, yes, he is a man that all nice good-natured people should naturally hate!

"He speaks no meaner of the ridiculous faith-healers and chiropractors than he does of the doctors that want to snatch our science before it is tested and rush around hoping they heal people, and spoiling all the clues with their footsteps; and worse than the men like hogs, worse than the imbeciles who have not even heard of science, he hates pseudo-scientists, guess-scientists — like these psycho-analysts; and worse than those comic dream-scientists he hates the men that are allowed in a clean kingdom like biology but know only one textbook and how to lecture to nincompoops all so popular! He is the only real revolutionary, the authentic scientist, because he alone knows how liddle he knows.

"He must be heartless. He lives in a cold, clear light. Yet dis is a funny t'ing: really, in private, he is not cold nor heartless — so much less cold than the Professional Optimists. The world has always been ruled by the Philanthropists: by the doctors that want to use therapeutic methods they do not understand, by the soldiers that want something to defend their country against, by the preachers that yearn to make everybody listen to them, by the kind manufacturers that love their workers, by the eloquent statesmen and soft-hearted authors — and see once what a fine mess of hell they haf made of the world! Maybe now it is time for the scientist, who works and searches and never goes around howling how he loves everybody!

"But once again always remember that not all the men who work at science are scientists. So few! The rest — secretaries, press-agents, camp-followers! To be a scientist is like being a Goethe: it is born in you. Sometimes I t'ink you have a liddle of it born in you. If you haf, there is only one t'ing — no, there is two t'ings you must do: work twice as hard as you can, and keep people from using you. I will try to protect you from Success. It is all I can do. So.... I should wish, Martin, that you will be very happy here. May Koch bless you!"

## II

Five rapt minutes Martin spent in the laboratory which was to be his — smallish but efficient, the bench exactly the right height, a proper sink with pedal taps. When he had closed the door and let his spirit flow out and fill that minute apartment with his own essence, he felt secure.

No Pickerbaugh or Rouncefield could burst in here and drag him away to be explanatory and plausible and public; he would be free to work, instead of being summoned to the package-wrapping and dictation of breezy letters which men call work.

He looked out of the broad window above his bench and saw that he did have the coveted Woolworth Tower, to keep and gloat on. Shut in to a joy of precision, he would nevertheless not be walled out from flowing life. He had, to the north, not the Woolworth Tower alone but the Singer Building, the arrogant magnificence of the City Investing Building. To the west, tall ships were riding, tugs were bustling, all the world went by. Below his cliff, the streets were feverish. Suddenly he loved humanity as he loved the decent, clean rows of test-tubes, and he prayed then the prayer of the scientist:

"God give me unclouded eyes and freedom from haste. God give me a quiet and relentless anger against all pretense and all pretentious work and all work left slack and unfinished. God give me a restlessness whereby I may neither sleep nor accept praise till my observed results equal my calculated results or in pious glee I discover and assault my error. God give me strength not to trust to God!"

## III

He walked all the way up to their inconsiderable hotel in the Thirties, and all the way the crowds stared at him — this slim, pale, black-eyed, beaming young man who thrust among them, half-running, seeing nothing yet in a blur seeing everything: gallant buildings, filthy streets, relentless traffic, soldiers of fortune, fools, pretty women, frivolous shops, windy sky. His feet raced to the tune of "I've found my work, I've found my work, I've found my work!"

Leora was awaiting him — Leora whose fate it was ever to wait for him in creaky rocking-chairs in cheapish rooms. As he galloped in she smiled, and all her thin, sweet body was illumined. Before he spoke she cried:

"Oh, Sandy, I'm so glad!"

She interrupted his room-striding panegyrics on Max Gottlieb, on the McGurk Institute, on New York, on the charms of staphylolysin, by a meek "Dear, how much are they going to pay you?"

He stopped with a bump. "Gosh! I forgot to ask!"

"Oh!"

"Now you look here! This isn't a Rouncefield Clinic! I hate these buzzards that can't see anything but making money — "

"I know, Sandy. Honestly, I don't care. I was just wondering what kind of a flat we'll be able to afford, so I can begin looking for it. Go on. Dr. Gottlieb said — "

It was three hours after, at eight, when they went to dinner.

## IV

The city of magic was to become to Martin neither a city nor any sort of magic but merely a route: their flat, the subway, the Institute, a favorite inexpensive restaurant, a few streets of laundries and delicatessens and movie theaters. But tonight it was a fog of wonder. They dined at the Brevoort, of which Gustaf Sondelius had told him. This was in 1916, before the country had become wholesome and sterile, and the Brevoort was a tumult of French uniforms, caviar, Louis, dangling neckties, Nuits St. Georges, illustrators, Grand Marnier, British Intelligence officers, brokers, conversation, and Martell, V.O.

"It's a fine crazy bunch," said Martin. "Do you realize we can stop being respectable now? Irving Watters isn't watching us, or Angus! Would we be too insane if we had a bottle of champagne?"

He awoke next day to fret that there must be a trick somewhere, as there had been in Nautilus, in Chicago. But as he set to work he seemed to be in a perfect world. The Institute deftly provided all the material and facilities he could desire — animals, incubators, glassware, cultures, media — and he had a thoroughly trained technician — "garçon" they called him at the Institute. He really was let alone; he really was encouraged to do individual work; he really was associated with men who thought not in terms of poetic posters or of two-thousand-dollar operations but of colloids and sporulation and electrons, and of the laws and energies which governed them.

On his first day there came to greet him the head of the Department of Physiology, Dr. Rippleton Holabird.

Holabird seemed, though Martin had found his name starred in physiological journals, too young and too handsome to be the head of a department: a tall, slim, easy man with a trim mustache. Martin had been reared in the school of Clif Clawson; he had not realized, till he heard Dr. Holabird's quick greeting, that a man's voice may be charming without effeminacy.

Holabird guided him through the two floors of the Institute, and Martin beheld all the wonders of which he had ever dreamed. If it was not so large, McGurk ranked in equipment with Rockefeller, Pasteur, McCormick, Lister. Martin saw rooms for sterilizing glass and preparing media, for glass-blowing, for the polariscope and the spectroscope, and a steel-and-cement-walled combustion-chamber. He saw a museum of pathology and bacteriology to which he longed to add. There was a department of publications, whence were issued the Institute reports, and the *American Journal of Geographic Pathology* , edited by the Director, Dr. Tubbs; there was a room for photography, a glorious library, an aquarium for the Department of Marine Biology, and (Dr. Tubbs's own idea) a row of laboratories which visiting foreign scientists were invited to use as their own. A Belgian biologist and a Portuguese bio-chemist were occupying guest laboratories now, and once, Martin thrilled to learn, Gustaf Sondelius had been here.

Then Martin saw the Berkeley-Saunders centrifuge.

The principle of the centrifuge is that of the cream-separator. It collects as sediment the solids scattered through a liquid, such as bacteria in a solution. Most centrifuges are hand- or water-power contrivances the size of a large cocktail-shaker, but this noble implement was four feet across, electrically driven, the central bowl enclosed in armor plate fastened with levers like a submarine hatch, the whole mounted on a cement pillar.

Holabird explained, "There're only three of these in existence. They're made by Berkeley-Saunders in England. You know the normal speed, even for a good centrifuge, is about four thousand revolutions a minute. This does twenty thousand a minute — fastest in the world. Eh?"

"Jove, they do give you the stuff to work with!" gloated Martin. (He really did, under Holabird's handsome influence, say Jove, not Gosh.)

"Yes, McGurk and Tubbs are the most generous men in the scientific world. I think you'll find it very pleasant to be here, Doctor."

"I know I will — shall. And Jove, it's awfully nice of you to take me around this way."

"Can't you see how much I'm enjoying my chance to display my knowledge? There's no form of egotism so agreeable and so safe as being a cicerone. But we still have the real wonder of the Institute for to behold, Doctor. Down this way."

The real wonder of the Institute had nothing visible to do with science. It was the Hall, in which lunched the staff, and in which occasional scientific dinners were given, with Mrs. McGurk as hostess. Martin gasped and his head went back as his glance ran from glistening floor to black and gold ceiling. The Hall rose the full height of the two floors of the Institute. Clinging to the soaring wall, above the dais on which lunched the Director and the seven heads of departments, was a carved musicians'-gallery. Against the oak paneling of the walls were portraits of the pontiffs of science, in crimson robes, with a vast mural by Maxfield Parrish, and above all was an electrolier of a hundred globes.

"Gosh — *Jove!* " said Martin. "I never knew there was such a room!"

Holabird was generous. He did not smile. "Oh, perhaps it's almost too gorgeous. It's Capitola's pet creation — Capitola is Mrs. Ross McGurk, wife of the founder; she's really an awfully nice woman but she does love Movements and Associations. Terry Wickett, one of the chemists here, calls this 'Bonanza Hall.' Yet it does inspire you when you come in to lunch all tired and grubby. Now let's go call on the Director. He told me to bring you in."

After the Babylonian splendor of the Hall, Martin expected to find the office of Dr. A. DeWitt Tubbs fashioned like a Roman bath, but it was, except for a laboratory bench at one end, the most rigidly business-like apartment he had ever seen.

Dr. Tubbs was an earnest man, whiskered like a terrier, very scholarly, and perhaps the most powerful American exponent of co-operation in science, but he was also a man of the world, fastidious of boots and waistcoats. He had graduated from Harvard, studied on the Continent, been professor of pathology in the University of Minnesota, president of Hartford University, minister to Venezuela, editor of the *Weekly Statesman* and president of the Sanity League, finally Director of McGurk.

He was a member both of the American Academy of Arts and Letters and of the Academy of Sciences. Bishops, generals, liberal rabbis, and musical bankers dined with him. He was one of the Distinguished Men to whom the newspapers turned for authoritative interviews on all subjects.

You realized before he had talked to you for ten minutes that here was one of the few leaders of mankind who could discourse on any branch of knowledge, yet could control practical affairs and drive stumbling mankind on to sane and reasonable ideals. Though a Max Gottlieb might in his research show a certain talent, yet his narrowness, his sour and antic humor, kept him from developing the broad view of education, politics, commerce, and all other noble matters which marked Dr. A. DeWitt Tubbs.

But the Director was as cordial to the insignificant Martin Arrowsmith as though Martin were a visiting senator. He shook his hand warmly; he unbent in a smile; his baritone was mellow.

"Dr. Arrowsmith, I trust we shall do more than merely say you are welcome here; I trust we shall show you how welcome you are! Dr. Gottlieb tells me that you have a natural aptitude for cloistered investigation but that you have been looking over the fields of medical practice and public health before you settled down to the laboratory. I can't tell you how wise I consider you to have made that broad preliminary survey. Too many would-be scientists lack the tutored vision which comes from coordinating all mental domains."

Martin was dazed to discover that he had been making a broad survey.

"Now you'll doubtless wish to take some time, perhaps a year or more, in getting into your stride, Dr. Arrowsmith. I shan't ask you for any reports. So long as Dr. Gottlieb feels that you yourself are satisfied with your progress, I shall be content. Only if there is anything in which I can advise you, from a perhaps somewhat longer career in science, please believe that I shall be delighted to be of aid, and I am quite sure the same obtains with Dr. Holabird here, though he really ought to be jealous, because he is one of our youngest workers — in fact I call him my *enfant terrible* — but you, I believe, are only thirty-three, and you quite put the poor fellow's nose out!"

Holabird merrily suggested, "Oh, no, Doctor, it's been put out long ago. You forget Terry Wickett. He's under forty."

"Oh. *Him!* " murmured Dr. Tubbs.

Martin had never heard a man disposed of so poisonously with such politeness. He saw that in Terry Wickett there might be a serpent even in this paradise.

"Now," said Dr. Tubbs, "perhaps you might like to glance around my place here. I pride myself on keeping our card-indices and letter-files as unimaginatively as though I were an insurance agent. But there is a certain exotic touch in these charts." He trotted across the room to show a nest of narrow drawers filled with scientific blue-prints.

Just what they were charts of, he did not say, nor did Martin ever learn.

He pointed to the bench at the end of the room, and laughingly admitted:

"You can see there what an inefficient fellow I really am. I keep asserting that I have given up all the idyllic delights of pathological research for the less fascinating but so very important and fatiguing cares of the directorship. Yet such is the weakness of *genus homo* that sometimes, when I ought to be attending to practical details, I become obsessed by some probably absurd pathological concept, and so ridiculous am I that I can't wait to hasten down the hall to my regular laboratory — I must always have a bench at hand and an experiment going on. Oh, I'm afraid I'm not the moral man that I pose as being in public! Here I am married to executive procedure, and still I hanker for my first love, Milady Science!"

"I think it's fine you still have an itch for it," Martin ventured.

He was wondering just what experiments Dr. Tubbs had been doing lately. The bench seemed rather unused.

"And now, Doctor, I want you to meet the real Director of the Institute — my secretary, Miss Pearl Robbins."

Martin had already noticed Miss Robbins. You could not help noticing Miss Robbins. She was thirty-five and stately, a creamy goddess. She rose to shake hands — a firm, competent grasp — and to cry in her glorious contralto, "Dr. Tubbs is so complimentary only because he knows that otherwise I wouldn't give him his afternoon tea. We've heard so much about your cleverness from Dr. Gottlieb that I'm almost afraid to welcome you, Dr. Arrowsmith, but I do want to."

Then, in a glow, Martin stood in his laboratory looking at the Woolworth Tower. He was dizzy with these wonders — his own wonders, now! In Rippleton Holabird, so gaily elegant yet so distinguished, he hoped to have a friend. He found Dr. Tubbs somewhat sentimental, but he was moved by his kindness and by Miss Robbins's recognition. He was in a haze of future glory when his door was banged open by a hard-faced, red-headed, soft-shirted man of thirty-six or -eight.

"Arrowsmith?" the intruder growled. "My name is Wickett, Terry Wickett. I'm a chemist. I'm with Gottlieb. Well, I noticed the Holy Wren was showing you the menagerie."

"Dr. Holabird?"

"Him.... Well, you must be more or less intelligent, if Pa Gottlieb let you in. How's it starting? Which kind are you going to be? One of the polite birds that uses the Institute for social climbing and catches him a rich wife, or one of the roughnecks like me and Gottlieb?"

Terry Wickett's croak was as irritating a sound as Martin had ever heard. He answered in a voice curiously like that of Rippleton Holabird:

"I don't think you need to worry. I happen to be married already!"

"Oh, don't let that fret you, Arrowsmith. Divorces are cheap, in this man's town. Well, did the Holy Wren show you Gladys the Tart?"

"Huh?"

"Gladys the Tart, or the Galloping Centrifuge."

"Oh. You mean the Berkeley-Saunders?"

"I do, soul of my soul. Whajuh think of it?"

"It's the finest centrifuge I've ever seen. Dr. Holabird said — "

"Hell, he ought to say something! He went and got old Tubbs to buy it. He just loves it, Holy Wren does."

"Why not? It's the fastest — "

"Sure. Speediest centrifuge in the whole *Vereinigten* , and made of the best toothpick steel. The only trouble is, it always blows out fuses, and it spatters the bugs so that you need a gas-mask if you're going to use it.... And did you love dear old Tubbsy and the peerless Pearl?"

"I did!"

"Fine. Of course Tubbs is an illiterate jackass but still, at that, he hasn't got persecution-mania, like Gottlieb."

"Look here, Wickett — is it Dr. Wickett?"

"Uh-huh.... M.D., Ph.D., but a first-rate chemist just the same."

"Well, Dr. Wickett, it seems to me a shame that a man of your talents should have to associate with idiots like Gottlieb and Tubbs and Holabird. I've just left a Chicago clinic where everybody is nice and sensible. I'd be glad to recommend you for a job there!"

"Wouldn't be so bad. At least I'd avoid all the gassing at lunch in Bonanza Hall. Well, sorry I got your goat, Arrowsmith, but you look all right to me."

"Thanks!"

Wickett grinned obscenely — red-headed, rough-faced, wiry — and snorted, "By the way, did Holabird tell you about being wounded in the first month of the war, when he was a field marshal or a hospital orderly or something in the British Army?"

"He did not! He didn't mention the war!"

"He will! Well, Brer Arrowsmith, I look forward to many happy, happy years together, playing at the feet of Pa Gottlieb. So long. My lab is right next to yours."

"Fool!" Martin decided, and, "Well, I can stand him as long as I can fall back on Gottlieb and Holabird. But — The conceited idiot! Gosh, so Holabird was in the war! Invalided out, I guess. I certainly got back at Wickett on that! 'Did he tell you about his being a jolly old hero in the blinkin' war?' he said, and I came right back at him, 'I'm sorry to displease you,' I said, 'but Dr. Holabird did not mention the war.' The idiot! Well, I won't let him worry me."

And indeed, as Martin met the staff at lunch, Wickett was the only one whom he did not find courteous, however brief their greetings. He did not distinguish among them; for days most of the twenty researchers remained a blur. He confused Dr. Yeo, head of the Department of Biology, with the carpenter who had come to put up shelves.

The staff sat in Hall at two long tables, one on the dais, one below: tiny insect groups under the massy ceiling. They were not particularly noble of aspect, these possible Darwins and Huxleys and Pasteurs. None of them were wide-browed Platos. Except for Rippleton Holabird and Max Gottlieb and perhaps Martin himself, they looked like lunching grocers: brisk featureless young men; thick mustached elders; and wimpish little men with spectacles, men whose collars did not meet. But there was a steady calm about them; there was, Martin believed, no anxiety over money in their voices nor any restlessness of envy and scandalous gossip. They talked gravely or frivolously of their work, the one sort of work that, since it becomes part of the chain of discovered fact, is eternal, however forgotten the worker's name.

As Martin listened to Terry Wickett (rude and slangy as ever, referring to himself as "the boy chemist," speaking of "this gaudy Institute" and "our trusting new lil brother, Arrowsmith") debating with a slight thin-bearded man — Dr. William T. Smith, assistant in bio-chemistry — the possibility of increasing the effects of all enzymes by doses of X-rays, as he heard one associate-member vituperate another for his notions of cell-chemistry and denounce Ehrlich as "the Edison of medical science," Martin perceived new avenues of exciting research; he stood on a mountain, and unknown valleys, craggy tantalizing paths, were open to his feet.

## V

Dr. and Mrs. Rippleton Holabird invited them to dinner, a week after their coming.

As Holabird's tweeds made Clay Tredgold's smartness seem hard and pretentious, so his dinner revealed Angus Duer's affairs in Chicago as mechanical and joyless and a little anxious. Everyone whom Martin met at the Holabirds' flat was a Somebody, though perhaps a minor Somebody: a goodish editor or a rising ethnologist; and all of them had Holabird's graceful casualness.

The provincial Arrowsmiths arrived on time, therefore fifteen minutes early. Before the cocktails appeared, in old Venetian glass, Martin demanded, "Doctor, what problems are you getting after now in your physiology?"

Holabird was transformed into an ardent boy. With a deprecatory "Would you really like to hear about 'em — you needn't be polite, you know!" he dashed into an exposition of his experiments, drawing sketches on the blank spaces in newspaper advertisements, on the back of a wedding invitation, on the flyleaf of a presentation novel, looking at Martin apologetically, learned yet gay.

"We're working on the localization of brain functions. I think we've gone beyond Bolton and Flechsig. Oh, it's jolly exciting, exploring the brain. Look here!"

His swift pencil was sketching the cerebrum; the brain lived and beat under his fingers.

He threw down the paper. "I say, it's a shame to inflict my hobbies on you. Besides, the others are coming. Tell me, how is your work going? Are you comfortable at the Institute? Do you find you like people?"

"Everybody except — To be frank, I'm jarred by Wickett."

Generously, "I know. His manner is slightly aggressive. But you mustn't mind him; he's really an extraordinarily gifted bio-chemist. He's a bachelor — gives up everything for his work. And he doesn't really mean half the rude things he says. He detests me, among others. Has he mentioned me?"

"Why, not especially — "

"I have a feeling he goes around saying that I talk about my experiences in the war, which really isn't quite altogether true."

"Yes," in a burst, "he did say that."

"I do rather wish he wouldn't. So sorry to have offended him by going and getting wounded. I'll remember and not do it again! Such a fuss for a war record as insignificant as mine! What happened was: when the war broke out in '14 I was in England, studying under Sherrington. I pretended to be a Canadian and joined up with the medical corps and got mine within three weeks and got hoofed out, and that was the end of my magnificent career! Here's somebody arriving."

His easy gallantry won Martin complete. Leora was equally captivated by Mrs. Holabird, and they went home from the dinner in new enchantment.

So began for them a white light of happiness. Martin was scarce more blissful in his undisturbed work than in his life outside the laboratory.

All the first week he forgot to ask what his salary was to be. Then it became a game to wait until the end of the month. Evenings, in little restaurants, Leora and he would speculate about it.

The Institute would surely not pay him less than the twenty-five hundred dollars a year he had received at the Rouncefield Clinic, but on evenings when he was tired it dropped to fifteen hundred, and one evening when they had Burgundy he raised it to thirty-five hundred.

When his first monthly check came, neat in a little sealed envelope, he dared not look at it. He took it home to Leora. In their hotel room they stared at the envelope as though it was likely to contain poison. Martin opened it shakily; he stared, and whispered, "Oh, those decent people! They're paying me — this is for four hundred and twenty dollars — they're paying me five thousand a year!"

Mrs. Holabird, a white kitten of a woman, helped Leora find a three-room flat with a spacious living-room, in an old house near Gramercy Park, and helped her furnish it with good bits, second-hand. When Martin was permitted to look he cried, "I hope we stay here for fifty years!"

This was the Grecian isle where they found peace. Presently they had friends: the Holabirds, Dr. Billy Smith — the thin-bearded bio-chemist, who had an intelligent taste in music and German beer — an anatomist whom Martin met at a Winnemac alumni dinner, and always Max Gottlieb.

Gottlieb had found his own serenity. In the Seventies he had a brown small flat, smelling of tobacco and leather books. His son Robert had graduated from City College and gone bustlingly into business. Miriam kept up her music while she guarded her father — a dumpling of a girl, holy fire behind the deceptive flesh. After an evening of Gottlieb's acrid doubting, Martin was inspired to hasten to the laboratory and attempt a thousand new queries into the laws of microorganisms, a task which usually began with blasphemously destroying all the work he had recently done.

Even Terry Wickett became more tolerable. Martin perceived that Wickett's snarls were partly a Clif Clawson misconception of humor, but partly a resentment, as great as Gottlieb's, of the morphological scientists who ticket things with the nicest little tickets, who name things and rename them and never analyze them. Wickett often worked all night; he was to be seen in shirt-sleeves, his sulky red hair rumpled, sitting with a stop-watch before a constant temperature bath for hours. Now and then it was a relief to have the surly intentness of Wickett instead of the elegance of Rippleton Holabird, which demanded from Martin so much painful elegance in turn, at a time when he was sunk beyond sounding in his experimentation.

## Chapter 27

His work began fumblingly. There were days when, for all the joy of it, he dreaded lest Tubbs stride in and bellow, "What are you doing here? You're the wrong Arrowsmith! Get out!"

He had isolated twenty strains of staphylococcus germs and he was testing them to discover which of them was most active in producing a hemolytic, a blood-disintegrating toxin, so that he might produce an antitoxin.

There were picturesque moments when, after centrifuging, the organisms lay in coiling cloudy masses at the bottoms of the tubes; or when the red corpuscles were completely dissolved and the opaque brick-red liquid turned to the color of pale wine. But most of the processes were incomparably tedious: removing samples of the culture every six hours, making salt suspensions of corpuscles in small tubes, recording the results.

He never knew they were tedious.

Tubbs came in now and then, found him busy, patted his shoulder, said something which sounded like French and might even have been French, and gave vague encouragement; while Gottlieb imperturbably told him to go ahead, and now and then stirred him by showing his own note-books (they were full of figures and abbreviations, stupid-seeming as invoices of calico) or by speaking of his own work, in a vocabulary as heathenish as Tibetan magic:

"Arrhenius and Madsen have made a contribution toward bringing immunity reactions under the mass action law, but I hope to show that antigen-antibody combinations occur in stoicheiometric proportions when certain variables are held constant."

"Oh, yes, I see," said Martin; and to himself: "Well, I darn near a quarter understand that! Oh, Lord, if they'll only give me a little time and not send me back to tacking up diphtheria posters!"

When he had obtained a satisfactory toxin, Martin began his effort to find an antitoxin. He made vast experiments with no results. Sometimes he was certain that he had something, but when he rechecked his experiments he was bleakly certain that he hadn't. Once he rushed into Gottlieb's laboratory with the announcement of the antitoxin, whereupon with affection and several discomforting questions and the present of a box of real Egyptian cigarettes, Gottlieb showed him that he had not considered certain dilutions.

With all his amateurish fumbling, Martin had one characteristic without which there can be no science: a wide-ranging, sniffing, snuffling, undignified, unself-dramatizing curiosity, and it drove him on.

### II

While he puttered his insignificant way through the early years of the Great European War, the McGurk Institute had a lively existence under its placid surface.

Martin may not have learned much in the matter of antibodies but he did learn the secret of the Institute, and he saw that behind all its quiet industriousness was Capitola McGurk, the Great White Uplifter.

Capitola, Mrs. Ross McGurk, had been opposed to woman suffrage — until she learned that women were certain to get the vote — but she was a complete controller of virtuous affairs. Ross McGurk had bought the Institute not only to glorify himself but to divert Capitola and keep her itching fingers out of his shipping and mining and lumber interests, which would not too well have borne the investigations of a Great White Uplifter.

Ross McGurk was at the time a man of fifty-four, second generation of California railroad men; a graduate of Yale; big, suave, dignified, cheerful, unscrupulous. Even in 1908, when he had founded the Institute, he had had too many houses, too many servants, too much food, and no children, because Capitola considered "that sort of thing detrimental to women with large responsibilities." In the Institute he found each year more satisfaction, more excuse for having lived.

When Gottlieb arrived, McGurk went up to look him over. McGurk had bullied Dr. Tubbs now and then; Tubbs was compelled to scurry to his office as though he were a messenger boy; yet when he saw the saturnine eyes of Gottlieb, McGurk looked interested; and the two men, the bulky, clothes-conscious, powerful, reticent American and the cynical, simple, power-despising European, became friends. McGurk would slip away from a conference affecting the commerce of a whole West Indian island to sit on a high stool, silent, and watch Gottlieb work.

"Some day when I quit hustling and wake up, I'm going to become your garçon, Max," said McGurk, and Gottlieb answered, "I don't know — you haf imagination, Ross, but I t'ink you are too late to get a training in reality. Now if you do not mind eating at Childs's, we will avoid your very expostulatory Regal Hall, and I shall invite you to lunch."

But Capitola did not join their communion.

Gottlieb's arrogance had returned, and with Capitola McGurk he needed it. She had such interesting little problems for her husband's pensioners to attack. Once, in excitement, she visited Gottlieb's laboratory to tell him that large numbers of persons die of cancer, and why didn't he drop this anti-whatever-it-was and find a cure for cancer, which would be ever so nice for all of them.

But her real grievance arose when, after Rippleton Holabird had agreed to give midnight supper on the roof of the Institute to one of her most intellectual dinner-parties, she telephoned to Gottlieb, merely asking, "Would it be too much trouble for you to go down and open your lab, so we can all enjoy just a tiny peep at it?" and he answered:

"It would! Good night!"

Capitola protested to her husband. He listened — at least he seemed to listen — and remarked:

"Cap, I don't mind your playing the fool with the footmen. They've got to stand it. But if you get funny with Max, I'll simply shut up the whole Institute, and then you won't have anything to talk about at the Colony Club. And it certainly does beat the deuce that a man worth thirty million dollars — at least a fellow that's got that much — can't find a clean pair of pajamas. No, I *won't* have a valet! Oh, please now, Capitola, please quit being high-minded and let me go to sleep, will you!"

But Capitola was uncontrollable, especially in the matter of the monthly dinners which she gave at the Institute.

## III

The first of the McGurk Scientific Dinners which Martin and Leora witnessed was a particularly important and explanatory dinner, because the guest of honor was Major-General Sir Isaac Mallard, the London surgeon, who was in America with a British War Mission. He had already beautifully let himself be shown through the Institute; he had been Sir Isaac'd by Dr. Tubbs and every researcher except Terry Wickett; he remembered meeting Rippleton Holabird in London, or said he remembered; and he admired Gladys the Centrifuge.

The dinner began with one misfortune in that Terry Wickett, who hitherto could be depended upon to stay decently away, now appeared, volunteering to the wife of an ex-ambassador, "I simply couldn't duck this spread, with dear Sir Isaac coming. Say, if I hadn't told you, you wouldn't hardly think my dress-suit was rented, would you! Have you noticed that Sir Isaac is getting so he doesn't tear the carpet with his spurs any more? I wonder if he still kills all his mastoid patients?"

There was vast music, vaster food; there were uncomfortable scientists explaining to golden cooing ladies, in a few words, just what they were up to and what in the next twenty years they hoped to be up to; there were the cooing ladies themselves, observing in tones of pretty rebuke, "But I'm afraid you haven't yet made it as clear as you might." There were the cooing ladies' husbands — college graduates, manipulators of oil stocks or of corporation law — who sat ready to give to anybody who desired it their opinion that while antitoxins might be racy, what we really needed was a good substitute for rubber.

There was Rippleton Holabird, being charming.

And in the pause of the music, there suddenly was Terry Wickett, saying to quite an important woman, one of Capitola's most useful friends, "Yes, his name is spelled G-o-t-t-l-i-e-b but it's pronounced Gottdamn."

But such outsiders as Wickett and such silent riders as Martin and Leora and such totally absent members as Max Gottlieb were few, and the dinner waxed magnificently to a love-feast when Dr. Tubbs and Sir Isaac Mallard paid compliments to each other, to Capitola, to the sacred soil of France, to brave little Belgium, to American hospitality, to British love of privacy, and to the extremely interesting things a young man with a sense of co-operation might do in modern science.

The guests were conducted through the Institute. They inspected the marine biology aquarium, the pathological museum, and the animal house, at sight of which one sprightly lady demanded of Wickett, "Oh, the poor little guinea pigs and darling rabbicks! Now honestly, Doctor, don't you think it would be ever so much nicer if you let them go free, and just worked with your test-tubes?"

A popular physician, whose practice was among rich women, none of them west of Fifth Avenue, said to the sprightly lady, "I think you're absolutely right. I never have to kill any poor wee little beasties to get my knowledge!"

With astounding suddenness Wickett took his hat and went away.

The sprightly lady said, "You see, he didn't dare stand up to a real argument. Oh, Dr. Arrowsmith, of course I know how wonderful Ross McGurk and Dr. Tubbs and all of you are, but I must say I'm disappointed in your laboratories. I'd expected there'd be such larky retorts and electric furnaces and everything but, honestly, I don't see a single thing that's interesting, and I do think all you clever people ought to do *something* for us, now that you've coaxed us all the way down here. Can't you or somebody create life out of turtle eggs, or whatever it is? Oh, please do! Pretty please! Or at least, do put on one of these cunnin' dentist coats that you wear."

Then Martin also went rapidly away, accompanied by a furious Leora, who in the taxicab announced that she had desired to taste the champagne-cup which she had observed on the buffet, and that her husband was little short of a fool.

## IV

Thus, however satisfying his work, Martin began to wonder about the perfection of his sanctuary; to wonder why Gottlieb should be so insulting at lunch to neat Dr. Sholtheis, the industrious head of the Department of Epidemiology, and why Dr. Sholtheis should endure the insults; to wonder why Dr. Tubbs, when he wandered into one's laboratory, should gurgle, "The one thing for you to keep in view in all your work is the ideal of co-operation"; to wonder why so ardent a physiologist as Rippleton Holabird should all day long be heard conferring with Tubbs instead of sweating at his bench.

Holabird had, five years before, done one bit of research which had taken his name into scientific journals throughout the world: he had studied the effect of the extirpation of the anterior lobes of a dog's brain on its ability to find its way through the laboratory. Martin had read of that research before he had thought of going to McGurk; on his arrival he was thrilled to have it chronicled by the master himself; but when he had heard Holabird refer to it a dozen times he was considerably less thrilled, and he speculated whether all his life Holabird would go on being "the man — *you* remember — the chap that did the big stunt, whatever it was, with locomotion in dogs or something."

Martin speculated still more as he perceived that all his colleagues were secretly grouped in factions.

Tubbs, Holabird, and perhaps Tubbs's secretary, Pearl Robbins, were the ruling caste. It was murmured that Holabird hoped some day to be made Assistant Director, an office which was to be created for him. Gottlieb, Terry Wickett, and Dr. Nicholas Yeo, that long-mustached and rustic biologist whom Martin had first taken for a carpenter, formed an independent faction of their own, and however much he disliked the boisterous Wickett, Martin was dragged into it.

Dr. William Smith, with his little beard and a notion of mushrooms formed in Paris, kept to himself. Dr. Sholtheis, who had been born to a synagogue in Russia but who was now the most zealous high-church Episcopalian in Yonkers, was constantly in his polite small way trying to have his scientific work commended by Gottlieb. In the Department of Bio-Physics, the good-natured chief was reviled and envied by his own assistant. And in the whole Institute there was not one man who would, in all states of liquor, assert that the work of any other scientist anywhere was completely sound, or that there was a single one of his rivals who had not stolen ideas from him. No rocking-chair clique on a summer-hotel porch, no knot of actors, ever whispered more scandal or hinted more warmly of complete idiocy in their confrères than did these uplifted scientists.

But these discoveries Martin could shut out by closing his door, and he had that to do now which deafened him to the mutters of intrigue.

## V

For once Gottlieb did not amble into his laboratory but curtly summoned him. In a corner of Gottlieb's office, a den opening from his laboratory, was Terry Wickett, rolling a cigarette and looking sardonic.

Gottlieb observed, "Martin, I haf taken the privilege of talking you over with Terry, and we concluded that you haf done well enough now so it is time you stop puttering and go to work."

"I thought I was working, sir!"

All the wide placidness of his halcyon days was gone; he saw himself driven back to Pickerbaughism.

Wickett intruded, "No, you haven't. You've just been showing that you're a bright boy who might work if he only knew something."

While Martin turned on Wickett with a "Who the devil are you?" expression, Gottlieb went on:

"The fact is, Martin, you can do nothing till you know a little mathematics. If you are not going to be a cookbook bacteriologist, like most of them, you must be able to handle some of the fundamentals of science. All living things are physicochemical machines. Then how can you make progress if you do not know physical chemistry, and how can you know physical chemistry without much mathematics?"

"Yuh," said Wickett, "you're lawn-mowing and daisy-picking, not digging."

Martin faced them. "But rats, Wickett, a man can't know everything. I'm a bacteriologist, not a physicist. Strikes me a fellow ought to use his insight, not just a chest of tools, to make discoveries. A good sailor could find his way at sea even if he didn't have instruments, and a whole *Lusitania* -ful of junk wouldn't make a good sailor out of a dub. Man ought to develop his brain, not depend on tools."

"Ye-uh, but if there were charts and quadrants in existence, a sailor that cruised off without 'em would be a chump!"

For half an hour Martin defended himself, not too politely, before the gem-like Gottlieb, the granite Wickett. All the while he knew that he was sickeningly ignorant.

They ceased to take interest. Gottlieb was looking at his note-books, Wickett was clumping off to work. Martin glared at Gottlieb. The man meant so much that he could be furious with him as he would have been with Leora, with his own self.

"I'm sorry you think I don't know anything," he raged, and departed with the finest dramatic violence. He slammed into his own laboratory, felt freed, then wretched. Without volition, like a drunken man, he stormed to Wickett's room, protesting, "I suppose you're right. My physical chemistry is nix, and my math rotten. What am I going to do — what am I going to do?"

The embarrassed barbarian grumbled, "Well, for Pete's sake, Slim, don't worry. The old man and I were just egging you on. Fact is, he's tickled to death about the careful way you're starting in. About the math — probably you're better off than the Holy Wren and Tubbs right now; you've forgotten all the math you ever knew, and they never knew any. Gosh all fishhooks! Science is supposed to mean Knowledge — from the Greek, a handsome language spoken by the good old booze-hoisting Hellenes — and the way most of the science boys resent having to stop writing little jeweled papers or giving teas and sweat at getting some knowledge certainly does make me a grand booster for the human race. My own math isn't any too good, Slim, but if you'd like to have me come around evenings and tutor you — Free, I mean!"

Thus began the friendship between Martin and Terry Wickett; thus began a change in Martin's life whereby he gave up three or four hours of wholesome sleep each night to grind over matters which everyone is assumed to know, and almost everyone does not know.

He took up algebra; found that he had forgotten most of it; cursed over the competition of the indefatigable A and the indolent B who walk from Y to Z; hired a Columbia tutor; and finished the subject, with a spurt of something like interest in regard to quadratic equations, in six weeks ... while Leora listened, watched, waited, made sandwiches, and laughed at the tutor's jokes.

By the end of his first nine months at McGurk, Martin had reviewed trigonometry and analytic geometry and he was finding differential calculus romantic. But he made the mistake of telling Terry Wickett how much he knew.

Terry croaked, "Don't trust math too much, son," and he so confused him with references to the thermo-dynamical derivation of the mass action law, and to the oxidation reduction potential, that he stumbled again into raging humility, again saw himself an impostor and a tenth-rater.

He read the classics of physical science: Copernicus and Galileo, Lavoisier, Newton, LaPlace, Descartes, Faraday. He became completely bogged in Newton's "Fluxions"; he spoke of Newton to Tubbs and found that the illustrious Director knew nothing about him. He cheerfully mentioned this to Terry, and was shockingly cursed for his conceit as a "nouveau cultured," as a "typical enthusiastic convert," and so returned to the work whose end is satisfying because there is never an end.

His life did not seem edifying nor in any degree amusing. When Tubbs peeped into his laboratory he found a humorless young man going about his tests of hemolytic toxins with no apparent flair for the Real Big Thing in Science, which was co-operation and being efficient. Tubbs tried to set him straight with "Are you quite sure you're following a regular demarked line in your work?"

It was Leora who bore the real tedium.

She sat quiet (a frail child, only up to one's shoulder, not nine minutes older than at marriage, nine years before), or she napped inoffensively, in the long living-room of their flat, while he worked over his dreary digit-infested books till one, till two, and she politely awoke to let him worry at her, "But look here now, I've got to keep up my research at the same time. God, I am so tired!"

She dragged him away for an illegal five-day walk on Cape Cod, in March. He sat between the Twin Lights at Chatham, and fumed, "I'm going back and tell Terry and Gottlieb they can go to the devil with their crazy physical chemistry. I've had enough, now I've done math," and she commented, "Yes, I certainly would — though isn't it funny how Dr. Gottlieb always seems to be right?"

He was so absorbed in staphylolysin and in calculus that he did not realize the world was about to be made safe for democracy. He was a little dazed when America entered the war.

## VI

Dr. Tubbs dashed to Washington to offer the services of the Institute to the War Department.

All the members of the staff, except Gottlieb and two others who declined to be so honored, were made officers and told to run out and buy nice uniforms.

Tubbs became a Colonel, Rippleton Holabird a Major, Martin and Wickett and Billy Smith were Captains. But the garçons had no military rank whatever, nor any military duties except the polishing of brown riding-boots and leather puttees, which the several warriors wore as pleased their fancies or their legs. And the most belligerent of all, Miss Pearl Robbins, she who at tea heroically slaughtered not only German men but all their women and viperine children, was wickedly unrecognized and had to make up a uniform for herself.

The only one of them who got nearer to the front than Liberty Street was Terry Wickett, who suddenly asked for leave, was transferred to the artillery, and sailed off to France.

He apologized to Martin: "I'm ashamed of chucking my work like this, and I certainly don't want to kill Germans — I mean not any more'n I want to kill most people — but I never could resist getting into a big show. Say, Slim, keep an eye on Pa Gottlieb, will you? This has hit him bad. He's got a bunch of nephews and so on in the German army, and the patriots like Big Foot Pearl will give an exhibit of idealism by persecuting him. So long, Slim, take care y'self."

Martin had vaguely protested at being herded into the army. The war was to him chiefly another interruption to his work, like Pickerbaughism, like earning his living at Wheatsylvania. But when he had gone strutting forth in uniform, it was so enjoyable that for several weeks he was a standard patriot. He had never looked so well, so taut and erect, as in khaki. It was enchanting to be saluted by privates, quite as enchanting to return the salute in the dignified, patronizing, all-comrades-together splendor which Martin shared with the other doctors, professors, lawyers, brokers, authors, and former socialist intellectuals who were his fellow-officers.

But in a month the pleasures of being a hero became mechanical, and Martin longed for soft shirts, easy shoes, and clothes with reasonable pockets. His puttees were a nuisance to wear and an inferno to put on; his collar pinched his neck and jabbed his chin; and it was wearing on a man who sat up till three, on the perilous duty of studying calculus, to be snappy at every salute.

Under the martinet eye of Col. Director Dr. A. DeWitt Tubbs he had to wear his uniform, at least recognizable portions of it, at the Institute, but by evening he slipped into the habit of sneaking into citizen clothes, and when he went with Leora to the movies he had an agreeable feeling of being Absent Without Leave, of risking at every street corner arrest by the Military Police and execution at dawn.

Unfortunately no M.P. ever looked at him. But one evening when in an estimable and innocent manner he was looking at the remains of a gunman who had just been murdered by another gunman, he realized that Major Rippleton Holabird was standing by, glaring. For once the Major was unpleasant:

"Captain, does it seem to you that this is quite playing the game, to wear mufti? We, unfortunately, with our scientific work, haven't the privilege of joining the Boys who are up against the real thing, but we are under orders just as if we were in the trenches — where *some* of us would so much like to be again! Captain, I trust I shall never again see you breaking the order about being in uniform, or — uh — "

Martin blurted to Leora, later:

"I'm sick of hearing about his being wounded. Nothing that I can see to prevent his going back to the trenches. Wound's all right now. I want to be patriotic, but my patriotism is chasing antitoxins, doing my job, not wearing a particular kind of pants and a particular set of ideas about the Germans. Mind you, I'm anti-German all right — I think they're probably just as bad as we are. Oh, let's go back and do some more calculus.... Darling, my working nights doesn't bore you too much, does it?"

Leora had cunning. When she could not be enthusiastic, she could be unannoyingly silent.

At the Institute Martin perceived that he was not the only defender of his country who was not comfortable in the garb of heroes. The most dismal of the staff-members was Dr. Nicholas Yeo, the Yankee sandy-mustached head of the Department of Biology.

Yeo had put on Major's uniform, but he never felt neighborly with it. (He knew he was a Major, because Col. Dr. Tubbs had told him he was, and he knew that this was a Major's uniform because the clothing salesman said so.) He walked out of the McGurk Building in a melancholy, deprecatory way, with one breeches leg bulging over his riding-boots; and however piously he tried, he never remembered to button his blouse over the violet-flowered shirts which, he often confided, you could buy ever so cheap on Eighth Avenue.

But Major Dr. Yeo had one military triumph. He hoarsely explained to Martin, as they were marching to the completely militarized dining-hall:

"Say, Arrowsmith, do you ever get balled up about this saluting? Darn it, I never can figure out what all these insignia mean. One time I took a Salvation Army Lieutenant for a Y.M.C.A. General, or maybe he was a Portygee. But I've got the idea now!" Yeo laid his finger beside his large nose, and produced wisdom: "Whenever I see any fellow in uniform that looks older than I am, I salute him — my nephew, Ted, has drilled me so I salute swell now — and if he don't salute back, well, Lord, I just think about my work and don't fuss. If you look at it scientifically, this military life isn't so awful' hard after all!"

## VII

Always, in Paris or in Bonn, Max Gottlieb had looked to America as a land which, in its freedom from Royalist tradition, in its contact with realities of cornfields and blizzards and town-meetings, had set its face against the puerile pride of war. He believed that he had ceased to be a German, now, and become a countryman of Lincoln.

The European War was the one thing, besides his discharge from Winnemac, which had ever broken his sardonic serenity. In the war he could see no splendor nor hope, but only crawling tragedy. He treasured his months of work and good talk in France, in England, in Italy; he loved his French and English and Italian friends as he loved his ancient *Korpsbrüder* , and very well indeed beneath his mocking did he love the Germans with whom he had drudged and drunk.

His sister's sons — on home-craving vacations he had seen them, in babyhood, in boyhood, in ruffling youngmanhood — went out with the Kaiser's colors in 1914; one of them became an Oberst, much decorated, one existed insignificantly, and one was dead and stinking in ten days. This he sadly endured, as later he endured his son Robert's going out as an American lieutenant, to fight his own cousins. What struck down this man to whom abstractions and scientific laws were more than kindly flesh was the mania of hate which overcame the unmilitaristic America to which he had emigrated in protest against Junkerdom.

Incredulously he perceived women asserting that all Germans were baby-killers, universities barring the language of Heine, orchestras outlawing the music of Beethoven, professors in uniform bellowing at clerks, and the clerks never protesting.

It is uncertain whether the real hurt was to his love for America or to his egotism, that he should have guessed so grotesquely; it is curious that he who had so denounced the machine-made education of the land should yet have been surprised when it turned blithely to the old, old, mechanical mockeries of war.

When the Institute sanctified the war, he found himself regarded not as the great and impersonal immunologist but as a suspect German Jew.

True, the Terry who went off to the artillery did not look upon him dourly, but Major Rippleton Holabird became erect and stiff when they passed in the corridor. When Gottlieb insisted to Tubbs at lunch, "I am villing to admit every virtue of the French — I am very fond of that so individual people — but on the theory of probabilities I suggest that there must be some good Germans out of sixty millions," then Col. Dr. Tubbs commanded, "In this time of world tragedy, it does not seem to me particularly becoming to try to be flippant, Dr. Gottlieb!"

In shops and on the elevated train, little red-faced sweaty people when they heard his accent glared at him, and growled one to another, "There's one of them damn' barb'rous well-poisoning Huns!" and however contemptuous he might be, however much he strove for ignoring pride, their nibbling reduced him from arrogant scientist to an insecure, raw-nerved, shrinking old man.

And once a hostess who of old time had been proud to know him, a hostess whose maiden name was Straufnabel and who had married into the famous old Anglican family of Rosemont when Gottlieb bade her "*Auf Wiedersehen* " cried out upon him, "Dr. Gottlieb, I'm very sorry, but the use of that disgusting language is not permitted in this house!"

He had almost recovered from the anxieties of Winnemac and the Hunziker factory; he had begun to expand, to entertain people — scientists, musicians, talkers. Now he was thrust back into himself. With Terry gone, he trusted only Miriam and Martin and Ross McGurk; and his deep-set wrinkle-lidded eyes looked ever on sadness.

But he could still be tart. He suggested that Capitola ought to have in the window of her house a Service Flag with a star for every person at the Institute who had put on uniform.

She took it quite seriously, and did it.

## VIII

The military duties of the McGurk staff did not consist entirely in wearing uniforms, receiving salutes, and listening to Col. Dr. Tubbs's luncheon lectures on "the part America will inevitably play in the reconstruction of a Democratic Europe."

They prepared sera; the assistant in the Department of Bio-Physics was inventing electrified wire entanglements; Dr. Billy Smith, who six months before had been singing *Studentenlieder* at Lüchow's, was working on poison gas to be used against all singers of *Lieder* ; and to Martin was assigned the manufacture of lipovaccine, a suspension of finely ground typhoid and paratyphoid organisms in oil. It was a greasy job, and dull. Martin was faithful enough about it, and gave to it almost every morning, but he blasphemed more than usual and he unholily welcomed scientific papers in which lipovaccines were condemned as inferior to ordinary salt solutions.

He was conscious of Gottlieb's sorrowing and tried to comfort him.

It was Martin's most pitiful fault that he was not very kind to shy people and lonely people and stupid old people; he was not cruel to them, he simply was unconscious of them or so impatient of their fumbling that he avoided them. Whenever Leora taxed him with it he grumbled:

"Well, but — I'm too much absorbed in my work, or in doping stuff out, to waste time on morons. And it's a good thing. Most people above the grade of hog do so much chasing around after a lot of vague philanthropy that they never get anything done — and most of your confounded shy people get spiritually pauperized. Oh, it's so much easier to be good-natured and purring and self-congratulatory and generally footless than it is to pound ahead and keep yourself strictly for your own work, the work that gets somewhere. Very few people have the courage to be decently selfish — not answer letters — and demand the right to work. If they had their way, these sentimentalists would've had a Newton — yes, or probably a Christ! — giving up everything they did for the world to address meetings and listen to the troubles of cranky old maids. Nothing takes so much courage as to keep hard and clear-headed."

And he hadn't even that courage.

When Leora had made complaint, he would be forcibly kind to all sorts of alarmed stray beggars for a day or two, then drift back into his absorption. There were but two people whose unhappiness could always pierce him: Leora and Gottlieb.

Though he was busier than he had known anyone could ever be, with lipovaccines in the morning, physical chemistry in the evening and, at all sorts of intense hours between, the continuation of his staphylolysin research, he gave what time he could to seeking out Gottlieb and warming his vanity by reverent listening.

Then his research wiped out everything else, made him forget Gottlieb and Leora and all his briskness about studying, made him turn his war work over to others, and confounded night and day in one insane flaming blur as he realized that he had something not unworthy of a Gottlieb, something at the mysterious source of life.

## Chapter 28

Captain Martin Arrowsmith, M.R.C., came home to his good wife Leora, wailing, "I'm so rotten tired, and I feel kind of discouraged. I haven't accomplished a darn' thing in this whole year at McGurk. Sterile. No good. And I'm hanged if I'll study calculus this evening. Let's go to the movies. Won't even change to regular human clothes. Too tired."

"All right, honey," said Leora. "But let's have dinner here. I bought a wonderful ole fish this afternoon."

Through the film Martin gave his opinion, as a captain and as a doctor, that it seemed improbable a mother should not know her daughter after an absence of ten years. He was restless and rational, which is not a mood in which to view the cinema. When they came blinking out of that darkness lit only from the shadowy screen, he snorted, "I'm going back to the lab. I'll put you in a taxi."

"Oh, let the beastly thing go for one night."

"Now that's unfair! I haven't worked late for three or four nights now!"

"Then take me along."

"Nope. I have a hunch I may be working all night."

Liberty Street, as he raced along it, was sleeping below its towers. It was McGurk's order that the elevator to the Institute should run all night, and indeed three or four of the twenty staff-members did sometimes use it after respectable hours.

That morning Martin had isolated a new strain of staphylococcus bacteria from the gluteal carbuncle of a patient in the Lower Manhattan Hospital, a carbuncle which was healing with unusual rapidity. He had placed a bit of the pus in broth and incubated it. In eight hours a good growth of bacteria had appeared. Before going wearily home he had returned the flask to the incubator.

He was not particularly interested in it, and now, in his laboratory, he removed his military blouse, looked down to the lights on the blue-black river, smoked a little, thought what a dog he was not to be gentler to Leora, and damned Bert Tozer and Pickerbaugh and Tubbs and anybody else who was handy to his memory before he absent-mindedly wavered to the incubator, and found that the flask, in which there should have been a perceptible cloudy growth, had no longer any signs of bacteria — of staphylococci.

"Now what the hell!" he cried. "Why, the broth's as clear as when I seeded it! Now what the — Think of this fool accident coming up just when I was going to start something new!"

He hastened from the incubator, in a closet off the corridor, to his laboratory and, holding the flask under a strong light, made certain that he had seen aright. He fretfully prepared a slide from the flask contents and examined it under the microscope. He discovered nothing but shadows of what had been bacteria: thin outlines, the form still there but the cell substance gone; minute skeletons on an infinitesimal battlefield.

He raised his head from the microscope, rubbed his tired eyes, reflectively rubbed his neck — his blouse was off, his collar on the floor, his shirt open at the throat. He considered:

"Something funny here. This culture was growing all right, and now it's committed suicide. Never heard of bugs doing that before. I've hit something! What caused it? Some chemical change? Something organic?"

Now in Martin Arrowsmith there were no decorative heroisms, no genius for amours, no exotic wit, no edifyingly borne misfortunes. He presented neither picturesque elegance nor a moral message. He was full of hasty faults and of perverse honesty; a young man often unkindly, often impolite. But he had one gift: curiosity whereby he saw nothing as ordinary. Had he been an acceptable hero, like Major Rippleton Holabird, he would have chucked the contents of the flask into the sink, avowed with pretty modesty, "Silly! I've made some error!" and gone his ways. But Martin, being Martin, walked prosaically up and down his laboratory, snarling. "Now there was some *cause* for that, and I'm going to find out what it was."

He did have one romantic notion: he would telephone to Leora and tell her that splendor was happening, and she wasn't to worry about him. He fumbled down the corridor, lighting matches, trying to find electric switches.

At night all halls are haunted. Even in the smirkingly new McGurk Building there had been a bookkeeper who committed suicide. As Martin groped he was shakily conscious of feet padding behind him, of shapes which leered from doorways and insolently vanished, of ancient bodiless horrors, and when he found the switch he rejoiced in the blessing and security of sudden light that re-created the world.

At the Institute telephone switchboard he plugged in wherever it seemed reasonable. Once he thought he was talking to Leora, but it proved to be a voice, sexless and intolerant, which said "Number pleeeeeze" with a taut alertness impossible to anyone so indolent as Leora. Once it was a voice which slobbered, "Is this Sarah?" then, "I don't want *you* ! Ring off, will yuh!" Once a girl pleaded, "Honestly, Billy, I did try to get there but the boss came in at five and he said — "

As for the rest it was only a blurring; the sound of seven million people hungry for sleep or love or money.

He observed, "Oh, rats, I guess Lee'll have gone to bed by now," and felt his way back to the laboratory.

A detective, hunting the murderer of bacteria, he stood with his head back, scratching his chin, scratching his memory for like cases of microorganisms committing suicide or being slain without perceptible cause. He rushed upstairs to the library, consulted the American and English authorities and, laboriously, the French and German. He found nothing.

He worried lest there might, somehow, have been no living staphylococci in the pus which he had used for seeding the broth — none there to die. At a hectic run, not stopping for lights, bumping corners and sliding on the too perfect tile floor, he skidded down the stairs and galloped through the corridors to his room. He found the remains of the original pus, made a smear on a glass slide, and stained it with gentian-violet, nervously dribbling out one drop of the gorgeous dye. He sprang to the microscope. As he bent over the brass tube and focused the objective, into the gray-lavender circular field of vision rose to existence the grape-like clusters of staphylococcus germs, purple dots against the blank plane.

"Staph in it, all right!" he shouted.

Then he forgot Leora, war, night, weariness, success, everything, as he charged into preparations for an experiment, his first great experiment. He paced furiously, rather dizzy. He shook himself into calmness and settled down at a table, among rings and spirals of cigarette smoke, to list on small sheets of paper all the possible causes of suicide in the bacteria — all the questions he had to answer and the experiments which should answer them.

It might be that alkali in an improperly cleaned flask had caused the clearing of the culture. It might be some anti-staph substance existing in the pus, or something liberated by the staphylococci themselves. It might be some peculiarity of this particular broth.

Each of these had to be tested.

He pried open the door of the glass-storeroom, shattering the lock. He took new flasks, cleaned them, plugged them with cotton, and placed them in the hot-air oven to sterilize. He found other batches of broth — as a matter of fact he stole them, from Gottlieb's private and highly sacred supply in the ice-box. He filtered some of the clarified culture through a sterile porcelain filter, and added it to his regular staphylococcus strains.

And, perhaps most important of all, he discovered that he was out of cigarettes.

Incredulously he slapped each of his pockets, and went the round and slapped them all over again. He looked into his discarded military blouse; had a cheering idea about having seen cigarettes in a drawer; did not find them; and brazenly marched into the room where hung the aprons and jackets of the technicians. Furiously he pilfered pockets, and found a dozen beautiful cigarettes in a wrinkled and flattened paper case.

To test each of the four possible causes of the flask's clearing he prepared and seeded with bacteria a series of flasks under varying conditions, and set them away in the incubator at body temperature. Till the last flask was put away, his hand was steady, his worn face calm. He was above all nervousness, free from all uncertainty, a professional going about his business.

By this time it was six o'clock of a fine wide August morning, and as he ceased his swift work, as taut nerves slackened, he looked out of his lofty window and was conscious of the world below: bright roofs, jubilant towers, and a high-decked Sound steamer swaggering up the glossy river.

He was completely fagged; he was, like a surgeon after a battle, like a reporter during an earthquake, perhaps a little insane; but sleepy he was not. He cursed the delay involved in the growth of the bacteria, without which he could not discover the effect of the various sorts of broths and bacterial strains, but choked his impatience.

He mounted the noisy slate stairway to the lofty world of the roof. He listened at the door of the Institute's animal house. The guinea pigs, awake and nibbling, were making a sound like that of a wet cloth rubbed on glass in window-cleaning. He stamped his foot, and in fright they broke out in their strange sound of fear, like the cooing of doves.

He marched violently up and down, refreshed by the soaring sky, till he was calmed to hunger. Again he went pillaging. He found chocolate belonging to an innocent technician; he even invaded the office of the Director and in the desk of the Diana-like Pearl Robbins unearthed tea and a kettle (as well as a lip-stick, and a love-letter beginning "My Little Ickles"). He made himself a profoundly bad cup of tea, then, his whole body dragging, returned to his table to set down elaborately, in a shabby, nearly-filled note-book, every step of his experiment.

After seven he worked out the operation of the telephone switchboard and called Lower Manhattan Hospital. Could Dr. Arrowsmith have some more pus from the same carbuncle? What? It'd healed? Curse it! No more of that material.

He hesitated over waiting for Gottlieb's arrival, to tell him of the discovery, but determined to keep silence till he should have determined whether it was an accident. Eyes wide, too wrought up to sleep in the subway, he fled uptown to tell Leora. He had to tell someone! Waves of fear, doubt, certainty, and fear again swept over him; his ears rang and his hands trembled.

He rushed up to the flat; he bawled "Lee! Lee!" Before he had unlocked the door. And she was gone.

He gaped. The flat breathed emptiness. He searched it again. She had slept there, she had had a cup of coffee, but she had vanished.

He was at once worried lest there had been an accident, and furious that she should not have been here at the great hour. Sullenly he made breakfast for himself.... It is strange that excellent bacteriologists and chemists should scramble eggs so waterily, should make such bitter coffee and be so casual about dirty spoons.... By the time he had finished the mess he was ready to believe that Leora had left him forever. He quavered, "I've neglected her a lot." Sluggishly, an old man now, he started for the Institute, and at the entrance to the subway he met her.

She wailed, "I was so worried! I couldn't get you on the 'phone. I went clear down to the Institute to see what'd happened to you."

He kissed her, very competently, and raved, "God, woman, I've got it! The real big stuff! I've found something, not a chemical you put in I mean, that eats bugs — dissolves 'em — kills 'em. May be a big new step in therapeutics. Oh, no, rats, I don't suppose it really is. Prob'ly just another of my bulls."

She sought to reassure him but he did not wait. He dashed down to the subway, promising to telephone to her. By ten, he was peering into his incubator.

There was a cloudy appearance of bacteria in all the flasks except those in which he had used broth from the original alarming flask. In these, the mysterious murderer of germs had prevented the growth of the new bacteria which he had introduced.

"Great stuff," he said.

He returned the flasks to the incubator, recorded his observations, went again to the library, and searched handbooks, bound proceedings of societies, periodicals in three languages. He had acquired a reasonable scientific French and German. It is doubtful whether he could have bought a drink or asked the way to the Kursaal in either language, but he understood the universal

Hellenistic scientific jargon, and he pawed through the heavy books, rubbing his eyes, which were filled with salty fire.

He remembered that he was an army officer and had lipovaccine to make this morning. He went to work, but he was so twitchy that he ruined the batch, called his patient garçon a fool, and after this injustice sent him out for a pint of whisky.

He had to have a confidant. He telephoned to Leora, lunched with her expensively, and asserted, "It still looks as if there were something to it." He was back in the Institute every hour that afternoon, glancing at his flasks, but between he tramped the streets, creaking with weariness, drinking too much coffee.

Every five minutes it came to him, as a quite new and ecstatic idea, "Why don't I go to sleep?" then he remembered, and groaned, "No, I've got to keep going and watch every step. Can't leave it, or I'll have to begin all over again. But I'm so sleepy! Why don't I go to sleep?"

He dug down, before six, into a new layer of strength, and at six his examination showed that the flasks containing the original broth still had no growth of bacteria, and the flasks which he had seeded with the original pus had, like the first eccentric flask, after beginning to display a good growth of bacteria cleared up again under the slowly developing attack of the unknown assassin.

He sat down, drooping with relief. He had it! He stated in the conclusions of his first notes:

"I have observed a principle, which I shall temporarily call the X Principle, in pus from a staphylococcus infection, which checks the growth of several strains of staphylococcus, and which dissolves the staphylococci from the pus in question."

When he had finished, at seven, his head was on his note-book and he was asleep.

He awoke at ten, went home, ate like a savage, slept again, and was in the laboratory before dawn. His next rest was an hour that afternoon, sprawled on his laboratory table, with his garçon on guard; the next, a day and a half later, was eight hours in bed, from dawn till noon.

But in dreams he was constantly upsetting a rack of test-tubes or breaking a flask. He discovered an X Principle which dissolved chairs, tables, human beings. He went about smearing it on Bert Tozers and Dr. Bissexes and fiendishly watching them vanish, but accidentally he dropped it on Leora and saw her fading, and he woke screaming to find the real Leora's arms about him, while he sobbed, "Oh, I couldn't do anything without you! Don't ever leave me! I do love you so, even if this damned work does keep me tied up. Stay with me!"

While she sat by him on the frowsy bed, gay in her gingham, he went to sleep, to wake up three hours later and start off for the Institute, his eyes blood-glaring and set. She was ready for him with strong coffee, waiting on him silently, looking at him proudly, while he waved his arms, babbling:

"Gottlieb better not talk any more about the importance of new observations! The X Principle may not just apply to staph. Maybe you can sic it on any bug — cure any germ disease by it. Bug that lives on bugs! Or maybe it's a chemical principle, an enzyme. Oh, I don't know. But I will!"

As he bustled to the Institute he swelled with the certainty that after years of stumbling he had arrived. He had visions of his name in journals and textbooks; of scientific meetings cheering him. He had been an unknown among the experts of the Institute, and now he pitied all of them. But when he was back at his bench the grandiose aspirations faded and he was the sniffing, snuffling beagle, the impersonal worker. Before him, supreme joy of the investigator, new mountain-passes of work opened, and in him was new power.

## II

For a week Martin's life had all the regularity of an escaped soldier in the enemy's country, with the same agitation and the same desire to prowl at night. He was always sterilizing flasks, preparing media of various hydrogen-ion concentrations, copying his old notes into a new book lovingly labeled "X Principle, Staph," and adding to it further observations. He tried, elaborately, with many flasks and many reseedings, to determine whether the X Principle would perpetuate itself indefinitely, whether when it was transmitted from tube to new tube of bacteria it would reappear, whether, growing by cell-division automatically, it was veritably a germ, a sub-germ infecting germs.

During the week Gottlieb occasionally peered over his shoulder, but Martin was unwilling to report until he should have proof, and one good night's sleep, and perhaps even a shave.

When he was sure that the X Principle did reproduce itself indefinitely, so that in the tenth tube it grew to have as much effect as in the first, then he solemnly called on Gottlieb and laid before him his results, with his plans for further investigation.

The old man tapped his thin fingers on the report, read it intently, looked up and, not wasting time in congratulations, vomited questions:

"Have you done dis? Why have you not done dat? At what temperature is the activity of the Principle at its maximum? Is its activity manifested on agar-solid medium?"

"This is my plan for new work. I think you'll find it includes most of your suggestions."

"Huh!" Gottlieb ran through it and snorted, "Why have you not planned to propagate it on dead staph? That is most important of all."

"Why?"

Gottlieb flew instantly to the heart of the jungle in which Martin had struggled for many days: "Because that will show whether you are dealing with a living virus."

Martin was humbled, but Gottlieb beamed:

"You haf a big thing. Now do not let the Director know about this and get enthusiastic too soon. I am glad, Martin!"

There was that in his voice which sent Martin swanking down the corridor, back to work — and to not sleeping.

What the X Principle was — chemical or germ — he could not determine, but certainly the original Principle flourished. It could be transmitted indefinitely; he determined the best temperature for it and found that it did not propagate on dead staphylococcus. When he added a drop containing the Principle to a growth of staphylococcus which was a gray film on the solid surface of agar, the drop was beautifully outlined by bare patches, as the enemy made its attack, so that the agar slant looked like moth-eaten beeswax. But within a fortnight one of the knots of which Gottlieb warned him appeared.

Wary of the hundreds of bacteriologists who would rise to slay him once his paper appeared, he sought to make sure that his results could be confirmed. At the hospital he obtained pus from many boils, of the arms, the legs, the back; he sought to reduplicate his results — and failed, complete. No X Principle appeared in any of the new boils, and sadly he went to Gottlieb.

The old man meditated, asked a question or two, sat hunched in his cushioned chair, and demanded:

"What kind of a carbuncle was the original one?"

"Gluteal."

"Ah, den the X Principle may be present in the intestinal contents. Look for it, in people with boils and without."

Martin dashed off. In a week he had obtained the Principle from intestinal contents and from other gluteal boils, finding an especial amount in boils which were "healing of themselves"; and he transplanted his new Principle, in a heaven of triumph, of admiration for Gottlieb. He extended his investigation to the intestinal group of organisms and discovered an X Principle against the colon bacillus. At the same time he gave some of the original Principle to a doctor in the Lower Manhattan Hospital for the treatment of boils, and from him had excited reports of cures, more excited inquiries as to what this mystery might be.

With these new victories he went parading in to Gottlieb, and suddenly he was being trounced:

"Oh! So! Beautiful! You let a doctor try it before you finished your research? You want fake reports of cures to get into the newspapers, to be telegraphed about places, and have everybody in the world that has a pimple come tumbling in to be cured, so you will never be able to work? You want to be a miracle man, and not a scientist? You do not want to complete things? You wander off monkey-skipping and flap-doodling with colon bacillus before you have finish with staph — before you haf really begun your work — before you have found what is the *nature* of the X Principle? Get out of my office! You are a — a — a college president! Next I know you will be dining with Tubbs, and get your picture in the papers for a smart cure-vendor!"

Martin crept out, and when he met Billy Smith in the corridor and the little chemist twittered, "Up to something big? Haven't seen you lately," Martin answered in the tone of Doc Vickerson's assistant in Elk Mills:

"Oh — no — gee — I'm just grubbing along, I guess."

### III

As sharply and quite as impersonally as he would have watched the crawling illness of an infected guinea pig, Martin watched himself, in the madness of overwork, drift toward neurasthenia. With considerable interest he looked up the symptoms of neurasthenia, saw one after another of them twitch at him, and casually took the risk.

From an irritability which made him a thoroughly impossible person to live with, he passed into a sick nervousness in which he missed things for which he reached, dropped test-tubes, gasped at sudden footsteps behind him. Dr. Yeo's croaking voice became to him a fever, an insult, and he waited with his whole body clenched, muttering, "Shut up — shut up — oh, shut *up* !" when Yeo stopped to talk to someone outside his door.

Then he was obsessed by the desire to spell backward all the words which snatched at him from signs.

As he stood dragging out his shoulder on a subway strap, he pored over the posters, seeking new words to spell backward. Some of them were remarkably agreeable: No Smoking became a jaunty and agreeable "gnikoms on," and Broadway was tolerable as "yawdaorb," but he was displeased by his attempts on Punch, Health, Rough; while Strength, turning into "htgnerts" was abominable.

When he had to return to his laboratory three times before he was satisfied that he had closed the window, he sat down, coldly, informed himself that he was on the edge, and took council as to whether he dared go on. It was not very good council: he was so glorified by his unfolding work that his self could not be taken seriously.

At last Fear closed in on him.

It began with childhood's terror of the darkness. He lay awake dreading burglars; footsteps in the hall were a creeping cutthroat; an unexplained scratching on the fire-escape was a murderer with an automatic in his fist. He beheld it so clearly that he had to spring from bed and look timorously out, and when in the street below he did actually see a man standing still, he was cold with panic.

Every sky glow was a fire. He was going to be trapped in his bed, be smothered, die writhing.

He knew absolutely that his fears were absurd, and that knowledge did not at all keep them from dominating him.

He was ashamed at first to acknowledge his seeming cowardice to Leora. Admit that he was crouching like a child? But when he had lain rigid, almost screaming, feeling the cord of an assassin squeezing his throat, till the safe dawn brought back a dependable world, he muttered of "insomnia" and after that, night on night, he crept into her arms and she shielded him from the horrors, protected him from garroters, kept away the fire.

He made a checking list of the favorite neurasthenic fears: agoraphobia, claustrophobia, pyrophobia, anthropophobia, and the rest, ending with what he asserted to be "the most fool, pretentious, witch-doctor term of the whole bloomin' lot," namely, siderodromophobia, the fear of a railway journey. The first night, he was able to check against pyrophobia, for at the vaudeville with Leora, when on the stage a dancer lighted a brazier, he sat waiting for the theater to take fire. He looked cautiously along the row of seats (raging at himself the while for doing it), he estimated his chance of reaching an exit, and became easy only when he had escaped into the street.

It was when anthropophobia set in, when he was made uneasy by people who walked too close to him, that, sagely viewing his list and seeing how many phobias were now checked, he permitted himself to rest.

He fled to the Vermont hills for a four-day tramp — alone, that he might pound on the faster. He went at night, by sleeper, and was able to make the most interesting observations of siderodromophobia.

He lay in a lower berth, the little pillow wadded into a lump. He was annoyed by the waving of his clothes as they trailed from the hanger beside him, at the opening of the green curtains. The window-shade was up six inches; it left a milky blur across which streaked yellow lights, emphatic in the noisy darkness of his little cell. He was shivering with anxiety. Whenever he tried to relax, he was ironed back into apprehension. When the train stopped between stations and from the engine came a questioning, fretful whistle, he was aghast with certainty that something had gone wrong — a bridge was out, a train was ahead of them; perhaps another was coming just behind them, about to smash into them at sixty miles an hour —

He imagined being wrecked, and he suffered more than from the actual occurrence, for he pictured not one wreck but half a dozen, with assorted miseries.... The flat wheel just beneath him — surely it shouldn't pound like that — why hadn't the confounded man with the hammer detected it at the last big station? — the flat wheel cracking; the car lurching, falling, being dragged on its side.... A collision, a crash, the car instantly a crumpled, horrible heap, himself pinned in the telescoped berth, caught between seat and seat. Shrieks, death groans, the creeping flames.... The car turning, falling, plumping into a river on its side; himself trying to crawl through a window as the water seeped about his body. ... Himself standing by the wrenched car, deciding whether to keep away and protect his sacred work or go back, rescue people, and be killed.

So real were the visions that he could not endure lying here, waiting. He reached for the berth light, and could not find the button. In agitation he tore a match-box from his coat pocket, scratched a match, snapped on the light. He saw himself, under the sheets, reflected in the polished wooden ceiling of his berth like a corpse in a coffin. Hastily he crawled out, with trousers and coat over his undergarments (he had somehow feared to show so much trust in the train as to put on pajamas), and with bare disgusted feet he paddled up to the smoking compartment. The porter was squatting on a stool, polishing an amazing pile of shoes.

Martin longed for his encouraging companionship, and ventured, "Warm night."

"Uh-huh," said the porter.

Martin curled on the chill leather seat of the smoking compartment, profoundly studying a brass wash-bowl. He was conscious that the porter was disapproving, but he had comfort in calculating that the man must make this run thrice a week, tens of thousands of miles yearly, apparently without being killed, and there might be a chance of their lasting till morning.

He smoked till his tongue was raw and till, fortified by the calmness of the porter, he laughed at the imaginary catastrophes. He staggered sleepily to his berth.

Instantly he was tense again, and he lay awake till dawn.

For four days he tramped, swam in cold brooks, slept under trees or in straw stacks, and came back (but by day) with enough reserve of energy to support him till his experiment should have turned from overwhelming glory into sane and entertaining routine.

## Chapter 29

When the work on the X Principle had gone on for six weeks, the Institute staff suspected that something was occurring, and they hinted to Martin that he needed their several assistances. He avoided them. He did not desire to be caught in any of the log-rolling factions, though for Terry Wickett, still in France, and for Terry's rough compulsion to honesty he was sometimes lonely.

How the Director first heard that Martin was finding gold is not known.

Dr. Tubbs was tired of being a Colonel — there were too many Generals in New York — and for two weeks he had not had an Idea which would revolutionize even a small part of the world. One morning he burst in, whiskers alive, and reproached Martin:

"What is this mysterious discovery you're making, Arrowsmith? I've asked Dr. Gottlieb, but he evades me; he says you want to be sure, first. I must know about it, not only because I take a very friendly interest in your work but because I am, after all, your Director!"

Martin felt that his one ewe lamb was being snatched from him but he could see no way to refuse. He brought out his note-books and the agar slants with their dissolved patches of bacilli. Tubbs gasped, assaulted his whiskers, did a moment of impressive thinking, and clamored:

"Do you mean to say you think you've discovered an infectious disease of bacteria, and you haven't told me about it? My dear boy, I don't believe you quite realize that you may have hit on the supreme way to kill pathogenic bacteria. ...And you didn't tell me!"

"Well, sir, I wanted to make certain — "

"I admire your caution, but you must understand, Martin, that the basic aim of this Institution is the conquest of disease, not making pretty scientific notes! You *may* have hit on one of the discoveries of a generation; the sort of thing that Mr. McGurk and I are looking for....If your results are confirmed....I shall ask Dr. Gottlieb's opinion."

He shook Martin's hand five or six times and bustled out. Next day he called Martin to his office, shook his hand some more, told Pearl Robbins that they were honored to know him, then led him to a mountain top and showed him all the kingdoms of the world:

"Martin, I have some plans for you. You have been working brilliantly, but without a complete vision of broader humanity. Now the Institute is organized on the most flexible lines. There are no set departments, but only units formed about exceptional men like our good friend Gottlieb. If any new man has the real right thing, we'll provide him with every facility, instead of letting him merely plug along doing individual work. I have given your results the most careful consideration, Martin; I have talked them over with Dr. Gottlieb — though I must say he does not altogether share my enthusiasm about immediate practical results. And I have decided to submit to the Board of Trustees a plan for a Department of Microbic Pathology, with you as head! You will have an assistant — a real trained Ph.D. — and more room and technicians, and you will report to me directly, talk things over with me daily, instead of with Gottlieb. You will be relieved of all war work, by my order — though you can retain your uniform and everything. And your salary will be, I should think, if Mr. McGurk and the other Trustees confirm me, ten thousand a year instead of five.

"Yes, the best room for you would be that big one on the upper floor, to the right of the elevators. That's vacant now. And your office across the hall.

"And all the assistance you require. Why, my boy, you won't need to sit up nights using your hands in this wasteful way, but just think things out and take up possible extensions of the work — cover all the possible fields. We'll extend this to everything! We'll have scores of physicians in hospitals helping us and confirming our results and widening our efforts....We might have a weekly council of all these doctors and assistants, with you and me jointly presiding....If men like Koch and Pasteur had only had such a system, how much more scope their work might have had! Efficient universal *co-operation* — that's the thing in science today — the time of this silly, jealous, fumbling individual research has gone by.

"My boy, we may have found the real thing — another salvarsan! We'll publish together! We'll have the whole world talking! Why, I lay awake last night thinking of our magnificent opportunity! In a few months we may be curing not only staph infections but typhoid, dysentery! Martin, as your colleague, I do not for a moment wish to detract from the great credit which is yours, but I must say that if you had been more closely allied with Me you would have extended your work to practical proofs and results long before this."

Martin wavered back to his room, dazzled by the view of a department of his own, assistants, a cheering world — and ten thousand a year. But his work seemed to have been taken from him, his own self had been taken from him; he was no longer to be Martin, and Gottlieb's disciple, but a Man of Measured Merriment, Dr. Arrowsmith, Head of the Department of Microbic Pathology, who would wear severe collars and make addresses and never curse.

Doubts enfeebled him. Perhaps the X Principle would develop only in the test-tube; perhaps it had no large value for human healing. He wanted to know — to *know*.

Then Rippleton Holabird burst in on him:

"Martin, my dear boy, the Director has just been telling me about your discovery and his splendid plans for you. I want to congratulate you with all my heart, and to welcome you as a fellow department-head — and you so young — only thirty-four, isn't it? What a magnificent future! Think, Martin" — Major Holabird discarded his dignity, sat astride a chair — "think of all you have ahead! If this work really pans out, there's no limit to the honors that'll come to you, you lucky young dog! Acclaim by scientific societies, any professorship you might happen to want, prizes, the biggest men begging to consult you, a ripping place in society!

"Now listen, old boy: Perhaps you know how close I am to Dr. Tubbs, and I see no reason why you shouldn't come in with us, and we three run things here to suit ourselves. Wasn't it simply too decent of the Director to be so eager to recognize and help you in every way! So cordial — and so helpful. Now you really understand him. And the three of us — Some day we might be able to erect a superstructure of co-operative science which would control not only McGurk but every institute and every university scientific department in the country, and so produce really efficient research. When Dr. Tubbs retires, I have — I'm speaking with the most complete confidence — I have some reason to suppose that the Board of Trustees will consider me as his successor. Then, old boy, if this work succeeds, you and I can do things together!

"To be ever so frank, there are very few men in our world (think of poor old Yeo!) who combine presentable personalities with first-rate achievement, and if you'll just get over some of your abruptness and your unwillingness to appreciate big executives and charming women (because, thank God, you do wear your clothes well — when you take the trouble!) why, you and I can become the dictators of science throughout the whole country!"

Martin did not think of an answer till Holabird had gone.

He perceived the horror of the shrieking bawdy thing called Success, with its demand that he give up quiet work and parade forth to be pawed by every blind devotee and mud-spattered by every blind enemy.

He fled to Gottlieb as to the wise and tender father, and begged to be saved from Success and Holabirds and A. DeWitt Tubbses and their hordes of address-making scientists, degree-hunting authors, pulpit orators, popular surgeons, valeted journalists, sentimental merchant princes, literary politicians, titled sportsmen, statesmenlike generals, interviewed senators, sententious bishops.

Gottlieb was worried:

"I knew Tubbs was up to something idealistic and nasty when he came purring to me, but I did not t'ink he would try to turn you into a megaphone all so soon in one day! I will gird up my loins and go oud to battle with the forces of publicity!"

He was defeated.

"I have let you alone, Dr. Gottlieb," said Tubbs, "but, hang it, I am the Director! And I must say that, perhaps owing to my signal stupidity, I fail to see the horrors of enabling Arrowsmith to cure thousands of suffering persons and to become a man of weight and esteem!"

Gottlieb took it to Ross McGurk.

"Max, I love you like a brother, but Tubbs is the Director, and if he feels he needs this Arrowsmith (Is he the thin young fellow I see around your lab?) then I have no right to stop him. I've got to back him up the same as I would the master of one of our ships," said McGurk.

Not till the Board of Trustees, which consisted of McGurk himself, the president of the University of Wilmington, and three professors of science in various universities, should meet and give approval, would Martin be a department-head. Meantime Tubbs demanded:

"Now, Martin, you must hasten and publish your results. Get right to it. In fact you should have done it before this. Throw your material together as rapidly as possible and send a note in to the Society for Experimental Biology and Medicine, to be published in their next proceedings."

"But I'm not ready to publish! I want to have every loophole plugged up before I announce anything whatever!"

"Nonsense! That attitude is old-fashioned. This is no longer an age of parochialism but of competition, in art and science just as much as in commerce — co-operation with your own group, but with those outside it, competition to the death! Plug up the holes thoroughly, later, but we can't have somebody else stealing a march on us. Remember you have your name to make. The way to make it is by working with me — toward the greatest good for the greatest number."

As Martin began his paper, thinking of resigning but giving it up because Tubbs seemed to him at least better than the Pickerbaughs, he had a vision of a world of little scientists, each busy in a roofless cell. Perched on a cloud, watching them, was the divine Tubbs, a glory of whiskers, ready to blast any of the little men who stopped being earnest and wasted time on speculation about anything which he had not assigned to them. Back of their welter of coops, unseen by the tutelary Tubbs, the lean giant figure of Gottlieb stood sardonic on a stormy horizon.

Literary expression was not easy to Martin. He delayed with his paper, while Tubbs became irritable and whipped him on. The experiments had ceased; there were misery and pen-scratching and much tearing of manuscript paper in Martin's particular roofless cell.

For once he had no refuge in Leora. She cried:

"Why not? Ten thousand a year would be awfully nice, Sandy. Gee! We've always been so poor, and you do like nice flats and things. And to boss your own department — And you could consult Dr. Gottlieb just the same. He's a department-head, isn't he, and yet he keeps independent of Dr. Tubbs. Oh, I'm for it!"

And slowly, under the considerable increase in respect given to him at Institute lunches, Martin himself was "for it."

"We could get one of those new apartments on Park Avenue. Don't suppose they cost more than three thousand a year," he meditated. "Wouldn't be so bad to be able to entertain people there. Not that I'd let it interfere with my work.... Kind of nice."

It was still more kind of nice, however agonizing in the taking, to be recognized socially.

Capitola McGurk, who hitherto had not perceived him except as an object less interesting than Gladys the Centrifuge, telephoned: "... Dr. Tubbs so enthusiastic and Ross and I are so pleased. Be delighted if Mrs. Arrowsmith and you could dine with us next Thursday at eight-thirty."

Martin accepted the royal command.

It was his conviction that after glimpses of Angus Duer and Rippleton Holabird he had seen luxury, and understood smart dinner parties. Leora and he went without too much agitation to the house of Ross McGurk, in the East Seventies, near Fifth Avenue. The house did, from the street, seem to have an unusual quantity of graystone gargoyles and carven lintels and bronze grills, but it did not seem large.

Inside, the vaulted stone hallway opened up like a cathedral. They were embarrassed by the footmen, awed by the automatic elevator, oppressed by a hallway full of vellum folios and Italian chests and a drawing-room full of water-colors, and reduced to rusticity by Capitola's queenly white satin and pearls.

There were eight or ten Persons of Importance, male and female, looking insignificant but bearing names as familiar as Ivory Soap.

Did one give his arm to some unknown lady and "take her in," Martin wondered. He rejoiced to find that one merely straggled into the dining-room under McGurk's amiable basso herding.

The dining-room was gorgeous and very hideous, in stamped leather and hysterias of gold, with collections of servants watching one's use of asparagus forks. Martin was seated (it is doubtful if he ever knew that he was the guest of honor) between Capitola McGurk and a woman of whom he could learn only that she was the sister of a countess.

Capitola leaned toward him in her great white splendor.

"Now, Dr. Arrowsmith, just what is this you are discovering?"

"Why, it's — uh — I'm trying to figure — "

"Dr. Tubbs tells us that you have found such wonderful new ways of controlling disease." Her L's were a melody of summer rivers, her R's the trill of birds in the brake. "Oh, what — *what* could be more beau-tiful than relieving this sad old world of its burden of illness! But just precisely what *is* it that you're doing?"

"Why, it's awfully early to be sure but — You see, it's like this. You take certain bugs like staph — "

"Oh, how interesting science is, but how frightfully difficult for simple people like me to grasp! But we're all so humble. We're just waiting for scientists like you to make the world secure for friendship — "

Then Capitola gave all her attention to her other man. Martin looked straight ahead and ate and suffered. The sister of the countess, a sallow and stringy woman, was glowing at him. He turned with unhappy meekness (noting that she had one more fork than he, and wondering where he had got lost).

She blared, "You are a scientist, I am told."

"Ye-es."

"The trouble with scientists is that they do not understand beauty. They are so cold."

Rippleton Holabird would have made pretty mirth, but Martin could only quaver, "No, I don't think that's true," and consider whether he dared drink another glass of champagne.

When they had been herded back to the drawing-room, after masculine but achingly elaborate passings of the port, Capitola swooped on him with white devouring wings:

"Dear Dr. Arrowsmith, I really didn't get a chance at dinner to ask you just exactly *what* you are doing.... Oh! Have you seen my dear little children at the Charles Street settlement? I'm sure ever so many of them will become the most fascinating scientists. You must come lecture to them."

That night he fretted to Leora, "Going to be hard to keep up this twittering. But I suppose I've got to learn to enjoy it. Oh, well, think how nice it'll be to give some dinners of our own, with real people, Gottlieb and everybody, when I'm a department-head."

Next morning Gottlieb came slowly into Martin's room. He stood by the window; he seemed to be avoiding Martin's eyes. He sighed, "Something sort of bad — perhaps not altogether bad — has happened."

"What is it, sir? Anything I can do?"

"It does not apply to me. To you."

Irritably Martin thought, "Is he going into all this danger-of-rapid-success stuff again? I'm getting tired of it!"

Gottlieb ambled toward him. "It iss a pity, Martin, but you are not the discoverer of the X Principle."

"Wh-what — "

"Someone else has done it."

"They have not! I've searched all the literature, and except for Twort, not one person has even hinted at anticipating — Why, good Lord, Dr. Gottlieb, it would mean that all I've done, all these weeks, has just been waste, and I'm a fool — "

"Vell. Anyvay. D'Hérelle of the Pasteur Institute has just now published in the *Comptes Rendus, Académie des Sciences* , a report — it is your X Principle, absolute. Only he calls it 'bacteriophage.' So."

"Then I'm — "

In his mind Martin finished it, "Then I'm not going to be a department-head or famous or anything else. I'm back in the gutter." All strength went out of him and all purpose, and the light of creation faded to dirty gray.

"Now of course," said Gottlieb, "you could claim to be co-discoverer and spend the rest of your life fighting to get recognized. Or you could forget it, and write a nice letter congratulating D'Hérelle, and go back to work."

Martin mourned, "Oh, I'll go back to work. Nothing else to do. I guess Tubbs'll chuck the new department now. I'll have time to really finish my research — maybe I've got some points that D'Hérelle hasn't hit on — and I'll publish it to corroborate him.... Damn him!... Where is his report?... I suppose you're glad that I'm saved from being a Holabird."

"I ought to be. It is a sin against my religion that I am not. But I am getting old. And you are my friend. I am sorry you are not to have the fun of being pretentious and successful — for a while.... Martin, it iss nice that you will corroborate D'Hérelle. That is science: to work and not to care — too much — if somebody else gets the credit.... Shall I tell Tubbs about D'Hérelle's priority, or will you?"

Gottlieb straggled away, looking back a little sadly.

Tubbs came in to wail, "If you had only published earlier, as I told you, Dr. Arrowsmith! You have really put me in a most embarrassing position before the Board of Trustees. Of course there can be no question now of a new department."

"Yes," said Martin vacantly.

He carefully filed away the beginnings of his paper and turned to his bench. He stared at a shining flask till it fascinated him like a crystal ball. He pondered:

"Wouldn't have been so bad if Tubbs had let me alone. Damn these old men, damn these Men of Measured Merriment, these Important Men that come and offer you honors. Money. Decorations. Titles. Want to make you windy with authority. Honors! If you get 'em, you become pompous, and then when you're used to 'em, if you lose 'em you feel foolish.

"So I'm not going to be rich. Leora, poor kid, she won't have her new dresses and flat and everything. We — Won't be so much fun in the lil old flat, now. Oh, quit whining!

"I wish Terry were here.

"I love that man Gottlieb. He might have gloated —

"Bacteriophage, the Frenchman calls it. Too long. Better just call it *phage* . Even got to take his name for it, for my own X Principle! Well, I had a lot of fun, working all those nights. Working — "

He was coming out of his trance. He imagined the flask filled with staph-clouded broth. He plodded into Gottlieb's office to secure the journal containing D'Hérelle's report, and read it minutely, enthusiastically.

"There's a man, there's a scientist!" he chuckled.

On his way home he was planning to experiment on the Shiga dysentery bacillus with phage (as henceforth he called the X Principle), planning to volley questions and criticisms at D'Hérelle, hoping that Tubbs would not discharge him for a while, and expanding with relief that he would not have to do his absurd premature paper on phage, that he could be lewd and soft-collared and easy, not judicious and spied-on and weighty.

He grinned, "Gosh, I'll bet Tubbs was disappointed! He'd figured on signing all my papers with me and getting the credit. Now for this Shiga experiment — Poor Lee, she'll have to get used to my working nights, I guess."

Leora kept to herself what she felt about it — or at least most of what she felt.

## Chapter 30

For a year broken only by Terry Wickett's return after the Armistice, and by the mockeries of that rowdy intelligence, Martin was in a grind of drudgery. Week on week he toiled at complicated phage experiments. His work — his hands, his technique — became more adept, and his days more steady, less fretful.

He returned to his evening studying. He went from mathematics into physical chemistry; began to understand the mass action law; became as sarcastic as Terry about what he called the "bedside manner" of Tubbs and Holabird; read much French and German; went canoeing on the Hudson on Sunday afternoons; and had a bawdy party with Leora and Terry to celebrate the day when the Institute was purified by the sale of Holabird's pride, Gladys the Centrifuge.

He suspected that Dr. Tubbs, now magnificent with the ribbon of the Legion of Honor, had retained him in the Institute only because of Gottlieb's intervention. But it may be that Tubbs and Holabird hoped he would again blunder into publicity-bringing miracles, for they were both polite to him at lunch — polite and wistfully rebuking, and full of meaty remarks about publishing one's discoveries early instead of dawdling.

It was more than a year after Martin's anticipation by D'Hérelle when Tubbs appeared in the laboratory with suggestions:

"I've been thinking, Arrowsmith," said Tubbs.

He looked it.

"D'Hérelle's discovery hasn't aroused the popular interest I thought it would. If he'd only been here with us, I'd have seen to it that he got the proper attention. Practically no newspaper comment at all. Perhaps we can still do something. As I understand it, you've been going along with what Dr. Gottlieb would call 'fundamental research.' I think it may now be time for you to use phage in practical healing. I want you to experiment with phage in pneumonia, plague, perhaps typhoid, and when your experiments get going, make some practical tests in collaboration with the hospitals. Enough of all this mere frittering and vanity. Let's really *cure* somebody!"

Martin was not free from a fear of dismissal if he refused to obey. And he was touched as Tubbs went on:

"Arrowsmith, I suspect you sometimes feel I lack a sense of scientific precision when I insist on practical results. I — Somehow I don't see the really noble and transforming results coming out of this Institute that we ought to be getting, with our facilities. I'd like to do something big, my boy, something fine for poor humanity, before I pass on. Can't you give it to me? Go cure the plague!"

For once Tubbs was a tired smile and not an earnestness of whiskers.

That day, concealing from Gottlieb his abandonment of the quest for the fundamental nature of phage, Martin set about fighting pneumonia, before attacking the Black Death. And when Gottlieb learned of it, he was absorbed in certain troubles of his own.

Martin cured rabbits of pleuro-pneumonia by the injection of phage, and by feeding them with it he prevented the spread of pneumonia. He found that phage-produced immunity could be as infectious as a disease.

He was pleased with himself, and expected pleasure from Tubbs, but for weeks Tubbs did not heed him. He was off on a new enthusiasm, the most virulent of his whole life: he was organizing the League of Cultural Agencies.

He was going to standardize and co-ordinate all mental activities in America, by the creation of a bureau which should direct and pat and gently rebuke and generally encourage chemistry and batik-making, poetry and Arctic exploration, animal husbandry and Bible study, Negro spirituals and business-letter writing. He was suddenly in conference with conductors of symphony orchestras, directors of art-schools, owners of itinerant Chautauquas, liberal governors, ex-clergymen who wrote tasty philosophy for newspaper syndicates, in fact all the proprietors of American intellectuality — particularly including a millionaire named Minnigen who had recently been elevating the artistic standards of the motion pictures.

Tubbs was all over the Institute inviting the researchers to join him in the League of Cultural Agencies with its fascinating committee-meetings and dinners. Most of them grunted, "The Old Man is erupting again," and forgot him, but one ex-major went out every evening to confer with serious ladies who wore distinguished frocks, who sobbed over "the loss of spiritual and intellectual horsepower through lack of co-ordination," and who went home in limousines.

There were rumors. Dr. Billy Smith whispered that he had gone in to see Tubbs and heard McGurk shouting at him, "Your job is to run this shop and not work for that land-stealing, four-flushing, play-producing son of evil, Pete Minnigen!"

The morning after, when Martin ambled to his laboratory, he discovered a gasping, a muttering, a shaking in the corridors, and incredulously he heard:

"Tubbs has resigned!"

"No!"

"They say he's gone to his League of Cultural Agencies. This fellow Minnigen has given the League a scad of money, and Tubbs is to get twice the salary he had here!"

## II

Instantly, for all but the zealots like Gottlieb, Terry, Martin, and the bio-physics assistant, research was halted. There was a surging of factions, a benevolent and winning buzz of scientists who desired to be the new Director of the Institute.

Rippleton Holabird, Yeo the carpenter-like biologist, Gillingham the joky chief in bio-physics, Aaron Sholtheis the neat Russian Jewish High Church Episcopalian, all of them went about with expressions of modest willingness. They were affectionate with everybody they met in the corridors, however violent they were in private discussions. Added to them were no few outsiders, professors and researchers in other institutes, who found it necessary to come and confer about rather undefined matters with Ross McGurk.

Terry remarked to Martin, "Probably Pearl Robbins and your garçon are pitching horseshoes for the Directorship. My garçon ain't — the only reason, though, is because I've just murdered him. At that, I think Pearl would be the best choice. She's been Tubbs's secretary so long that she's learned all his ignorance about scientific technique."

Rippleton Holabird was the most unctuous of the office seekers, and the most hungry. The war over, he missed his uniform and his authority. He urged Martin:

"You know how I've always believed in your genius, Martin, and I know how dear old Gottlieb believes in you. If you would get Gottlieb to back me, to talk to McGurk — Of course in taking the Directorship I would be making a sacrifice, because I'd have to give up my research, but I'd be willing because I feel, really, that somebody with a Tradition ought to carry on the control. Tubbs is backing me, and if Gottlieb did — I'd see that it was to Gottlieb's advantage. I'd give him a lot more floor-space!"

Through the Institute it was vaguely known that Capitola was advocating the election of Holabird as "the only scientist here who is also a gentleman." She was seen sailing down corridors, a frigate, with Holabird a sloop in her wake.

But while Holabird beamed, Nicholas Yeo looked secret and satisfied.

The whole Institute fluttered on the afternoon when the Board of Trustees met in the Hall, for the election of a Director. They were turned from investigators into boarding-school girls. The Board debated, or did something annoying, for draining hours.

At four, Terry Wickett hastened to Martin with, "Say, Slim, I've got a straight tip that They've elected Silva, dean of the Winnemac medical school. That's your shop, isn't it? Wha's like?"

"He's a fine old — No! He and Gottlieb hate each other. Lord! Gottlieb'll resign, and I'll have to get out. Just when my work's going nice!"

At five, past doors made of attentive eyes, the Board of Trustees marched to the laboratory of Max Gottlieb.

Holabird was heard saying bravely, "Of course with me, I wouldn't give my research up for any administrative job." And Pearl Robbins informed Terry, "Yes, it's true — Mr. McGurk himself just told me — the Board has elected Dr. Gottlieb the new Director."

"Then they're fools," said Terry. "He'll refuse it, with wilence. 'Dot dey should ask me to go monkey-skipping mit committee meetings!' Fat chance!"

When the Board had gone, Martin and Terry flooded into Gottlieb's laboratory and found the old man standing by his bench, more erect than they had seen him for years.

"Is it true — they want you to be Director?" panted Martin.

"Yes, they have asked me."

"But you'll refuse? You won't let 'em gum up your work!"

"Vell.... I said my real work must go on. They consent I should appoint an Assistant Director to do the detail. You see — Of course nothing must interfere with my immunology, but dis gives me the chance to do big t'ings and make a free scientific institute for all you boys. And those fools at Winnemac that laughed at my idea of a real medical school, now maybe they will see — Do you know who was my rival for Director — do you know who it was, Martin? It was that man Silva! Ha!"

In the corridor Terry groaned, "*Requiescat in pace* ."

## III

To the dinner in Gottlieb's honor (the only dinner that ever was given in Gottlieb's honor) there came not only the men of impressive but easy affairs who attend all dinners of honor, but the few scientists whom Gottlieb admired.

He appeared late, rather shaky, escorted by Martin. When he reached the speakers' table, the guests rose to him, shouting. He peered at them, he tried to speak, he held out his long arms as if to take them all in, and sank down sobbing.

There were cables from Europe; ardent letters from Tubbs and Dean Silva bewailing their inability to be present; telegrams from college presidents; and all of these were read to admiring applause.

But Capitola murmured, "Just the same, we shall miss dear Dr. Tubbs. He was so forward-looking. Don't play with your fork, Ross."

So Max Gottlieb took charge of the McGurk Institute of Biology, and in a month that Institute became a shambles.

## IV

Gottlieb planned to give only an hour a day to business. As Assistant Director he appointed Dr. Aaron Sholtheis, the epidemiologist, the Yonkers churchman and dahlia-fancier. Gottlieb explained to Martin that, though of course Sholtheis was a fool, yet he was the only man in sight who combined at least a little scientific ability with a willingness to endure the routine and pomposity and compromises of executive work.

By continuing his ancient sneers at all bustling managers, Gottlieb obviously felt that he excused himself for having become a manager.

He could not confine his official work to an hour a day. There were too many conferences, too many distinguished callers, too many papers which needed his signature. He was dragged into dinner-parties; and the long, vague, palavering luncheons to which a Director has to go, and the telephoning to straighten out the dates of these tortures, took nervous hours. Each day his executive duties crawled into two hours or three or four, and he raged, he became muddled by complications of personnel and economy, he was ever more autocratic, more testy; and the loving colleagues of the Institute, who had been soothed or bullied into surface peace by Tubbs, now jangled openly.

While he was supposed to radiate benevolence from the office recently occupied by Dr. A. DeWitt Tubbs, Gottlieb clung to his own laboratory and to his narrow office as a cat clings to its cushion under a table. Once or twice he tried to sit and look impressive in the office of the Director, but fled from that large clean vacuity and from Miss Robbins's snapping typewriter to his own den that smelled not of forward-looking virtue but only of cigarettes and old papers.

To McGurk, as to every scientific institution, came hundreds of farmers and practical nurses and suburban butchers who had paid large fares from Oklahoma or Oregon to get recognition for the unquestionable cures which they had discovered: oil of Mississippi catfish which saved every case of tuberculosis, arsenic pastes guaranteed to cure all cancers. They came with letters and photographs amid the frayed clean linen in their shabby suit-cases — at any opportunity they would stoop over their bags and hopefully bring out testimonials from their Pastors; they begged for a chance to heal humanity, and for themselves only enough money to send The Girl to musical conservatory. So certain, so black-crapely beseeching were they that no reception-clerk could be trained to keep them all out.

Gottlieb found them seeping into his office. He was sorry for them. They did take his working hours, they did scratch his belief that he was hard-hearted, but they implored him with such wretched timorousness that he could not get rid of them without making promises, and admitting afterward that to have been more cruel would have been less cruel.

It was the Important People to whom he was rude.

The Directorship devoured enough time and peace to prevent Gottlieb from going on with the ever more recondite problems of his inquiry into the nature of specificity, and his inquiry prevented him from giving enough attention to the Institute to keep it from falling to pieces. He depended on Sholtheis, passed decisions on to him, but Sholtheis, since in any case Gottlieb would get all the credit for a successful Directorship, kept up his own scientific work and passed the decisions to Miss Pearl Robbins, so that the actual Director was the handsome and jealous Pearl.

There was no craftier or crookeder Director in the habitable world. Pearl enjoyed it. She so warmly and modestly assured Ross McGurk of the merits of Gottlieb and of her timorous devotion to him, she so purred to the flattery of Rippleton Holabird, she so blandly answered the hoarse hostility of Terry Wickett by keeping him from getting materials for his work, that the Institute reeled with intrigue.

Yeo was not speaking to Sholtheis. Terry threatened Holabird to "paste him one." Gottlieb constantly asked Martin for advice, and never took it. Joust, the vulgar but competent biophysicist, lacking the affection which kept Martin and Terry from reproaching the old man, told Gottlieb that he was a "rotten Director and ought to quit," and was straightway discharged and replaced by a muffin.

Max Gottlieb had ever discoursed to Martin of "the jests of the gods." Among these jests Martin had never beheld one so pungent as this whereby the pretentiousness and fussy unimaginativeness which he had detested in Tubbs should have made him a good manager, while the genius of Gottlieb should have made him a feeble tyrant; the jest that the one thing worse than a too managed and standardized institution should be one that was not managed and standardized at all. He would once have denied it with violence, but nightly now he prayed for Tubbs's return.

If the business of the Institute was not more complicated thereby, certainly its placidity was the more disturbed by the appearance of Gustaf Sondelius, who had just returned from a study of sleeping sickness in Africa and who noisily took one of the guest laboratories.

Gustaf Sondelius, the soldier of preventive medicine whose lecture had sent Martin from Wheatsylvania to Nautilus, had remained in his gallery of heroes as possessing a little of Gottlieb's perception, something of Dad Silva's steady kindliness, something of Terry's tough honesty though none of his scorn of amenities, and with these a spicy, dripping richness altogether his own. It is true that Sondelius did not remember Martin. Since their evening in Minneapolis he had drunk and debated and flamboyantly ridden to obscure but vinuous destinations with too many people. But he was made to remember, and in a week Sondelius and Terry and Martin were to be seen tramping and dining, or full of topics and gin at Martin's flat.

Sondelius's wild flaxen hair was almost gray, but he had the same bull shoulders, the same wide brow, and the same tornado of plans to make the world aseptic, without neglecting to enjoy a few of the septic things before they should pass away.

His purpose was, after finishing his sleeping sickness report, to found a school of tropical medicine in New York.

He besieged McGurk and the wealthy Mr. Minnigen who was Tubbs's new patron, and in and out of season he besieged Gottlieb.

He adored Gottlieb and made noises about it. Gottlieb admired his courage and his hatred of commercialism, but his presence Gottlieb could not endure. He was flustered by Sondelius's hilarity, his compliments, his bounding optimism, his inaccuracy, his boasting, his oppressive bigness. It may be that Gottlieb resented the fact that though Sondelius was only eleven years younger — fifty-eight to Gottlieb's sixty-nine — he seemed thirty years younger, half a century gayer.

When Sondelius perceived this grudgingness he tried to overcome it by being more noisy and complimentary and enthusiastic than ever. On Gottlieb's birthday he gave him a shocking smoking-jacket of cherry and mauve velvet, and when he called at Gottlieb's flat, which was often, Gottlieb had to put on the ghastly thing and sit humming while Sondelius assaulted him with roaring condemnations of mediocre soup and mediocre musicians.... That Sondelius gave up surprisingly decorative dinner-parties for these calls, Gottlieb never knew.

Martin turned to Sondelius for courage as he turned to Terry for concentration. Courage and concentration were needed, in these days of an Institute gone insane, if a man was to do his work.

And Martin was doing it.

## V

After a consultation with Gottlieb and a worried conference with Leora about the danger of handling the germs, he had gone on to bubonic plague, to the possibilities of preventing it and curing it with phage.

To have heard him asking Sondelius about his experience in plague epidemics, one would have believed that Martin found the Black Death delightful. To have beheld him infecting lean snaky rats with the horror, all the while clucking to them and calling them pet names, one would have known him mad.

He found that rats fed with phage failed to come down with plague; that after phage-feeding, *Bacillus pestis* disappeared from carrier rats which, without themselves being killed thereby, harbored and spread chronic plague; and that, finally, he could cure the disease. He was as absorbed and happy and nervous as in the first days of the X Principle. He worked all night.... At the microscope, under a lone light, fishing out with a glass pipette drawn fine as a hair one single plague bacillus.

To protect himself from infection by the rat-fleas he wore, while he worked with the animals, rubber gloves, high leather boots, straps about his sleeves. These precautions thrilled him, and to the others at McGurk they had something of the esoteric magic of the alchemists. He became a bit of a hero and a good deal of a butt. No more than hearty business men in offices or fussy old men in villages are researchers free from the tedious vice of jovial commenting. The chemists and biologists called him "The Pest," refused to come to his room, and pretended to avoid him in the corridors.

As he went fluently on from experiment to experiment, as the drama of science obsessed him, he thought very well of himself and found himself taken seriously by the others. He published one cautious paper on phage in plague, which was mentioned in numerous scientific journals. Even the harassed Gottlieb was commendatory, though he could give but little attention and no help. But Terry Wickett remained altogether cool. He showed for Martin's somewhat brilliant work only enough enthusiasm to indicate that he was not jealous; he kept poking in to ask whether, with his new experimentation, Martin was continuing his quest for the fundamental nature of all phage, and his study of physical chemistry.

Then Martin had such an assistant as has rarely been known, and that assistant was Gustaf Sondelius.

Sondelius was discouraged regarding his school of tropical medicine. He was looking for new trouble. He had been through several epidemics, and he viewed plague with affectionate hatred. When he understood Martin's work he gloated, "Hey, Yesus! Maybe you got the t'ing that will be better than Yersin or Haffkine or anybody! Maybe you cure all the world of plague — the poor devils in India — millions of them. Let me in!"

He became Martin's collaborator; unpaid, tireless, not very skillful, valuable in his buoyancy. As well as Martin he loved irregularity; by principle he never had his meals at the same hours two days in succession, and by choice he worked all night and made poetry, rather bad poetry, at dawn.

Martin had always been the lone prowler. Possibly the thing he most liked in Leora was her singular ability to be cheerfully non-existent even when she was present. At first he was annoyed by Sondelius's disturbing presence, however interesting he found his fervors about plague-bearing rats (whom Sondelius hated not at all but whom, with loving zeal, he had slaughtered by the million, with a romantic absorption in traps and poison gas). But the Sondelius who was raucous in conversation could be almost silent at work. He knew exactly how to hold the animals while Martin did intrapleural injections; he made cultures of *Bacillus pestis*; when Martin's technician had gone home at but a little after midnight (the garçon liked Martin and thought well enough of science, but he was prejudiced in favor of six hours' daily sleep and sometimes seeing his wife and children in Harlem), then Sondelius cheerfully sterilized glassware and needles, and lumbered up to the animal house to bring down victims.

The change whereby Sondelius was turned from Martin's master to his slave was so unconscious, and Sondelius, for all his Pickerbaughian love of sensationalism, cared so little about mastery or credit, that neither of them considered that there had been a change. They borrowed cigarettes from each other; they went out at the most improbable hours to have flap-jacks and coffee at an all-night lunch; and together they candled test-tubes charged with death.

## Chapter 31

From Yunnan in China, from the clattering bright bazaars, crept something invisible in the sun and vigilant by dark, creeping, sinister, ceaseless; creeping across the Himalayas, down through walled market-places, across a desert, along hot yellow rivers, into an American missionary compound — creeping, silent, sure; and here and there on its way a man was black and stilled with plague.

In Bombay a new dock-guard, unaware of things, spoke boisterously over his family rice of a strange new custom of the rats.

Those princes of the sewer, swift to dart and turn, had gone mad. They came out on the warehouse floor, ignoring the guard springing up as though (the guard said merrily) they were trying to fly, and straightway falling dead. He had poked at them, but they did not move.

Three days later that dock-guard died of the plague.

Before he died, from his dock a ship with a cargo of wheat steamed off to Marseilles. There was no sickness on it all the way; there was no reason why at Marseilles it should not lie next to a tramp steamer, nor why that steamer, pitching down to Montevideo with nothing more sensational than a discussion between the supercargo and the second officer in the matter of a fifth ace, should not berth near the *S.S. Pendown Castle* , bound for the island of St. Hubert to add cocoa to its present cargo of lumber.

On the way to St. Hubert, a Goanese seedie boy and after him the messroom steward on the *Pendown Castle* died of what the skipper called influenza. A greater trouble was the number of rats which, ill satisfied with lumber as diet, scampered up to the food-stores, then into the forecastle, and for no reason perceptible died on the open decks. They danced comically before they died, and lay in the scuppers stark and ruffled.

So the *Pendown Castle* came to Blackwater, the capital and port of St. Hubert.

It is a little isle of the southern West Indies, but St. Hubert supports a hundred thousand people — English planters and clerks, Hindu road-makers, Negro cane-hands, Chinese merchants. There is history along its sands and peaks. Here the buccaneers careened their ships; here the Marquess of Wimsbury, when he had gone mad, took to repairing clocks and bade his slaves burn all the sugar-cane.

Hither that peasant beau, Gaston Lopo, brought Madame de Merlemont, and dwelt in fashionableness till the slaves whom he had often relished to lash came on him shaving, and straightway the lather was fantastically smeared with blood.

Today, St. Hubert is all sugar-cane and Ford cars, oranges and plantains and the red and yellow pods of cocoa, bananas and rubber trees and jungles of bamboo, Anglican churches and tin chapels, colored washerwomen busy at the hollows in the roots of silk-cotton trees, steamy heat and royal palms and the immortelle that fills the valleys with crimson; today it is all splendor and tourist dullness and cabled cane-quotations, against the unsparing sun.

Blackwater, flat and breathless town of tin-roofed plaster houses and incandescent bone-white roads, of salmon-red hibiscus and balconied stores whose dark depths open without barrier from the stifling streets, has the harbor to one side and a swamp to the other. But behind it are the Penrith Hills, on whose wholesome and palm-softened heights is Government House, looking to the winking sails.

Here lived in bulky torpor His Excellency the Governor of St. Hubert, Colonel Sir Robert Fairlamb.

Sir Robert Fairlamb was an excellent fellow, a teller of messroom stories, one who in a heathen day never smoked till the port had gone seven times round; but he was an execrable governor and a worried governor. The man whose social rank was next to his own — the Hon. Cecil Eric George Twyford, a lean, active, high-nosed despot who owned and knew rod by snakewrithing rod some ten thousand acres of cane in St. Swithin's Parish — Twyford said that His Excellency was a "potty and snoring fool," and versions of the opinion came not too slowly to Fairlamb. Then, to destroy him complete, the House of Assembly, which is the St. Hubert legislature, was riven by the feud of Kellett the Red Leg and George William Vertigan.

The Red Legs were a tribe of Scotch-Irish poor whites who had come to St. Hubert as indentured servants two hundred years before. Most of them were still fishermen and plantation-foremen, but one of them, Kellett, a man small-mouthed and angry and industrious, had risen from office-boy to owner of a shipping company, and while his father still spread his nets on the beach at Point Carib, Kellett was the scourge of the House of Assembly and a hound for economy — particularly any economy which would annoy his fellow legislator, George William Vertigan.

George William, who was sometimes known as "Old Jeo Wm." and sometimes as "The King of the Ice House" (that enticing and ruinous bar), had been born behind a Little Bethel in Lancashire. He owned The Blue Bazaar, the hugest stores in St. Hubert; he caused tobacco to be smuggled into Venezuela; he was as full of song and incaution and rum as Kellett the Red Leg was full of figures and envy and decency.

Between them, Kellett and George William split the House of Assembly. There could be, to a respectable person, no question as to their merits: Kellett the just and earnest man of domesticity whose rise was an inspiration to youth; George William the gambler, the lusher, the smuggler, the liar, the seller of shoddy cottons, a person whose only excellence was his cheap good nature.

Kellett's first triumph in economy was to pass an ordinance removing the melancholy Cockney (a player of oboes) who was the official rat-catcher of St. Hubert.

George William Vertigan insisted in debate, and afterward privily to Sir Robert Fairlamb, that rats destroy food and perhaps spread disease, and His Excellency must veto the bill. Sir Robert was troubled. He called in The Surgeon General, Dr. R. E. Inchcape Jones (but he preferred to be called Mister, not Doctor).

Dr. Inchcape Jones was a thin, tall, fretful, youngish man, without bowels. He had come out from Home only two years before, and he wanted to go back Home, to that particular part of Home represented by tennis-teas in Surrey. He remarked to Sir Robert that rats and their ever faithful fleas do carry diseases — plague and infectious jaundice and rat-bite fever and possibly leprosy — but these diseases did not and therefore could not exist in St. Hubert, except for leprosy, which was a natural punishment of outlandish Native Races. In fact, noted Inchcape Jones, nothing did exist in St. Hubert except malaria, dengue, and a general beastly dullness, and if Red Legs like Kellett longed to die of plague and rat-bite fever, why should decent people object?

So by the sovereign power of the House of Assembly of St. Hubert, and of His Excellency the Governor, the Cockney rat-catcher and his jiggling young colored assistant were commanded to cease to exist. The rat-catcher became a chauffeur. He drove Canadian and American tourists, who stopped over at St. Hubert for a day or two between Barbados and Trinidad, along such hill-trails as he considered most easy to achieve with a second-hand motor, and gave them misinformation regarding the flowers. The rat-catcher's assistant became a respectable smuggler and leader of a Wesleyan choir. And as for the rats themselves, they flourished, they were glad in the land, and each female produced from ten to two hundred offspring every year.

They were not often seen by day. "The rats aren't increasing; the cats kill 'em," said Kellett the Red Leg. But by darkness they gamboled in the warehouses and in and out of the schooners along the quay. They ventured countryward, and lent their fleas to a species of ground squirrels which were plentiful about the village of Carib.

A year and a half after the removal of the rat-catcher, when the *Pendown Castle* came in from Montevideo and moored by the Councillor Pier, it was observed by ten thousand glinty small eyes among the piles.

As a matter of routine, certainly not as a thing connected with the deaths from what the skipper had called influenza, the crew of the *Pendown Castle* put rat-shields on the mooring hawsers, but they did not take up the gangplank at night, and now and then a rat slithered ashore to find among its kin in Blackwater more unctuous fare than hardwood lumber. The *Pendown* sailed amiably for home, and from Avonmouth came to Surgeon General Inchcape Jones a cable announcing that the ship was held, that others of the crew had died ... and died of plague.

In the curt cablegram the word seemed written in bone-scorching fire.

Two days before the cable came, a Blackwater lighterman had been smitten by an unknown ill, very unpleasant, with delirium and buboes. Inchcape Jones said that it could not be plague, because there never was plague in St. Hubert. His confrère, Stokes, retorted that perhaps it couldn't be plague, but it damn' well *was* plague.

Dr. Stokes was a wiry, humorless man, the parish medical officer of St. Swithin Parish. He did not remain in the rustic reaches of St. Swithin, where he belonged, but snooped all over the island, annoying Inchcape Jones. He was an M.B. of Edinburgh; he had served in the African bush; he had had blackwater fever and cholera and most other reasonable afflictions; and he had come to St. Hubert only to recover his red blood corpuscles and to disturb the unhappy Inchcape Jones. He was not a nice man; he had beaten Inchcape Jones at tennis, with a nasty, unsporting serve — the sort of serve you'd expect from an American.

And this Stokes, rather a bounder, a frightful bore, fancied himself as an amateur bacteriologist! It was a bit thick to have him creeping about the docks, catching rats, making cultures from the bellies of their fleas, and barging in — sandy-headed and red-faced, thin and unpleasant — to insist that they bore plague.

"My dear fellow, there's always some *Bacillus pestis* among rats," said Inchcape Jones, in a kindly but airy way.

When the lighterman died, Stokes irritatingly demanded that it be openly admitted that the plague had come to St. Hubert.

"Even if it was plague, which is not certain," said Inchcape Jones, "there's no reason to cause a row and frighten everybody. It was a sporadic case. There won't be any more."

There were more, immediately. In a week three other waterfront workers and a fisherman at Point Carib were down with something which, even Inchcape Jones acknowledged, was uncomfortably like the description of plague in "Manson's Tropical Diseases": "a prodromal stage characterized by depression, anorexia, aching of the limbs," then the fever, the vertigo, the haggard features, the bloodshot and sunken eyes, the buboes in the groin. It was not a pretty disease. Inchcape Jones ceased being chattery and ever so jolly about picnics, and became almost as grim as Stokes. But publicly he still hoped and denied and St. Hubert did not know ... did not know.

## II

To drinking men and wanderers, the pleasantest place in the rather dull and tin-roofed town of Blackwater is the bar and restaurant called the Ice House.

It is on the floor above the Kellett Shipping Agency and the shop where the Chinaman who is supposed to be a graduate of Oxford sells carved tortoise, and cocoanuts in the horrible likeness of a head shrunken by headhunters. Except for the balcony, where one lunches and looks down on squatting breech-clouted Hindu beggars, and unearthly pearl-pale English children at games in the savannah, all of the Ice House is a large and dreaming dimness wherein you are but half conscious of Moorish grills, a touch of gilt on white-painted walls, a heavy, amazingly long mahogany bar, slot machines, and marble-topped tables beyond your own.

Here, at the cocktail-hour, are all the bloodless, sun-helmeted white rulers of St. Hubert who haven't quite the caste to belong to the Devonshire Club: the shipping-office clerks, the merchants who have no grandfathers, the secretaries to the Inchcape Joneses, the Italians and Portuguese who smuggle into Venezuela.

Calmed by rum swizzles, those tart and commanding apéritifs which are made in their deadly perfection only by the twirling swizzle-sticks of the darkies at the Ice House bar, the exiles become peaceful, and have another swizzle, and grow certain again (as for twenty-four hours, since the last cocktail-hour, they have not been certain) that next year they will go Home. Yes, they will taper off, take exercise in the dawn coolness, stop drinking, become strong and successful, and go Home ... the Lotus Eaters, tears in their eyes when in the dimness of the Ice House they think of Piccadilly or the heights of Quebec, of Indiana or Catalonia or the clogs of Lancashire.... They never go Home. But always they have new reassuring cocktail-hours at the Ice House, until they die, and the other lost men come to their funerals and whisper one to another that they *are* going Home.

Now of the Ice House, George William Vertigan, owner of The Blue Bazaar, was unchallenged monarch. He was a thick, ruddy man, the sort of Englishman one sees in the Midlands, the sort that is either very Non-Conformist or very alcoholic, and George William was not Non-Conformist. Each day from five to seven he was tilted against the bar, never drunk, never altogether sober, always full of melody and kindliness; the one man who did not long for Home, because outside the Ice House he remembered no home.

When it was whispered that a man had died of something which might be plague, George William announced to his court that if it were true, it would serve Kellett the Red Leg jolly well right. But everyone knew that the West Indian climate prevented plague.

The group, quivering on the edge of being panicky, were reassured.

It was two nights afterward that there writhed into the Ice House a rumor that George William Vertigan was dead.

## III

No one dared speak of it, whether in the Devonshire Club or the Ice House or the breeze-fluttered, sea-washed park where the Negroes gather after working hours, but they heard, almost without hearing, of this death — and this — and another. No one liked to shake hands with his oldest friend; everyone fled from everyone else, though the rats loyally stayed with them; and through the island galloped the Panic, which is more murderous than its brother, the Plague.

Still there was no quarantine, no official admission. Inchcape Jones vomited feeble proclamations of the inadvisability of too-large public gatherings, and wrote to London to inquire about Haffkine's prophylactic, but to Sir Robert Fairlamb he protested, "Honestly, there's only been a few deaths and I think it's all passed over. As for these suggestions of Stokes that we burn the village of Carib, merely because they've had several cases — why, it's barbarous! And it's been conveyed to me that if we were to establish a quarantine, the merchants would take the strongest measures against the administration. It would ruin the tourist and export business."

But Stokes of St. Swithin's secretly wrote to Dr. Max Gottlieb, Director of the McGurk Institute, that the plague was ready to flare up and consume all the West Indies, and would Dr. Gottlieb do something about it?

## Chapter 32

There may have been in the shadowy heart of Max Gottlieb a diabolic insensibility to divine pity, to suffering humankind; there may have been mere resentment of the doctors who considered his science of value only as it was handy to advertising their business of healing; there may have been the obscure and passionate and unscrupulous demand of genius for privacy. Certainly he who had lived to study the methods of immunizing mankind against disease had little interest in actually using those methods. He was like a fabulous painter, so contemptuous of popular taste that after a lifetime of creation he should destroy everything he has done, lest it be marred and mocked by the dull eyes of the crowd.

The letter from Dr. Stokes was not his only intimation that plague was striding through St. Hubert, that tomorrow it might be leaping to Barbados, to the Virgin Islands ... to New York. Ross McGurk was an emperor of the new era, better served than any cloistered satrap of old. His skippers looked in at a hundred ports; his railroads penetrated jungles; his correspondents whispered to him of the next election in Colombia, of the Cuban cane-crop, of what Sir Robert Fairlamb had said to Dr. R. E. Inchcape Jones on his bungalow porch. Ross McGurk, and after him Max Gottlieb, knew better than did the Lotus Eaters of the Ice House how much plague there was in St. Hubert.

Yet Gottlieb did not move, but pondered the unknown chemical structure of antibodies, interrupted by questions as to whether Pearl Robbins had enough pencils, whether it would be quite all right for Dr. Holabird to receive the Lettish scientific mission this afternoon, so that Dr. Sholtheis might attend the Anglican Conference on the Reservation of the Host.

He was assailed by inquirers: public health officials, one Dr. Almus Pickerbaugh, a congressman who was said to be popular in Washington, Gustaf Sondelius, and a Martin Arrowsmith who could not (whether because he was too big or too small) quite attain Gottlieb's concentrated indifference.

It was rumored that Arrowsmith of McGurk had something which might eradicate plague. Letters demanded of Gottlieb, "Can you stand by, with the stuff of salvation in your hands, and watch thousands of these unfortunate people dying in St. Hubert, and what is more are you going to let the dreaded plague gain a foothold in the Western hemisphere? My dear man, this is the time to come out of your scientific reverie and act!"

Then Ross McGurk, over a comfortable steak, hinted, not too diffidently, that this was the opportunity for the Institute to acquire world-fame.

Whether it was the compulsion of McGurk or the demands of the public-spirited, or whether Gottlieb's own imagination aroused enough to visualize the far-off misery of the blacks in the canefields, he summoned Martin and remarked:

"It comes to me that there is pneumonic plague in Manchuria and bubonic in St. Hubert, in the West Indies. If I could trust you, Martin, to use the phage with only half your patients and keep the others as controls, under normal hygienic conditions but without the phage, then you could make an absolute determination of its value as complete as what we have of mosquito transmission of yellow fever, and then I would send you down to St. Hubert. What do you t'ink?"

Martin swore by Jacques Loeb that he would observe test conditions; he would determine forever the value of phage by the contrast between patients treated and untreated and so, perhaps, end all plague forever; he would harden his heart and keep clear his eyes.

"We will get Sondelius to go along," said Gottlieb. "He will do the big boom-boom and so bring us the credit in the newspapers which, I am now told, a Director must obtain."

Sondelius did not merely consent — he insisted.

Martin had never seen a foreign country — he could not think of Canada, where he had spent a vacation as hotel-waiter, as foreign to him. He could not comprehend that he was really going to a place of palm trees and brown faces and languid Christmas Eves. He was busy (while Sondelius was out ordering linen suits and seeking a proper new sun helmet) making anti-plague phage on a large scale: a hundred liters of it, sealed in tiny ampules. He felt like the normal Martin, but conferences and powers were considering him.

There was a meeting of the Board of Trustees to advise Martin and Sondelius as to their methods. For it the President of the University of Wilmington gave up a promising interview with a millionaire alumnus, Ross McGurk gave up a game of golf, and one of the three university scientists arrived by aeroplane. Called in from the laboratory, a rather young man in a wrinkled soft collar, dizzy still with the details of Erlenmeyer flasks, infusorial earth, and sterile filters, Martin was confronted by the Men of Measured Merriment, and found that he was no longer concealed in the invisibility of insignificance but regarded as a leader who was expected not only to produce miracles but to explain beforehand how important and mature and miraculous he was.

He was shy before the spectacled gravity of the five Trustees as they sat, like a Supreme Court, at the dais table in Bonanza Hall — Gottlieb a little removed, also trying to look grave and supreme. But Sondelius rolled in, enthusiastic and tremendous, and suddenly Martin was not shy, nor was he respectful to his one-time master in public health.

Sondelius wanted to exterminate all the rodents in St. Hubert, to enforce a quarantine, to use Yersin's serum and Haffkine's prophylactic, and to give Martin's phage to everybody in St. Hubert, all at once, all with everybody.

Martin protested. For the moment it might have been Gottlieb speaking.

He knew, he flung at them, that humanitarian feeling would make it impossible to use the poor devils of sufferers as mere objects of experiment, but he must have at least a few real test cases, and he was damned, even before the Trustees he was damned, if he would have his experiment so mucked up by multiple treatment that they could never tell whether the cures were due to Yersin or Haffkine or phage or none of them.

The Trustees adopted his plan. After all, while they desired to save humanity, wasn't it better to have it saved by a McGurk representative than by Yersin or Haffkine or the outlandish Sondelius?

It was agreed that if Martin could find in St. Hubert a district which was comparatively untouched by the plague, he should there endeavor to have test cases, one half injected with phage, one half untreated. In the badly afflicted districts, he might give the phage to everyone, and if the disease slackened unusually, that would be a secondary proof.

Whether the St. Hubert government, since they had not asked for aid, would give Martin power to experiment and Sondelius police authority, the Trustees did not know. The Surgeon General, a chap named Inchcape Jones, had replied to their cables: "No real epidemic not need help." But McGurk promised that he would pull his numerous wires to have the McGurk Commission (Chairman, Martin Arrowsmith, B.A., M.D.) welcomed by the authorities.

Sondelius still insisted that in this crisis mere experimentation was heartless, yet he listened to Martin's close-reasoned fury with enthusiasm which this bull-necked eternal child had for anything which sounded new and preferably true. He did not, like Almus Pickerbaugh, regard a difference of scientific opinion as an attack on his character.

He talked of going on his own, independent of Martin and McGurk, but he was won back when the Trustees murmured that though they really did wish the dear man wouldn't fool with sera, they would provide him with apparatus to kill all the rats he wanted.

Then Sondelius was happy:

"And you watch me! I am the captain-general of rat-killers! I yoost walk into a warehouse and the rats say, 'There's that damn' old Uncle Gustaf — what's the use?' and they turn up their toes and die! I am yoost as glad I have you people behind me, because I am broke — I went and bought some oil stock that don't look so good now — and I shall need a lot of hydrocyanic acid gas. Oh, those rats! You watch me! Now I go and telegraph I can't keep a lecture engagement next week — huh! me lecture to a women's college, me that can talk rat-language and know seven beautiful deadly kind of traps!"

## II

Martin had never known greater peril than swimming a flood as a hospital intern. From waking to midnight he was too busy making phage and receiving unsolicited advice from all the Institute staff to think of the dangers of a plague epidemic, but when he went to bed, when his brain was still revolving with plans, he pictured rather too well the chance of dying, unpleasantly.

When Leora received the idea that he was going off to a death-haunted isle, to a place of strange ways and trees and faces (a place, probably, where they spoke funny languages and didn't have movies or tooth-paste), she took the notion secretively away with her, to look at it and examine it, precisely as she often stole little foods from the table and hid them and meditatively ate them at odd hours of the night, with the pleased expression of a bad child. Martin was glad that she did not add to his qualms by worrying. Then, after three days, she spoke:

"I'm going with you."

"You are not!"

"Well.... I am!"

"It's not safe."

"Silly! Of course it is. You can shoot your nice old phage into me, and then I'll be absolutely all right. Oh, I have a husband who cures things, I have! I'm going to blow in a lot of money for thin dresses, though I bet St. Hubert isn't any hotter than Dakota can be in August."

"Listen! Lee, darling! Listen! I do think the phage will immunize against the plague — you bet I'll be mighty well injected with it myself! — but I don't *know*, and even if it were practically perfect, there'd always be some people it wouldn't protect. You simply can't go, sweet. Now I'm terribly sleepy — "

Leora seized his lapels, as comic fierce as a boxing kitten, but her eyes were not comic, nor her wailing voice; age-old wail of the soldiers' women:

"Sandy, don't you know I haven't any life outside of you? I might've had, but honestly, I've been glad to let you absorb me. I'm a lazy, useless, ignorant scut, except as maybe I keep you comfortable. If you were off there, and I didn't know you were all right, or if you died and somebody else cared for your body that I've loved so — haven't I loved it, dear? — I'd go mad. I mean it — can't you see I mean it — I'd go mad! It's just — I'm you, and I got to be with you. And I *will* help you! Make your media and everything. You know how often I've helped you. Oh, I'm not much good at McGurk, with all your awful' complicated jiggers, but I did help you at Nautilus — I *did* help you, didn't I? — and maybe in St. Hubert" — her voice was the voice of women in midnight terror — "maybe you won't find anybody that can help you even my little bit, and I'll cook and everything — "

"Darling, don't make it harder for me. Going to be hard enough in any case — "

"Damn you, Sandy Arrowsmith, don't you dare use those old stuck-up expressions that husbands have been drooling out to wives forever and ever! I'm not a wife, any more'n you're a husband. You're a rotten husband! You neglect me absolutely. The only time you know what I've got on is when some doggone button slips — and how they can pull off when a person has gone over 'em and sewed 'em all on again is simply beyond me! — and then you bawl me out. But I don't care. I'd rather have you than any decent husband.... Besides. I'm going."

Gottlieb opposed it, Sondelius roared about it, Martin worried about it, but Leora went, and — his only act of craftiness as Director of the Institute — Gottlieb made her "Secretary and Technical Assistant to the McGurk Plague and Bacteriophage Commission to the Lesser Antilles," and blandly gave her a salary.

## III

The day before the Commission sailed, Martin insisted that Sondelius take his first injection of phage. He refused.

"No, I will not touch it till you get converted to humanity, Martin, and give it to everybody in St. Hubert. And you will! Wait till you see them suffering by the thousand. You have not seen such a thing. Then you will forget science and try to save everybody. You shall not inject me till you will inject all my Negro friends down there too."

That afternoon Gottlieb called Martin in. He spoke with hesitation:

"You're off for Blackwater tomorrow."

"Yes, sir."

"Hm. You may be gone some time. I — Martin, you are my oldest friend in New York, you and the good Miriam. Tell me: At first you and Terry t'ought I should not take up the Directorship. Don't you t'ink I was wise?"

Martin stared, then hastily he lied and said that which was comforting and expected.

"I am glad you t'ink so. You have known so long what I have tried to do. I haf faults, but I t'ink I begin to see a real scientific note coming into the Institute at last, after the popoolarity-chasing of Tubbs and Holabird.... I wonder how I can discharge Holabird, that pants-presser of science? If only he dit not know Capitola so well — socially, they call it! But anyway —

"There are those that said Max Gottlieb could not do the child job of running an institution. Huh! Buying note-books! Hiring women that sweep floors! Or no — the floors are swept by women hired by the superintendent of the building, *nicht wahr* ? But anyway —

"I did not make a rage when Terry and you doubted. I am a great fellow for allowing everyone his opinion. But it pleases me — I am very fond of you two boys — the only real sons I have — " Gottlieb laid his withered hand on Martin's arm. "It pleases me that you see now I am beginning to make a real scientific Institute. Though I have enemies. Martin, you would t'ink I was joking, if I told you the plotting against me —

"Even Yeo. I t'ought he was my friend. I t'ought he was a real biologist. But just today he comes to me and says he cannot get enough sea-urchins for his experiments. As if I could make sea-urchins out of thin air! He said I keep him short of all materials. Me! That have always stood for — I do not care what they *pay* scientists, but always I have stood, against that fool Silva and all of them, all my enemies —

"You do not know how many enemies I have, Martin! They do not dare show their faces. They smile to me, but they whisper — I will show Holabird — always he plot against me and try to win over Pearl Robbins, but she is a good girl, she knows what I am doing, but — "

He looked perplexed; he peered at Martin as though he did not quite recognize him, and begged:

"Martin, I grow old — not in years — it is a lie I am over seventy — but I have my worries. Do you mind if I give you advice as I have done so often, so many years? Though you are not a schoolboy now in Queen City — no, at Winnemac it was. You are a man and you are a genuine worker. But —

"Be sure you do not let anything, not even your own good kind heart, spoil your experiment at St. Hubert. I do not make funniness about humanitarianism as I used to; sometimes now I t'ink the vulgar and contentious human race may yet have as much grace and good taste as the cats. But if this is to be, there must be knowledge. So many men, Martin, are kind and neighborly; so few have added to knowledge. You have the chance! You may be the man who ends all plague, and maybe old Max Gottlieb will have helped, too, *hein* , maybe?

"You must not be just a good doctor at St. Hubert. You must pity, oh, so much the generation after generation yet to come that you can refuse to let yourself indulge in pity for the men you will see dying.

"Dying.... It will be peace.

"Let nothing, neither beautiful pity nor fear of your own death, keep you from making this plague experiment complete. And as my friend — If you do this, something will yet have come out of my Directorship. If but one fine thing could come, to justify me — "

When Martin came sorrowing into his laboratory he found Terry Wickett waiting.

"Say, Slim," Terry blurted, "just wanted to butt in and suggest, now for St. Gottlieb's sake keep your phage notes complete and up-to-date, and keep 'em in ink!"

"Terry, it looks to me as if you thought I had a fine chance of not coming back with the notes myself."

"Aw, what's biting you!" said Terry feebly.

## IV

The epidemic in St. Hubert must have increased, for on the day before the McGurk Commission sailed, Dr. Inchcape Jones declared that the island was quarantined. People might come in, but no one could leave. He did this despite the fretting of the Governor, Sir Robert Fairlamb, and the protests of the hotel-keepers who fed on tourists, the ex-rat-catchers who drove the same, Kellett the Red Leg who sold them tickets, and all the other representatives of sound business in St. Hubert.

## V

Besides his ampules of phage and his Luer syringes for injection, Martin made personal preparations for the tropics. He bought, in seventeen minutes, a Palm Beach suit, two new shirts, and, as St. Hubert was a British possession and as he had heard that all Britishers carry canes, a stick which the shopkeeper guaranteed to be as good as genuine malacca.

## VI

They started, Martin and Leora and Gustaf Sondelius, on a winter morning, on the six-thousand-ton steamer *St. Buryan* of the McGurk Line, which carried machinery and flour and codfish and motors to the Lesser Antilles and brought back molasses, cocoa, avocados, and Trinidad asphalt. A score of winter tourists made the round trip, but only a score, and there was little handkerchief-waving.

The McGurk Line pier was in South Brooklyn, in a district of brown anonymous houses. The sky was colorless above dirty snow. Sondelius seemed well content. As they drove upon a wharf littered with hides and boxes and disconsolate steerage passengers, he peered out of their crammed taxicab and announced that the bow of the *St. Buryan* — all they could see of it — reminded him of the Spanish steamer he had taken to the Cape Verde Isles. But to Martin and Leora, who had read of the drama of departure, of stewards darting with masses of flowers, dukes and divorcees being interviewed, and bands playing "The Star-spangled Banner," the *St. Buryan* was unromantic and its ferry-like casualness was discouraging.

Only Terry came to see them off, bringing a box of candy for Leora.

Martin had never ridden a craft larger than a motor launch. He stared up at the black wall of the steamer's side. As they mounted the gangplank he was conscious that he was cutting himself off from the safe, familiar land, and he was embarrassed by the indifference of more experienced-looking passengers, staring down from the rail. Aboard, it seemed to him that the forward deck looked like the backyard of an old-iron dealer, that the *St. Buryan* leaned too much to one side, and that even in the dock she swayed undesirably.

The whistle snorted contemptuously; the hawsers were cast off. Terry stood on the pier till the steamer, with Martin and Leora and Sondelius above, their stomachs pressed against the rail, had slid past him, then he abruptly clumped away.

Martin realized that he was off for the perilous sea and the perilous plague; that there was no possibility of leaving the ship till they should reach some distant island. This narrow deck, with its tarry lines between planks, was his only home. Also, in the breeze across the wide harbor he was beastly cold, and in general God help him!

As the *St. Buryan* was warped out into the river, as Martin was suggesting to his Commission, "How about going downstairs and seeing if we can raise a drink?" there was the sound of a panicky taxicab on the pier, the sight of a lean, tall figure running — but so feebly, so shakily — and they realized that it was Max Gottlieb, peering for them, tentatively raising his thin arm in greeting, not finding them at the rail, and turning sadly away.

## VII

As representatives of Ross McGurk and his various works, evil and benevolent, they had the two suites de luxe on the boat deck.

Martin was cold off snow-blown Sandy Hook, sick off Cape Hatteras, and tired and relaxed between; with him Leora was cold, and in a ladylike manner she was sick, but she was not at all tired. She insisted on conveying information to him, from the West Indian guide-book which she had earnestly bought.

Sondelius was conspicuously all over the ship. He had tea with the Captain, scouse with the fo'c'sle, and intellectual conferences with the Negro missionary in the steerage. He was to be heard — always he was to be heard: singing on the promenade deck, defending Bolshevism against the boatswain, arguing oil-burning with the First Officer, and explaining to the bar steward how to make a gin sling. He held a party for the children in the steerage, and he borrowed from the First Officer a volume of navigation to study between parties.

He gave flavor to the ordinary cautious voyage of the *St. Buryan* , but he made a mistake. He was courteous to Miss Gwilliam; he tried to cheer her on a seemingly lonely adventure.

Miss Gwilliam came from one of the best families in her section of New Jersey; her father was a lawyer and a churchwarden, her grandfather had been a solid farmer. That she had not married, at thirty-three, was due entirely to the preference of modern young men for jazz-dancing hussies; and she was not only a young lady of delicate reservations but also a singer; in fact, she was going to the West Indies to preserve the wonders of primitive art for reverent posterity in the native ballads she would collect and sing to a delighted public — if only she learned how to sing.

She studied Gustaf Sondelius. He was a silly person, not in the least like the gentlemanly insurance-agents and office-managers she was accustomed to meet at the country club, and what was worse, he did not ask her opinions on art and good form. His stories about generals and that sort of people could be discounted as lies, for did he not associate with grimy engineers? He needed some of her gentle but merry chiding.

When they stood together at the rail and he chanted in his ludicrous up-and-down Swedish sing-song that it was a fine evening, she remarked, "Well, Mr. Roughneck, have you been up to something smart again today? Or have you been giving somebody else a chance to talk, for once?"

She was placidly astonished when he clumped away with none of the obedient reverence which any example of cultured American womanhood has a right to expect from all males, even foreigners.

Sondelius came to Martin lamenting, "Slim — if I may call you so, like Terry — I think you and your Gottlieb are right. There is no use saving fools. It's a great mistake to be natural. One should always be a stuffed shirt, like old Tubbs. Then one would have respect even from artistic New Jersey spinsters.... How strange is conceit! That I who have been cursed and beaten by so many Great Ones, who was once led out to be shot in a Turkish prison, should never have been annoyed by them as by this smug wench. Ah, smugness! That is the enemy!"

Apparently he recovered from Miss Gwilliam. He was seen arguing with the ship's doctor about sutures in Negro skulls, and he invented a game of deck cricket. But one evening when he sat reading in the "social hall," stooped over, wearing betraying spectacles and his mouth puckered, Martin walked past the window and incredulously saw that Sondelius was growing old.

## VIII

As he sat by Leora in a deck-chair, Martin studied her, really looked at her pale profile, after years when she had been a matter of course. He pondered on her as he pondered on phage; he weightily decided that he had neglected her, and weightily he started right in to be a good husband.

"Now I have a chance to be human, Lee, I realize how lonely you must have been in New York."

"But I haven't."

"Don't be foolish! Of course you've been lonely! Well, when we get back, I'll take a little time off every day and we'll — we'll have walks and go to the movies and everything. And I'll send you flowers, every morning. Isn't it a relief to just sit here! But I do begin to think and realize how I've prob'ly neglected — Tell me, honey, has it been too terribly dull?"

"Hunka. Really."

"No, but *tell* me."

"There's nothing to tell."

"Now hang it, Leora, here when I *do* have the first chance in eleven thousand years to think about you, and I come right out frankly and admit how slack I've been — And planning to send you flowers — "

"You look here, Sandy Arrowsmith! Quit bullying me! You want the luxury of harrowing yourself by thinking what a poor, bawling, wretched, story-book wife I am. You're working up to become perfectly miserable if you can't enjoy being miserable.... It would be terrible, when we got back to New York, if you did get on the job and devoted yourself to showing me a good time. You'd go at it like a bull. I'd have to be so dratted grateful for the flowers every day — the days you didn't forget! — and the way you'd sling me off to the movies when I wanted to stay home and snooze — "

"Well, by thunder, of all the — "

"No, please! You're dear and good, but you're so bossy that I've always got to be whatever *you* want, even if it's lonely. But — Maybe I'm lazy. I'd rather just snoop around than have to work at being well-dressed and popular and all those jobs. I fuss over the flat — hang it, wish I'd had the kitchen repainted while we're away, it's a *nice* little kitchen — and I make believe read my French books, and go out for a walk, and look in the windows, and eat an ice cream soda, and the day slides by. Sandy, I do love you awful' much; if I could, I'd be as ill-treated as the dickens, so you could enjoy it, but I'm no good at educated lies, only at easy little ones like the one I told you last week — I said I hadn't eaten any candy and didn't have a stomach-ache, and I'd eaten half a pound and I was as sick as a pup.... Gosh, I'm a good wife I am!"

They rolled from gray seas to purple and silver. By dusk they stood at the rail, and he felt the spaciousness of the sea, of life. Always he had lived in his imagination. As he had blundered through crowds, an inconspicuous young husband trotting out to buy cold roast beef for dinner, his brain-pan had been wide as the domed sky. He had seen not the streets, but microorganisms large as jungle monsters, miles of flasks cloudy with bacteria, himself giving orders to his garçon, Max Gottlieb awesomely congratulating him. Always his dreams had clung about his work. Now, no less passionately, he awoke to the ship, the mysterious sea, the presence of Leora, and he cried to her, in the warm tropic winter dusk:

"Sweet, this is only the first of our big hikes! Pretty soon, if I'm successful in St. Hubert, I'll begin to count in science, and we'll go abroad, to your France and England and Italy and everywhere!"

"Can we, do you think? Oh, Sandy! Going *places* !"

## IX

He never knew it but for an hour, in their cabin half-lighted from the lamps in their sitting-room beyond, she watched him sleeping.

He was not handsome; he was grotesque as a puppy napping on a hot afternoon. His hair was ruffled, his face was deep in the crumpled pillow he had encircled with both his arms. She looked at him, smiling, with the stretched corners of her lips like tiny flung arrows.

"I do love him so when he's frowsy! Don't you see, Sandy, I was wise to come! You're so worn out. *It* might get you, and nobody but me could nurse you. Nobody knows all your cranky ways — about how you hate prunes and everything. Night and day I'll nurse you — the least whisper and I'll be awake. And if you need ice bags and stuff — And I'll *have* ice, too, if I have to sneak into some millionaire's house and steal it out of his highballs! My dear!"

She shifted the electric fan so that it played more upon him, and on soft toes she crept into their stiff sitting-room. It did not contain much save a round table, a few chairs, and a Sybaritic glass and mahogany wall-cabinet whose purpose was never discovered.

"It's so sort of — Aah! Pinched. I guess maybe I ought to fix it up somehow."

But she had no talent for the composing of chairs and pictures which brings humanness into a dead room. Never in her life had she spent three minutes in arranging flowers. She looked doubtful, she smiled and turned out the light, and slipped in to him.

She lay on the coverlet of her berth, in the tropic languidness, a slight figure in a frivolous nightgown. She thought, "I like a small bedroom, because Sandy is nearer and I don't get so scared by things. What a dratted bully the man is! Some day I'm going to up and say to him: 'You go to the devil!' I will so! Darling, we will hike off to France together, just you and I, won't we!"

She was asleep, smiling, so thin a little figure —

## Chapter 33

Misty mountains they saw, and on their flanks the palm-crowned fortifications built of old time against the pirates. In Martinique were white-faced houses like provincial France, and a boiling market full of colored women with kerchiefs ultramarine and scarlet. They passed hot St. Lucia, and Saba that is all one lone volcano. They devoured pawpaws and breadfruit and avocados, bought from coffee-colored natives who came alongside in nervous small boats; they felt the languor of the isles, and panted before they approached Barbados.

Just beyond was St. Hubert.

None of the tourists had known of the quarantine. They were raging that the company should have taken them into danger. In the tepid wind they felt the plague.

The skipper reassured them, in a formal address. Yes, they would stop at Blackwater, the port of St. Hubert, but they would anchor far out in the harbor; and while the passengers bound for St. Hubert would be permitted to go ashore, in the port-doctor's launch, no one in St. Hubert would be allowed to leave — nothing from that pest-hole would touch the steamer except the official mail, which the ship's surgeon would disinfect.

(The ship's surgeon was wondering, the while, how you disinfected mail — let's see — sulfur burning in the presence of moisture, wasn't it?)

The skipper had been trained in oratory by arguments with wharf-masters, and the tourists were reassured. But Martin murmured to his Commission, "I hadn't thought of that. Once we go ashore, we'll be practically prisoners till the epidemic's over — if it ever does get over — prisoners with the plague around us."

"Why, of course!" said Sondelius.

### II

They left Bridgetown, the pleasant port of Barbados, by afternoon. It was late night, with most of the passengers asleep, when they arrived at Blackwater. As Martin came out on the damp and vacant deck, it seemed unreal, harshly unfriendly, and of the coming battleground he saw nothing but a few shore lights beyond uneasy water.

About their arrival there was something timorous and illicit. The ship's surgeon ran up and down, looking disturbed; the captain could be heard growling on the bridge; the first officer hastened up to confer with him and disappeared below again; and there was no one to meet them. The steamer waited, rolling in a swell, while from the shore seemed to belch a hot miasma.

"And here's where we're going to land and *stay* !" Martin grunted to Leora, as they stood by their bags, their cases of phage, on the heaving, black-shining deck near the top of the accommodation-ladder.

Passengers came out in dressing-gowns, chattering, "Yes, this must be the place, those lights there. Must be fierce. *What?* Somebody going ashore? Oh, sure those two doctors. Well, they got nerve. I certainly don't envy them!"

Martin heard.

From shore a pitching light made toward the ship, slid round the bow, and sidled to the bottom of the accommodation-ladder. In the haze of a lantern held by a steward at the foot of the steps, Martin could see a smart covered launch, manned by darky sailors in naval uniform and glazed black straw hats with ribbons, and commanded by a Scotch-looking man with some sort of a peaked uniform cap over a civilian jacket.

The captain clumped down the swinging steps beside the ship. While the launch bobbed, its wet canvas top glistening, he had a long and complaining conference with the commander of the launch, and received a pouch of mail, the only thing to come aboard.

The ship's surgeon took it from the captain with aversion, grumbling, "Now where can I get a barrel to disinfect these darn' letters in?"

Martin and Leora and Sondelius waited, without option.

They had been joined by a thin woman in black whom they had not seen all the trip — one of the mysterious passengers who are never noticed till they come on deck at landing. Apparently she was going ashore. She was pale, her hands twitching.

The captain shouted at them, "All right — all right — all right! You can go now. Hustle, please. I've got to get on.... Damn' nuisance."

The *St. Buryan* had not seemed large or luxurious, but it was a castle, steadfast among storms, its side a massy wall, as Martin crept down the swaying stairs, thinking all at once, "We're in for it; like going to the scaffold — they lead you along — no chance to resist," and, "You're letting your imagination run away with you; quit it now!" and, "Is it too late to make Lee stay behind, on the steamer?" and an agonized, "Oh, Lord, are the stewards handling that phage carefully?" Then he was on the tiny square platform at the bottom of the accommodation-ladder, the ship's side was high above him, lit by the round ports of cabins, and someone was helping him into the launch.

As the unknown woman in black came aboard, Martin saw in lantern light how her lips tightened once, then her whole face went blank, like one who waited hopelessly.

Leora squeezed his hand, hard, as he helped her in.

He muttered, while the steamer whistled, "Quick! You can still go back! You must!"

"And leave the pretty launch? Why, Sandy! Just look at the elegant engine it's got!... Gosh, I'm scared blue!"

As the launch sputtered, swung round, and headed for the filtering of lights ashore, as it bowed its head and danced to the swell, the sandy-headed official demanded of Martin:

"You're the McGurk Commission?"

"Yes."

"Good." He sounded pleased yet cold, a busy voice and humorless.

"Are you the port-doctor?" asked Sondelius.

"No, not exactly. I'm Dr. Stokes, of St. Swithin's Parish. We're all of us almost everything, nowadays. The port-doctor — In fact he died couple of days ago."

Martin grunted. But his imagination had ceased to agitate him.

"You're Dr. Sondelius, I imagine. I know your work in Africa, in German East — was out there myself. And you're Dr. Arrowsmith? I read your plague phage paper. Much impressed. Now I have just the chance to say before we go ashore — You'll both be opposed. Inchcape Jones, the S.G., has lost his head. Running in circles, lancing buboes — afraid to burn Carib, where most of the infection is. Arrowsmith, I have a notion of what you may want to do experimentally. If Inchcape balks, you come to me in my parish — if I'm still alive. Stokes, my name is.... Damn it, boy, what *are* you doing? Trying to drift clear down to Venezuela?... Inchcape and H.E. are so afraid that they won't even cremate the bodies — some religious prejudice among the blacks — obee or something."

"I see," said Martin.

"How many cases plague you got now?" said Sondelius.

"Lord knows. Maybe a thousand. And ten million rats ... I'm so sleepy!... Well, welcome, gentlemen — " He flung out his arms in a dry hysteria. "Welcome to the Island of Hesperides!"

Out of darkness Blackwater swung toward them, low flimsy barracks on a low swampy plain stinking of slimy mud. Most of the town was dark, dark and wickedly still. There was no face along the dim waterfront — warehouses, tram station, mean hotels — and they ground against a pier, they went ashore, without attention from customs officials. There were no carriages, and the hotel-runners who once had pestered tourists landing from the *St. Buryan* , whatever the hour, were dead now or hidden.

The thin mysterious woman passenger vanished, staggering with her suit-case — she had said no word, and they never saw her again. The Commission, with Stokes and the harbor-police who had manned the launch, carried the baggage (Martin weaving with a case of the phage) through the rutty balconied streets to the San Marino Hotel.

Once or twice faces, disembodied things with frightened lips, stared at them from alley-mouths; and when they came to the hotel, when they stood before it, a weary caravan laden with bags and boxes, the bulging-eyed manageress peered from a window before she would admit them.

As they entered, Martin saw under a street light the first stirring of life: a crying woman and a bewildered child following an open wagon in which were heaped a dozen stiff bodies.

"And I might have saved all of them, with phage," he whispered to himself.

His forehead was cold, yet it was greasy with sweat as he babbled to the manageress of rooms and meals, as he prayed that Leora might not have seen the Things in that slow creaking wagon.

"I'd have choked her before I let her come, if I'd known," he was shuddering.

The woman apologized, "I must ask you gentlemen to carry your things up to your rooms. Our boys — They aren't here any more."

What became of the walking stick which, in such pleased vanity, Martin had bought in New York, he never knew. He was too busy guarding the cases of phage, and worrying, "Maybe this stuff would save everybody."

Now Stokes of St. Swithin's was a reticent man and hard, but when they had the last bag upstairs, he leaned his head against a door, cried, "My God, Arrowsmith, I'm so glad you've got here," and broke from them, running.... One of the Negro harbor-police, expressionless, speaking the English of the Antilles with something of the accent of Piccadilly, said, "Sar, have you any other command for I? If you permit, we boys will now go home. Sar, on the table is the whisky Dr. Stokes have told I to bring."

Martin stared. It was Sondelius who said, "Thank you very much, boys. Here's a quid between you. Now get some sleep."

They saluted and were not.

Sondelius made the novices as merry as he could for half an hour.

Martin and Leora woke to a broiling, flaring, green and crimson morning, yet ghastly still; awoke and realized that about them was a strange land, as yet unseen, and before them the work that in distant New York had seemed dramatic and joyful and that stank now of the charnel house.

## III

A sort of breakfast was brought to them by a Negress who, before she would enter, peeped fearfully at them from the door.

Sondelius rumbled in from his room, in an impassioned silk dressing-gown. If ever, spectacled and stooped, he had looked old, now he was young and boisterous.

"Hey, ya, Slim, I think we get some work here! Let me at those rats! This Inchcape — to try to master them with strychnin! A noble melon! Leora, when you divorce Martin, you marry me, heh? Give me the salt. Yey, I sleep fine!"

The night before, Martin had scarce looked at their room. Now he was diverted by what he considered its foreignness: the lofty walls of wood painted a watery blue, the wide furnitureless spaces, the bougainvillaea at the window, and in the courtyard the merciless heat and rattling metallic leaves of palmettoes.

Beyond the courtyard walls were the upper stories of a balconied Chinese shop and the violent-colored skylight of The Blue Bazaar.

He felt that there should be a clamor from this exotic world, but there was only a rebuking stillness, and even Sondelius became dumb, though he had his moment. He waddled back to his room, dressed himself in surah silk last worn on the East Coast of Africa, and returned bringing a sun-helmet which secretly he had bought for Martin.

In linen jacket and mushroom helmet, Martin belonged more to the tropics than to his own harsh Northern meadows. But his pleasure in looking foreign was interrupted by the entrance of the Surgeon General, Dr. R. E. Inchcape Jones, lean but apple-cheeked, worried and hasty.

"Of course you chaps are welcome, but really, with all we have to do I'm afraid we can't give you the attention you doubtless expect," he said indignantly.

Martin sought for adequate answer. It was Sondelius who spoke of a non-existent cousin who was a Harley Street specialist, and who explained that all they wanted was a laboratory for Martin and, for himself, a chance to slaughter rats. How many times, in how many lands, had Gustaf Sondelius flattered pro-consuls and persuaded the heathen to let themselves be saved!

Under his hands the Surgeon General became practically human; he looked as though he really thought Leora was pretty; he promised that he might perhaps let Sondelius tamper with his rats. He would return that afternoon and conduct them to the house prepared for them, Penrith Lodge, on the safe secluded hills behind Blackwater. And (he bowed gallantly) he thought that Mrs. Arrowsmith would find the Lodge a topping bungalow, with three rather decent servants. The butler, though a colored chap, was an old mess-sergeant.

Inchcape Jones had scarce gone when at the door there was a pounding and it opened on Martin's classmate at Winnemac, Dr. the Rev. Ira Hinkley.

Martin had forgotten Ira, that bulky Christian who had tried to save him during otherwise dulcet hours of dissection. He recalled him confusedly. The man came in, vast and lumbering. His eyes were staring and altogether mad, and his voice was parched:

"Hello, Mart. Yump, it's old Ira. I'm in charge of all the chapels of the Sanctification Brotherhood here. Oh, Mart, if you only knew the wickedness of the natives, and the way they lie and sing indecent songs and commit all manner of vileness! And the Church of England lets them wallow in their sins! Only us to save them. I heard you were coming. I have been laboring, Mart. I've nursed the poor plague-stricken devils, and I've told them how hellfire is roaring about them. Oh, Mart, if you knew how my heart bleeds to see these ignorant fellows going unrepentant to eternal torture! After all these years I know you can't still be a scoffer. I come to you with open hands, begging you not merely to comfort the sufferers but to snatch their souls from the burning lakes of sulfur to which, in His everlasting mercy, the Lord of Hosts hath condemned those that blaspheme against His gospel, freely given — "

Again it was Sondelius who got Ira Hinkley out, not too discontented, while Martin could only sputter, "Now how do you suppose that maniac ever got here? This is going to be awful!"

Before Inchcape Jones returned, the Commission ventured out for their first sight of the town.... A Scientific Commission, yet all the while they were only boisterous Gustaf and doubtful Martin and casual Leora.

The citizens had been told that in bubonic plague, unlike pneumonic, there is no danger from direct contact with people developing the disease, so long as vermin were kept away, but they did not believe it. They were afraid of one another, and the more afraid of strangers. The Commission found a street dying with fear. House-shutters were closed, hot slatted patches in the sun; and the only traffic was an empty trolley-car with a frightened motorman who peered down at them and sped up lest they come aboard. Grocery shops and drugstores were open, but from their shady depths the shopkeepers looked out timidly, and when the Commission neared a fish-stall, the one customer fled, edging past them.

Once a woman, never explained, a woman with wild ungathered hair, ran by them shrieking, "My little boy — "

They came to the market, a hundred stalls under a long corrugated-iron roof, with stone pillars bearing the fatuous names of the commissioners who had built it — by voting bonds for the building. It should have been buzzing with jovial buyers and sellers, but in all the gaudy booths there were only one Negress with a row of twig besoms, one Hindu in gray rags squatting before his wealth of a dozen vegetables. The rest was emptiness, and a litter of rotted potatoes and scudding papers.

Down a grim street of coal yards, they found a public square, and here was the stillness not of sleep but of ancient death.

The square was rimmed with the gloom of mango trees, which shut out the faint-hearted breeze and cooped in the heat — stale lifeless heat, in whose misery the leering silence was the more dismaying. Through a break in the evil mangoes they beheld a plaster house hung with black crape.

"It's too hot to walk. Perhaps we'd better go back to the hotel," said Leora.

## IV

In the afternoon Inchcape Jones appeared with a Ford, whose familiarity made it the more grotesque in this creepy world, and took them to Penrith Lodge, on the cool hills behind Blackwater.

They traversed a packed native section of bamboo hovels and shops that were but unpainted, black-weathered huts, without doors, without windows, from whose recesses dark faces looked at them resentfully. They passed, at their colored driver's most jerky speed, a new brick structure in front of which stately Negro policemen with white gloves, white sun-helmets, and scarlet coats cut by white belts, marched with rifles at the carry.

Inchcape Jones sighed, "Schoolhouse. Turned it into pest-house. Hundred cases in there. Die every hour. Have to guard it — patients get delirious and try to escape."

After them trailed an odor of rotting.

Martin did not feel superior to humanity.

## V

With broad porches and low roof, among bright flamboyants and the cheerful sago palms, the bungalow of Penrith Lodge lay high on a crest, looking across the ugly flat of the town to the wash of sea. At its windows the reed jalousies whispered and clattered, and the high bare rooms were enlivened by figured Carib scarfs.... It had belonged to the port-doctor, dead these three days.

Inchcape Jones assured the doubtful Leora that she would nowhere else be so safe; the house was rat-proofed, and the doctor had caught the plague at the pier, had died without ever coming back to this well-beloved bungalow in which he, the professional bachelor, had given the most clamorous parties in St. Hubert.

Martin had with him sufficient equipment for a small laboratory, and he established it in a bedroom with gas and running water. Next to it was his and Leora's bedroom, then an apartment which Sondelius immediately made homelike by dropping his clothes and his pipe ashes all over it. There were two colored maids and an ex-soldier butler, who received them and unpacked their bags as though the plague did not exist.

Martin was perplexed by their first caller. He was a singularly handsome young Negro, quick-moving, intelligent of eye. Like most white Americans, Martin had talked a great deal about the inferiority of Negroes and had learned nothing whatever about them. He looked questioning as the young man observed:

"My name is Oliver Marchand."

"Yes?"

"Dr. Marchand — I have my M.D. from Howard."

"Oh."

"May I venture to welcome you, Doctor? And may I ask before I hurry off — I have three cases from official families isolated at the bottom of the hill — oh, yes, in this crisis they permit a Negro doctor to practice even among the whites! But — Dr. Stokes insists that D'Hérelle and you are right in calling bacteriophage an organism. But what about Bordet's contention that it's an enzyme?"

Then for half an hour did Dr. Arrowsmith and Dr. Marchand, forgetting the plague, forgetting the more cruel plague of race-fear, draw diagrams.

Marchand sighed, "I must go, Doctor. May I help you in any way I can? It is a great privilege to know you."

He saluted quietly and was gone, a beautiful young animal.

"I never thought a Negro doctor — I wish people wouldn't keep showing me how much I don't know!" said Martin.

## VI

While Martin prepared his laboratory, Sondelius was joyfully at work, finding out what was wrong with Inchcape Jones's administration, which proved to be almost anything that could be wrong.

A plague epidemic today, in a civilized land, is no longer an affair of people dying in the streets and of drivers shouting "Bring out your dead." The fight against it is conducted like modern warfare, with telephones instead of foaming chargers. The ancient horror bears a face of efficiency. There are offices, card indices, bacteriological examinations of patients and of rats. There is, or should be, a lone director with superlegal powers. There are large funds, education of the public by placard and newspaper, brigades of rat-killers, a corps of dis-infectors, isolation of patients lest vermin carry the germs from them to others.

In most of these particulars Inchcape Jones had failed. To have the existence of the plague admitted in the first place, he had had to fight the merchants controlling the House of Assembly, who had howled that a quarantine would ruin them, and who now refused to give him complete power and tried to manage the epidemic with a Board of Health, which was somewhat worse than navigating a ship during a typhoon by means of a committee.

Inchcape Jones was courageous enough, but he could not cajole people. The newspapers called him a tyrant, would not help win over the public to take precautions against rats and ground squirrels. He had tried to fumigate a few warehouses with sulfur dioxid, but the owners complained that the fumes stained fabrics and paint; and the Board of Health bade him wait — wait a little while — wait and see. He had tried to have the rats examined, to discover what were the centers of infection, but his only bacteriologists were the overworked Stokes and Oliver Marchand; and Inchcape Jones had often explained, at nice dinner-parties, that he did not trust the intelligence of Negroes.

He was nearly insane; he worked twenty hours a day; he assured himself that he was not afraid; he reminded himself that he had an honestly won D.S.O.; he longed to have someone besides a board of Red Leg merchants give him orders; and always in the blur of his sleepless brain he saw the hills of Surrey, his sisters in the rose-walk, and the basket-chairs and tea-table beside his father's tennis-lawn.

Then Sondelius, that crafty and often lying lobbyist, that unmoral soldier of the Lord, burst in and became dictator.

He terrified the Board of Health. He quoted his own experiences in Mongolia and India. He assured them that if they did not cease being politicians, the plague might cling in St. Hubert forever, so that they would no more have the amiable dollars of the tourists and the pleasures of smuggling.

He threatened and flattered, and told a story which they had never heard, even at the Ice House; and he had Inchcape Jones appointed dictator of St. Hubert.

Gustaf Sondelius stood extremely close behind the dictator.

He immediately started rat-killing. On a warrant signed by Inchcape Jones, he arrested the owner of a warehouse who had declared that he was not going to have his piles of cocoa ruined. He marched his policemen, stout black fellows trained in the Great War, to the warehouse, set them on guard, and pumped in hydrocyanic acid gas.

The crowd gathered beyond the police line, wondering, doubting. They could not believe that anything was happening, for the cracks in the warehouse walls had been adequately stuffed and there was no scent of gas. But the roof was leaky. The gas crept up through it, colorless, diabolic, and suddenly a buzzard circling above the roof tilted forward, fell slantwise, and lay dead among the watchers.

A man picked it up, goggling.

"Dead, right enough," everybody muttered. They looked at Sondelius, parading among his soldiers, with reverence.

His rat-crew searched each warehouse before pumping in the gas, lest someone be left in the place, but in the third one a tramp had been asleep, and when the doors were anxiously opened after the fumigation, there were not only thousands of dead rats but also a dead and very stiff tramp.

"Poor fella — bury him," said Sondelius.

There was no inquest.

Over a rum swizzle at the Ice House, Sondelius reflected, "I wonder how many men I murder, Martin? When I was disinfecting ships at Antofagasta, always afterward we find two or three stowaways. They hide too good. Poor fellas."

Sondelius arbitrarily dragged bookkeepers and porters from their work, to pursue the rats with poison, traps, and gas, or to starve them by concreting and screening stables and warehouses. He made a violent red and green rat map of the town. He broke every law of property by raiding shops for supplies. He alternately bullied and caressed the leaders of the House of Assembly. He called on Kellett, told stories to his children, and almost wept as he explained what a good Lutheran he was — and consistently (but not at Kellett's) he drank too much.

The Ice House, that dimmest and most peaceful among saloons, with its cool marble tables, its gilt-touched white walls, had not been closed, though only the oldest topers and the youngest bravos, fresh out from Home and agonizingly lonely for Peckham or Walthamstow, for Peel Park or the Cirencester High Street, were desperate enough to go there, and of the attendants there remained only one big Jamaica barman. By chance he was among them all the most divine mixer of the planter's punch, the New Orleans fizz, and the rum swizzle. His masterpieces Sondelius acclaimed, he alone placid among the scary patrons who came in now not to dream but to gulp and flee. After a day of slaughtering rats and disinfecting houses he sat with Martin, with Martin and Leora, or with whomever he could persuade to linger.

To Gustaf Sondelius, dukes and cobblers were alike remarkable, and Martin was sometimes jealous when he saw Sondelius turning to a cocoa-broker's clerk with the same smile he gave to Martin. For hours Sondelius talked, of Shanghai and epistemology and the painting of Nevinson; for hours he sang scurrilous lyrics of the Quarter, and boomed, "Yey, how I kill the rats at Kellett's wharf today! I don't t'ink one little swizzle would break down too many glomeruli in an honest man's kidneys."

He was cheerful, but never with the reproving and infuriating cheerfulness of an Ira Hinkley. He mocked himself, Martin, Leora, and their work. At home dinner he never cared what he ate (though he did care what he drank), which at Penrith Lodge was desirable, in view of Leora's efforts to combine the views of Wheatsylvania with the standards of West Indian servants and the absence of daily deliveries. He shouted and sang — and took precautions for working among rats and the agile fleas: the high boots, the strapped wrists, and the rubber neck-band which he had invented and which is known in every tropical supply shop today as the Sondelius Anti-vermin Neck Protector.

It happened that he was, without Martin or Gottlieb ever understanding it, the most brilliant as well as the least pompous and therefore least appreciated warrior against epidemics that the world has known.

Thus with Sondelius, though for Martin there were as yet but embarrassment and futility and the fear of fear.

## Chapter 34

To persuade the shopkeeping lords of St. Hubert to endure a test in which half of them might die, so that all plague might — perhaps — be ended forever, was impossible. Martin argued with Inchcape Jones, with Sondelius, but he had no favor, and he began to meditate a political campaign as he would have meditated an experiment.

He had seen the suffering of the plague and he had (though he still resisted) been tempted to forget experimentation, to give up the possible saving of millions for the immediate saving of thousands. Inchcape Jones, a little rested now under Sondelius's padded bullying and able to slip into a sane routine, drove Martin to the village of Carib, which, because of its pest of infected ground squirrels, was proportionately worse smitten than Blackwater.

They sped out of the capital by white shell roads agonizing to the sun-poisoned eyes; they left the dusty shanties of suburban Yamtown for a land cool with bamboo groves and palmettoes, thick with sugar-cane. From a hilltop they swung down a curving road to a beach where the high surf boomed in limestone caves. It seemed impossible that this joyous shore could be threatened by plague, the slimy creature of dark alleys.

The motor cut through a singing trade wind which told of clean sails and disdainful men. They darted on where the foam feathers below Point Carib and where, round that lone royal palm on the headland, the bright wind hums. They slipped into a hot valley, and came to the village of Carib and to creeping horror.

The plague had been dismaying in Blackwater; in Carib it was the end of all things. The rat-fleas had found fat homes in the ground squirrels which burrowed in every garden about the village. In Blackwater there had from the first been isolation of the sick, but in Carib death was in every house, and the village was surrounded by soldier police, with bayonets, who let no one come or go save the doctors.

Martin was guided down the stinking street of cottages palm-thatched and walled with cow-dung plaster on bamboo laths, cottages shared by the roosters and the goats. He heard men shrieking in delirium; a dozen times he saw that face of terror — sunken bloody eyes, drawn face, open mouth — which marks the Black Death; and once he beheld an exquisite girl child in coma on the edge of death, her tongue black and round her the scent of the tomb.

They fled away, to Point Carib and the trade wind, and when Inchcape Jones demanded, "After that sort of thing, can you really talk of experimenting?" then Martin shook his head, while he tried to recall the vision of Gottlieb and all their little plans: "half to get the phage, half to be sternly deprived."

It came to him that Gottlieb, in his secluded innocence, had not realized what it meant to gain leave to experiment amid the hysteria of an epidemic.

He went to the Ice House; he had a drink with a frightened clerk from Derbyshire; he regained the picture of Gottlieb's sunken, demanding eyes; and he swore that he would not yield to a compassion which in the end would make all compassion futile.

Since Inchcape Jones could not understand the need of experimentation, he would call on the Governor, Colonel Sir Robert Fairlamb.

### II

Though Government House was officially the chief residence of St. Hubert, it was but a thatched bungalow a little larger than Martin's own Penrith Lodge. When he saw it, Martin felt more easy, and he ambled up to the broad steps, at nine of the evening, as though he were dropping in to call on a neighbor in Wheatsylvania.

He was stopped by a Jamaican man-servant of appalling courtesy.

He snorted that he was Dr. Arrowsmith, head of the McGurk Commission, and he was sorry but he must see Sir Robert at once.

The servant was suggesting, in his blandest and most annoying manner, that really Dr. Uh would do better to see the Surgeon General, when a broad red face and a broad red voice projected themselves over the veranda railing, with a rumble of, "Send him up, Jackson, and don't be a fool!"

Sir Robert and Lady Fairlamb were finishing dinner on the veranda, at a small round table littered with coffee and liqueurs and starred with candles. She was a slight, nervous insignificance; he was rather puffy, very flushed, undoubtedly courageous, and altogether dismayed; and at a time when no laundress dared go anywhere, his evening shirt was luminous.

Martin was in his now beloved linen suit, with a crumply soft shirt which Leora had been meanin' to wash.

Martin explained what he wanted to do — what he must do, if the world was ever to get over the absurdity of having plague.

Sir Robert listened so agreeably that Martin thought he understood, but at the end he bellowed:

"Young man, if I were commanding a division at the front, with a dud show, an awful show, going on, and a War Office clerk asked me to risk the whole thing to try out some precious little invention of his own, can you imagine what I'd answer? There isn't much I can do now — these doctor Johnnies have taken everything out of my hands — but as far as possible I shall certainly prevent you Yankee vivisectionists from coming in and using us as a lot of sanguinary — sorry, Evelyn — sanguinary corpses. Good night, sir!"

### III

Thanks to Sondelius's crafty bullying, Martin was able to present his plan to a Special Board composed of the Governor, the temporarily suspended Board of Health, Inchcape Jones, several hearty members of the House of Assembly, and Sondelius himself, attending in the unofficial capacity which all over the world he had found useful for masking a cheerful tyranny. Sondelius even brought in the Negro doctor, Oliver Marchand, not on the ground that he was the most intelligent person on the island (which happened to be Sondelius's reason) but because he "represented the plantation hands."

Sondelius himself was as much opposed to Martin's unemotional experiments as was Fairlamb; he believed that all experiments should be, by devices not entirely clear to him, carried on in the laboratory without disturbing the conduct of agreeable epidemics, but he could never resist a drama like the innocent meeting of the Special Board.

The meeting was set for a week ahead ... with scores dying every day. While he waited for it Martin manufactured more phage and helped Sondelius murder rats, and Leora listened to the midnight debates of the two men and tried to make them acknowledge that it had been wise to let her come. Inchcape Jones offered to Martin the position of Government bacteriologist, but he refused lest he be sidetracked.

The Special Board met in Parliament House, all of them trying to look not like their simple and domestic selves but like judges. With them appeared such doctors of the island as could find the time.

While Leora listened from the back of the room, Martin addressed them, not unaware of the spectacle of little Mart Arrowsmith of Elk Mills taken seriously by the rulers of a tropic isle headed by a Sir Somebody. Beside him stood Max Gottlieb, and in Gottlieb's power he reverently sought to explain that mankind has ever given up eventual greatness because some crisis, some war or election or loyalty to a Messiah which at the moment seemed weighty, has choked the patient search for truth. He sought to explain that he could — perhaps — save half of a given district, but that to test for all time the value of phage, the other half must be left without it ... though, he craftily told them, in any case the luckless half would receive as much care as at present.

Most of the Board had heard that he possessed a magic cure for the plague which for unknown and probably discreditable reasons, he was withholding, and they were not going to have it withheld. There was a great deal of discussion rather unconnected with what he had said, and out of it came only the fact that everybody except Stokes and Oliver Marchand was against him; Kellett was angry with this American, Sir Robert Fairlamb was beefily disapproving, and Sondelius admitted that though Martin was quite a decent young man, he was a fanatic.

Into their argument plunged a fury in the person of Ira Hinkley, missionary of the Sanctification Brotherhood.

Martin had not seen him since the first morning in Blackwater. He gaped as he heard Ira pleading:

"Gentlemen, I know almost the whole bunch of you are Church of England, but I beg you to listen to me, not as a minister but as a qualified doctor of medicine. Oh, the wrath of God is upon you — But I mean: I was a classmate of Arrowsmith in the States. I'm onto him! He was such a failure that he was suspended from medical school. A scientist! And his boss, this fellow Gottlieb, he was fired from the University of Winnemac for incompetence! I know 'em! Liars and fools! Scorners of righteousness! Has anybody but Arrowsmith himself told you he's a qualified scientist?"

The face of Sondelius changed from curiosity to stolid Scandinavian wrath. He arose and shouted:

"Sir Robert, this man is crazy! Dr. Gottlieb is one of the seven distinguished living scientists, and Dr. Arrowsmith is his representative! I announce my agreement with him, complete. As you must have seen from my work, I'm perfectly independent of him and entirely at your service, but I know his standing and I follow him, quite humbly."

The Special Board coaxed Ira Hinkley out, for the meanest of reasons — in St. Hubert the whites do not greatly esteem the holy ecstasies of Negroes in the Sanctification Brotherhood chapels — but they voted only to "give the matter their consideration," while still men died by the score each day, and in Manchuria as in St. Hubert they prayed for rest from the ancient clawing pain.

Outside, as the Special Board trudged away, Sondelius blared at Martin and the indignant Leora, "Yey, a fine fight!"

Martin answered, "Gustaf, you've joined me now. The first darn' thing you do, you come have a shot of phage."

"No. Slim, I said I will not have your phage till you give it to everybody. I mean it, no matter how much I make fools of your Board."

As they stood before Parliament House, a small motor possessing everything but comfort and power staggered up to them, and from it vaulted a man lean as Gottlieb and English as Inchcape Jones.

"You Dr. Arrowsmith? My name is Twyford, Cecil Twyford of St. Swithin's Parish. Tried to get here for the Special Board meeting, but my beastly foreman had to take the afternoon off and die of plague. Stokes has told me your plans. Quite right. All nonsense to go on having plague. Board refused? Sorry. Perhaps we can do something in St. Swithin's. Goo' day."

All evening Martin and Sondelius were full of language. Martin went to bed longing for the regularity of working all night and foraging for cigarettes at dawn. He could not sleep, because an imaginary Ira Hinkley was always bursting in on him.

Four days later he heard that Ira was dead.

Till he had sunk in coma, Ira had nursed and blessed his people, the humble colored congregation in the hot tin chapel which he had now turned into a pest-house. He staggered from cot to cot, under the gospel texts he had lettered on the whitewashed wall, then he cried once, loudly, and dropped by the pine pulpit where he had joyed to preach.

## IV

One chance Martin did have. In Carib, where every third man was down with plague and one doctor to attend them all, he now gave phage to the entire village; a long strain of injections, not improved by the knowledge that one jaunty flea from any patient might bring him the plague.

The tedium of dread was forgotten when he began to find and make precise notes of a slackening of the epidemic, which was occurring nowhere except here at Carib.

He came home raving to Leora, "I'll show 'em! Now they'll let me try test conditions, and then when the epidemic's over we'll hustle home. It'll be lovely to be cold again! Wonder if Holabird and Sholtheis are any more friendly now? Be pretty good to see the little ole flat, eh?"

"Yes, won't it!" said Leora. "I wish I'd thought to have the kitchen painted while we're away.... I think I'll put that blue chair in the bedroom."

Though there was a decrease in the plague at Carib, Sondelius was worried, because it was the worst center for infected ground squirrels on the island. He made decisions quickly. One evening he explained certain things to Inchcape Jones and Martin, rode down their doubts, and snorted:

"Only way to disinfect that place is to burn it — burn th' whole thing. Have it done by morning, before anybody can stop us."

With Martin as his lieutenant he marshaled his troop of rat-catchers — ruffians all of them, with high boots, tied jacket sleeves, and ebon visages of piracy. They stole food from shops, tents and blankets and camp-stoves from the Government military warehouse, and jammed their booty into motor trucks. The line of trucks roared down to Carib, the rat-catchers sitting atop, singing pious hymns.

They charged on the village, drove out the healthy, carried the sick on litters, settled them all in tents in a pasture up the valley, and after midnight they burned the town.

The troops ran among the huts, setting them alight with fantastic torches. The palm thatch sent up thick smoke, dead sluggish white with currents of ghastly black through which broke sudden flames. Against the glare the palmettoes were silhouetted. The solid-seeming huts were instantly changed into thin bamboo frameworks, thin lines of black slats, with the thatch falling in sparks. The flame lighted the whole valley; roused the terrified squawking birds, and turned the surf at Point Carib to bloody foam.

With such of the natives as had strength enough and sense enough, Sondelius's troops made a ring about the burning village, shouting insanely as they clubbed the fleeing rats and ground squirrels. In the flare of devastation Sondelius was a fiend, smashing the bewildered rats with a club, shooting at them as they fled, and singing to himself all the while the obscene chantey of Bill the Sailor. But at dawn he was nursing the sick in the bright new canvas village, showing mammies how to use their camp-stoves, and in a benevolent way discussing methods of poisoning ground squirrels in their burrows.

Sondelius returned to Blackwater, but Martin remained in the tent village for two days, giving them the phage, making notes, directing the amateur nurses. He returned to Blackwater one mid-afternoon and sought the office of the Surgeon General, or what had been the office of the Surgeon General till Sondelius had come and taken it away from him.

Sondelius was there, at Inchcape Jones's desk, but for once he was not busy. He was sunk in his chair, his eyes bloodshot.

"Yey! We had a fine time with the rats at Carib, eh? How is my new tent willage?" he chuckled, but his voice was weak, and as he rose he staggered.

"What is it? What is it?"

"I t'ink — It's got me. Some flea got me. Yes," in a shaky but extremely interested manner, "I was yoost thinking I will go and quarantine myself. I have fever all right, and adenitis. My strength — Huh! I am almost sixty, but the way I can lift weights that no sailor can touch — And I could fight five rounds! Oh, my God, Martin, I am so weak! Not scared! No!"

But for Martin's arms he would have collapsed.

He refused to return to Penrith Lodge and Leora's nursing. "I who have isolated so many — it is my turn," he said.

Martin and Inchcape Jones found for Sondelius a meager clean cottage — the family had died there, all of them, but it had been fumigated. They procured a nurse and Martin himself attended the sick man, trying to remember that once he had been a doctor, who understood ice-bags and consolation. One thing was not to be had — mosquito netting — and only of this did Sondelius complain.

Martin bent over him, agonized to see how burning was his skin, how swollen his face and his tongue, how weak his voice as he babbled:

"Gottlieb is right about these jests of God. Yey! His best one is the tropics. God planned them so beautiful, flowers and sea and mountains. He made the fruit to grow so well that man need not work — and then He laughed, and stuck in volcanoes and snakes and damp heat and early senility and the plague and malaria. But the nastiest trick He ever played on man was inventing the flea."

His bloated lips widened, from his hot throat oozed a feeble croaking, and Martin realized that he was trying to laugh.

He became delirious, but between spasms he muttered, with infinite pain, tears in his eyes at his own weakness:

"I want you to see how an agnostic can die!

"I am not afraid, but yoost once more I would like to see Stockholm, and Fifth Avenue on the day the first snow falls and Holy Week at Sevilla. And one good last drunk! I am very peaceful, Slim. It hurts some, but life was a good game. And — I am a pious agnostic. Oh, Martin, give my people the phage! Save all of them — God, I did not think they could hurt me so!"

His heart had failed. He was still on his low cot.

## V

Martin had an unhappy pride that, with all his love for Gustaf Sondelius, he could still keep his head, still resist Inchcape Jones's demand that he give the phage to everyone, still do what he had been sent to do.

"I'm not a sentimentalist; I'm a scientist!" he boasted.

They snarled at him in the streets now; small boys called him names and threw stones. They had heard that he was willfully withholding their salvation. The citizens came in committees to beg him to heal their children, and he was so shaken that he had ever to keep before him the vision of Gottlieb.

The panic was increasing. They who had at first kept cool could not endure the strain of wakening at night to see upon their windows the glow of the pile of logs on Admiral Knob, the emergency crematory where Gustaf Sondelius and his curly gray mop had been shoveled into the fire along with a crippled Negro boy and a Hindu beggar.

Sir Robert Fairlamb was a blundering hero, exasperating the sick while he tried to nurse them; Stokes remained the Rock of Ages — he had only three hours' sleep a night, but he never failed to take his accustomed fifteen minutes of exercise when he awoke; and Leora was busy in Penrith Lodge, helping Martin prepare phage.

It was the Surgeon General who went to pieces.

Robbed of his dependence on the despised Sondelius, sunk again in a mad planlessness, Inchcape Jones shrieked when he thought he was speaking low, and the cigarette which was ever in his thin hand shook so that the smoke quivered up in trembling spirals.

Making his tour, he came at night on a sloop by which a dozen Red Legs were escaping to Barbados, and suddenly he was among them, bribing them to take him along.

As the sloop stood out from Blackwater Harbor he stretched his arms toward his sisters and the peace of the Surrey hills, but as the few frightened lights of the town were lost, he realized that he was a coward and came up out of his madness, with his lean head high.

He demanded that they turn the sloop and take him back. They refused, howling at him, and locked him in the cabin. They were becalmed; it was two days before they reached Barbados, and by then the world would know that he had deserted.

Altogether expressionless, Inchcape Jones tramped from the sloop to a waterfront hotel in Barbados, and stood for a long time in a slatternly room smelling of slop-pails. He would never see his sisters and the cool hills. With the revolver which he had carried to drive terrified patients back into the isolation wards, with the revolver which he had carried at Arras, he killed himself.

## VI

Thus Martin came to his experiment. Stokes was appointed Surgeon General, vice Inchcape Jones, and he made an illegal assignment of Martin to St. Swithin's Parish, as medical officer with complete power. This, and the concurrence of Cecil Twyford, made his experiment possible.

He was invited to stay at Twyford's. His only trouble was the guarding of Leora. He did not know what he would encounter in St. Swithin's, while Penrith Lodge was as safe as any place on the island. When Leora insisted that, during his experiment, the cold thing which had stilled the laughter of Sondelius might come to him and he might need her, he tried to satisfy her by promising that if there was a place for her in St. Swithin's, he would send for her.

Naturally, he was lying.

"Hard enough to see Gustaf go. By thunder she's not going to run risks!" he vowed.

He left her, protected by the maids and the soldier butler, with Dr. Oliver Marchand to look in when he could.

## VII

In St. Swithin's Parish the cocoa and bamboo groves and sharp hills of southern St. Hubert gave way to unbroken canefields. Here Cecil Twyford, that lean abrupt man, ruled every acre and interpreted every law.

His place, Frangipani Court, was a refuge from the hot humming plain. The house was old and low, of thick stone and plaster walls; the paneled rooms were lined with the china, the portraits, and the swords of Twyfords for three hundred years; and between the wings was a walled garden dazzling with hibiscus.

Twyford led Martin through the low cool hall and introduced him to five great sons and to his mother, who, since his wife's death, ten years ago, had been mistress of the house.

"Have tea?" said Twyford. "Our American guest will be down in a moment."

He would not have thought of saying it, but he had sworn that since for generations Twyfords had drunk tea here at a seemly hour, no panic should prevent their going on drinking it at that hour.

When Martin came into the garden, when he saw the old silver on the wicker table and heard the quiet voices, the plague seemed conquered, and he realized that, four thousand miles southwest of the Lizard, he was in England.

They were seated, pleasant but not too comfortable, when the American guest came down and from the door stared at Martin as strangely as he stared in turn.

He beheld a woman who must be his sister. She was perhaps thirty to his thirty-seven, but in her slenderness, her paleness, her black brows and dusky hair, she was his twin; she was his self enchanted.

He could hear his voice croaking, "But you're my sister!" and she opened her lips, yet neither of them spoke as they bowed at introduction. When she sat down, Martin had never been so conscious of a woman's presence.

He learned, before evening, that she was Joyce Lanyon, widow of Roger Lanyon of New York. She had come to St. Hubert to see her plantations and had been trapped by the quarantine. He had tentatively heard of her dead husband as a young man of wealth and family; he seemed to remember having seen in *Vanity Fair* a picture of the Lanyons at Palm Beach.

She talked only of the weather, the flowers, but there was a rising gaiety in her which stirred even the dour Cecil Twyford. In the midst of her debonair insults to the hugest of the huge sons, Martin turned on her:

"You *are* my sister!"

"Obviously. Well, since you're a scientist — Are you a good scientist?"

"Pretty good."

"I've met your Mrs. McGurk. And Dr. Rippleton Holabird. Met 'em in Hessian Hook. You know it, don't you?"

"No, I — Oh, I've heard of it."

"You know. It's that renovated old part of Brooklyn where writers and economists and all those people, some of them almost as good as the very best, consort with people who are almost as smart as the very smartest. You know. Where they dress for dinner but all of them have heard about James Joyce. Dr. Holabird is frightfully charming, don't you think?"

"Why — "

"Tell me. I really mean it. Cecil has been explaining what you plan to do experimentally. Could I help you — nursing or cooking or something — or would I merely be in the way?"

"I don't know yet. If I can use you, I'll be unscrupulous enough!"

"Oh, don't be earnest like Cecil here, and Dr. Stokes! They have no sense of play. Do you like that man Stokes? Cecil adores him, and I suppose he's simply infested with virtues, but I find him so dry and thin and unappetizing. Don't you think he might be a little gayer?"

Martin gave up all chance of knowing her as he hurled:

"Look here! You said you found Holabird 'charming.' It makes me tired to have you fall for his scientific tripe and not appreciate Stokes. Stokes is hard — thank God! — and probably he's rude. Why not? He's fighting a world that bellows for fake charm. No scientist can go through his grind and not come out more or less rude. And I tell you Stokes was born a researcher. I wish we had him at McGurk. Rude? Wish you could hear him being rude to me!"

Twyford looked doubtful, his mother looked delicately shocked, and the five sons beefily looked nothing at all, while Martin raged on, trying to convey his vision of the barbarian, the ascetic, the contemptuous acolyte of science. But Joyce Lanyon's lovely eyes were kind, and when she spoke she had lost something of her too-cosmopolitan manner of a diner-out:

"Yes. I suppose it's the difference between me, playing at being a planter, and Cecil."

After dinner he walked with her in the garden and sought to defend himself against he was not quite sure what, till she hinted:

"My dear man, you're so apologetic about never being apologetic! If you really must be my twin brother, do me the honor of telling me to go to the devil whenever you want to. I don't mind. Now about your Gottlieb, who seems to be so much of an obsession with you — "

"Obsession! Rats! He — "

They parted an hour after.

Least of all things Martin desired such another peeping, puerile, irritable restlessness as he had shared with Orchid Pickerbaugh, but as he went to bed in a room with old prints and a four-poster, it was disturbing to know that somewhere near him was Joyce Lanyon.

He sat up, aghast with truth. Was he going to fall in love with this desirable and quite useless young woman? (How lovely her shoulders, above black satin at dinner! She had a genius of radiant flesh; it made that of most women, even the fragile Leora, seem coarse and thick. There was a rosy glow behind it, as from an inner light.)

Did he really want Leora here, with Joyce Lanyon in the house? (Dear Leora, who was the source of life! Was she now, off there in Penrith Lodge, missing him, lying awake for him?)

How could he, even in the crisis of an epidemic, invite the formal Twyfords to invite Leora? (How honest was he? That afternoon he had recognized the rigid though kindly code of the Twyfords, but could he not set it aside by being frankly an Outlander?)

Suddenly he was out of bed, kneeling, praying to Leora.

## Chapter 35

The plague had only begun to invade St. Swithin's, but it was unquestionably coming, and Martin, with his power as official medical officer of the parish, was able to make plans. He divided the population into two equal parts. One of them, driven in by Twyford, was injected with plague phage, the other half was left without.

He began to succeed. He saw far-off India, with its annual four hundred thousand deaths from plague, saved by his efforts. He heard Max Gottlieb saying, "Martin, you haf done your experiment. I am very glat!"

The pest attacked the unphaged half of the parish much more heavily than those who had been treated. There did appear a case or two among those who had the phage, but among the others there were ten, then twenty, then thirty daily victims. These unfortunate cases he treated, giving the phage to alternate patients, in the somewhat barren almshouse of the parish, a whitewashed cabin the meaner against its vaulting background of banyans and breadfruit trees.

He could never understand Cecil Twyford. Though Twyford had considered his hands as slaves, though he had, in his great barony, given them only this barren almshouse, yet he risked his life now in nursing them, and the lives of all his sons.

Despite Martin's discouragement, Mrs. Lanyon came down to cook, and a remarkably good cook she was. She also made beds; she showed more intelligence than the Twyford men about disinfecting herself; and as she bustled about the rusty kitchen, in a gingham gown she had borrowed from a maid, she so disturbed Martin that he forgot to be gruff.

### II

In the evening, while they returned by Twyford's rattling little motor to Frangipani Court, Mrs. Lanyon talked to Martin as one who had shared his work, but when she had bathed and powdered and dressed, he talked to her as one who was afraid of her. Their bond was their resemblance as brother and sister. They decided, almost irritably, that they looked utterly alike, except that her hair was more patent-leather than his and she lacked his impertinent, cocking eyebrow.

Often Martin returned to his patients at night, but once or twice Mrs. Lanyon and he fled, as much from the family stolidity of the Twyfords as from the thought of fever-scorched patients, to the shore of a rocky lagoon which cut far in from the sea.

They sat on a cliff, full of the sound of the healing tide. His brain was hectic with the memory of charts on the whitewashed broad planks of the almshouse, the sun cracks in the wall, the puffy terrified faces of black patients, how one of the Twyford sons had knocked over an ampule of phage, and how itchingly hot it had been in the ward. But to his intensity the lagoon breeze was cooling, and cooling the rustling tide. He perceived that Mrs. Lanyon's white frock was fluttering about her knees; he realized that she too was strained and still. He turned somberly toward her, and she cried:

"I'm so frightened and so lonely! The Twyfords are heroic, but they're stone. I'm so marooned!"

He kissed her, and she rested against his shoulder. The softness of her sleeve was agitating to his hand. But she broke away with:

"No! You don't really care a hang about me. Just curious. Perhaps that's a good thing for me — tonight."

He tried to assure her, to assure himself, that he did care with peculiar violence, but languor was over him; between him and her fragrance were the hospital cots, a great weariness, and the still face of Leora. They were silent together, and when his hand crept to hers they sat unimpassioned, comprehending, free to talk of what they would.

He stood outside her door, when they had returned to the house, and imagined her soft moving within.

"No," he raged. "Can't do it. Joyce — women like her — one of the million things I've given up for work and for Lee. Well. That's all there is to it then. But if I were here two weeks — Fool! She'd be furious if you knocked! But — "

He was aware of the dagger of light under her door; the more aware of it as he turned his back and tramped to his room.

## III

The telephone service in St. Hubert was the clumsiest feature of the island. There was no telephone at Penrith Lodge — the port-doctor had cheerfully been wont to get his calls through a neighbor. The central was now demoralized by the plague, and when for two hours Martin had tried to have Leora summoned, he gave up.

But he had triumphed. In three or four days he would drive to Penrith Lodge. Twyford had blankly assented to his suggestion that Leora be invited hither, and if she and Joyce Lanyon should become such friends that Joyce would never again turn to him in loneliness, he was willing, he was eager — he was almost eager.

## IV

When Martin left her at the Lodge, in the leafy gloom high on the Penrith Hills, Leora felt his absence. They had been so little apart since he had first come on her, scrubbing a hospital room in Zenith.

The afternoon was unending; each time she heard a creaking she roused with the hope that it was his step, and realized that he would not be coming, all the blank evening, the terrifying night; would not be here anywhere, not his voice nor the touch of his hand.

Dinner was mournful. Often enough she had dined alone when Martin was at the Institute, but then he had been returning to her some time before dawn — probably — and she had reflectively munched a snack on the corner of the kitchen table, looking at the funnies in the evening paper. Tonight she had to live up to the butler, who served her as though she were a dinner-party of twenty.

She sat on the porch, staring at the shadowy roofs of Blackwater below, sure that she felt a "miasm" writhing up through the hot darkness.

She knew the direction of St. Swithin's Parish — beyond that delicate glimmer of lights from palm huts coiling up the hills. She concentrated on it, wondering if by some magic she might not have a signal from him, but she could get no feeling of his looking toward her. She sat long and quiet.... She had nothing to do.

Her night was sleepless. She tried to read in bed, by an electric globe inside the misty little tent of the mosquito-netting, but there was a tear in the netting and the mosquitoes crept through. As she turned out the light and lay tense, unable to give herself over to sleep, unable to sink into security, while to her blurred eyes the half-seen folds of the mosquito netting seemed to slide about her, she tried to remember whether these mosquitoes might be carrying plague germs. She realized how much she had depended on Martin for such bits of knowledge, as for all philosophy. She recalled how annoyed he had been because she could not remember whether the yellow fever mosquito was *Anopheles* or *Stegomyia* — or was it *Aëdes* ? — and suddenly she laughed in the night.

She was reminded that he had told her to give herself another injection of phage.

"Hang it, I forgot. Well, I must be sure to do that tomorrow."

"Do that t'morrow — do that t'morrow," buzzed in her brain, an irritating inescapable refrain, while she was suspended over sleep, conscious of how much she wanted to creep into his arms.

Next morning (and she did not remember to give herself another injection) the servants seemed twitchy, and her effort to comfort them brought out the news that Oliver Marchand, the doctor on whom they depended, was dead.

In the afternoon the butler heard that his sister had been taken off to the isolation ward, and he went down to Blackwater to make arrangements for his nieces. He did not return; no one ever learned what had become of him.

Toward dusk, when Leora felt as though a skirmish line were closing in on her, she fled into Martin's laboratory. It seemed filled with his jerky brimming presence. She kept away from the flasks of plague germs, but she picked up, because it was his, a half-smoked cigarette and lighted it.

Now there was a slight crack in her lips; and that morning, fumbling at dusting — here in the laboratory meant as a fortress against disease — a maid had knocked over a test-tube, which had trickled. The cigarette seemed dry enough, but in it there were enough plague germs to kill a regiment.

Two nights after, when she was so desperately lonely that she thought of walking to Blackwater, finding a motor, and fleeing to Martin, she woke with a fever, a headache, her limbs chilly. When the maids discovered her in the morning, they fled from the house. While lassitude flowed round her, she was left alone in the isolated house, with no telephone.

All day, all night, as her throat crackled with thirst, she lay longing for someone to help her. Once she crawled to the kitchen for water. The floor of the bedroom was an endless heaving sea, the hall a writhing dimness, and by the kitchen door she dropped and lay for an hour, whimpering.

"Got to — got to — can't remember what it was," her voice kept appealing to her cloudy brain.

Aching, fighting the ache, she struggled up, wrapped about her a shabby cloak which one of the maids had abandoned in flight, and in the darkness staggered out to find help. As she came to the highway she stumbled, and lay under the hedge, unmoving, like a hurt animal. On hands and knees she crawled back into the Lodge, and between times, as her brain went dark, she nearly forgot the pain in her longing for Martin.

She was bewildered; she was lonely; she dared not start on her long journey without his hand to comfort her. She listened for him — listened — tense with listening.

"You will come! I know you'll come and help me! I know. You'll come! Martin! Sandy! *Sandy!* " she sobbed.

Then she slipped down into the kindly coma. There was no more pain, and all the shadowy house was quiet but for her hoarse and struggling breath.

## V

Like Sondelius, Joyce Lanyon tried to persuade Martin to give the phage to everybody.

"I'm getting to be good and stern, with all you people after me. Regular Gottlieb. Nothing can make me do it, not if they tried to lynch me," he boasted.

He had explained Leora to Joyce.

"I don't know whether you two will like each other. You're so darn' different. You're awfully articulate, and you like these 'pretty people' that you're always talking about, but she doesn't care a hang for 'em. She sits back — oh, she never misses anything, but she never says much. Still, she's got the best instinct for honesty that I've ever known. I hope you two'll get each other. I was afraid to let her come here — didn't know what I'd find — but now I'm going to hustle to Penrith and bring her here today."

He borrowed Twyford's car and drove to Blackwater, up to Penrith, in excellent spirits. For all the plague, they could have a lively time in the evenings. One of the Twyford sons was not so solemn; he and Joyce, with Martin and Leora, could slip down to the lagoon for picnic suppers; they would sing —

He came up to Penrith Lodge bawling, "Lee! Leora! Come on! *Here* we are!"

The veranda, as he ran up on it, was leaf-scattered and dusty, and the front door was banging. His voice echoed in a desperate silence. He was uneasy. He darted in, found no one in the living-room, the kitchen, then hastened into their bedroom.

On the bed, across the folds of the torn mosquito netting, was Leora's body, very frail, quite still. He cried to her, he shook her, he stood weeping.

He talked to her, his voice a little insane, trying to make her understand that he had loved her and had left her here only for her safety —

There was rum in the kitchen, and he went out to gulp down raw full glasses. They did not affect him.

By evening he strode to the garden, the high and windy garden looking toward the sea, and dug a deep pit. He lifted her light stiff body, kissed it, and laid it in the pit. All night he wandered. When he came back to the house and saw the row of her little dresses with the lines of her soft body in them, he was terrified.

Then he went to pieces.

He gave up Penrith Lodge, left Twyford's, and moved into a room behind the Surgeon General's office. Beside his cot there was always a bottle.

Because death had for the first time been brought to him, he raged, "Oh, damn experimentation!" and, despite Stokes's dismay, he gave the phage to everyone who asked.

Only in St. Swithin's, since there his experiment was so excellently begun, did some remnant of honor keep him from distributing the phage universally; but the conduct of this experiment he turned over to Stokes.

Stokes saw that he was a little mad, but only once, when Martin snarled, "What do I care for your science?" did he try to hold Martin to his test.

Stokes himself, with Twyford, carried on the experiment and kept the notes Martin should have kept. By evening, after working fourteen or fifteen hours since dawn, Stokes would hasten to St. Swithin's by motor-cycle — he hated the joggling and the lack of dignity and he found it somewhat dangerous to take curving hill-roads at sixty miles an hour, but this was the quickest way, and till midnight he conferred with Twyford, gave him orders for the next day, arranged his clumsy annotations, and marveled at his grim meekness.

Meantime, all day, Martin injected a line of frightened citizens, in the Surgeon General's office in Blackwater. Stokes begged him at least to turn the work over to another doctor and take what interest he could in St. Swithin's, but Martin had a bitter satisfaction in throwing away all his significance, in helping to wreck his own purposes.

With a nurse for assistant, he stood in the bare office. File on file of people, black, white, Hindu, stood in an agitated cue a block long, ten deep, waiting dumbly, as for death. They crept up to the nurse beside Martin and in embarrassment exposed their arms, which she scrubbed with soap and water and dabbed with alcohol before passing them on to him. He brusquely pinched up the skin of the upper arm and jabbed it with the needle of the syringe, cursing at them for jerking, never seeing their individual faces. As they left him they fluttered with gratitude — "Oh, may God bless you, Doctor!" — but he did not hear.

Sometimes Stokes was there, looking anxious, particularly when in the queue he saw plantation-hands from St. Swithin's, who were supposed to remain in their parish under strict control, to test the value of the phage. Sometimes Sir Robert Fairlamb came down to beam and gurgle and offer his aid.... Lady Fairlamb had been injected first of all, and next to her a tattered kitchen wench, profuse with Hallelujah's.

After a fortnight when he was tired of the drama, he had four doctors making the injections, while he manufactured phage.

But by night Martin sat alone, tousled, drinking steadily, living on whisky and hate, freeing his soul and dissolving his body by hatred as once hermits dissolved theirs by ecstasy. His life was as unreal as the nights of an old drunkard. He had an advantage over normal cautious humanity in not caring whether he lived or died, he who sat with the dead, talking to Leora and Sondelius, to Ira Hinkley and Oliver Marchand, to Inchcape Jones and a shadowy horde of blackmen with lifted appealing hands.

After Leora's death he had returned to Twyford's but once, to fetch his baggage, and he had not seen Joyce Lanyon. He hated her. He swore that it was not her presence which had kept him from returning earlier to Leora, but he was aware that while he had been chattering with Joyce, Leora had been dying.

"Damn' glib society climber! Thank God I'll never see *her* again!"

He sat on the edge of his cot, in the constricted and airless room, his hair ruffled, his eyes blotched with red, a stray alley kitten, which he esteemed his only friend, asleep on his pillow. At a knock he muttered, "I can't talk to Stokes now. Let him do his own experiments. Sick of experiments!"

Sulkily, "Oh, come in!"

The door opened on Joyce Lanyon, cool, trim, sure.

"What do you want?" he grunted.

She stared at him; she shut the door; silently she straightened the litter of food, papers, and instruments on his table. She coaxed the indignant kitten to a mat, patted the pillow, and sat by him on the frowsy cot. Then:

"Please! I know what's happened. Cecil is in town for an hour and I wanted to bring — Won't it comfort you a little if you know how fond we are of you? Won't you let me offer you friendship?"

"I don't want anybody's friendship. I haven't any friends!"

He sat dumb, her hand on his, but when she was gone he felt a shiver of new courage.

He could not get himself to give up his reliance on whisky, and he could see no way of discontinuing the phage-injection of all who came begging for it, but he turned both injection and manufacture over to others, and went back to the most rigid observation of his experiment in St. Swithin's ... blotted as it now was by the unphaged portion of the parish going in to Blackwater to receive the phage.

He did not see Joyce. He lived at the almshouse, but most evenings now he was sober.

## VI

The gospel of rat-extermination had spread through the island; everybody from five-year-old to hobbling grandam was out shooting rats and ground squirrels. Whether from phage or rat-killing or Providence, the epidemic paused, and six months after Martin's coming, when the West Indian May was broiling and the season of hurricanes was threatened, the plague had almost vanished and the quarantine was lifted.

St. Hubert felt safe in its kitchens and shops, and amid the roaring spring the island rejoiced as a sick man first delivered from pain rejoices at merely living and being at peace.

That chaffering should be abusive and loud in the public market, that lovers should stroll unconscious of all save themselves, that loafers should tell stories and drink long drinks at the Ice House, that old men should squat cackling in the shade of the mangoes, that congregations should sing together to the Lord — this was no longer ordinary to them nor stupid, but the bliss of paradise.

They made a festival of the first steamer's leaving. White and black, Hindu and Chink and Caribbee, they crowded the wharf, shouting, waving scarfs, trying not to weep at the feeble piping of what was left of the Blackwater Gold Medal Band; and as the steamer, the *St. Ia* of the McGurk Line, was warped out, with her captain at the rail of the bridge, very straight, saluting them with a flourish but his eyes so wet that he could not see the harbor, they felt that they were no longer jailed lepers but a part of the free world.

On the steamer Joyce Lanyon sailed. Martin said good-by to her at the wharf.

Strong of hand, almost as tall as he, she looked at him without flutter, and rejoiced, "You've come through. So have I. Both of us have been mad, trapped here the way we've been. I don't suppose I helped you, but I did try. You see, I'd never been trained in reality. You trained me. Good-by."

"Mayn't I come to see you in New York?"

"If you'd really like to."

She was gone, yet she had never been so much with him as through that tedious hour when the steamer was lost beyond the horizon, a line edged with silver wire. But that night, in panic, he fled up to Penrith Lodge and buried his cheek in the damp soil above the Leora with whom he had never had to fence and explain, to whom he had never needed to say, "Mayn't I come to see you?"

But Leora, cold in her last bed, unsmiling, did not answer him nor comfort him.

## VII

Before Martin took leave he had to assemble the notes of his phage experiment; add the observation of Stokes and Twyford to his own first precise figures.

As the giver of phage to some thousands of frightened islanders, he had become a dignitary. He was called, in the first issue of the *Blackwater Guardian* after the quarantine was raised, "the savior of all our lives." He was the universal hero. If Sondelius had helped to cleanse them, had Sondelius not been his lieutenant? If it was the intervention of the Lord, as the earnest old Negro who succeeded Ira Hinkley in the chapels of the Sanctification Brotherhood insisted, had not the Lord surely sent him?

No one heeded a wry Scotch doctor, diligent but undramatic through the epidemic, who hinted that plagues have been known to slacken and cease without phage.

When Martin was completing his notes he had a letter from the McGurk Institute, signed by Rippleton Holabird.

Holabird wrote that Gottlieb was "feeling seedy," that he had resigned the Directorship, suspended his own experimentation, and was now at home, resting. Holabird himself had been appointed Acting Director of the Institute, and as such he chanted:

> *The reports of your work in the letters from Mr. McGurk's agents which the quarantine authorities have permitted to get through to us apprize us far more than does your own modest report what a really sensational success you have had. You have done what few other men living could do, both established the value of bacteriophage in plague by tests on a large scale, and saved most of the unfortunate population. The Board of Trustees and I are properly appreciative of the glory which you have added, and still more will add when your report is published, to the name of McGurk Institute, and we are thinking, now that we may for some months be unable to have your titular chief, Dr. Gottlieb, working with us, of establishing a separate Department, with you as its head.*

"Established the value — rats! I about half made the tests," sighed Martin, and: "Department! I've given too many orders here. Sick of authority. I want to get back to my lab and start all over again."

It came to him that now he would probably have ten thousand a year.... Leora would have enjoyed small extravagant dinners.

Though he had watched Gottlieb declining, it was a shock that he could be so unwell as to drop his work even for a few months.

He forgot his own self as it came to him that in giving up his experiment, playing the savior, he had been a traitor to Gottlieb and all that Gottlieb represented. When he returned to New York he would have to call on the old man and admit to him, to those sunken relentless eyes, that he did not have complete proof of the value of the phage.

If he could have run to Leora with his ten thousand a year —

## VIII

He left St. Hubert three weeks after Joyce Lanyon.

The evening before his sailing, a great dinner with Sir Robert Fairlamb in the chair was given to him and to Stokes. While Sir Robert ruddily blurted compliments and Kellett tried to explain things, and all of them drank to him, standing, after the toast to the King, Martin sat lonely, considering that tomorrow he would leave these trusting eyes and face the harsh demands of Gottlieb, of Terry Wickett.

The more they shouted his glory, the more he thought about what unknown, tight-minded scientists in distant laboratories would say of a man who had had his chance and cast it away. The more they called him the giver of life, the more he felt himself disgraced and a traitor; and as he looked at Stokes he saw in his regard a pity worse than condemnation.

## Chapter 36

It happened that Martin returned to New York, as he had come, on the *St. Buryan* . The ship was haunted with the phantoms of Leora dreaming, of Sondelius shouting on the bridge.

And on the *St. Buryan* was the country-club Miss Gwilliam who had offended Sondelius.

She had spent the winter importantly making notes on native music in Trinidad and Caracas; at least in planning to make notes. She saw Martin come aboard at Blackwater, and pertly noted the friends who saw him off — two Englishmen, one puffy, one rangy, and a dry-looking Scotsman.

"Your friends all seem to be British," she enlightened him, when she had claimed him as an old friend.

"Yes."

"You've spent the winter here."

"Yes."

"Hard luck to be caught by the quarantine. But I *told* you you were silly to go ashore! You must have managed to pick up quite a little money practicing. But it must have been unpleasant, really."

"Ye-es, I suppose it was."

"I *told* you it would be! You ought to have come on to Trinidad. Such a fascinating island! And tell me, how is the Roughneck?"

"Who?"

"Oh, you know — that funny Swede that used to dance and everything."

"He is dead."

"Oh, I *am* sorry. You know, no matter what the others said, I never thought he was so bad. I'm sure he had quite a nice cultured mind, when he wasn't carousing around. Your wife isn't with you, is she?"

"No — she isn't with me. I must go down and unpack now."

Miss Gwilliam looked after him with an expression which said that the least people could do was to learn some manners.

### II

With the heat and the threat of hurricanes, there were few first-class passengers on the *St. Buryan* , and most of these did not count, because they were not jolly, decent Yankee tourists but merely South Americans. As tourists do when their minds have been broadened and enriched by travel, when they return to New Jersey or Wisconsin with the credit of having spent a whole six months in the West Indies and South America, the respectable remnant studied one another fastidiously, and noted the slim pale man who seemed so restless, who all day trudged round the deck, who after midnight was seen standing by himself at the rail.

"That guy looks awful' restless to me!" said Mr. S. Sanborn Hibble of Detroit to the charming Mrs. Dawson of Memphis, and she answered, with the wit which made her so popular wherever she went, "Yes, don't he. I reckon he must be in love!"

"Oh, I know him!" said Miss Gwilliam. "He and his wife were on the *St. Buryan* when I came down. She's in New York now. He's some kind of a doctor — not awful' successful I don't believe. Just between ourselves, I don't think much of him or of her either. They sat and looked stupid all the way down."

### III

Martin was itching to get his fingers on his test-tubes. He knew, as once he had guessed, that he hated administration and Large Affairs.

As he tramped the deck, his head cleared and he was himself. Angrily he pictured the critics who would soon be pecking at whatever final report he might make. For a time he hated the criticism of his fellow laboratory-grinds as he had hated their competition; he hated the need of forever looking over his shoulder at pursuers. But on a night when he stood at the rail for hours, he admitted that he was afraid of their criticism, and afraid because his experiment had so many loopholes. He hurled overboard all the polemics with which he had protected himself: "Men who never have had the experience of trying, in the midst of an epidemic, to remain calm and keep experimental conditions, do not realize in the security of their laboratories what one has to contend with."

Constant criticism was good, if only it was not spiteful, jealous, petty —

No, even then it might be good! Some men had to be what easy-going workers called "spiteful." To them the joyous spite of crushing the almost-good was more natural than creation. Why should a great house-wrecker, who could clear the cumbered ground, be set at trying to lay brick?

"All right!" he rejoiced. "Let 'em come! Maybe I'll anticipate 'em and publish a roast of my own work. I have got something, from the St. Swithin test, even if I did let things slide for a while. I'll take my tables to a biometrician. He may rip 'em up. Good! What's left, I'll publish."

He went to bed feeling that he could face the eyes of Gottlieb and Terry, and for the first time in weeks he slept without terror.

## IV

At the pier in Brooklyn, to the astonishment and slight indignation of Miss Gwilliam, Mr. S. Sanborn Hibble, and Mrs. Dawson, Martin was greeted by reporters who agreeably though vaguely desired to know what were these remarkable things he had been doing to some disease or other, in some island some place.

He was rescued from them by Rippleton Holabird, who burst through them with his hands out, crying, "Oh, my dear fellow! We know all that's happened. We grieve for you so, and we're so glad you were spared to come back to us."

Whatever Martin might, under the shadow of Max Gottlieb, have said about Holabird, now he wrung his hands and muttered, "It's good to be home."

Holabird (he was wearing a blue shirt with a starched blue collar, like an actor) could not wait till Martin's baggage had gone through the customs. He had to return to his duties as Acting Director of the Institute. He delayed only to hint that the Board of Trustees were going to make him full Director, and that certainly, my dear fellow, he would see that Martin had the credit and the reward he deserved.

When Holabird was gone, driving away in his neat coupé (he often explained that his wife and he could afford a chauffeur, but they preferred to spend the money on other things), Martin was conscious of Terry Wickett, leaning against a gnawed wooden pillar of the wharf-house, as though he had been there for hours.

Terry strolled up and snorted, "Hello, Slim. All O.K.? Lez shoot the stuff through the customs. Great pleasure to see the Director and you kissing."

As they drove through the summer-walled streets of Brooklyn, Martin inquired, "How's Holabird working out as Director? And how is Gottlieb?"

"Oh, the Holy Wren is no worse than Tubbs; he's even politer and more ignorant....Me, you watch me! One of these days I'm going off to the woods — got a shack in Vermont — going to work there without having to produce results for the Director! They've stuck me in the Department of Biochemistry. And Gottlieb — " Terry's voice became anxious. "I guess he's pretty shaky — They've pensioned him off. Now look, Slim: I hear you're going to be a gilded department-head, and I'll never be anything but an associate member. Are you going on with me, or are you going to be one of the Holy Wren's pets — hero-scientist?"

"I'm with you, Terry, you old grouch." Martin dropped the cynicism which had always seemed proper between him and Terry. "I haven't got anybody else. Leora and Gustaf are gone and now maybe Gottlieb. You and I have got to stick together!"

"It's a go!"

They shook hands, they coughed gruffly, and talked of straw hats.

## V

When Martin entered the Institute, his colleagues galloped up to shake hands and to exclaim, and if their praise was flustering, there is no time at which one can stomach so much of it as at home-coming.

Sir Robert Fairlamb had written to the Institute a letter glorifying him. The letter arrived on the same boat with Martin, and next day Holabird gave it out to the press.

The reporters, who had been only a little interested at his landing, came around for interviews, and while Martin was sulky and jerky Holabird took them in hand, so that the papers were able to announce that America, which was always rescuing the world from something or other, had gone and done it again. It was spread in the prints that Dr. Martin Arrowsmith was not only a powerful witch-doctor and possibly something of a laboratory-hand, but also a ferocious rat-killer, village-burner, Special Board addresser, and snatcher from death. There was at the time, in certain places, a doubt as to how benevolent the United States had been to its Little Brothers — Mexico, Cuba, Haiti, Nicaragua — and the editors and politicians were grateful to Martin for this proof of their sacrifice and tender watchfulness.

He had letters from the Public Health service; from an enterprising Midwestern college which desired to make him a Doctor of Civil Law; from medical schools and societies which begged him to address them. Editorials on his work appeared in the medical journals and the newspapers; and Congressman Almus Pickerbaugh telegraphed him from Washington, in what the Congressman may conceivably have regarded as verse: "They got to go some to get ahead of fellows that come from old Nautilus." And he was again invited to dinner at the McGurks', not by Capitola but by Ross McGurk, whose name had never had such a whitewashing.

He refused all invitations to speak, and the urgent organizations which had invited him responded with meekness that they understood how intimidatingly busy Dr. Arrowsmith was, and if he ever *could* find the time, they would be most highly honored —

Rippleton Holabird was elected full Director now, in succession to Gottlieb, and he sought to use Martin as the prize exhibit of the Institute. He brought all the visiting dignitaries, all the foreign Men of Measured Merriment, in to see him, and they looked pleased and tried to think up questions. Then Martin was made head of the new Department of Microbiology at twice his old salary.

He never did learn what was the difference between micro-biology and bacteriology. But none of his glorification could he resist. He was still too dazed — he was more dazed when he had seen Max Gottlieb.

## VI

The morning after his return he had telephoned to Gottlieb's flat, had spoken to Miriam and received permission to call in the late afternoon.

All the way uptown he could hear Gottlieb saying, "You were my son! I gave you eferyt'ing I knew of truth and honor, and you haf betrayed me. Get out of my sight!"

Miriam met him in the hall, fretting, "I don't know if I should have let you come at all, Doctor."

"Why? Isn't he well enough to see people?"

"It isn't that. He doesn't really seem ill, except that he's feeble, but he doesn't know anyone. The doctors say it's senile dementia. His memory is gone. And he's just suddenly forgotten all his English. He can only speak German, and I can't speak it, hardly at all. If I'd only studied it, instead of music! But perhaps it may do him good to have you here. He was always so fond of you. You don't know how he talked of you and the splendid experiment you've been doing in St. Hubert."

"Well, I — " He could find nothing to say.

Miriam led him into a room whose walls were dark with books. Gottlieb was sunk in a worn chair, his thin hand lax on the arm.

"Doctor, it's Arrowsmith, just got back!" Martin mumbled.

The old man looked as though he half understood; he peered at him, then shook his head and whimpered, "*Versteh' nicht*." His arrogant eyes were clouded with ungovernable slow tears.

Martin understood that never could he be punished now and cleansed. Gottlieb had sunk into his darkness still trusting him.

## VII

Martin closed his flat — their flat — with a cold swift fury, lest he yield to his misery in finding among Leora's possessions a thousand fragments which brought her back: the frock she had bought for Capitola McGurk's dinner, a petrified chocolate she had hidden away to munch illegally by night, a memorandum, "Get almonds for Sandy." He took a grimly impersonal room in a hotel, and sunk himself in work. There was nothing for him but work and the harsh friendship of Terry Wickett.

His first task was to check the statistics of his St. Swithin treatments and the new figures still coming in from Stokes. Some of them were shaky, some suggested that the value of phage certainly had been confirmed, but there was nothing final. He took his figures to Raymond Pearl the biometrician, who thought less of them than did Martin himself.

He had already made a report of his work to the Director and the Trustees of the Institute, with no conclusion except "the results await statistical analysis and should have this before they are published." But Holabird had run wild, the newspapers had reported wonders, and in on Martin poured demands that he send out phage; inquiries as to whether he did not have a phage for tuberculosis, for syphilis; offers that he take charge of this epidemic and that.

Pearl had pointed out that his agreeable results in first phaging the whole of Carib village must be questioned, because it was possible that when he began, the curve of the disease had already passed its peak. With this and the other complications, viewing his hot work in St. Hubert as coldly as though it were the pretense of a man whom he had never seen, Martin decided that he had no adequate proof, and strode in to see the Director.

Holabird was gentle and pretty, but he sighed that if this conclusion were published, he would have to take back all the things he had said about the magnificence which, presumably, he had inspired his subordinate to accomplish. He was gentle and pretty, but firm; Martin was to suppress (Holabird did not say "suppress" — he said "leave to me for further consideration") the real statistical results, and issue the report with an ambiguous summary.

Martin was furious, Holabird delicately relentless. Martin hastened to Terry, declaring that he would resign — would denounce — would expose — Yes! He would! He no longer had to support Leora. He'd work as a drug-clerk. He'd go back right now and tell the Holy Wren —

"Hey! Slim! Wait a minute! Hold your horses!" observed Terry. "Just get along with Holy for a while, and we'll work out something we can do together and be independent. Meanwhile you have got your lab here, and you still have some physical chemistry to learn! And, uh — Slim, I haven't said anything about your St. Hubert stuff, but you know and I know you bunged it up badly. Can you come into court with clean hands, if you're going to indict the Holy One? Though I do agree that aside from being a dirty, lying, social-climbing, sneaking, power-grabbing hypocrite, he's all right. Hold on. We'll fix up something. Why, son, we've just been learning our science; we're just beginning to work."

Then Holabird published officially, under the Institute's seal, Martin's original report to the Trustees, with such quaint revisions as a change of "the results should have analysis" to "while statistical analysis would seem desirable, it is evident that this new treatment has accomplished all that had been hoped."

Again Martin went mad, again Terry calmed him; and with a hard fury unlike his eagerness of the days when he had known that Leora was waiting for him he resumed his physical chemistry.

He learned the involved mysteries of freezing-point determinations, osmotic pressure determinations, and tried to apply Northrop's generalizations on enzymes to the study of phage.

He became absorbed in mathematical laws which strangely predicted natural phenomena; his world was cold, exact, austerely materialistic, bitter to those who founded their logic on impressions. He was daily more scornful toward the counters of paving stones, the renamers of species, the compilers of irrelevant data. In his absorption the pleasant seasons passed unseen.

Once he raised his head in astonishment to perceive that it was spring; once Terry and he tramped two hundred miles through the Pennsylvania hills, by summer roads; but it seemed only a day later when it was Christmas, and Holabird was being ever so jolly and yuley about the Institute.

The absence of Gottlieb may have been good for Martin, since he no longer turned to the master for solutions in tough queries. When he took up diffusion problems, he began to develop his own apparatus, and whether it was from inborn ingenuity or merely from a fury of labor, he was so competent that he won from Terry the almost overwhelming praise: "Why, that's not so darn' bad, Slim!"

The sureness to which Max Gottlieb seems to have been born came to Martin slowly, after many stumblings, but it came. He desired a perfection of technique in the quest for absolute and provable fact; he desired as greatly as any Pater to "burn with a hard gem-like flame," and he desired not to have ease and repute in the market-place, but rather to keep free of those follies, lest they confuse him and make him soft.

Holabird was as much bewildered as Tubbs would have been by the ramifications of Martin's work. What did he think he was anyway — a bacteriologist or a bio-physicist? But Holabird was won by the scientific world's reception of Martin's first important paper, on the effect of X-rays, gamma rays, and beta rays on the anti-Shiga phage. It was praised in Paris and Brussels and Cambridge as much as in New York, for its insight and for "the clarity and to perhaps be unscientifically enthusiastic, the sheer delight and style of its presentation," as Professor Berkeley Wurtz put it; which may be indicated by quoting the first paragraph of the paper:

> *In a preliminary publication, I have reported a marked qualitative destructive effect of the radiations from radium emanations on Bacteriophage-anti-Shiga. In the present paper it is shown that X-rays, gamma rays, and beta rays produce identical inactivating effects on this bacteriophage. Furthermore, a quantitative relation is demonstrated to exist between this inactivation and the radiations that produce it. The results obtained from this quantitative study permit the statement that the percentage of inactivation, as measured by determining the units of bacteriophage remaining after irradiation by gamma and beta rays of a suspension of fixed virulence, is a function of the two variables, nillicuries and hours. The following equation accounts quantitatively for the experimental results obtained:*

$$\lambda \log e \frac{u_0}{u}$$

$$K = \frac{\qquad}{E_0(\varepsilon - \lambda t_1)}$$

When Director Holabird saw the paper — Yeo was vicious enough to take it in and ask his opinion — he said, “Splendid, oh, I say, simply splendid! I’ve just had the chance to skim through it, old boy, but I shall certainly read it carefully, the first free moment I have.”

## Chapter 37

Martin did not see Joyce Lanyon for weeks after his return to New York. Once she invited him to dinner, but he could not come, and he did not hear from her again.

His absorption in osmotic pressure determinations did not content him when he sat in his prim hotel room and was reduced from Dr. Arrowsmith to a man who had no one to talk to. He remembered how they had sat by the lagoon in the tepid twilight; he telephoned asking whether he might come in for tea.

He knew in an unformulated way that Joyce was rich, but after seeing her in gingham, cooking in the kitchen of St. Swithin's almshouse, he did not grasp her position; and he was uncomfortable when, feeling dusty from the laboratory, he came to her great house and found her the soft-voiced mistress of many servants. Hers was a palace, and palaces, whether they are such very little ones as Joyce's, with its eighteen rooms, or Buckingham or vast Fontainebleau, are all alike; they are choked with the superfluities of pride, they are so complete that one does not remember small endearing charms, they are indistinguishable in their common feeling of polite and uneasy grandeur, they are therefore altogether tedious.

But amid the pretentious splendor which Roger Lanyon had accumulated, Joyce was not tedious. It is to be suspected that she enjoyed showing Martin what she really was, by producing footmen and too many kinds of sandwiches, and by boasting, "Oh, I never do know what they're going to give me for tea."

But she had welcomed him, crying, "You look so much better. I'm frightfully glad. Are you still my brother? I was a good cook at the almshouse, wasn't I!"

Had he been suave then and witty, she would not have been greatly interested. She knew too many men who were witty and well-bred, ivory smooth and competent to help her spend the four or five million dollars with which she was burdened. But Martin was at once a scholar who made osmotic pressure determinations almost interesting, a taut swift man whom she could fancy running or making love, and a lonely youngster who naïvely believed that here in her soft security she was still the girl who had sat with him by the lagoon, still the courageous woman who had come to him in a drunken room at Blackwater.

Joyce Lanyon knew how to make men talk. Thanks more to her than to his own articulateness, he made living the Institute, the members, their feuds, and the drama of coursing on the trail of a discovery.

Her easy life here had seemed tasteless after the risks of St. Hubert, and in his contempt for ease and rewards she found exhilaration.

He came now and then to tea, to dinner; he learned the ways of her house, her servants, the more nearly intelligent of her friends. He liked — and possibly he was liked by — some of them. With one friend of hers Martin had a state of undeclared war. This was Latham Ireland, an achingly well-dressed man of fifty, a competent lawyer who was fond of standing in front of fireplaces and being quietly clever. He fascinated Joyce by telling her that she was subtle, then telling her what she was being subtle about.

Martin hated him.

In midsummer Martin was invited for a week-end at Joyce's vast blossom-hid country house at Greenwich. She was half apologetic for its luxury; he was altogether unhappy.

The strain of considering clothes, of galloping out to buy white trousers when he wanted to watch the test-tubes in the constant-temperature bath, of trying to look easy in the limousine which met him at the station, and of deciding which servants to tip and how much and when, was dismaying to a simple man. He felt rustic when, after he had blurted, "Just a minute til I go up and unpack my suit-case," she said gently, "Oh, that will have been done for you."

He discovered that a valet had laid out for him to put on, that first evening, all the small store of underclothes he had brought, and had squeezed out on his brush a ribbon of tooth-paste.

He sat on the edge of his bed, groaning, "This is too rich for my blood!"

He hated and feared that valet, who kept stealing his clothes, putting them in places where they could not be found, then popping in menacingly when Martin was sneaking about the enormous room looking for them.

But his chief unhappiness was that there was nothing to do. He had no sport but tennis, at which he was too rusty to play with these chattering unidentified people who filled the house and, apparently with perfect willingness, worked at golf and bridge. He had met but few of the friends of whom they talked. They said, "You know dear old R. G.," and he said, "Oh, *yes* ," but he never did know dear old R. G.

Joyce was as busily amiable as when they were alone at tea, and she found for him a weedy flapper whose tennis was worse than his own, but she had twenty guests — forty at Sunday lunch — and he gave up certain agreeable notions of walking with her in fresh lanes and, after excitedly saying this and that, perhaps kissing her. He had one moment with her. As he was going, she ordered, "Come here, Martin," and led him apart.

"You haven't really enjoyed it."

"Why, sure, course I — "

"Of course you haven't! And you despise us, rather, and perhaps you're partly right. I do like pretty people and gracious manners and good games, but I suppose they seem piffling after nights in a laboratory."

"No, I like 'em too. In a way. I like to look at beautiful women — at you! But — Oh, darn it, Joyce, I'm not up to it. I've always been poor and horribly busy. I haven't learned your games."

"But, Martin, you could, with the intensity you put into everything."

"Even getting drunk in Blackwater!"

"And I hope in New York, too! Dear Roger, he did have such an innocent, satisfying time getting drunk at class-dinners! But I mean: if you went at it, you could play bridge and golf — and talking — better than any of them. If you only knew how frightfully recent most of the ducal class in America are! And Martin: wouldn't it be good for you? Wouldn't you work all the better if you got away from your logarithmic tables now and then? And are you going to admit there's anything you can't conquer?"

"No, I — "

"Will you come to dinner on Tuesday week, just us two, and we'll fight it out?"

"Be glad to."

For a number of hours, on the train to Terry Wickett's vacation place in the Vermont hills, Martin was convinced that he loved Joyce Lanyon, and that he was going to attack the art of being amusing as he had attacked physical chemistry. Ardently, and quite humorlessly, as he sat stiffly in a stale Pullman chaircar with his feet up on his suit-case, he pictured himself wearing a club-tie (presumably first acquiring the tie and the club), playing golf in plus-fours, and being entertaining about dear old R. G. and incredibly witty about dear old Latham Ireland's aged Rolls-Royce.

But these ambitions he forgot as he came to Terry's proud proprietary shanty, by a lake among oaks and maples, and heard Terry's real theories of the decomposition of quinine derivatives.

Being perhaps the least sentimental of human beings, Terry had named his place "Birdies' Rest." He owned five acres of woodland, two miles from a railroad station. His shanty was a two-room affair of logs, with bunks for beds and oilcloth for table-linen.

"Here's the layout, Slim," said Terry. "Some day I'm going to figure out a way of making a lab here pay, by manufacturing sera or something, and I'll put up a couple more buildings on the flat by the lake, and have one absolutely independent place for science — two hours a day on the commercial end, and say about six for sleeping and a couple for feeding and telling dirty stories. That leaves — two and six and two make ten, if I'm any authority on higher math — that leaves fourteen hours a day for research (except when you got something special on), with no Director and no Society patrons and no Trustees that you've got to satisfy by making fool reports. Of course there won't be any scientific dinners with ladies in candy-box dresses, but I figure we'll be able to afford plenty of salt pork and corncob pipes, and your bed will be made perfectly — if you make it yourself. Huh? Lez go and have a swim."

Martin returned to New York with the not very compatible plans of being the best-dressed golfer in Greenwich and of cooking beef-stew with Terry at Birdies' Rest.

But the first of these was the more novel to him.

## II

Joyce Lanyon was enjoying a conversion. Her St. Hubert experiences and her natural variability had caused her to be dissatisfied with Roger's fast-motoring set.

She let the lady Maecenases of her acquaintance beguile her into several of their Causes, and she enjoyed them as she had enjoyed her active and entirely purposeless war work in 1917, for Joyce Lanyon was to some degree an Arranger, which was an epithet invented by Terry Wickett for Capitola McGurk.

An Arranger and even an Improver was Joyce, but she was not a Capitola; she neither waved a feathered fan and spoke spaciously, nor did she take out her sex-passion in talking. She was fine and occasionally gorgeous, with tiger in her, though she was as far from perfumed-boudoir and black-lingerie passion as she was from Capitola's cooling staleness. Hers was sheer straight white silk and cherished skin.

Behind all her reasons for valuing Martin was the fact that the only time in her life when she had felt useful and independent was when she had been an almshouse cook.

She might have drifted on, in her world of drifters, but for the interposition of Latham Ireland, the lawyer-dilettante-lover.

"Joy," he observed, "there seems to be an astounding quantity of that Dr. Arrowsmith person about the place. As your benign uncle — "

"Latham, my sweet, I quite agree that Martin is too aggressive, thoroughly unlicked, very selfish, rather a prig, absolutely a pedant, and his shirts are atrocious. And I rather think I shall marry him. I almost think I love him!"

"Wouldn't cyanide be a neater way of doing suicide?" said Latham Ireland.

## III

What Martin felt for Joyce was what any widowed man of thirty-eight would feel for a young and pretty and well-spoken woman who was attentive to his wisdom. As to her wealth, there was no problem at all. He was no poor man marrying money! Why, he was making ten thousand a year, which was eight thousand more than he needed to live on!

Occasionally he was suspicious of her dependence on luxury. With tremendous craft he demanded that instead of their dining in her Jacobean hall of state, she come with him on his own sort of party. She came, with enthusiasm. They went to abysmal Greenwich Village restaurants with candles, artistic waiters, and no food; or to Chinatown dives with food and nothing else. He even insisted on their taking the subway — though after dinner he usually forgot that he was being Spartan, and ordered a taxicab. She accepted it all without either wincing or too much gurgling.

She played tennis with him in the court on her roof; she taught him bridge, which, with his concentration and his memory, he soon played better than she and enjoyed astonishingly; she persuaded him that he had a leg and would look well in golf clothes.

He came to take her to dinner, on a serene autumn evening. He had a taxi waiting.

"Why don't we stick to the subway?" she said.

They were standing on her doorstep, in a blankly expensive and quite unromantic street off Fifth Avenue.

"Oh, I hate the rotten subway as much as you do! Elbows in my stomach never did help me much to plan experiments. I expect when we're married I'll enjoy your limousine."

"Is this a proposal? I'm not at all sure I'm going to marry you. Really, I'm *not*! You have no sense of ease!"

They were married the following January, in St. George's Church, and Martin suffered almost as much over the flowers, the bishop, the relatives with high-pitched voices, and the top hat which Joyce had commanded, as he did over having Rippleton Holabird wring his hand with a look of, "At last, dear boy, you have come out of barbarism and become One of Us."

Martin had asked Terry to be his best man. Terry had refused, and asserted that only with pain would he come to the wedding at all. The best man was Dr. William Smith, with his beard trimmed for the occasion, and distressing morning clothes and a topper which he had bought in London eleven years before, but both of them were safe in charge of a cousin of Joyce who was guaranteed to have extra handkerchiefs and to recognize the Wedding March. He had understood that Martin was Groton and Harvard, and when he discovered that he was Winnemac and nothing at all, he became suspicious.

In their stateroom on the steamer Joyce murmured, "Dear, you were brave! I didn't know what a damn' fool that cousin of mine was. Kiss me!"

Thenceforth ... except for a dreadful second when Leora floated between them, eyes closed and hands crossed on her pale cold breast ... they were happy and in each other found adventurous new ways.

## IV

For three months they wandered in Europe.

On the first day Joyce had said, "Let's have this beastly money thing over. I should think you are the least mercenary of men. I've put ten thousand dollars to your credit in London — oh, yes, and fifty thousand in New York — and if you'd like, when you have to do things for me, I'd be glad if you'd draw on it. No! Wait! Can't you see how easy and decent I want to make it all? You won't hurt me to save your own self-respect?"

## V

They really had, it seemed, to stay with the Principessa del Oltraggio (formerly Miss Lucy Deemy Bessy of Dayton), Madame des Basses Loges (Miss Brown of San Francisco), and the Countess of Marazion (who had been Mrs. Arthur Snaipe of Albany, and several things before that), but Joyce did go with him to see the great laboratories in London, Paris, Copenhagen. She swelled to perceive how Nobel-Prize winners received Her Husband, knew of him, desired to be violent with him about phage, and showed him their work of years. Some of them were hasty and graceless, she thought. Her Man was prettier than any of them, and if she would but be patient with him, she could make him master polo and clothes and conversation ... but of course go on with his science ... a pity he could not have a knighthood, like one or two of the British scientists they met. But even in America there were honorary degrees....

While she discovered and digested Science, Martin discovered Women.

## VI

Aware only of Madeline Fox and Orchid Pickerbaugh, who were Nice American Girls, of soon-forgotten ladies of the night, and of Leora, who, in her indolence, her indifference to decoration and good fame, was neither woman nor wife but only her own self, Martin knew nothing whatever about Women. He had expected Leora to wait for him, to obey his wishes, to understand without his saying them all the flattering things he had planned to say. He was spoiled, and Joyce was not timorous about telling him so.

It was not for her to sit beaming and wordless while he and his fellow-researchers arranged the world. With many jolts he perceived that even outside the bedroom he had to consider the fluctuations and variables of his wife, as A Woman, and sometimes as A Rich Woman.

It was confusing to find that where Leora had acidly claimed sex-loyalty but had hummingly not cared in what manner he might say Good Morning, Joyce was indifferent as to how many women he might have fondled (so long as he did not insult her by making love to them in her presence) but did require him to say Good Morning as though he meant it. It was confusing to find how starkly she discriminated between his caresses when he was absorbed in her and his hasty interest when he wanted to go to sleep. She could, she said, kill a man who considered her merely convenient furniture, and she uncomfortably emphasized the "kill."

She expected him to remember her birthday, her taste in wine, her liking for flowers, and her objection to viewing the process of shaving. She wanted a room to herself; she insisted that he knock before entering; and she demanded that he admire her hats.

When he was so interested in the work at Pasteur Institute that he had a clerk telephone that he would not be able to meet her for dinner, she was tight-lipped with rage.

"Oh, you got to expect that," he reflected, feeling that he was being tactful and patient and penetrating.

It annoyed him, sometimes, that she would never impulsively start off on a walk with him. No matter how brief the jaunt, she must first go to her room for white gloves — placidly stand there drawing them on.... And in London she made him buy spats ... and even wear them.

Joyce was not only an Arranger — she was a Loyalist. Like most American cosmopolites she revered the English peerage, adopted all their standards and beliefs — or what she considered their standards and beliefs — and treasured her encounters with them. Three and a half years after the War of 1914-18, she still said that she loathed all Germans, and the one complete quarrel between her and Martin occurred when he desired to see the laboratories in Berlin and Vienna.

But for all their differences it was a romantic pilgrimage. They loved fearlessly; they tramped through the mountains and came back to revel in vast bathrooms and ingenious dinners; they idled before cafés, and save when he fell silent as he remembered how much Leora had wanted to sit before cafés in France, they showed each other all the eagernesses of their minds.

Europe, her Europe, which she had always known and loved, Joyce offered to him on generous hands, and he who had ever been sensitive to warm colors and fine gestures — when he was not frenzied with work — was grateful to her and boyish with wonder. He believed that he was learning to take life easily and beautifully; he criticized Terry Wickett (but only to himself) for provincialism; and so in a golden leisure they came back to America and prohibition and politicians charging to protect the Steel Trust from the communists, to conversation about bridge and motors and to osmotic pressure determinations.

## Chapter 38

Director Rippleton Holabird had also married money, and whenever his colleagues hinted that since his first ardent work in physiology he had done nothing but arrange a few nicely selected flowers on the tables hewn out by other men, it was a satisfaction to him to observe that these rotters came down to the Institute by subway, while he drove elegantly in his coupé. But now Arrowsmith, once the poorest of them all, came by limousine with a chauffeur who touched his hat, and Holabird's coffee was salted.

There was a simplicity in Martin, but it cannot be said that he did not lick his lips when Holabird mooned at the chauffeur.

His triumph over Holabird was less than being able to entertain Angus Duer and his wife, on from Chicago; to introduce them to Director Holabird, to Salamon the king of surgeons, and to a medical baronet; and to have Angus gush, "Mart, do you mind my saying we're all awfully proud of you? Rouncefield was speaking to me about it the other day. 'It may be presumptuous,' he said, 'but I really feel that perhaps the training we tried to give Dr. Arrowsmith here in the Clinic did in some way contribute to his magnificent work in the West Indies and at McGurk.' What a lovely woman your wife is, old man! Do you suppose she'd mind telling Mrs. Duer where she got that frock?"

Martin had heard about the superiority of poverty to luxury, but after the lunch-wagons of Mohalis, after twelve years of helping Leora check the laundry and worry about the price of steak, after a life of waiting in the slush for trolleys, it was not at all dismaying to have a valet who produced shirts automatically; not at all degrading to come to meals which were always interesting, and, in the discretion of his car, to lean an aching head against softness and think how clever he was.

"You see, by having other people do the vulgar things for you, it saves your own energy for the things that only you can do," said Joyce.

Martin agreed, then drove to Westchester for a lesson in golf.

A week after their return from Europe, Joyce went with him to see Gottlieb. He fancied that Gottlieb came out of his brooding to smile on them.

"After all," Martin considered, "the old man did like beautiful things. If he'd had the chance, he might've liked a big Establishment, too, maybe."

Terry was surprisingly complaisant.

"I'll tell you, Slim — if you want to know. Personally I'd hate to have to live up to servants. But I'm getting old and wise. I figure that different folks like different things, and awful' few of 'em have the sense to come and ask me what they ought to like. But honest, Slim, I don't think I'll come to dinner. I've gone and bought a dress-suit — *bought* it! got it in my room — damn' landlady keeps filling it with moth-balls — but I don't think I could stand listening to Latham Ireland being clever."

It was, however, Rippleton Holabird's attitude which most concerned Martin, for Holabird did not let him forget that unless he desired to drift off and be merely a ghostly Rich Woman's husband, he would do well to remember who was Director.

Along with the endearing manners which he preserved for Ross McGurk, Holabird had developed the remoteness, the inhuman quiet courtesy, of the Man of Affairs, and people who presumed on his old glad days he courteously put in their places. He saw the need of repressing insubordination, when Arrowsmith appeared in a limousine. He gave him one week after his return to enjoy the limousine, then blandly called on him in his laboratory.

"Martin," he sighed, "I find that our friend Ross McGurk is just a bit dissatisfied with the practical results that are coming out of the Institute and, to convince him, I'm afraid I really must ask you to put less emphasis on bacteriophage for the moment and take up influenza. The Rockefeller Institute has the right idea. They've utilized their best minds, and spent money magnificently, on such problems as pneumonia, meningitis, cancer. They've already lessened the terrors of meningitis and pneumonia, and yellow fever is on the verge of complete abolition through Noguchi's work, and I have no doubt that their hospital, with its enormous resources and splendidly co-operating minds, will be the first to find something to alleviate diabetes. Now, I understand, they're hot after the cause of influenza. They're not going to permit another great epidemic of it. Well, dear chap, it's up to us to beat them on the flu, and I've chosen you to represent us in the race."

Martin was at the moment hovering over a method of reproducing phage on dead bacteria, but he could not refuse, he could not risk being discharged. He was too rich! Martin the renegade medical student could flounder off and be a soda-clerk, but if the husband of Joyce Lanyon should indulge in such insanity, he would be followed by reporters and photographed at the soda handles. Still less could he chance becoming merely her supported husband — a butler of the boudoir.

He assented, not very pleasantly.

He began to work on the cause of influenza with a half-heartedness almost magnificent. In the hospitals he secured cultures from cases which might be influenza and might be bad colds — no one was certain just what the influenza symptoms were; nothing was clean cut. He left most of the work to his assistants, occasionally giving them sardonic directions to "put on another hundred tubes of the A medium — hell, make it another thousand!" and when he found that they were doing as they pleased, he was not righteous nor rebuking. If he did not guiltily turn his hand from the plow it was only because he never touched the plow. Once his own small laboratory had been as fussily neat as a New Hampshire kitchen. Now the several rooms under his charge were a disgrace, with long racks of abandoned test-tubes, many half-filled with mold, none of them properly labeled.

Then he had his idea. He began firmly to believe that the Rockefeller investigators had found the cause of flu. He gushed in to Holabird and told him so. As for himself, he was going back to his search for the real nature of phage.

Holabird argued that Martin must be wrong. If Holabird wanted the McGurk Institute — and the Director of the McGurk Institute — to have the credit for capturing influenza, then it simply could not be possible that Rockefeller was ahead of them. He also said weighty things about phage. Its essential nature, he pointed out, was an academic question.

But Martin was by now too much of a scientific dialectician for Holabird, who gave up and retired to his den (or so Martin gloomily believed) to devise new ways of plaguing him. For a time Martin was again left free to wallow in work.

He found a means of reproducing phage on dead bacteria by a very complicated, very delicate use of partial oxygen-carbon dioxide tension — as exquisite as cameo-carving, as improbable as weighing the stars. His report stirred the laboratory world, and here and there (in Tokio, in Amsterdam, in Winnemac) enthusiasts believed he had proven that phage was a living organism; and other enthusiasts said, in esoteric language with mathematical formulae, that he was a liar and six kinds of a fool.

It was at this time, when he might have become a Great Man, that he pitched over most of his own work and some of the duties of being Joyce's husband to follow Terry Wickett, which showed that he lacked common sense, because Terry was still an assistant while he himself was head of a department.

Terry had discovered that certain quinine derivatives when introduced into the animal body slowly decompose into products which are highly toxic to bacteria but only mildly toxic to the body. There was hinted here a whole new world of therapy. Terry explained it to Martin, and invited him to collaborate. Buoyant with great things they got leave from Holabird — and from Joyce — and though it was winter they went off to Birdies' Rest, in the Vermont hills. While they snowshoed and shot rabbits, and all the long dark evenings while they lay on their bellies before the fire, they ranted and planned.

Martin had not been so long silk-wrapped that he could not enjoy gobbling salt pork after the northwest wind and the snow. It was not unpleasant to be free of thinking up new compliments for Joyce.

They had, they saw, to answer an interesting question: Do the quinine derivatives act by attaching themselves to the bacteria, or by changing the body fluids? It was a simple, clear, definite question which required for answer only the inmost knowledge of chemistry and biology, a few hundred animals on which to experiment, and perhaps ten or twenty or a million years of trying and failing.

They decided to work with the pneumococcus, and with the animal which should most nearly reproduce human pneumonia. This meant the monkey, and to murder monkeys is expensive and rather grim. Holabird, as Director, could supply them, but if they took him into confidence he would demand immediate results.

Terry meditated, "'Member there was one of these Nobel-Prize winners, Slim, one of these plumb fanatics that instead of blowing in the prize spent the whole thing on chimps and other apes, and he got together with another of those whiskery old birds, and they ducked up alleys and kept the anti-viv folks from prosecuting them, and settled the problem of the transfer of syphilis to lower animals? But we haven't got any Nobel Prize, I grieve to tell you, and it doesn't look to me — "

"Terry, I'll do it, if necessary! I've never sponged on Joyce yet, but I will now, if the Holy Wren holds out on us."

## II

They faced Holabird in his office, sulkily, rather childishly, and they demanded the expenditure of at least ten thousand dollars for monkeys. They wished to start a research which might take two years without apparent results — possibly without any results. Terry was to be transferred to Martin's department as co-head, their combined salaries shared equally.

Then they prepared to fight.

Holabird stared, assembled his mustache, departed from his Diligent Director manner, and spoke:

"Wait a minute, if you don't mind. As I gather it, you are explaining to me that occasionally it's necessary to take some time to elaborate an experiment. I really must tell you that I was formerly a researcher in an Institute called McGurk, and learned several of these things all by myself! Hell, Terry, and you, Mart, don't be so egotistic! You're not the only scientists who like to work undisturbed! If you poor fish only knew how I long to get away from signing letters and get my fingers on a kymograph drum again! Those beautiful long hours of search for truth! And if you knew how I've fought the Trustees for the chance to keep you fellows free! All right. You shall have your monkeys. Fix up the joint department to suit yourselves. And work ahead as seems best. I doubt if in the whole scientific world there's two people that can be trusted as much as you two surly birds!"

Holabird rose, straight and handsome and cordial, his hand out. They sheepishly shook it and sneaked away, Terry grumbling, "He's spoiled my whole day! I haven't got a single thing to kick about! Slim, where's the catch? You can bet there is one — there always is!"

In a year of divine work, the catch did not appear. They had their monkeys, their laboratories and garçons, and their unbroken leisure; they began the most exciting work they had ever known, and decidedly the most nerve-jabbing. Monkeys are unreasonable animals; they delight in developing tuberculosis on no provocation whatever; in captivity they have a liking for epidemics; and they make scenes by cursing at their masters in seven dialects.

"They're so up-and-coming," sighed Terry. "I feel like lettin' 'em go and retiring to Birdies' Rest to grow potatoes. Why should we murder live-wires like them to save pasty-faced, big-bellied humans from pneumonia?"

Their first task was to determine with accuracy the tolerated dose of the quinine derivative, and to study its effects on the hearing and vision, and on the kidneys, as shown by endless determinations of blood sugar and blood urea. While Martin did the injections and observed the effect on the monkeys and lost himself in chemistry, Terry toiled (all night, all next day, then a drink and a frowsy nap and all night again) on new methods of synthesizing the quinine derivative.

This was the most difficult period of Martin's life. To work, staggering sleepy, all night, to drowse on a bare table at dawn and to breakfast at a greasy lunch-counter, these were natural and amusing, but to explain to Joyce why he had missed her dinner to a lady sculptor and a lawyer whose grandfather had been a Confederate General, this was impossible. He won a brief tolerance by explaining that he really had longed to kiss her good-night, that he did appreciate the basket of sandwiches which she had sent, and that he was about to remove pneumonia from the human race, a statement which he healthily doubted.

But when he had missed four dinners in succession; when she had raged, "Can you imagine how awful it was for Mrs. Thorn to be short a man at the last moment?" when she had wailed, "I didn't so much mind your rudeness on the other nights, but this evening, when I had nothing to do and sat home alone and waited for you" — then he writhed.

Martin and Terry began to produce pneumonia in their monkeys and to treat them, and they had success which caused them to waltz solemnly down the corridor. They could save the monkeys from pneumonia invariably, when the infection had gone but one day, and most of them on the second day and the third.

Their results were complicated by the fact that a certain number of monkeys recovered by themselves, and this they allowed for by simple-looking figures which took days of stiff, shoulder-aching sitting over papers ... one wild-haired collarless man at a table, while the other walked among stinking cages of monkeys, clucking to them, calling them Bess and Rover, and grunting placidly, "Oh, you would bite me, would you, sweetheart!" and all the while, kindly but merciless as the gods, injecting them with the deadly pneumonia.

They came into a high upland where the air was thin with failures. They studied in the test-tube the break-down products of pneumococci — and failed. They constructed artificial body fluids (carefully, painfully, inadequately), they tried the effect of the derivative on germs in this artificial blood — and failed.

Then Holabird heard of their previous success, and came down on them with laurels and fury.

He understood, he said, that they had a cure for pneumonia. Very well! The Institute could do with the credit for curing that undesirable disease, and Terry and Martin would kindly publish their findings (mentioning McGurk) at once.

"We will not! Look here, Holabird!" snarled Terry, "I thought you were going to let us alone!"

"I have! Nearly a year! Till you should complete your research. And now you've completed it. It's time to let the world know what you're doing."

"If I did, the world would know a doggone sight more'n I do! Nothing doing, Chief. Maybe we can publish in a year from now."

"You'll publish now or — "

"All right, Holy. The blessed moment has arrived. I quit! And I'm so gentlemanly that I do it without telling you what I think of you!"

Thus was Terry Wickett discharged from McGurk. He patented the process of synthesizing his quinine derivative and retired to Birdies' Rest, to build a laboratory out of his small savings and spend a life of independent research supported by a restricted sale of sera and of his drug.

For Terry, wifeless and valetless, this was easy enough, but for Martin it was not simple.

## III

Martin assumed that he would resign. He explained it to Joyce. How he was to combine a town house and a Greenwich castle with flannel-shirt collaboration at Birdies' Rest he had not quite planned, but he was not going to be disloyal.

"Can you beat it! The Holy Wren fires Terry but doesn't dare touch me! I waited simply because I wanted to watch Holabird figure out what I'd do. And now — "

He was elucidating it to her in their — in her — car, on the way home from a dinner at which he had been so gaily charming to an important dowager that Joyce had crooned, "What a fool Latham Ireland was to say he couldn't be polite!"

"I'm free, by thunder at last I'm free, because I've worked up to something that's worth being free for!" he exulted.

She laid her fine hand on his, and begged, "Wait! I want to think. Please! Do be quiet for a moment."

Then: "Mart, if you went on working with Mr. Wickett, you'd have to be leaving me constantly."

"Well — "

"I really don't think that would be quite nice — I mean especially now, because I fancy I'm going to have a baby."

He made a sound of surprise.

"Oh, I'm not going to do the weeping mother. And I don't know whether I'm glad or furious, though I do believe I'd like to have one baby. But it does complicate things, you know. And personally, I should be sorry if you left the Institute, which gives you a solid position, for a hole-and-corner existence. Dear, I have been fairly nice, haven't I? I really do like you, you know! I don't want you to desert me, and you would if you went off to this horrid Vermont place."

"Couldn't we get a little house near there, and spend part of the year?"

"Pos-sibly. But we ought to wait till this beastly job of bearing a Dear Little One is over, then think about it."

Martin did not resign from the Institute, and Joyce did not think about taking a house near Birdies' Rest to the extent of doing it.

## Chapter 39

With Terry Wickett gone, Martin returned to phage. He made a false start and did the worst work of his life. He had lost his fierce serenity. He was too conscious of the ordeal of a professional social life, and he could never understand that esoteric phenomenon, the dinner-party — the painful entertainment of people whom one neither likes nor finds interesting.

So long as he had had a refuge in talking to Terry, he had not been too irritated by well-dressed nonentities, and for a time he had enjoyed the dramatic game of making Nice People accept him. Now he was disturbed by reason.

Clif Clawson showed him how tangled his life had grown.

When he had first come to New York, Martin had looked for Clif, whose boisterousness had been his comfort among Angus Duers and Irving Watterses in medical school. Clif was not to be found, neither at the motor agency for which he had once worked nor elsewhere on Automobile Row. For fourteen years Martin had not seen him.

Then to his laboratory at McGurk was brought a black-and-red card:

CLIFFORD L. CLAWSON
(Clif)
TOP NOTCH GUARANTEED OIL INVESTMENTS

*Higham Block*
*Butte*

"Clif! Good old Clif! The best friend a man ever had! That time he lent me the money to get to Leora! Old Clif! By golly I need somebody like him, with Terry out of it and all these tea-hounds around me!" exulted Martin.

He dashed out and stopped abruptly, staring at a man who was, not softly, remarking to the girl reception-clerk:

"Well, sister, you scientific birds certainly do lay on the agony! Never struck a sweller layout than you got here, except in crook investment-offices — and I've never seen a nicer cutie than you anywhere. How 'bout lil dinner one of these beauteous evenings? I expect I'll parley-vous with thou full often now — I'm a great friend of Doc Arrowsmith. Fact I'm a doc myself — honest — real sawbones — went to medic school and everything. Ah! *Here's* the boy!"

Martin had not allowed for the changes of fourteen years. He was dismayed.

Clif Clawson, at forty, was gross. His face was sweaty, and puffy with pale flesh; his voice was raw, he fancied checked Norfolk jackets, tight across his swollen shoulders and his beefy hips.

He bellowed, while he belabored Martin's back:

"Well, well, well, well, well, well! Old Mart! Why, you old son of a gun! Why, you old son of a gun! Why, you damn' old chicken-thief! Say you skinny little runt, I'm a son of a gun if you look one day older'n when I saw you last in Zenith!"

Martin was aware of the bright leering of the once humble reception-clerk. He said, "Well, gosh, it certainly is good to see you," and hastened to get Clif into the privacy of his office.

"You look fine," he lied, when they were safe. "What you been doing with yourself? Leora and I did our best to look you up, when we first came to New York. Uh — Do you know about, uh, about her?"

"Yuh, I read about her passing away. Fierce luck. And about your swell work in the West Indies — where was it? I guess you're a great man now — famous plague-chaser and all that stuff, and world-renowned skee-entist. I don't suppose you remember your old friends now."

"Oh, don't be a chump! It's — it's — it's fine to see you."

"Well, I'm glad to observe you haven't got the *capitus enlargatus*, Mart. Golly, I says to meself says I, if I blew in and old Mart high-hatted me, I'd just about come nigh unto letting him hear the straight truth, after all the compliments he's been getting from the sassiety dames. I'm glad you've kept your head. I thought about writing you from Butte — been selling some bum oil-stock there and kind of got out quick to save the inspectors the trouble of looking over my books. 'Well,' I thought, 'I'll just sit down and write the whey-faced runt a letter, and make him feel good by telling him how tickled I am over his nice work.' But you know how it is — time kind of slips by. Well, this is excellentus! We'll have a chance to see a whole lot of each other now. I'm going in with a fellow on an investment stunt here in New York. Great pickings, old kid! I'll take you out and show you how to order a real feed, one of these days. Well, tell me what you been doing since you got back from the West Indies. I suppose you're laying your plans to try and get in as the boss or president or whatever they call it of this gecelebrated Institute."

"No — I, uh, well, I shouldn't much care to be Director. I prefer sticking to my lab. I — Perhaps you'd like to hear about my work on phage."

Rejoicing to discover something of which he could talk, Martin sketched his experiments.

Clif spanked his forehead with a spongy hand and shouted:

"Wait! Say, I've got an idea — and you can come right in on it. As I apperceive it, the dear old Gen. Public is just beginning to hear about this bac — what is it? — bacteriophage junk. Look here! Remember that old scoundrel Benoni Carr, that I introduced as a great pharmacologist at the medical banquet? Had din-din with him last eventide. He's running a sanitarium out on Long Island — slick idea, too — practically he's a bootlegger; gets a lot of high-rollers out there and let's 'em have all the hooch they want, on prescriptions, absolutely legal and water-tight! The parties they throw at that joint, dames and everything! Believe me, Uncle Clif is sore stricken with tootelus bootelus and is going to the Carr Sanitarium for what ails him! But now look: Suppose we got him or somebody to rig up a new kind of cure — call it phageotherapy — oh, it takes Uncle Clif to invent the names that claw in the bounteous dollars! Patients sit in a steam cabinet and eat tablets made of phage, with just a little strychnin to jazz up their hearts! Bran-new! Million in it! What-cha-think?"

Martin was almost feeble. "No. I'm afraid I'm against it."

"Why?"

"Well, I — Honestly, Clif, if you don't understand it, I don't know how I can explain the scientific attitude to you. You know — that's what Gottlieb used to call it — scientific attitude. And as I'm a scientist — least I hope I am — I couldn't — Well, to be associated with a thing like that — "

"But, you poor louse, don't you suppose I understand the scientific attitude? Gosh, I've seen a dissecting-room myself! Why, you poor crab, of course I wouldn't expect you to have your name associated with it! You'd keep in the background and slip us all the dope, and get a lot of publicity for phage in general so the Dee-ah People would fall easier, and we'd pull all the strong-arm work."

"But — I hope you're joking, Clif. If you weren't joking, I'd tell you that if anybody tried to pull a thing like that, I'd expose 'em and get 'em sent to jail, no matter who they were!"

"Well, gosh, if you feel that way about it — !"

Clif was peering over the fatty pads beneath his eyes. He sounded doubtful:

"I suppose you have the right to keep other guys from grabbing your own stuff. Well, all right, Mart. Got to be teloddeling. Tell you what you *might* do, though, if that don't hurt your tender conscience, too: you might invite old Clif up t' the house for dinner, to meet the new lil wifey that I read about in the sassiety journals. You might happen to remember, old bean, that there have been times when you were glad enough to let poor fat old Clif slip you a feed and a place to sleep!"

"Oh, I know. You bet there have! Nobody was ever decenter to me; nobody. Look. Where you staying? I'll find out from my wife what dates we have ahead, and telephone you tomorrow morning."

"So you let the Old Woman keep the work-sheet for you, huh? Well, I never butt into anybody's business. I'm staying at the Berrington Hotel, room 617 — 'member that, 617 — and you might try and 'phone me before ten tomorrow. Say, that's one grand sweet song of a cutie you got on the door here. What cha think? How's chances on dragging her out to feed and shake a hoof with Uncle Clif?"

As primly as the oldest, most staid scientist in the Institute, Martin protested, "Oh, she belongs to very nice family. I don't think I should try it. Really, I'd rather you didn't."

Clif's gaze was sharp, for all its fattiness.

With excessive cordiality, with excessive applause when Clif remarked, "You better go back to work and put some salt on a coupla bacteria's tails," Martin guided him to the reception-room, safely past the girl clerk, and to the elevator.

For a long time he sat in his office and was thoroughly wretched.

He had for years pictured Clif Clawson as another Terry Wickett. He saw that Clif was as different from Terry as from Rippleton Holabird. Terry was rough, he was surly, he was colloquial, he despised many fine and gracious things, he offended many fine and gracious people, but these acerbities made up the haircloth robe wherewith he defended a devotion to such holy work as no cowled monk ever knew. But Clif —

"I'd do the world a service by killing that man!" Martin fretted. "Phageotherapy at a yegg sanitarium! I stand him only because I'm too much of a coward to risk his going around saying that 'in the days of my Success, I've gone back on my old friends.' (Success! Puddling at work! Dinners! Talking to idiotic women! Being furious because you weren't invited to the dinner to the Portuguese minister!) No. I'll 'phone Clif we can't have him at the house."

Over him came remembrance of Clif's loyalty in the old barren days, and Clif's joy to share with him every pathetic gain.

"Why *should* he understand my feeling about phage? Was his scheme any worse than plenty of reputable drug-firms? How much was I righteously offended, and how much was I sore because he didn't recognize the high social position of the rich Dr. Arrowsmith?"

He gave up the question, went home, explained almost frankly to Joyce what her probable opinion of Clif would be, and contrived that Clif should be invited to dinner with only the two of them.

"My dear Mart," said Joyce, "why do you insult me by hinting that I'm such a snob that I'll be offended by racy slang and by business ethics very much like those of dear Roger's grandpapa? Do you think I've never ventured out of the drawing-room? I thought you'd seen me outside it! I shall probably like your Clawson person very much indeed."

The day after Martin had invited him to dinner, Clif telephoned to Joyce:

"This Mrs. Arrowsmith? Well, say, this is old Clif."

"I'm afraid I didn't quite catch it."

"Clif! Old Clif!"

"I'm frightfully sorry but — Perhaps there's a bad connection."

"Why, it's Mr. *Clawson* , that's going to feed with you on — "

"Oh, of course. I *am* so sorry."

"Well, look: What I wanted to know is: Is this going to be just a homey grub-grabbing or a real soirée? In other words, honey, shall I dress natural or do I put on the soup-and-fish? Oh, I got 'em — swallow-tail and the whole darn' outfit!"

"I — Do you mean — Oh. Shall you dress for dinner? I think perhaps I would."

"Attaboy! I'll be there, dolled up like a new saloon. I'll show you folks the cutest lil line of jeweled studs you ever laid eyes on. Well, it's been a great pleezhure to meet Mart's Missus, and we will now close with singing 'Till We Meet Again' or 'Au Reservoir.' "

When Martin came home, Joyce faced him with, "Sweet, I can't do it! The man must be mad. Really, dear, you just take care of him and let me go to bed. Besides: you two won't want me — you'll want to talk over old times, and I'd only interfere. And with baby coming in two months now, I ought to go to bed early."

"Oh, Joy, Clif'd be awfully offended, and he's always been so decent to me and — And you've often asked me about my cub days. Don't you *want* ," plaintively, "to hear about 'em?"

"Very well, dear. I'll try to be a little sunbeam to him, but I warn you I sha'n't be a success."

They worked themselves up to a belief that Clif would be raucous, would drink too much, and slap Joyce on the back. But when he appeared for dinner he was agonizingly polite and flowery — till he became slightly drunk. When Martin said "damn," Clif reproved him with, "Of course I'm only a hick, but I don't think a lady like the Princess here would like you to cuss."

And, "Well, I never expected a rube like young Mart to marry the real bon-ton article."

And, "Oh, maybe it didn't cost something to furnish this dining-room, oh, not a-tall!"

And, "Champagne, heh? Well, you're certainly doing poor old Clif proud. Your Majesty, just tell your High Dingbat to tell his valay to tell my secretary the address of your bootlegger, will you?"

In his cups, though he severely retained his moral and elegant vocabulary, Clif chronicled the jest of selling oil-wells unprovided with oil and of escaping before the law closed in; the cleverness of joining churches for the purpose of selling stock to the members; and the edifying experience of assisting Dr. Benoni Carr to capture a rich and senile widow for his sanitarium by promising to provide medical consultation from the spirit-world.

Joyce was silent through it all, and so superbly polite that everyone was wretched.

Martin struggled to make a liaison between them, and he had no elevating remarks about the strangeness of a man's boasting of his own crookedness, but he was coldly furious when Clif blundered:

"You said old Gottlieb was sort of down on his luck now."

"Yes, he's not very well."

"Poor old coot. But I guess you've realized by now how foolish you were when you used to fall for him like seven and a half brick. Honestly, Lady Arrowsmith, this kid used to think Pa Gottlieb was the cat's pajamas — begging your pardon for the slanguageness."

"What do you mean?" said Martin.

"Oh, I'm onto Gottlieb! Of course you know as well as I do that he always was a self-advertiser, getting himself talked about by confidin' to the whole *ops terrara* what a strict scientist he was, and putting on a lot of dog and emitting these wise cracks about philosophy and what fierce guys the regular docs were. But what's worse than — Out in San Diego I ran onto a fellow that used to be an instructor in botany in Winnemac, and he told me that with all this antibody stuff of his, Gottlieb never gave any credit to — well, he was some Russian that did most of it before and Pa Gottlieb stole all his stuff."

That in this charge against Gottlieb there was a hint of truth, that he knew the great god to have been at times ungenerous, merely increased the rage which was clenching Martin's fist in his lap.

Three years before, he would have thrown something, but he was an adaptable person. He had yielded to Joyce's training in being quietly instead of noisily disagreeable; and his only comment was "No, I think you're wrong, Clif. Gottlieb has carried the antibody work 'way beyond all the others."

Before the coffee and liqueurs had come into the drawing-room, Joyce begged, at her prettiest, "Mr. Clawson, do you mind awfully if I slip up to bed? I'm so frightfully glad to have had the opportunity of meeting one of my husband's oldest friends, but I'm not feeling very well, and I do think I'd be wise to have some rest."

"Madam the Princess, I noticed you were looking peeked."

"Oh! Well — Good-night!"

Martin and Clif settled in large chairs in the drawing-room, and tried to play at being old friends happy in meeting. They did not look at each other.

After Clif had cursed a little and told three sound smutty stories, to show that he had not been spoiled and that he had been elegant only to delight Joyce, he flung:

"Huh! So that is that, as the Englishers remark. Well, I could see your Old Lady didn't cotton to me. She was just as chummy as an iceberg. But gosh, I don't mind. She's going to have a kid, and of course women, all of 'em, get cranky when they're that way. But — "

He hiccuped, looked sage, and bolted his fifth cognac.

"But what I never could figure out — Mind you, I'm not criticizing the Old Lady. She's as swell as they make 'em. But what I can't understand is how after living with Leora, who was the real thing, you can stand a hoity-toity skirt like Joycey!"

Then Martin broke.

The misery of not being able to work, these months since Terry had gone, had gnawed at him.

"Look here, Clif. I won't have you discuss my wife. I'm sorry she doesn't please you, but I'm afraid that in this particular matter — "

Clif had risen, not too steadily, though his voice and his eyes were resolute.

"All right. I figured out you were going to high-hat me. Of course I haven't got a rich wife to slip me money. I'm just a plain old hobo. I don't belong in a place like this. Not smooth enough to be a butler. You are. All right. I wish you luck. And meanwhile you can go plumb to hell, my young friend!"

Martin did not pursue him into the hall.

As he sat alone he groaned, "Thank Heaven, that operation's over!"

He told himself that Clif was a crook, a fool, and a fat waster; he told himself that Clif was a cynic without wisdom, a drunkard without charm, and a philanthropist who was generous only because it larded his vanity. But these admirable truths did not keep the operation from hurting any more than it would have eased the removal of an appendix to be told that it was a bad appendix, an appendix without delicacy or value.

He had loved Clif — did love him and always would. But he would never see him again. Never!

The impertinence of that flabby blackguard to sneer at Gottlieb! His boorishness! Life was too short for —

"But hang it — yes, Clif is a tough, but so am I. He's a crook, but wasn't I a crook to fake my plague figures in St. Hubert — and the worse crook because I got praise for it?"

He bobbed up to Joyce's room. She was lying in her immense four-poster, reading "Peter Whiffle."

"Darling, it was all rather dreadful, wasn't it!" she said. "He's gone?"

"Yes.... He's gone.... I've driven out the best friend I ever had — practically. I let him go, let him go off feeling that he was a rotter and a failure. It would have been decenter to have killed him. Oh, why couldn't you have been simple and jolly with him? You were so confoundedly polite! He was uneasy and unnatural, and showed up worse than he really is. He's no tougher than — he's a lot better than the financiers who cover up their stuff by being suave.... Poor devil! I'll bet right now Clif's tramping in the rain, saying, 'The one man I ever loved and tried to do things for has turned against me, now he's — now he has a lovely wife. What's the use of ever being decent?' he's saying.... Why couldn't you be simple and chuck your high-falutin' manners for once?"

"See here! You disliked him quite as much as I did, and I will not have you blame it on me! You've grown beyond him. You that are always blaring about Facts — can't you face the fact? For once, at least, it's not my fault. You may perhaps remember, my king of men, that I had the good sense to suggest that I shouldn't appear tonight; not meet him at all."

"Oh — well — yes — gosh — but — Oh, I suppose so. Well, anyway — It's over, and that's all there is to it."

"Darling, I do understand how you feel. But isn't it good it is over! Kiss me good-night."

"*But*" — Martin said to himself, as he sat feeling naked and lost and homeless, in the dressing-gown of gold dragon-flies on black silk which she had bought for him in Paris — "but if it'd been Leora instead of Joyce — Leora would've known Clif was a crook, and she'd've accepted it as a fact. (Talk about your facing facts!) She wouldn't've insisted on sitting as a judge. She wouldn't've said, 'This is different from me, so it's wrong.' She'd've said, 'This is different from me, so it's interesting.' Leora — "

He had a sharp, terrifying vision of her, lying there coffin-less, below the mold in a garden on the Penrith Hills.

He came out of it to growl, "What was it Clif said? 'You're not her husband — you're her butler — you're too smooth.' He was right! The whole point is: I'm not allowed to see who I want to. I've been so clever that I've made myself the slave of Joyce and Holy Holabird."

He was always going to, but he never did see Clif Clawson again.

## II

It happened that both Joyce's and Martin's paternal grandfathers had been named John, and John Arrowsmith they called their son. They did not know it, but a certain John Arrowsmith, mariner of Bideford, had died in the matter of the Spanish Armada, taking with him five valorous Dons.

Joyce suffered horribly, and renewed all of Martin's love for her (he did love pitifully this slim, brilliant girl).

"Death's a better game than bridge — you have no partner to help you!" she said, when she was grotesquely stretched on a chair of torture and indignity; when before they would give her the anesthetic, her face was green with agony.

John Arrowsmith was straight of back and straight of limb — ten good pounds he weighed at birth — and he was gay of eye when he had ceased to be a raw wrinkled grub and become a man-child. Joyce worshiped him, and Martin was afraid of him, because he saw that this minuscule aristocrat, this child born to the self-approval of riches, would some day condescend to him.

Three months after child-bearing, Joyce was more brisk than ever about putting and back-hand service and hats and Russian emigrés.

## III

For science Joyce had great respect and no understanding. Often she asked Martin to explain his work, but when he was glowing, making diagrams with his thumb-nail on the tablecloth, she would interrupt him with a gracious "Darling — do you mind — just a second — Plinder, isn't there any more of the sherry?"

When she turned back to him, though her eyes were kind his enthusiasm was gone.

She came to his laboratory, asked to see his flasks and tubes, and begged him to bully her into understanding, but she never sat back watching for silent hours.

Suddenly, in his bogged floundering in the laboratory, he touched solid earth. He blundered into the effect of phage on the mutation of bacterial species — very beautiful, very delicate — and after plodding months when he had been a sane citizen, an almost good husband, an excellent bridge-player, and a rotten workman, he knew again the happiness of high taut insanity.

He wanted to work nights, every night. During his uninspired fumbling, there had been nothing to hold him at the Institute after five, and Joyce had become used to having him flee to her. Now he showed an inconvenient ability to ignore engagements, to snap at delightful guests who asked him to explain all about science, to forget even her and the baby.

"I've *got* to work evenings!" he said. "I can't be regular and easy about it when I'm caught by a big experiment, any more than you could be regular and easy and polite when you were gestating the baby."

"I know but — Darling, you get so nervous when you're working like this. Heavens, I don't care how much you offend people by missing engagements — well, after all, I wish you wouldn't, but I do know it may be unavoidable. But when you make yourself so drawn and trembly, are you gaining time in the long run? It's just for your own sake. Oh, I have it! Wait! You'll see what a scientist I am! No, I won't explain — not yet!"

Joyce had wealth and energy. A week later, flushed, slim, gallant, joyous, she said to him after dinner, "I've got a surprise for you!"

She led him to the unoccupied rooms over the garage, behind their house. In that week, using a score of workmen from the most immaculate and elaborate scientific supply-house in the country, she had created for him the best bacteriological laboratory he had ever seen — white-tile floor and enameled brick walls, ice-box and incubator, glassware and stains and microscope, a perfect constant-temperature bath — and a technician, trained in Lister and Rockefeller, who had his bedroom behind the laboratory and who announced his readiness to serve Dr. Arrowsmith day or night.

"There!" sang Joyce. "Now when you simply must work evenings, you won't have to go clear down to Liberty Street. You can duplicate your cultures or whatever you call 'em. If you're bored at dinner — all right! You can slip out here afterward and work as late as ever you want. Is — Sweet, is it all right? Have I done it right? I tried so hard — I got the best men I could — "

While his lips were against hers he brooded, "To have done this for me! And to be so humble!... And now, curse it, I'll *never* be able to get away by myself!"

She so joyfully demanded his finding some fault that, to give her the novel pleasure of being meek, he suggested that the centrifuge was inadequate.

"You wait, my man!" she crowed.

Two evenings after, when they had returned from the opera, she led him to the cement-floored garage beneath his new laboratory, and in a corner, ready to be set up, was a second-hand but adequate centrifuge, a most adequate centrifuge, the masterpiece of the great firm of Berkeley-Saunders — in fact none other than Gladys, whose dismissal from McGurk for her sluttish ways had stirred Martin and Terry to go out and get bountifully drunk.

It was less easy for him, this time, to be grateful, but he worked at it.

## IV

Through both the economico-literary and the Rolls-Royce section of Joyce's set the rumor panted that there was a new diversion in an exhausted world — going out to Martin's laboratory and watching him work, and being ever so silent and reverent, except perhaps when Joyce murmured, "Isn't he adorable the way he teaches his darling bacteria to say 'Pretty Polly'!" or when Latham Ireland convulsed them by arguing that scientists had no sense of humor, or Sammy de Lembre burst out in his marvelous burlesque of jazz:

*Oh, Mistah Back-sil-lil-us, don't you gri-in at me;*
*You mi-cro-bi-o-log-ic cuss, I'm o-on-to thee.*
*When Mr. Dr. Arrowsmith's done looked at de clues,*
*You'll sit in jail a-singin' dem Bac-ter-i-uh Blues.*

Joyce's cousin from Georgia sparkled, "Mart is so cute with all those lil vases of his. But Ah can always get him so mad by tellin' him the trouble with *him* is, he don't go to church often enough!"

While Martin sought to concentrate.

They flocked from the house to his laboratory only once a week, which was certainly not enough to disturb a resolute man — merely enough to keep him constantly waiting for them.

When he sedately tried to explain this and that to Joyce, she said, "Did we bother you this evening? But they do admire you so."

He remarked, "Well," and went to bed.

## V

R. A. Hopburn, the eminent patent-lawyer, as he drove away from the Arrowsmith-Lanyon mansion grunted at his wife:

"I don't mind a host throwing the port at you, if he thinks you're a chump, but I do mind his being bored at your daring to express any opinion whatever.... Didn't he look silly, out in his idiotic laboratory!... How the deuce do you suppose Joyce ever came to marry him?"

"I can't imagine."

"I can only think of one reason. Of course she may — "

"Now please don't be filthy!"

"Well, anyway — She who might have picked any number of well-bred, agreeable, intelligent chaps — and I *mean* intelligent, because this Arrowsmith person may know all about germs, but he doesn't know a symphony from a savory.... I don't think I'm too fussy, but I don't quite see why we should go to a house where the host apparently enjoys flatly contradicting you.... Poor devil, I'm really sorry for him; probably he doesn't even know when he's being rude."

"No. Perhaps. What hurts is to think of old Roger — so gay, so strong, real Skull and Bones — and to have this abrupt Outsider from the tall grass sitting in his chair, failing to appreciate his Pol Roger — What Joyce ever saw in him! Though he does have nice eyes and such funny strong hands — "

## VI

Joyce's busyness was on his nerves. Why she was so busy it was hard to ascertain; she had an excellent housekeeper, a noble butler, and two nurses for the baby. But she often said that she was never allowed to attain her one ambition: to sit and read.

Terry had once called her The Arranger, and though Martin resented it, when he heard the telephone bell he groaned, "Oh, Lord, there's The Arranger — wants me to come to tea with some high-minded hen."

When he sought to explain that he must be free from entanglements, she suggested, "Are you such a weak, irresolute, *little* man that the only way you can keep concentrated is by running away? Are you afraid of the big men who can do big work, and still stop and play?"

He was likely to turn abusive, particularly as to her definition of Big Men, and when he became hot and vulgar, she turned *grande dame* , so that he felt like an impertinent servant and was the more vulgar.

He was afraid of her then. He imagined fleeing to Leora, and the two of them, frightened little people, comforting each other and hiding from her in snug corners.

But often enough Joyce was his companion, seeking new amusements as surprises for him, and in their son they had a binding pride. He sat watching little John, rejoicing in his strength.

It was in early winter, after she had royally taken the baby South for a fortnight, that Martin escaped for a week with Terry at Birdies' Rest.

He found Terry tired and a little surly, after months of working absolutely alone. He had constructed beside the home cabin a shanty for laboratory, and a rough stable for the horses which he used in the preparation of his sera. Terry did not, as once he would have, flare into the details of his research, and not till evening, when they smoked before the rough fireplace of the cabin, loafing in chairs made of barrels cushioned with elk skin, could Martin coax him into confidences.

He had been compelled to give up much of his time to mere housework and the production of the sera which paid his expenses. "If you'd only been with me, I could have accomplished something." But his quinine derivative research had gone on solidly, and he did not regret leaving McGurk. He had found it impossible to work with monkeys; they were too expensive and too fragile to stand the Vermont winter; but he had contrived a method of using mice infected with pneumococcus and —

"Oh, what's the use of my telling you this, Slim? You're not interested, or you'd have been up here at work with me, months ago. You've chosen between Joyce and me. All right, but you can't have both."

Martin snarled, "I'm very sorry I intruded on you, Wickett," and slammed out of the cabin. Stumbling through the snow, blundering in darkness against stumps, he knew the agony of his last hour, the hour of failure.

"I've lost Terry, now (though I won't stand his impertinence!). I've lost everybody, and I've never really had Joyce. I'm completely alone. And I can only half work! I'm through! They'll never let me get to work again!"

Suddenly, without arguing it out, he knew that he was not going to give up.

He floundered back to the cabin and burst in, crying, "You old grouch, we got to stick together!"

Terry was as much moved as he; neither of them was far from tears; and as they roughly patted each other's shoulders they growled, "Fine pair of fools, scrapping just because we're tired!"

"I will come and work with you, somehow!" Martin swore. "I'll get a six months' leave from the Institute, and have Joyce stay at some hotel near here, or do *some* thing. Gee! Back to real work.... *Work!* ... Now tell me: When I come up here, what d'you say we — "

They talked till dawn.

## Chapter 40

Dr. and Mrs. Rippleton Holabird had invited only Joyce and Martin to dinner. Holabird was his most charming self. He admired Joyce's pearls, and when the squabs had been served he turned on Martin with friendly intensity:

"Now will Joyce and you listen to me most particularly? Things are happening, Martin, and I want you — no, Science wants you! — to take your proper part in them. I needn't, by the way, hint that this is absolutely confidential. Dr. Tubbs and his League of Cultural Agencies are beginning to accomplish marvels, and Colonel Minnigen has been extraordinarily liberal.

"They've gone at the League with exactly the sort of thoroughness and taking-it-slow that you and dear old Gottlieb have always insisted on. For four years now they've stuck to making plans. I happen to know that Dr. Tubbs and the council of the League have had the most wonderful conferences with college-presidents and editors and clubwomen and labor-leaders (the sound, sensible ones, of course) and efficiency-experts and the more advanced advertising-men and ministers, and all the other leaders of public thought.

"They've worked out elaborate charts classifying all intellectual occupations and interests, with the methods and materials and tools, and especially the goals — the aims, the ideals, the moral purposes — that are suited to each of them. Really tremendous! Why, a musician or an engineer, for example, could look at his chart and tell accurately whether he was progressing fast enough, at his age, and if not, just what his trouble was, and the remedy. With this basis, the League is ready to go to work and encourage all brain-workers to affiliate.

"McGurk Institute simply must get in on this co-ordination, which I regard as one of the greatest advances in thinking that has ever been made. We are at last going to make all the erstwhile chaotic spiritual activities of America really conform to the American ideal; we're going to make them as practical and supreme as the manufacture of cash-registers! I have certain reasons for supposing I can bring Ross McGurk and Minnigen together, now that the McGurk and Minnigen lumber interests have stopped warring, and if so I shall probably quit the Institute and help Tubbs guide the League of Cultural Agencies. Then we'll need a new Director of McGurk who will work with us and help bring Science out of the monastery to serve Mankind."

By this time Martin understood everything about the League except what the League was trying to do.

Holabird went on:

"Now I know, Martin, that you've always rather sneered at Practicalness, but I have faith in you! I believe you've been too much under the influence of Wickett, and now that he's gone and you've seen more of life and of Joyce's set and mine, I believe I can coax you to take (oh! without in any way neglecting the severities of your lab work!) a broader view.

"I am authorized to appoint an Assistant Director, and I think I'm safe in saying he would succeed me as full Director. Sholtheis wants the place, and Dr. Smith and Yeo would leap at it, but I haven't yet found any of them that are quite Our Own Sort, and I offer it to you! I daresay in a year or two, you will be Director of McGurk Institute!"

Holabird was uplifted, as one giving royal favor. Mrs. Holabird was intense, as one present on an historical occasion and Joyce was ecstatic over the honor to her Man.

Martin stammered, "W-why, I'll have to think it over. Sort of unexpected — "

The rest of the evening Holabird so brimmingly enjoyed himself picturing an era in which Tubbs and Martin and he would rule, co-ordinate, standardize, and make useful the whole world of intelligence, from trousers-designing to poetry, that he did not resent Martin's silence. At parting he chanted, "Talk it over with Joyce, and let me have your decision tomorrow. By the way, I think we'll get rid of Pearl Robbins; she's been useful but now she considers herself indispensable. But that's a detail.... Oh, I do have faith in you, Martin, dear old boy! You've grown and calmed down, and you've widened your interests so much, this past year!"

In their car, in that moving curtained room under the crystal dome-light, Joyce beamed at him.

"Isn't it too wonderful, Mart! And I do feel Rippleton can bring it off. Think of your being Director, head of that whole great Institute, when just a few years ago you were only a cub there! But haven't I perhaps helped, just a little?"

Suddenly Martin hated the blue-and-gold velvet of the car, the cunningly hid gold box of cigarettes, all this soft and smothering prison. He wanted to be out beside the unseen chauffeur — His Own Sort! — facing the winter. He tried to look as though he were meditating, in an awed, appreciative manner, but he was merely being cowardly, reluctant to begin the slaughter. Slowly:

"Would you really like to see me Director?"

"Of course! All that — Oh, you know; I don't just mean the prominence and respect, but the power to accomplish good."

"Would you like to see me dictating letters, giving out interviews, buying linoleum, having lunch with distinguished fools, advising men about whose work I don't know a blame' thing?"

"Oh, don't be so superior! Someone has to do these things. And that'd be only a small part of it. Think of the opportunity of encouraging some youngster who wanted a chance to do splendid science!"

"And give up my own chance?"

"Why need you? You'd be head of your own department just the same. And even if you did give up — You are so stubborn! It's lack of imagination. You think that because you've started in on one tiny branch of mental activity, there's nothing else in the world. It's just as when I persuaded you that if you got out of your stinking laboratory once a week or so, and actually bent your powerful intellect to a game of golf, the world of science wouldn't immediately stop! No imagination! You're precisely like these business men you're always cursing because they can't see anything in life beyond their soap-factories or their banks!"

"And you really would have me give up my work — "

He saw that with all her eager complaisances she had never understood what he was up to, had not comprehended one word about the murderous effect of the directorship on Gottlieb.

He was silent again, and before they reached home she said only, "You know I'm the last person to speak of money, but really, it's you who have so often brought up the matter of hating to be dependent on me, and you know as Director you would make so much more that — Forgive me!"

She fled before him into her palace, into the automatic elevator.

He plodded up the stairs, grumbling, "Yes, it is the first chance I've had to really contribute to the expenses here. Sure! Willing to take her money, but not to do anything in return, and then call it 'devotion to science!' Well, I've got to decide right now — "

He did not go through the turmoil of deciding; he leaped to decision without it. He marched into Joyce's room, irritated by its snobbishness of discreet color. He was checked by the miserable way in which she sat brooding on the edge of her day couch, but he flung:

"I'm not going to do it, even if I have to leave the Institute — and Holabird will just about make me quit. I will not get buried in this pompous fakery of giving orders and — "

"Mart! Listen! Don't you want your son to be proud of you?"

"Um. Well — *No* , not if he's to be proud of me for being a stuffed shirt, a sideshow barker — "

"Please don't be vulgar."

"Why not? Matter of fact, I haven't been vulgar enough lately. What I ought to do is to go to Birdies' Rest right now, and work with Terry."

"I wish I had some way of showing you — Oh, for a 'scientist' you do have the most incredible blind-spots! I wish I could make you see just how weak and futile that is. The wilds! The simple life! The old argument. It's just the absurd, cowardly sort of thing these tired highbrows do that sneak off to some Esoteric Colony and think they're getting strength to conquer life, when they're merely running away from it."

"No. Terry has his place in the country only because he can live cheaper there. If we — if he could afford it, he'd probably be right here in town, with garçons and everything, like McGurk, but with no Director Holabird, by God — and no Director Arrowsmith!"

"Merely a cursing, ill-bred, intensely selfish Director Terry Wickett!"

"Now, by God, let me tell you — "

"Martin, do you need to emphasize your arguments by a 'by God' in every sentence, or have you a few other expressions in your highly scientific vocabulary?"

"Well, I have enough vocabulary to express the idea that I'm thinking of joining Terry."

"Look here, Mart. You feel so virtuous about wanting to go off and wear a flannel shirt and be peculiar and very, very pure. Suppose everybody argued that way. Suppose every father deserted his children whenever his nice little soul ached? Just what would become of the world? Suppose I were poor, and you left me, and I had to support John by taking in washing — "

"It'd probably be fine for you but fierce on the washing! No! I beg your pardon. That was an obvious answer. But — I imagine it's just that argument that's kept almost everybody, all these centuries, from being anything but a machine for digestion and propagation and obedience. The answer is that very few ever do, under any condition, willingly leave a soft bed for a shanty bunk in order to be pure, as you very properly call it, and those of us that are pioneers — Oh, this debate could go on forever! We could prove that I'm a hero or a fool or a deserter or anything you like, but the fact is I've suddenly seen I must go! I want my freedom to work, and I herewith quit whining about it and grab it. You've been generous to me. I'm grateful. But you've never been mine. Good-by."

"Darling, darling — We'll talk it over again in the morning, when you aren't so excited.... And an hour ago I was so proud of you!"

"All right. Good-night."

But before morning, taking two suit-cases and a bag of his roughest clothes, leaving for her a tender note which was the hardest thing he had ever written, kissing his son and muttering, "Come to me when you grow up, old man," he went to a cheap side-street hotel. As he stretched on the rickety iron bed, he grieved for their love. Before noon he had gone to the Institute, resigned, taken certain of his own apparatus and notes and books and materials, refused to answer a telephone call from Joyce, and caught a train for Vermont.

Cramped on the red-plush seat of the day-coach (he who of late had ridden in silken private cars), he grinned with the joy of no longer having to toil at dinner-parties.

He drove up to Birdies' Rest in a bob-sled. Terry was chopping wood, in a mess of chip-littered snow.

"Hello, Terry. Come for keeps."

"Fine, Slim. Say, there's a lot of dishes in the shack need washing."

## II

He had become soft. To dress in the cold shanty and to wash in icy water was agony; to tramp for three hours through fluffy snow exhausted him. But the rapture of being allowed to work twenty-four hours a day without leaving an experiment at its juiciest moment to creep home for dinner, of plunging with Terry into arguments as cryptic as theology and furious as the indignation of a drunken man, carried him along, and he felt himself growing sinewy. Often he meditated on yielding to Joyce so far as to allow her to build a better laboratory for them, and more civilized quarters.

With only one servant, though, or two at the very most, and just a simple decent bathroom —

She had written, "You have been thoroughly beastly, and any attempt at reconciliation, if that is possible now, which I rather doubt, must come from you."

He answered, describing the ringing winter woods and not mentioning the platform word Reconciliation.

## III

They wanted to study further the exact mechanism of the action of their quinine derivatives. This was difficult with the mice which Terry had contrived to use instead of monkeys, because of their size. Martin had brought with him strains of *Bacillus lepisepticus* , which causes a pleuro-pneumonia in rabbits, and their first labor was to discover whether their original compound was effective against this bacillus as well as against pneumococcus. Profanely they found that it was not; profanely and patiently they trudged into an infinitely complicated search for a compound that should be.

They earned their living by preparing sera which rather grudgingly they sold to physicians of whose honesty they were certain, abruptly refusing the popular drug-vendors. They thus received surprisingly large sums, and among all clever people it was believed that they were too coyly shrewd to be sincere.

Martin worried as much over what he considered his treachery to Clif Clawson as over his desertion of Joyce and John, but this worrying he did only when he could not sleep. Regularly, at three in the morning, he brought both Joyce and honest Clif to Birdies' Rest; and regularly, at six, when he was frying bacon, he forgot them.

Terry the barbarian, once he was free of the tittering and success-pawing of Holabird, was an easy campmate. Upper berth or lower was the same to him, and till Martin was hardened to cold and fatigue, Terry did more than his share of wood-cutting and supply-toting, and with great melody and skill he washed their clothes.

He had the genius to see that they two alone, shut up together season on season, would quarrel. He planned with Martin that the laboratory scheme should be extended to include eight (but never more!) maverick and undomestic researchers like themselves, who should contribute to the expenses of the camp by manufacturing sera, but otherwise do their own independent work — whether it should be the structure of the atom, or a disproof of the results of Drs. Wickett and Arrowsmith. Two rebels, a chemist now caught in a drug-firm and a university professor, were coming next autumn.

"It's kind of a mis'able return to monasteries," grumbled Terry, "except that we're not trying to solve anything for anybody but our own fool selves. Mind you! When this place becomes a shrine, and a lot of cranks begin to creep in here, then you and I got to beat it, Slim. We'll move farther back in the woods, or if we feel too old for that, we'll take another shot at professorships or Dawson Hunziker or even the Rev. Dr. Holabird."

For the first time Martin's work began definitely to draw ahead of Terry's.

His mathematics and physical chemistry were now as sound as Terry's, his indifference to publicity and to flowery hangings as great, his industry as fanatical, his ingenuity in devising new apparatus at least comparable, and his imagination far more swift. He had less ease but more passion. He hurled out hypotheses like sparks. He began, incredulously, to comprehend his freedom. He would yet determine the essential nature of phage; and as he became stronger and surer — and no doubt less human — he saw ahead of him innumerous inquiries into chemotherapy and immunity; enough adventures to keep him busy for decades.

It seemed to him that this was the first spring he had ever seen and tasted. He learned to dive into the lake, though the first plunge was an agony of fiery cold. They fished before breakfast, they supped at a table under the oaks, they tramped twenty miles on end, they had bluejays and squirrels for interested neighbors; and when they had worked all night, they came out to find serene dawn lifting across the sleeping lake.

Martin felt sun-soaked and deep of chest, and always he hummed.

And one day he peeped out, beneath his new horn-rimmed almost-middle-aged glasses, to see a gigantic motor crawling up their woods road. From the car, jolly and competent in tweeds, stepped Joyce.

He wanted to flee through the back door of the laboratory shanty. Reluctantly he edged out to meet her.

"It's a sweet place, really!" she said, and amiably kissed him. "Let's walk down by the lake."

In a stilly place of ripples and birch boughs, he was moved to grip her shoulders.

She cried, "Darling, I *have* missed you! You're wrong about lots of things, but you're right about this — you must work and not be disturbed by a lot of silly people. Do you like my tweeds? Don't they look wildernessy? You see, I've come to stay! I'll build a house near here; perhaps right across the lake. Yes. That will make a sweet place, over there on that sort of little plateau, if I can get the land — probably some horrid tight-fisted old farmer owns it. Can't you just *see* it: a wide low house, with enormous verandas and red awnings — "

"And visitors coming?"

"I suppose so. Sometimes. Why?"

Desperately, "Joyce, I do love you. I want awfully, just now, to kiss you properly. But I will not have you bringing a lot of people — and there'd probably be a rotten noisy motor launch. Make our lab a joke. Roadhouse. New sensation. Why, Terry would go crazy! You *are* lovely! But you want a playmate, and I want to work. I'm afraid you can't stay. No."

"And our son is to be left without your care?"

"He — Would he have my care if I died?... He is a nice kid, too! I hope he won't be a Rich Man!... Perhaps ten years from now he'll come to me here."

"And live like *this* ?"

"Sure — unless I'm broke. Then he won't live so well. We have meat practically every day now!"

"I see. And suppose your Terry Wickett should marry some waitress or some incredibly stupid rustic? From what you've told me, he rather fancies that sort of girl!"

"Well, either he and I would beat her, together, or it would be the one thing that could break me."

"Martin, aren't you perhaps a little insane?"

"Oh, absolutely! And how I enjoy it! Though you — You look here now, Joy! We're insane but we're not cranks! Yesterday an 'esoteric healer' came here because he thought this was a free colony, and Terry walked him twenty miles, and then I think he threw him in the lake. No. Gosh. Let me think." He scratched his chin. "I don't believe we're insane. We're farmers."

"Martin, it's too infinitely diverting to find you becoming a fanatic, and all the while trying to wriggle out of being a fanatic. You've left common sense. I *am* common sense. I believe in bathing! Good-by!"

"Now you look here. By golly — "

She was gone, reasonable and triumphant.

As the chauffeur maneuvered among the stumps of the clearing, for a moment Joyce looked out from her car, and they stared at each other, through tears. They had never been so frank, so pitiful, as in this one unarmored look which recalled every jest, every tenderness, every twilight they had known together. But the car rolled on unhalted, and he remembered that he had been doing an experiment —

## IV

On a certain evening of May, Congressman Almus Pickerbaugh was dining with the President of the United States.

"When the campaign is over, Doctor," said the President, "I hope we shall see you a cabinet-member — the first Secretary of Health and Eugenics in the country!"

That evening, Dr. Rippleton Holabird was addressing a meeting of celebrated thinkers, assembled by the League of Cultural Agencies. Among the Men of Measured Merriment on the platform were Dr. Aaron Sholtheis, the new Director of McGurk Institute, and Dr. Angus Duer, head of the Duer Clinic and professor of surgery in Fort Dearborn Medical College.

Dr. Holabird's epochal address was being broadcast by radio to a million ardently listening lovers of science.

That evening, Bert Tozer of Wheatsylvania, North Dakota, was attending mid-week prayer-meeting. His new Buick sedan awaited him outside, and with modest satisfaction he heard the minister gloat:

"The righteous, even the Children of Light, they shall be rewarded with a great reward and their feet shall walk in gladness, saith the Lord of Hosts; but the mockers, the Sons of Belial, they shall be slain betimes and cast down into darkness and failure, and in the busy marts shall they be forgot."

That evening, Max Gottlieb sat unmoving and alone, in a dark small room above the banging city street. Only his eyes were alive.

That evening, the hot breeze languished along the palm-waving ridge where the ashes of Gustaf Sondelius were lost among cinders, and a depression in a garden marked the grave of Leora.

That evening, after an unusually gay dinner with Latham Ireland, Joyce admitted, "Yes, if I do divorce him, I may marry you. I know! He's never going to see how egotistical it is to think he's the only man living who's always right!"

That evening, Martin Arrowsmith and Terry Wickett lolled in a clumsy boat, an extraordinarily uncomfortable boat, far out on the water.

"I feel as if I were really beginning to work now," said Martin. "This new quinine stuff may prove pretty good. We'll plug along on it for two or three years, and maybe we'll get something permanent — and probably we'll fail!"

Made in the USA
Middletown, DE
01 June 2020